The
Stories of
James
Stern

The
Stories of
James
Stern

Harcourt, Brace & World, Inc.

New York

for
TANIA KURELLA
with love and gratitude

The stories in the book are fictional with the following exceptions:

A Stranger Among Miners is an eye-witness account of some days which the author spent in coal-mining districts of South Wales and Derbyshire during the winter of 1931–2. It was first published in *New Writing*.

A Peaceful Place and *Home* are stories extracted from *The Hidden Damage*, a book based on the author's experiences while on a U.S. government assignment in Germany during the spring and summer of 1945.

Contents

The Man Who Was Loved

EVEN OVER the wide asphalt streets of the town the old Ford bobbed along uncomfortably enough, but here on this road, which was merely the veld shorn of its scrub, the difficulty was to retain one's seat at all as the wheezing machine bounded over the bumps. Every now and then the native behind was thrown over on top of us, then with a wallop he crashed back into his seat again. My one resolve was to prevent my head hitting the wind-screen in front.

Major Carter sat at the wheel as if he had spent all his life in that position—his left leg thrust straight out before him, the other bent so that the foot rested on the rusty throttle. Not a muscle of the Major moved; he might have been made of clay. The skin of his face was the colour of the earth beneath the long sun-scorched grasses, which was also the colour of the houses in the town. Worn and lined it was, parched by the thin air and the sun. I looked at the plaster-like cheeks and wondered had they ever been kissed; it would be like kissing the walls of a house, I thought. His hands gripping the thin steering wheel were much the same, gnarled, huge and misshapen, like chunks of wood hewn from a pale tree. His iron-grey hair looked as if it might once have covered the head of a bear, but it had always been his, and possibly it had grown like this because he never wore a hat. How he escaped sunstroke remained one of the minor mysteries of the Major, whom no one considered in any sense mysterious. I thought that if a tree were female and a wooden monument of Cecil Rhodes her mate, none but the Major could possibly be the result of such a union.

His clothes, too, were almost earth-brown, made of that thin sand-coloured material commonly worn in the tropics, and his open khaki shirt displayed the reddish hairs on his tanned chest. When Major Carter walked he limped badly, and it was said that his left leg was made of wood, but proof of this fact there was none. Sometimes when he stood drinking in the Bar, his whole body appeared to me as if carved from wood. Motionless, the Major was a majestic figure, huge and rather frightening: but the moment he moved one felt a twinge of sympathy, for, though he covered the ground with amazing rapidity, yet he hardly combined speed with grace. He hopped forward on his right leg, rather in the manner of a kangaroo, then drew the other leg along behind him as if it had been given him purposely to impede his progress. Some of the children in the town used to look at him and laugh, but their elders would raise their eyes and say: "Ah, there's the Major; wonderful man, marvellous how he gets along!"

A Scot by birth, he had achieved his military rank in the Black Watch. Several years of his life had been spent in Australia before he came to live in Africa. It was in the former country that he had learnt the art of killing snakes with such facility. There, I gathered, he gained confidence through destroying snakes that were not deadly. For I never met a South African of any colour who would touch a dangerous snake with his bare hand, let alone attempt to kill one without the aid of some weapon, as was the custom of the Major. It was this feat that had made him famous in the town.

By profession a buyer and seller of horses, cattle, sheep, and dogs, he liked, however, more than all else, to be summoned to a farm or house in the town to dispose of a snake. He had only one method for their destruction. He would creep up behind them, grab them by the tail-end, then swing them round and round till he cracked their heads off in the air, as a huntsman cracks a riding crop. It may sound improbable, but this and the fact that he had pleasing manners with mothers and their manless daughters, could tell good stories and drink much whisky with men, account for his having earned the love and admiration of the people of every colour in the town.

Though few, if any, of the whites knew the Major well, one and all professed an intimate friendship. Men came to drink tea and whisky in his little office; to his house, in a suburb of the town, he was never known to have invited a soul. Nevertheless, he himself was invited Everywhere by Everyone. Had there been a dozen majors, he would still have remained The Major.

Everyone, in this case, was represented by perhaps one hundred persons, approximately one-fiftieth of the white population. At the head of the list stood Sir James Channon and his wife and daughter at Government House, followed by the governor's two private secretaries, Townsend and Clitheroe. There was the Reverend Arthur Virtue, of the Protestant Church. Next in order of social reverence came Mr Charles Northland, manager of the Standard Bank, and his family. (The unfortunate name of Isaac Goldstein deprived the charming manager of the National Bank from inclusion in such a list.) Then there was Doctor Richard Murry from "Barts" and Doctor Chute from Middlesex Hospital, both only three years "out from home." These two suffered horribly from professional jealousy, but since they were both English Eligibles and fair tennis players, every afternoon they met Everyone and each other, separated only by a net. Finally, there came the secretary of The Club and the manager of the Grand Hotel. Though the town boasted of several clubs and innumerable hotels, Everyone drank only in The Bar at The Club and, outside their homes, entertained only at The Grand. Yet above all these people —who knew each other so deplorably well that should one of the men turn up at a tennis party with his hair parted in a different way Everyone would not only notice it immediately but would also want to know the reason why—yet above them all the Major's name might be said to reign supreme, for among them he was The Man of The World, who had fought for His Country which had Won The War. Even the piccaninnies playing in the gutters of the native quarters recognized in the distance his limp, and held in awe this white man who could perform such miracles with the snakes of which they lived in constant dread.

When distinguished visitors arrived from the South it was the Major who met their train, conducted the party to their rooms in The Grand. It was the Major who produced horses for them to ride in the early mornings, and it was he who rode with them with his stiff leg, showed them the sights, introduced them to the

Representative of His Majesty at Government House. Once seen walking down Rhodes Street with the Major and you were good for several free drinks and dinners under the corrugated-iron roofs of Everyone: while, secretly, you were the envy of All.

And here was I, bouncing over the veld with him in his old Ford car. I am afraid I had known the Major so long that I did not look upon my present position beside him as the honour many others would have deemed it. No doubt they would have scratched their heads between each bump to think of something to say, then shouted into the spluttering grinding noise some commonplace which the Major would have smiled at but not heard. But since long acquaintance gives one the pleasure of easy silence in another's company, I said nothing and thought only how many more miles we should have to travel before we arrived at the farm where the Major wished to show me a horse he proposed to buy.

The heat of the roaring engine at my feet only made more oppressive the glare of the sun overhead. It was as if we were between two fires, the natural silent flame from above trying to combat the rage of the greater mechanical heat rising from below. Between the two I sat in a state of perspiring discomfort. We could never see the way very far ahead, and now and then the Major half turned to question the native as to whether he were certain we were on the right road. The Major spoke the native language with extraordinary fluency. Though he had lived little more than a third of his life in the country, I had heard no white man born and brought up there speak it with greater accuracy and ease. He could twist his tongue into almost all the difficult clicks that some say no white mouth can ever master. I had a fair knowledge of Sindabele, but were I blind I would have sworn that I was sitting next to an African while the Major chatted with his boy behind him.

For several miles we passed no living thing on the awful road. The heat danced up and down in front of us, waves of it rising from the car's furious bonnet whose sides flapped wide like the wings of an eagle as we pitched down from one boulder and rose again with a snort to the crest of the next. I felt all the time that something was about to give way and the three of us would be thrown headlong into the dry and dusty bush, or that the engine would blow up in a rage and the cap of the radiator go whizzing up to join the cooler flames of the sun. The road wound in and out in the manner of a reptile, the tall grasses in front—as I saw them through a haze of dirty glass and transparent waves of heat —appearing to leap about like a concentrated mass of slender lunatics. One or two isolated kopjes in the distance seemed un-naturally still and lonely, hills I could see without looking through the wind-screen and the mirage caused by the anger of the engine.

Almost suddenly the reptilian road took a sharper turn, as though this were the curve of its neck, and it stretched out before us into a straight brown and bumpy line. We could now see some distance ahead, and not far off, lodged in the middle of the line, quite motionless, stood a wagon and a span of oxen. As we approached, the Major began to slow down, for to pass the wagon was impossible: the road was blocked. Hearing the noise, a native appeared from beyond the oxen, his face curiously anxious. But when he saw the driver of our car, his body and his face relaxed and his closed mouth opened wide in a grin of genuine pleasure.

As the Major switched off the exhausted engine, he halted beside the car and, touching his black head with the fingers of his right hand, he uttered, as do all Africans when surprised and pleased, the syllable "Ah!" Immediately two more natives ap-peared, a poor, rather ashamed-looking couple with next to nothing on. They, too, at sight of the driver, took on a far less humble appearance, grinned, stood still, touched their heads with their hands, and together breathed the syllable "Ah!"

"*Quenjani wena?* How are you?" enquired Major Carter, look-ing at the three silent natives standing in a row. When the Major spoke to a native he addressed him much as one Englishman addresses another, with a half-smile, a nod, and a "How are you!" But unlike the Englishman whose usual answer to the conven-tional greeting is a limp handshake and, even though he be suffer-ing from cancer, a repetition of the "How are *you!*" the three natives again touched their heads, assumed more serious expres-sions, and said what they very evidently meant: "Not very well, *Inkos.*"

Judging from the way they all turned their heads simultaneously in the same direction, the cause of them being "not very well" seemed clearly to lie on the road beyond the wagon and the oxen. I looked at the natives, then glanced at the Major's plaster-like face, which, although he was barely out of the car, I could see was split across in a smile of excited eagerness. Once on the ground he leaped forward with his right leg, while the left chased it like the minute-hand of Big Ben keeping pace with the hour-hand of Time. Then, suddenly remembering me in his excitement, he turned.

"Come on!" he cried. "Here's some fun!"

In a moment both the native who had travelled in the back of the car and myself were at the Major's side. We had to run to keep up with him. The other three natives followed behind, at a trot. As we passed the wagon I noticed that the whole span of sixteen oxen was drawn in as far as possible to one side of the road, and that the leaders were so far off the beaten track that they stood belly-deep in the long grasses. Then it struck me that they were all staring towards the centre of the road, their necks arched away from what they saw, stamping with their forelegs, whipping their tails over their backs and snorting as cattle do when they scent danger. The leaders appeared more concerned than the rest; the one nearest the road kept taking a quick fearful look, then turning and stampeding with its feet as though so terrified at what it had seen that it must needs take to its heels at once. The other ox, harnessed to it, and bound by ropes of hide to the beam between them, could do no more to help than turn its head and pretend also to gallop away. But their impotent hoofs covered not a foot of ground, for a wagon-load of wood was beyond the power of one pair of oxen to pull unaided.

I saw all this at a glance and when I turned my eyes in the direction of the rest of the span, I stopped, stood still, hardly breathing. At the same moment I was aware that the Major and all four natives were standing motionless beside me. There, ten yards in front, in the middle of the road, its sharp and venomous-looking head pointing towards the terrified oxen, lay the shining coils of the longest snake I had ever seen.

Now, my fear of snakes is incurable: the fact that I had seen hundreds in Africa lessened not at all the horror in which I held them. At a fairly safe distance I had shot and killed them, but even their dead bodies I left for another to dispose of. And I knew enough about them to realize that this living rope on the road was a green mamba, the most deadly reptile in Africa.

When at last I turned to see the Major with his coat off, his sleeves rolled up, rubbing his hands, his eyes fixed in glee to the hateful object on the ground, I stepped back.

"Major!" I yelled. "You're mad! It's a mamba! We've no serum —nothing! You're crazy!"

I retreated farther into the bush, while the natives, wide-eyed, frightened, yet hypnotized with curiosity and admiration, only too willingly followed me—a fact I observed with relief: in their company I should perhaps appear less of a coward.

The Major took not the slightest notice of my cries of warning. I dare say he was too absorbed to hear them, and I knew that further words would be wasted. By now he was on the road beyond the snake, whose head was still raised in vicious anger towards the terrified oxen, its divided tongue slipping silently in and out of its mouth. I held my breath and wished I were in the car, aware that the speed at which a mamba can travel is such that the human eye can hardly follow its lightning progress as it rips along over the surface of the ground.

The Major had now bent himself almost double: stretching his left leg straight out behind him, he moved towards his poisonous prey by pressing the foot of his stiff leg into the ground to steady himself, while his right foot in some extraordinary manner stole silently forward, inch by inch. His right arm he held out but a yard from the snake, whose entire attention was still occupied watching the antics of the frightened oxen, and his open shirt hung so loose from his shoulders that I could see his chest and the red hairs growing down to his navel.

Suddenly, with a bound and a cry like that of an animal as it leaps upon another in fury, the Major had snatched the snake from the earth and was whirling it round and round his head at such a speed that it was unable to coil itself, and the sound it made whistling through the air was like that of wind whining through the rigging of a ship. As the snake's head drooped on its

wild circuit through space and ceased to make further effort to
coil, the Major seemed to lift the whole weight of his body on to
his right foot as suddenly he changed the course of his whirling,
and, as a huntsman wields a long-lashed riding-crop, cracked the
length of the reptile above his head in the air. As he did this he
uttered a low whoop of triumph and let go the tail-end of the
snake. I watched it soar into the sky, and then, though obviously
headless, saw it coil itself and fall yards away into the depths of
the bush.

I had just taken a deep breath of relief and was about to clap
my hands with joy at the Major's fantastic performance, when I
heard a howl, and looking up, saw him clutch his stomach as he
dropped like a falling tree to the ground.

With the natives I rushed to his side, and in a strangled voice
heard him cry: "A knife! Quick! For God's sake! It's got me! It's
... *got* me!" And with the last word his hand fell away from his
stomach, his head rolled back upon the ground. . . .

In one quick and feverish movement the Major's own native
tore away the shirt from his master's body. And at the same
moment, uttering a sharp scream, he jumped back. We all jumped
away from what we saw. For lying on the Major's bare stomach
was the bleeding, fangless, though not yet motionless head of
the mamba!

With the toe of my boot I kicked away the head, and a native
cut a hole in the white abdomen where, only too clearly, I could
see the two fangs embedded in the flesh. But the Major's boy
groaned and shook his head. With tears in his eyes, he gazed into
his master's face, which was now so horribly contorted and his
neck and eyes so swollen that he was hardly recognizable as the
man who, but a few minutes ago, had sat beside me in the car.

There was nothing to be done. As the four of us lifted the great
weight and placed it on the back seat of the old Ford, and I
jumped into the driver's seat and started the wheezing engine,
the native and I knew that hurry was in vain.

Before we had covered two miles of the return journey, the life
went out of the unconscious man as he lay in the arms of his
sobbing servant. Negroes weep easily, but I, thinking of all the
enjoyable hours I had spent in the dead man's company, hours

that I should never spend again, found tears in my own eyes too.

II

Seldom have I known a man's death cause so much universal consternation and genuine grief as did that of Major Carter.

News in the desert-places of Africa where few men live spreads fast: on the day after the tragic event, of which I had been the sole white witness, it is doubtful if there existed even a Negro child in the town who was ignorant of the end of the man whom All had been so long accustomed to see limping about the streets with a cheerful smile.

Orders came from Government House, where the Union Jack drooped drearily at half-mast, that the whole town should demonstrate its deep sorrow by closing down all the shops and drawing the blinds in every house. Readily was the summons obeyed. Never had the Clubs and Hotels sold so much whisky in so short a time. The Bar at The Club overflowed with men who, instead of laughing and joking over the glasses in their hands, peered sorrowfully into the yellow liquid and saw there the sun-tanned, laughing face of the dead man who in his lifetime had "stood" them so many. But they made wry little faces while they drank: Johnnie Walker, White Horse, Black Label, John Haig—their taste was not the same this morning when their consumers knew they should never again hear that loud familiar laugh, that heavy, uneven tread crossing the threshold of The Bar, no more listen to those stories which only one man could tell, nor even be able to walk into his little office, sit down over a fresh bottle, and be shaken by the great hand which had brought destruction to so many deadly snakes and, in the end, death to its owner. They talked, these men, in shy, subdued tones, as though it pained them to speak. Yet the more they drank, the more they spoke, the more gloomy they became; for the subtle powers of whisky can more easily exaggerate the melancholy of melancholy thoughts than enlarge upon the happiness of happy ones. They threw themselves into an orgy of reminiscence: one old story succeeded another even older, which the same chairs upon which we sat had heard so often that their seats had caved in from the weight of memory. The smoke- and whisky-ridden air rang with: "I remember," "in Australia," "in France," "in the old days," "the first time I saw him kill a snake, my God, it was a near thing . . . a wonderful man, the best friend *I* ever . . ."

Pitiful, selfish tears filled all our alcoholic eyes while our voices droned on and on, till it seemed almost as if we ourselves wished to follow our dead friend into the sun-baked earth.

And yet—I thought—and yet, next Wednesday at Government House there's a Garden Party. . . . Everyone will be there, all these sentiments will be repeated once more, word for word, but our voices—they won't drone on like a dull wind at night, they will be pitched high in a tone of polite false gaiety. This man now saying "I remember" in a funereal, almost inaudible mutter will be standing, talking, smiling into the uplifted aristocracy of Lady Channon's face. And with his top-hatted head thrown high in the air he will laugh as—the words running from his mouth like a joyous river in spate—he intones: "Yes, marvellous, wasn't he! Really the most appropriate end! *I* remember. . . ."

As The Club clock struck twelve we all filed out of the gloom into the glare of the sun. The body of the Major was lying in deathly state in the great room of the Town Hall, whose floor, on Saturday nights, the dead man's legs had so lately covered in limping, dancing strides. Since it was generally known that the deceased possessed no relations in the town, the affairs of his funeral and the arrangements for the moving of his remains were kindly conducted by one of his warmest friends, the Reverend Arthur Virtue, of the Protestant Church.

As we turned off Rhodes Street into another less wide, where the entrance to the Town Hall could be plainly seen, we found it almost impossible to move any farther in its direction. The dense crowd confronting us on all sides was impenetrable, and the smell of perspiring coloured flesh rose in strong pungent waves to my nostrils. It was a curious sight, and one that I have never forgotten. The fact that the white people among the mass of Negroes were draped in black made the spectacle even darker than perhaps, had everyone come naked, it would then have appeared. Nevertheless, as I pushed my way through the thick odour of

humans and the more solid resistance of their bodies, I don't
think I passed more than a dozen white faces in the silent crowd.
To some extent this was explained when, approaching the steps
to the Hall, a notice in large black letters above the entrance
caught my eye:

NATIVES NOT ADMITTED

Then beside me I heard the voice of the Reverend Arthur
Virtue, who, pale and harassed, was endeavouring to perform the
somewhat difficult task of collecting in a large bag money for a
memorial to our lost friend. "You'll see a drawing of the proposed
plaque inside," he whispered in my ear as, looking back, I saw
him besieged by crowds of natives, mostly women and girls, who
sobbingly dropped coin after coin into his bag. Children, too,
little brown pot-bellied piccaninnies, hardly knowing what they
did and certainly not why they did it (save that they believed,
perhaps, that in some mysterious way it would benefit the soul of
the man they had so much admired and respected), ran after the
Reverend, clutched at his black garments, and cried: "Baas Virtoo,
Baas Virtoo, me a penny, me a penny!" Wherewith they thrust
their little black hands into the opening of the bag and heard
their coppers drop with a clink among the hundreds of others.
"Thank you, children, thank you!" came the ceaseless answer of
the Reverend. "Thank you, dear people, God bless your kindness!" And on he was thrust through the sweating mass. Indeed,
the crowd now below the steps was such that two mounted
policemen were finding it beyond the power of their horses and
their whips to divide between them some kind of pathway up
which the white folk might drive to the door in their cars.

When at last within the Hall, I found the scene there strangely
different from that outside. It reminded me rather of the interior
of an Italian cathedral on any day of the week but Sunday. The
immense room was entirely void of furniture, and the many silent,
darkly-draped figures moving about like panthers on the prowl
for prey were creeping in ones and twos round the outskirts of
the Hall or standing in little clumps near the doorway. At the
end of the room, unattended save by a vast heap of wreaths and

pile upon pile of multi-coloured flowers, stood the bier whereon lay the body of the Major, draped in the voluminous folds of a great Union Jack.

Round the room I recognized at once the presence of every white person I had ever seen in the town, and many others whose faces were unknown to me. And one and all, like devout Italians gazing at the distant altar in an otherwise empty cathedral, were staring towards the lonely flower-covered figure on the dais. Tip-toeing my way round the edge of the room towards the object of their eyes, I saw, drawn on a large piece of cardboard placed among the floral cushions, the sketch of the proposed memorial for which, outside among the natives in the sun, the Reverend Arthur Virtue was so kindly collecting money. On it I read:

TO THE MEMORY OF
Major Oswald Perth Carter
A TRUE SON OF BRITAIN
WHOSE HEROIC CONDUCT IN LIFE SAVED
MANY LIVES AND EARNED FOR HIM THE
EVERLASTING GRATITUDE AND ADMIRATION
OF THOSE OF HIS RACE IN THIS TOWN
WHO HAVE HELPED TO ERECT
THIS STONE

For others he lived
For others he died

LOVED BY ALL

And above this fitting epitaph, clothed tight in a white shroud and covered over by the Union Jack, lay the body of the loved one. I took one look at it, then glanced away. In life I had never seen it like this. Only the crisp hair, like that of a bear, remained as I had known it. The yellow, weather-beaten face, its eyes closed, slept in a grimace hideous with silent mockery. The mouth drooped a little at one end, the lips were parted, showing two yellow teeth, and the wall-like flesh sagged away from the now prominent cheek-bones. In my one quick glance I saw what, in life, I had never seen on the Major's face—a look of calm contempt. I turned, and tiptoed out of the silent Hall.

In Africa, dead men are buried with little delay.

I was already ten minutes late when I left my room, dressed in a hired suit of black. The sun was low behind the houses, and the reflection of its fading light made pink the sky above and cast a mauve glow of mourning over the emptiness of the silent streets. All I could hear was the hum of a solitary motor-car in the direction of the Protestant Church, whence the funeral procession was to proceed to the cemetery, and to which I now hurriedly made my way.

When I had covered more than half the distance and come into the straight street where the tall spire towered above a medley of old iron roofs, I was astonished to see long lines of cars being driven away from the church's entrance. Some were coming towards me, all occupied by their white, black-clothed owners whom I knew; others were going off in the opposite direction, but none turned down the road to the cemetery. And more mysterious still was the fact that the hearse and its two black horses were standing, surrounded by a multitude of Negroes, waiting in the street at the gate of the church. Was the burial postponed? Why were all these cars driving away? Why were all these natives crowding round the empty hearse?

I quickened my step, my thoughts in a whirl of wondering. I approached the outskirts of the immense crowd. As I elbowed my way through, I was suddenly aware that among all these people only one white face was visible. It shone out like a distant pale lamp on a dark night, amongst all the surrounding black ones. This face belonged to the hearse's driver, who, sitting high up on his box, stared out, like a tired and lonely star, without interest or intent, upon a cruel world.

Then, into the low murmur of the waiting Negroes, who with luminous eyes were all gazing anxiously at the crowded entrance to the church, there broke a hush, a sigh, and a silence, as, with one accord, the mass withdrew a little from the close proximity of the wagon of death.

I followed their eyes, hemmed in as I was and unable to move, and saw, through a gap made in the doorway, a coffin being borne down the steps on the shoulders of four young Africans who in a white man's country would have been classed as giants. All four were dressed alike, from neck to naked feet in pure white linen, and I noticed that their faces, strangely brown, all bore a definite resemblance one with the other, and that each face shone with tears.

Immediately behind them, also dressed in white, came a dozen very dark Negro women, some middle-aged, others young and beautiful, weeping audibly into their hands. Beyond these there trotted, in what seemed to me an endless stream, a crowd of brown-faced boys, girls, and tiny piccaninnies, all holding hands.

I watched the four brown giants reverently place the coffin in the hearse, cover it with many hundreds of wreaths and a living carpet of multi-coloured flowers, leaves, and petals, then silently close the glass door.

For a moment there was tense silence, as though Africa were praying; then the one tired white star raised a whip against the evening sky. I heard the wheels of the hearse go grating over the road, and the vast procession, like one wing of a gigantic magpie, formed up behind and followed the bones of the man who was loved.

The Cloud

THE FARM IN THE LITTLE VALLEY belonged neither to Van Huyten
nor myself. In fact, we had no share in it. He was managing it;
I was helping him to manage it.

Van Huyten was a man of about forty, born in the Transvaal,
so he said. I was just under half his age, and Irish by birth. The
owner of the farm was a wealthy Belgian who had left the Congo
to come to a more healthy climate farther south, just below the
southern border of the Congo. Of him I knew practically nothing.
I never saw him; he was one of those men who take periodic
visits from their European homes to their "ranches in Africa,"
where such men are as a rule despised, and where no farm is
known as a ranch.

Van Huyten was a large, grizzly Dutchman, and there was no
one else, no other white man. At one time his face might have
possessed a certain dignity, but now it had a swollen appearance;
his skin was parched—such skin as was visible, for his face was
always covered by a growth of red stubble. The hairs on his arms
reminded me of tiny brown twigs, crisp and hard. And his fingers
were stained a deep orange-brown, the nails bitten down to the
quick.

Thirty miles away, as the vulture flew, lived another Dutchman,
alone. But him I had never seen. It was not my business to leave
the farm; I was helping Van Huyten to manage it. That was my
job, for which I was paid £7 a month; and that was good money,
just after the War. Each month I saved five of those seven pounds;
the rest I spent on tobacco and whisky: one had to smoke—and
drink.

But it was no good. For three whole months, from late April

to the end of July, Van Huyten and I managed to remain together. At first it was all right. It was all new to me. I was excited. During those first days together in the sun he used to show me things I had not seen before, tell me things I never knew, but without enthusiasm. I could see even then that Van Huyten had had enough, though all the time I was with him I never learnt anything of his past. Later on, when he began to drink more, before he had finished his nightly bottle and thrown himself on the bed just as he was in his canvas slacks and shirt, wandering in his speech, he silently refused to confide anything of himself to me. At this moment I know no more of the life of Van Huyten than the little I am about to speak of. Soured as he was—I imagine by misfortune leading to great loneliness and frustration—he seldom ceased grumbling. Nothing was ever right. He hated the little world he was in, though I doubt if he had known any other very dissimilar; but more than his lonely little world, inside him, he despised himself. That was the tragedy. It was always apparent. And he loathed the natives, who possessed an unholy terror of him, not without reason. For he ill-treated them and bullied them. Once, imagining he was unobserved, I saw him pounce on a single wandering African—a big youth, coal-black, called Plate, of whom I had grown very fond. I saw him lead the native a little way into the bush. It seemed that he then told the boy to walk on a few yards in front. Van Huyten began to steal up behind him. When within a yard he lifted the heavy sjambok he always carried and dealt the boy a terrible blow across the side of the face. The boy fell, writhing on the ground in agony and holding his injured face between his two hands. The next day the whole jaw had swollen to an abnormal size. Plate tried to smile when I looked at him in horror. "Toothache," he whispered, "awful toothache!" He told me long afterwards he knew I had not believed him, but I never told him what I had seen, a sight that made nightmares of my dreams for several weeks.

All his anger and unhappiness Van Huyten vented on innocent and defenceless natives, and in those first three months I was in constant fear for him. When I grew, little by little, to understand their language I could hear the Africans talking about him in the compound during the silent nights. And their chatter sounded excitable and ominous in my ears.

Natives came to work for a month, then left. Some failed to remain even that length of time; they fled, as often as not unpaid for the work they had done. I know Van Huyten received notes of warning from the Native Commissioner, notes due to reports that had come to his ears in various ways. But he paid no heed; perhaps it was an impossibility for him to reform at his age. He just hated life, and I believe his hate was incurable.

Soon Van Huyten found it difficult to find labour. Groups of boys had to be sent for from different parts of the Congo, even from Tanganyika, on annual contracts. I pitied these natives, for they were unable to find employment on any farm but this, and it was hundreds of miles back to their homes. It seemed incredible to me that they had walked all the way. The first batch that arrived—they were a wild lot with sharpened teeth and a passion for eating the dead frogs they found floating in the wells—told me they had started out from their kraals before the previous rainy season, some nine months prior to the date they arrived.

But in the immediate neighbourhood Van Huyten had become too well known. The natives shook their woolly heads. "No, we no work for Baas Huyten, he bad man, he bad." They would not come. The knowledge of this increased his wrath, and it was not long before his rage reacted upon me. For I was always there. *I* would not go; that he knew.

The one-time four-roomed house we had was almost a complete ruin, fallen in from neglect. They used to say it was one of the first brick houses built north of the Limpopo. It crouched on the side of a kopje overlooking the little valley, with the mealie lands below, and another flat-topped scrubby hill rising up from it on the other side. Beyond this was the blue sky. This was all you could see from the paneless windows of the ruin.

The little valley ran along at right angles to the house and opened out eventually into a vast flat and desert-like plain, right away to the horizon beyond which the great orange sun settled down in a cloud of glory every evening. . . .

We lived not actually under the same roof, for the roof of the one-time living-room (there were no ceilings) had come crashing down during the rainy season of the previous year. But our rooms being on either side of the fatality had escaped, and they still remained more or less rain- and sun-proof under those pieces of corrugated-iron still intact. But the open space between, far from being a living-room, was now a mass of rusty iron, broken ox-cart wheels and shafts, yokes, bridles, saddles, ropes, old decayed and smelling skins, and many coils of barbed and plain wire dumped here after the boundary of the farm had first been fenced off, perhaps thirty years ago.

I used to like this derelict space, since part of it, where a strip of roof still stuck upward into space, afforded a little shade. And I had made a rough stool which I propped against the wall, and on this I used to sit and re-read one of my three books brought out in my one suit-case from Ireland. I sat there for an hour during the middle of the day, when the sun was strong and fierce overhead.

But that was all over now. Van Huyten stopped that. It was one of my habits he simply could not tolerate, to see me read; he could not bear to see me contented. As a rule, he did not return to the ruin in the middle of the day; a hut had been put up for him down in the valley, near the mealie lands where he worked; it saved him from walking to and fro. But from the very beginning I felt instinctively I was not wanted in that hut at noon; not that I felt a desire to go there, but some instinct bade me make a point of avoiding its vicinity at that time of day. I knew he drank there, for in the afternoons he was often quite light-hearted, sometimes he would even smile, but the moment he opened his mouth there was always that awful acrid smell which came to me on his breath in the heat of the afternoon. Then, later on in the day, he would become morose and moody, then thoroughly bad-tempered and cruel, until sundown came, when we drank together in the ruin and said things we didn't mean and feared to look each other in the eyes, and I would take ten grains of quinine with my whisky. . . .

When I first arrived he used to say to me: "Never drink before sundown in Africa, but when you do, take quinine in it, though don't imagine the old fever won't get you in the end." I used to feel sorry for him then; he suffered so much from the malignant form of malaria. Sometimes at night I could hear the whole of his bed shaking under the prolonged paroxysms of his fevered trembling, and he would groan and scream in delirium. He told me once that his mother had had it on her when he was born.

But one day, instead of going to the hut as usual for his lunch, he came back to the ruin just before noon to fetch some barbed wire. I had just come in and was sitting on the stool, eating some bread. On my knees lay my much-soiled copy of *Moby Dick*. I believe I had already read it six times. I looked up as he entered behind me. He was a big man; standing there between me and the door, he towered over me in silence. His shirt-sleeves were rolled up and there was the grime of weeks on his arms, for once a day he washed only his hands and face. His old sun-helmet seemed to be clinging to the back of his semi-bald head, and a nasty look gleamed from out of his little grey blood-shot eyes as they stared down at the book on my knees. Then he took one step towards me and grabbed it. Holding it up in his great gnarled, stained fingers, he scrutinized the dirty cover.

"Mo-Moby Dick!" he growled. "Moby bloody Dick!" And he threw the book into a corner, where it landed on a heap of barbed wire and fell asunder in two halves. One half dropped down behind the rusty coil, while the other tumbled fluttering to the wooden floor, where it lay stretched and open and curiously still, like a mortally wounded bird. Van Huyten strode away. I picked up my bread and went on eating.

That night was my last in the ruin. In the evening I refused to drink with Van Huyten. I had despised him before; now I hated him, suddenly. But I think I was more frightened of myself than I was of him. I could not bear to see him any more. Something unknown to me leapt up in my chest as I thought of him, something that made me catch my breath and my mouth go dry, and my eyes see nothing, nothing but the form of Van Huyten casting my book away. . . . It was fear in me; fear that I might be driven to attack him, in spite of myself. And I refused to think of the possible consequences if I did. I knew he hated me. There had been hate in his gleaming eyes as he grabbed the book.

So that evening I refused to drink with him. He was already

slightly drunk when he came in. And he was sitting, swaying a little, on the edge of his camp-bed when I told him so.

"Oh, you do, do you?" he leered, threateningly.

"Yes, I do. I'm fed up," I said, and with this I slammed the door and jumped over the space between my room and his, then slammed mine, which had no lock. So I pulled over the bed, thrust it against the door, and lay on it. While I lay there I decided I could no longer live in the ruin, in the constant company of Van Huyten. Since it was a big farm some five miles in length, I thought I could quite easily get a hut put up in a day at the other end of it; and since I now looked after the cattle and all the livestock without his help, while he attended to the mealies and the few acres of cotton, there was no longer any need for either of us to see each other again, save perhaps upon some urgent matter. In the middle of the night I scribbled him a note to this effect and put it outside his door. As I did so I could hear him still stamping up and down his room. Then suddenly there was a groan and the sound of his body falling on the bed, and I closed my own door in peace, knowing that I should not be disturbed.

At dawn I left with my boy, Maradza, and all my belongings on his head for the farm's most distant kraal, near which I told Maradza to build two huts, one for himself and one for me.

Maradza giggled with happiness almost incessantly for several days before he settled down at last to our new life without Van Huyten.

II

I called my new hut the "Refuge." It shared very little resemblance with the "Refuges" I had known in the suburbs of Dublin and London, but I think there was a certain real significance in the name I gave it.

Like most African huts it was round, and built of mopani wood and mud plaster. Originally I had had it thatched with bleached grass, but now some old pieces of corrugated iron covered it, less dangerous in the event of fire. Two small paneless windows relieved the otherwise almost complete darkness within. The door I made out of thin posts strung together with wire, somewhat similar to those fences that go to form paddocks in an English park. After infinite trouble I had put down a rough cement floor, covering the ugliest, holiest parts of it with some uncured jackal skins. Altogether Maradza and I were proud of our job. Out of a multitude of twigs and leafy bush he had fashioned for himself a small broom with which once a week he industriously swept the skins and the cement floor. He took an extraordinary joy in doing this; he would have continued to sweep every day had he been allowed. For his trouble and ingenuity I presented him with an old moth-eaten vest which, having first of all washed it, he took round the whole farm, showing it to everyone before he eventually put it on, and wore till it was little more than a grey rag, hanging limp and useless from his black neck.

The "Refuge" and Maradza's hut stood on a slight promontory at the end of the little valley that gave out on to the vast plain, spreading away on all sides to the straight black line of horizon. That straight line was the end of my world; I could conceive of nothing existing beyond that line; for me it was the beginning and the end of Africa, the whole of the earth. Beyond was mystery, and I never thought about that. . . .

A few hundred yards away was a large native kraal, deep in a recess of the valley, near the little river. Half a mile farther on was the cattle kraal, while some three miles beyond this stood the ruin—and Van Huyten.

It was now nearly four months since I had left the ruin. During the whole of that time only twice had I cast eyes upon the manager, and then only in the distance. One-third of a year I had lived here without speaking to a man of my own colour.

One week had elapsed from that afternoon when Van Huyten had thrown away my book before I received from him a small piece of paper. Plate, the boy I had seen Van Huyten knock down with a sjambok, brought it one evening just after sundown. There was a tap on the now rather dilapidated door of my hut. Plate stood in the doorway, an immense grin displaying his perfect white teeth, holding in his hand a piece of crumpled paper.

"From Baas Huyten, *Inkosi*," said Plate, offering me the message.

Scrawled over the paper in pencil were three words: "Go to Hell." I read the words again, then looked up at the great black form standing on the threshold.

"*Inkosi?*" he said.

"Well, what is it, Plate?"

"I want to stay here, leave Baas Huyten," he almost pleaded in his own language. I thought for a few moments. It was more than natural Plate wished to leave Van Huyten. I should never forget what I had seen happen that day between this boy and the Dutchman. But what would Van Huyten do if I kept him? Would he demand him back? But how would he be able to get him unless he appeared in person and took him away by force? And once the others came to know of his deserting Van Huyten, would not they also desert? I released these thoughts in speech to Plate.

"The others?" he said, rather surprised. "The others—if they leave Baas Huyten they leave the farm—they go long way away —or—or——" and his eyes turned inward suddenly, their whites glistening large and liquid in his black face, "or, *Inkosi*, they kill Baas Huyten, they kill him."

I tried to appear incredulous of this statement, though I was far from disbelieving one word he said. Then he went on. "*Inkosi* does not know what Baas Huyten does to us. He thrashes *all* natives, he bad man. I stay there one more day I—I—kill Baas Huyten." As the Negro spat out the last few words, it seemed that all the muscles in his body drew themselves taut in a paroxysm of stifled hate.

I decided to risk it. Plate stayed. He shared the hut of Maradza from that day.

That was four months ago. It was now early December, and I had heard no more of Van Huyten save through some indirect reports of his continued cruelty. In the distance only had I caught sight of him twice. Nor did I think of him, except just lately in connection with that note he had sent me months before. Those three words kept recurring in my memory. "Go to Hell," he had written. Which, generally speaking, means nothing. But even now I look back upon that November and December as my conception of an earthly Hell. I feel sure it will not seem so, in words read during a cold winter's evening in England. Some things, most things are "not so bad when they are over," but tonight I am still shuddering at the thought of those months in the little African valley.

You see, the rains are expected in early September. It was now close upon Christmas, and I had not seen so much as a shower since last March in Capetown. There was nothing but sun, sun, sun. Every day was the same. And this morning, once more that sun. It hovered above the little window-ledge like a vast orange on a blue enamel plate. It heralded yet another day of heat. I rose from my camp-bed and peered out through the paneless hole that acted as one of the windows to the "Refuge." Boys wandered along down in the valley. They used to sing and whistle as they wandered to their work. But now they were dumb. And I knew that silence to be more eloquent than a cry. . . .

I looked up at the corrugated-iron roof above me and saw, through its many holes, the blue sky. Blue, pure azure blue, always blue. How many times had I not gazed upon it in wonder in other lands? Now it had lost all its beauty for me. To me, now, it was the symbol of pain and suffering, even of death. For weeks I had looked forward to the sight of a cloud as the coming of a great event, as the salvation to the animals I tended, as a relief to myself. It seemed a lifetime since I had beheld a cloud. Many moments of each day were occupied in thinking of it, trying to visualize it, wondering what shape, form, or size the first blessed sign of rain would take. But each day, every day, sun, sun, sun. And with it that clear, lucid blueness. Blue, pure blue, nothing but blueness. Walking away from the "Refuge" I noticed the baked earth and the wide cracks cutting their way through the reddish, brick-like soil. Even the feet of the cattle were cracked, and I had to burn cross-cuts on their dwindling hoofs to prevent the creatures from losing the foot and decay from reaching the leg. They were more than thin, their flanks were hollow and emaciated. Their bones stuck out all over their lean bodies; their skins hung upon them rather than covered them, skins that were riddled by bleeding, fly-infested tick sores.

As I wandered down the valley I saw them standing, all

huddled together under one of the few trees that ever gave shade, their tongues hanging out, their mouths motionless, and a hopeless look of ghastly suffering, patiently endured, in their watery eyes. They thirsted and were starving, for there was very little food and hardly any water to give them. It was not a strange sight to find the carcase of a wild buck lying in the dry river-bed, or the body of a week-old calf, dead, under the eyes of its grief-stricken mother. Only the birds lived on, undismayed, finding nourishment in the dried berries and the cow-dung before it became baked by the ruthless sun.

I was compelled to abandon the disinfectant dip; the mixing of this *mouti* required too much water. Instead, with the help of a scraper and some foul-smelling powder, I did what I could for the miserable brutes whose hides were almost rotten with vermin. But they suffered horribly. They flicked their tails with infuriated force, they stamped their feet, they bit their bleeding sores, they gnawed the barks of leafless trees and groaned aloud in their misery. The two ponies seemed to suffer least of all. They were under cover in comparative coolness, and their thirst was to a certain extent assuaged by blocks of salt-stone placed within their reach. But even they drooped their heads as if in mourning for those less fortunate than themselves.

In the evening I came home as usual by way of the river. It was only that in name, like most African rivers, and all the moisture that had lurked late in the now brown, parched grass had long since been absorbed by the merciless sun. Sun, sun, sun, always sun.

The deepest wells were low, almost dry. They had to be guarded day and night to prevent thieves from taking their precious substance. As I approached the "Refuge" I saw that Maradza had already hung up my watersack over the door of the "Refuge" and placed a cup beneath it to catch the treasured drops. Washing had long since been abandoned. I behaved and smelled like a native, for it is principally dirt that gives the African skin its peculiar smell.

From the back window of the hut I could see that the line suspended from two bushes, from which I was accustomed to hang my drying shorts and shirt, was now alone, bare and useless—for nothing was wet that might be dried.

I remember that night very well, though there was little difference between it and all the weeks of previous nights. I remember falling asleep on the narrow bed and wondering, as usual, which I dreaded least—the long days of sun or the longer nights without it. You see, if you lie naked on a bed at night and manage to fall asleep when the thermometer has already risen beyond the heat of your own blood, you are woken every few minutes by the perspiration of your body running in little rivers all over your skin. Tributaries from the larger rivers in the hair trickle down your forehead into your eyes; there they stop and form two pools. And when the little eye-basins are full, off flow two larger rivers again —one down the cheek and eventually on to the wet sheets, the other down the nose, round the corner, and in at the mouth. By that time the streams of perspiration have cooled off, and the cold water in a feverish mouth keeps waking you up. If this fails, the mosquitoes succeed. They pay you out in the end for having a comparatively clean body. They love cleanliness even more than do those who contend that it is next to Godliness; their sting is quite impotent when opposed by layers of dirt. Mosquitoes command you when in Africa to do as Africans do, and you stupidly wait until forced by circumstances before you obey.

They hummed and screamed at me all night long outside the net. Some, of course, found their way inside, and at first, when I heard one little hum approaching, I used to bang at the hum with my hand. But if you bang at hums fifty times in five minutes your arm gets tired. So now I just waited till the hum, coming closer, increased in volume of sound to a whining scream almost inside my ear, when it ceased suddenly—and I was bitten. And while it was biting I gave myself a box on the ear and hoped that the doctor who told me whining mosquitoes don't carry malaria was speaking the truth.

I remember that night, not because Maradza stole into the hut as usual towards dawn to tell me that God said it was going to rain immediately, but because he leapt through the door about an hour after with probably the only news that could have brought from me more than a murmur of surprise and hope.

"*Inkosi!*" he shouted. "*Inkosi!* A cloud! A cloud!"

When I was aware that it was he, and not a strange voice heard in my last nightmare, I tore a long rent in my mosquito net in a violent endeavour to break out of the bed.

"*Ubi?*" I cried, in his language, standing naked in front of him. "*Ubi?*"

Maradza, his eyes alight with excitement, pointed through the window towards the top of the opposite hill. I rushed from the "Refuge" and stood scanning the horizon of the hill, beyond the valley. Yes. Yes, there was certainly a great black cloud rising up like a parachute in the grey dawn-sky from behind the line of the hill's horizon. Greyer, darker than the dawn it was, and rising fast, looming up in a belching black mass. As I stood watching it, hardly breathing, I thought I felt a very slight puff of hot wind fan my face. I pulled a long hair out of my head and held it at arm's length. For a moment I watched it hang there from my fingers, when, to my surprise and joy, the end of the hair rose, followed by the rest, and it floated off behind me, drawn away as if by an invisible magnet.

In Africa they say that a wind always precedes a storm.

Then, looking back at the hill-top, what met my eyes made my hands grow wet. The grey sky beyond was already blotted out by a great cloud—a cloud of *smoke!* I could smell it, smell the burning grass fumes coming to me on the air. . . .

"Fire!" cried Maradza. "Fire! I can hear it! I can hear it!"

I listened for a moment and heard the sharp, crackling sound coming gradually nearer, being borne down to us on the faint breeze.

Of all the sights and sounds on the African veld, perhaps what instils most anxiety into those who see and hear it is the sight of a cloud of smoke and the noise of crackling fire. Man becomes then an impotent and puny person confronted by a wind fanning the blazing plain.

Maradza, whose experience of fires was far greater than mine, was already inside the native kraal, rousing every man, woman, and child from their sleep. I could see them dashing from their huts, scanning for a moment the dark explosion leaping from the hill into the empty heavens; then I saw them rushing in a body up the steep slope. My eyes followed them until they looked like large black ants on a dirty brown wall, stopping here and there as they climbed, to break some twig and leaf-covered branches from off a bush. There was an evergreen, half-way up the hill. I saw them all make for this, which, by the time they had left it, was branchless; nothing remained but the naked trunk. On they climbed, higher and higher, the little body of black ants, carrying over their shoulders what in the distance appeared like so many brooms, some dragging them along behind and others holding several in a bunch before them as they struggled up the stony incline towards the ominous crackling beyond the summit of the hill.

Then I, too, took to my heels. As I rushed through the cattle kraal I yelled at two milk-boys to leave off work and follow. They dropped their pails and came at a run.

I don't suppose I shall easily forget what I saw from the top of that hill. In front of me, and on either side away as far as I could see, concealing three horizons, a regiment of roaring orange flame was bearing down upon the defenceless valley where it seemed I had spent all my life. I have never felt so ridiculously powerless as I did during that moment, when for the first time I was looking at a ten-mile line of advancing fire. I remember what shocked and astounded me most at first was the noise it made. When I had come within a hundred yards of it I yelled at some natives to rush back to the kraal and fetch some more axes, and I found I was yelling at myself; my voice came back at me in that mocking, humiliating tone of a natural echo. I was merely telling *myself* to fetch the axes. A boy ten yards away failed to hear my cry.

One often hears that a certain man "works like a nigger"—a saying emanating probably from the slave-trade days of the seventeenth and eighteenth centuries. But I had never seen one Negro work as I had seen some white people work—till that day.

Before me was a long, uninterrupted line of natives, half in and half out of the flames which rose, tall and black and orange, yards above and before their bent backs. They were bending over in line before the blaze, thrashing the flames at their feet with branches snatched from the bushes as they mounted the hill.

They thrashed as if all their lives they had been waiting for this one chance of proving that power of endurance for which, throughout the world, they have become both famous and infamous. For wasn't the Negro once bought and sold? And wasn't a black slave despicable, rather less than human; horribly near a monkey, wasn't he, in the eyes of those born under another sky?

They planted their naked feet on the creeping fire, feet gnarled and cut and split and hard as leather, feet immune to pain; with these they stamped out the little jumping fits of flame that flitted from one tuft of dried grass to another, though there was no visible connection of fire between the tufts. A shoot of fire shot up there, and the moment it burst into a long tongue a blade from another tuft would be caught, and it burst out here, burst out everywhere.

Thus hour after hour, until there was no longer any hope of saving the little valley, we continued to stamp and thrash out the flames.

The natives thrashed like men possessed of devils, with their eyes, nose, and mouth closed to the anæsthetic fumes that rose in clouds from off the black, burnt ground.

As the fire rolled along the belly of the earth the reinforced tongues of flame leapt up the little trees, coursed like hungry red snakes along their barren branches, lapping up the crisp paper-like leaves, and snapping off the branches as if they were so many matches. And down came the trees in a crackling blaze, and they lay there on the ground, inert, like charred corpses on a battlefield of fire.

And while I thrashed and stamped till the soles of my boots caught alight and fell away from my feet, I could hear all the time beside me a native leap in, thrash and stamp, stamp and thrash, then leap out again; and every time he came I heard him mutter what sounded like a strangled oath.

Soon I was borne down upon him by a gust of wind bringing with it a cloud of fire-flaming branches, twigs, and scorching leaves, blistering my skin as they fell. And as I stumbled close to him, at each stamp of his feet I heard him spit out the word "Baas," and with each sweep of his arms at the advancing flames

I heard him, in a voice full of frightful vengeance, crying "*Huyten —Huyten—Huyten!*"

I half-turned towards him, and as I turned I managed to open one of my smarting eyes. There beside me, dimly through a cloud of dense smoke, I saw the great figure of Plate beating with a heavy sjambok the body of the manager. The Dutchman was lying on his back with his mouth open; the semi-bald head was black; the twig-like hairs on his arms were scorched away to the skin; and I remember hearing the scrunch of his ribs as they broke under the blows of the sjambok.

The Force

It was what they call in the British South African Police a One-Man Station—a two-roomed, one-storey house made of sun-burned brick, with a corrugated-iron roof. And it was one hundred and fifty miles from a town and seventy miles from a railway.

Big-boned, mature, strong and healthy men, such as George Newman was, were chosen from the Force to take over One-Man Stations. At one time they thought married men were more suited than single men to occupy these posts, but the wives did not share this view, and it was a failure. So bachelors were sent alone to Administer Justice and Keep the Peace in remote, unimportant places. Their pay was very good, and they could save money; they had to save money, for there was nothing to buy. And big men were chosen: the smaller, younger members of the Force being given stations near towns, in towns; and the good-looking, more refined boys were sent to the Matoppo Hills and the Victoria Falls, where wealthy tourists came to gaze at the resting-place of Cecil Rhodes and to hear the tremendous roar of the falling Zambesi river. Occasionally one of these young men would disappear and never be seen again. But, as a rule, during the week-ends they got drunk at the tourists' expense, and tried to go to bed with unattached American girls of the party. They did not always succeed, but at least they had a chance to try. Some paid no heed to the tourists, contenting themselves with their own company.

George Newman was a large man of thirty, with small eyes, a swollen nose, and a sallow, parched skin. He had been on the station, in his two-roomed house, for nine months before he was given a fortnight's leave. During those months he had not seen a white man, nor spoken a word of English. And when the day came for him to leave he was in a chronic nervous condition. He had looked forward so much, for so long, to this short holiday that he realized suddenly, at the last moment, he was loath to go. Perhaps even then, if a stranger had come to spend a few days at the station, he would have remained, welcoming wholeheartedly the stranger's arrival, which would give him an excuse to spend his fortnight where he had been for so long. It was a four days' ride into town, and Newman was aware that when he got there he would know no one, for he came from hundreds of miles farther south and in his life he had spent only one night in the town. What he would do there was the chief subject that had occupied his mind on the station. As he rode out to patrol the kraals, when he talked to the native chiefs, while he collected their tax-money and paid his own boys' wages, while he spent his spare hours cultivating his own few acres of mealies, while he listened to the natives who came to him with their wrongs, and when in the evenings he sat alone with a bottle of whisky and a cheap book he had read before—all the time, day and night, he thought of what he would do when he got his leave and arrived in the town. And the town itself, possessing little more than a thousand whites, grew in Newman's brain to resemble at last some fantastic city with glaring lights revealing the delirious night-life of a West European capital. He would arrive, and with all the money he had saved he would be able to buy the greatest pleasure and comfort the town could offer! He would have a large bedroom at the Grand Hotel, a real bath, and he would drink at the Club and make friends who would introduce him to a woman, two women, lots of women—and he would dance and drink, and after the dance—ah, God knows!—a large bedroom in the Grand Hotel and handfuls of money! Would there be such resistance? He could offer anything within reason that money could buy, and with it his clean, inviolate, tortured self. Maybe—maybe he would not return alone! And when at last he got into bed at nights, he would smile to himself at the thought of his approaching freedom.

But when the day came he did not smile. Instead, as he set off with his few belongings strapped to his horse, a feeling of dread possessed him, his mouth was dry, and many times he was on the point of returning to the lonely station. When the world jumped to reality before his eyes, when his dreams faded and he saw the friendless town as it actually was, with its sordid low houses and mean shops and empty hotels, then he would waver in disbelief of himself, plunge back into his loneliness, fearing the thought of social contact with men and women who would look at him and talk to him while he would gaze at them and be left with nothing to say. He could not hear himself talking, could not hear strange English sentences issuing from his mouth. And he asked himself what he *would* say, how he would carry on a conversation—and there was no answer. He had nothing to talk about but himself; he had said nothing for nine months, and now thought and words had left him. He had talked only to Africans, in their strange dialect, in a strained, half-furtive way. There was no communion between man and man—the black and the white—even in the loneliness of the latter. It could not be. Newman was not a man who despised the Negro, though he was conscious, as a civilized white, of the superiority of his own race. This he took for granted, although the dubious fact has never been proved. He did not despise them; unconsciously he was deeply envious of them, of their innate happiness, their freedom, their lives void of responsibility. He was wounded by their calm acceptance of living, troubled neither by ambition nor malice. It made him harbour a bitterness that smouldered within him, but which he kept under control so successfully that to the world at large it would have seemed like a brooding smoulder of smoke, lacking any fire. And the women, the native women, he feared, as a child fears to trespass upon forbidden ground; but it was a fear all the more desirable to overcome for the very reason that it was prompted by a taboo. And Newman found the desire very strong: in him there was a force working that often came near to overpowering him, near to shattering his "race-respect." To the African himself he paid no heed; Newman resented him, but for their women his normal, ever-increasing life-force rolled about and surged in him like a turbulent sea caught in the grip of a gorge, unable to free itself, thrust back on its own tide till the force of that tide urged it forward again, to smash its waters against the relentless rocks called colour.

And now he was to be free. He *was* free, riding into the town towards men and women whence he himself had sprung, to a world constructed by the hands of civilized people, who every day made the sight of the earth more and more grotesque and hideous. These men would not accept the freedom they were offered: there was innate striving wherever they lived. And he shrank from it, feeling cut off, inferior, lacking in grace, and alone.

And then he would think of himself back in the station again, sitting alone by a candle, while the whisky sunk lower and lower in the bottle—and instantly a sharp revolt would spring up in him. To turn back was impossible, the sense of failure and humiliation too strong to bear; so, fortifying himself with dreams he did not really believe in, he rode on.

In his imagination he had seen the town many hundreds of times, but in none of his visions had it looked so dreary and friendless as it did when he entered it on the afternoon of the fourth day's ride. It was very hot and the bare wide streets were empty but for a few ragged natives leaning against the walls of dilapidated shanties or sitting playing marbles with pebbles in the gutter. As Newman rode into the yard to stable his horse a man in a panama hat and a tropical suit walked leisurely across the arid square in front of the Grand Hotel. And that was all; there was no one else, nothing more, nothing but silence and the empty streets and drab houses whence waves of shimmering heat rose into the clear, spotless sky.

When he had ordered a room he left the hotel. But at the end of two hours he had walked through every street in the town and he had seen no one to whom he even wished to say a word. He went to the Club, where he signed on for a week's membership: he sat down to read the papers, but it was so long since he had heard any news of the world that the word-covered sheets now failed to interest him. And the Club was empty. He returned to the hotel, hating the town, hating the Police Force, hating Africa, despising himself. He had a bath, and then, throwing himself on the bed, fell fast asleep.

It was already late when he woke with a shock to find himself in a hotel bedroom. He got up quickly, washed, and went to the Club. Over the bar a group of big, brown-faced farmers sat drinking and talking about the latest prices of stock, their own immediate woes, and the prospects of rain in the near future. Newman listened, drinking whiskies and water. But nothing he heard either concerned or interested him. And the farmers seemed unaware of his presence. A member of the town police came in in uniform. Newman knew the man by sight, but until he came over and asked him if he were in the Force, Newman found it impossible to bring himself to make the other any sign of recognition. He told Newman his name was Bright, and then Newman remembered he had met him in the town the day before he had gone to the station. At first Bright talked not without difficulty, for to whatever question he asked of him the other always answered with a curt yes or no. Newman wished to talk, longed to talk, longed to appear friendly to this man who had gone so far towards helping him as to introduce himself. But he could not conquer his reserve, and he kept thinking what he would say if he spoke: he framed a sentence between each gulp of whisky, choosing his words with infinite care: he would think of asking Bright if there were anything to do in the town during the coming few days, but when he had almost formed the sentence and the words were on his lips it occurred to him suddenly that Bright might imagine he were seeking his companionship during that time. And the fact that this was in part true prevented him speaking, and he would drink again to conceal his embarrassment. He was about to ask Bright in what part of the town he lived, but even this question he could not force out of himself for fear that Bright would think he wished to come with him to his home. And he refrained from saying more than a few words about himself because he felt well-disposed towards the other man and did not wish to bore him with depressing details of his monotonous existence on the station. And that was all the conversation he had, that and asking questions, and questions he felt constrained to avoid in case Bright should think him too curious. And Bright talked on at random about his wife and his child and the hope they had of saving enough money to take a short holiday by the sea. It would be good for the child. Was Newman married? No? Well, in his opinion, life wasn't worth living up-country in Africa until you were married. He had not had much to do with women himself, he had always prided himself on being a "woman-hater," until he met his wife; but now he realized how wrong he had been, and since then he did not believe there was such a person as a "woman-hater." Oh, Newman must get married. And Newman smiled. It was a curious sensation, smiling. Quite strange to Newman. He was not smiling at anything humorous, but merely at the ironic thought that crossed his mind. He must get married! Bright might just as well have told him he must get wings and take a trip to the moon! Give him the wings, give him the woman! Yes, Newman could quite well believe life was almost pleasant with a wife. He began to visualize Bright's life. His wife, yes, she was probably charming, young, good-looking. Where was she now? Sitting at home, waiting for him to come back, while he stood at the bar drinking his seventh whisky and telling a strange man how wonderful it was to be married! Newman supposed this must be the case. Would he, would he stand about in bars and drink whisky if he had a woman? He doubted it. But even if he wanted to there were no bars, nowhere to stand about away from one's wife, on the station. But then if he were married he would not be on the station. Newman thought of Bright as a man who did not appreciate his luck, did not appreciate precisely what he was telling him he appreciated, and he began to resent him. What right had he to a wife? He felt bitter. But when, just before he left the bar, Bright asked him to come to a Saturday-night dance at the Grand Hotel with himself and his wife, the bitter look on Newman's face vanished and he accepted the invitation with eagerness. Saturday was the last day of his leave. Thank God there was something to look forward to!

"There are never many there," Bright said, "because there are so few unmarried girls in the town, but if you can find a partner —well, bring her along. Good-bye, Newman—glad to have met you. See you Saturday!" And they shook hands and Bright went out, a little unsteadily.

Newman ordered another whisky, feeling more cheerful than he had felt for a long time. He knew someone now. And Bright must have liked him or he would not have bothered to offer the invitation. But Newman wished the dance were tonight. It was only Monday, and he had five whole days to kill. And he had no wish to "kill" them. He was on leave, on holiday: he was supposed to be enjoying himself; every hour he had dreamed would be an hour of pleasure. And here he was drinking himself half stupid in a bar, looking forward almost with dread to the next few days and with pleasure to some little dance with another man's wife on the eve of the day when once more he would have to return to the station. The Station! He shuddered at the thought. He had only just arrived in the town, and already he was looking forward to the night before he had to return! A frail straw of hope entered his head when he thought of the possibility of meeting someone at the dance. It is odd to what little things an unhappy man will cling for happiness. But what had Bright said? "There are never many there, because there are so few girls in the town." No, the little hope grew smaller, nearly vanished. His spirits began to subside, and quite suddenly he knew he had drunk too much. His head was nodding and his eyes closed themselves against his will. With a noble effort he pulled himself together, paid for eight whiskies, and went to the dining-room to eat. Food would sober him. But he gobbled his food, not tasting it, and felt the sleepiness of much alcohol creeping over him. He knew he must get up, have one more drink to postpone the drowsiness, and then go out into the air.

The streets were poorly lighted, but a million stars sufficiently illuminated the night to show Newman the wide unpeopled streets. The sleeping town was without sound; not a stir among the leaves of the gum-trees lining the pavements. There was a singing in Newman's ears, fumes of alcohol floated in his head, and a wildness unknown to him rose from his bowels, taking possession of his body as tongues of flame envelop the coals of a newly lighted fire. He knew the way back to the hotel, could have walked it in his sleep, but he had no desire to go there. During the queer momentary glimpses of clarity in his befuddled brain he was aware of the visions that had come to him on the station, visions of the nights he would spend in town, of the glaring streets busy with traffic and the wild, exotic life of hundreds of men and women whose sole occupation till the hours appeared with dawn was pleasure. In the wide streets he saw corners that did not exist, where women stood watching, hoping, silent. And he gripped a wad of bank-notes in his trousers pocket, all the time turning away from his hotel, down darker, narrower streets, watching, hoping against hope. For Newman knew Africa. No white women walked the streets in up-country towns. White women were more rare than gold, more valuable than the most precious stone. Queens, they reigned supreme, respected, in a land their men annexed by force, bowed down to by all because of the colour of their skins. Spinsters were only that from their own wish, in up-country towns. And they had to fight even for spinsterhood. The streets, the meanest and the widest, were empty for Newman; no living thing accosted his hopeless wandering. He walked in circles, like a man lost in the desert, frustrated desire giving way slowly to despair, and in his loneliness he staggered back to his room. The night air had awakened fresh thirst in his parched throat, and he rang the bell. A native girl, dressed in black with a white apron, came to the door in answer, and Newman ordered a whisky. He watched her leave the room with her head lowered, and he watched her return with her face bent over the glass on the tray, and when she closed the door behind her he uttered a little stifled cry and threw himself on the bed and buried his face in the pillow. . . .

II

When George Newman put on his one suit and went down to the dance-room on Saturday night, conflicting emotions of hope and despair fought within him. He had spent the previous four days of his leave in much the same way as he had spent the first. But he had not seen Bright again, nor had he had the good fortune to fall in with anyone to whom he could talk. He had drunk a great deal in the Club and he had taken his meals there, and he had wandered aimlessly, hopelessly, round the town, visiting bars, shops, and the small hotel lounges; he had bought a new suit which he now wore, and every night he had staggered to his room and thrown himself on the bed in a drunken stupor. The excess of liquor was now apparent on his face; his eyes were bloodshot, the lids swollen, his hands shook, and the flesh on his

face was pale and puffy. Innumerable cigarettes had stained the
fingers of both his hands a deep brown.

As he stood at the entrance to the dance-room and heard the
music and the sound of people talking and laughing, he tried to
shut out his thoughts of the next day. He sat down on a chair and
ordered a whisky. Lighting a cigarette, he fell to wondering what
it would be like to dance again, to put his arm round a woman's
waist, and hold her hand and close himself up against her—when
he heard a voice near him: "Hullo, Newman! Let me introduce
my wife!"

Newman rose quickly from his chair and put out his hand. He
felt thin, lifeless fingers crumple in his grasp, and he looked up
into the face of Elsa Bright. It was a tired and faded face, drawn
and haggard, though Newman saw that she could not be older
than himself. There were shadows under her watery eyes, and the
thin rouged lips were too bright for the sallow, lightly powdered
face.

"Pleased to meet you, Mr Newman," she said weakly, but the
listless tone of her voice rather attracted Newman. He felt that
she was submissive, tired, and it gave him a sense of superiority
which he was far from feeling for the others in the room.

They sat at a small table near the band, where a little Jew
played the piano and another white accompanied him on a violin.
A boy made noises with his feet and banged when he felt like it
on a drum. It is strange that though music is in the very bones of
the African people, the white man continues in vain to try and
find it in stray dilettantes of his own colour. In Africa bar-tenders
and waiters in hotels are generally Indians; and in Paris, the
only capital in the world where all skins speak the same language
and black dances freely with white, the dance bands of the
greatest reputation in that city are composed of Negroes who
understand no tongue but American!

A dozen couples turned round and round, walked up and down
together, on the small dancing space: most of them danced with
no sense of rhythm, apologizing to each other for the mistakes
they made with their feet, and blushing and stammering little
sentences of encouragement in their efforts to believe that they
were enjoying themselves. Newman thought them very pathetic.

And he looked at Elsa Bright, and his hopes fell. Her thin green dress sagged from her shoulders, and she sat in a jaded fashion, her back slightly bent, so that to all appearances she might have been breastless. Then she glanced up, suddenly aware of his gaze, but looked away again, embarrassed. And Newman felt sorry for her, wishing to apologize for his lack of grace, wanting to excuse himself with the help of some insincere compliment. He would like to talk to her: he felt he *could* talk to this woman, for he felt she was unhappy; and they could share their mutual unhappiness with words of consolation and sympathy. But there was Bright, sitting opposite him with his eyes fixed on a girl at the next table. No, he couldn't talk to her as he wished while Bright was there. Then a waiter appeared, and Bright ordered food.

"Then you didn't find a fourth?" he suddenly asked of Newman.

"Er . . . no," stammered Newman; "you see, I really don't know anyone here."

"Too bad. I know some girls here tonight, but I'm afraid they're all with their partners. And—well, you know how it is, they don't like to be separated."

"Oh, that's all right," said Newman with embarrassment, suddenly terrified at the thought of being obliged to take a strange girl away from her partner, "quite all right, Bright. I'm not much of a dancer anyway—and I enjoy watching."

Having safely evaded what he thought might prove to be an awkward situation, Newman felt curiously pleased with himself. He glanced at Elsa Bright's pale face, and a longing came over him to lean forward and speak to her, to tell her he thought she looked tired and that he sympathized. He, too, was tired, and he too. . . . Then he realized with a shock that a man did not tell a woman he had just met even that she looked tired, although he might think so. And he felt hot and nervous at the thought of what he might have said. Food came, and from force of habit he put his hand round his tumbler to drink, and then was aware of its emptiness. He looked at the glass and his eyes brightened. With a certain appearance of excitement he leaned over the table.

"I say, Bright," he said, "you've been damn good to me; let

me stand you and your wife a bottle of fizz. I've saved a pot of money and have nothing to spend it on."

"That's very nice of you," said Bright with a smile. And he turned to his wife. "What about you, dear?"

"Oh, I'd love it!" Elsa exclaimed. And her pallid face almost beamed as she glanced quickly at Newman.

And Newman felt a thrill pass through him. For an instant he was quite happy, conscious of having rendered a little happiness.

The Brights excused themselves and rose to dance. Newman sat back and watched them. He saw Elsa place her hand on her husband's shoulder, put her other hand in his; and that was how they danced, apart from each other, Bright gazing disinterestedly about, and Elsa with an expressionless stare looking over his shoulder as though nothing on earth could attract her attention. There was no contact between them, they were entirely separate, man and woman, and the intimacy that even the slow and painful foxtrot can bring to the bodies and faces of some failed in this couple to produce so much as a word from either. They were lifeless. Newman drank a glass of champagne, and a feeling of resentment rose in him against his host. Why couldn't he show a little enthusiasm? He had a woman: this woman was his wife; it was barely ordinary civility to plough round a room as though he were not aware of her existence. It was an insult. Could he not show appreciation of her presence by so little as a smile, a word? People could be very cruel to one another. He watched them walk rather than dance round the room till the band ceased and they sat down. He poured some champagne into Elsa's glass and she smiled and thanked him. He thought she looked happy that the dance was ended and that she was back again at the table.

"You do dance, Mr Newman, don't you?" she asked suddenly, sipping her champagne.

"Oh, I used to once," he answered, smiling; "but one gets out of it, you know. One gets out of everything, living alone. You probably don't know what it's like——"

But instantly he cut himself short, suddenly aware that he was going too far. Bright was looking at him, and he fell silent under his gaze, lest he should be despised for talking of himself. The band struck up again, the "Blue Danube," just recognizable.

"Now, you two!" said Bright heartily, patting his wife on the back. "Now it's your turn. I'm just going over to talk to the Oaklands." And he left the table and walked over to the other end of the room.

Newman drank off his champagne and got up. He led Elsa out on to the floor and put his arm round her waist. She was slim and his arm enveloped her, his hand resting on her right hip. He smiled down at her unconsciously and she smiled back, as though she knew him, liked him, felt his nearness. And they swung out into the room, closed together, from their breasts to their knees. At one time Newman had known how to dance and he had not forgotten. They glided noiselessly over the floor in silence. He felt no need to talk, and something told him there was no urge for speech in Elsa. As they passed her husband Newman looked down at him and saw that he was engrossed in conversation with those at his table. He steered her to the other end of the room and they waltzed in circles away from where her husband sat. He took a fleeting glance at the face almost on a level with his, her cheek nearly touching his own, and he saw her eyes shining and a little ripple of a smile hovering about her red lips. She looked up at him.

"I thought you said you couldn't dance!" she said, breaking into a low laugh.

"I didn't think I could!" He smiled back.

"Well, *I* say you can!"

"That's very sweet of you. I used to love dancing, but it's so long since——"

"When d'you have to go back?" she broke in, a little eagerly Newman thought.

"I start tomorrow morning."

"Start?"

"Yes, it's a good four days' ride."

"Oh dear. I didn't know you were as far away as that. They must be terribly lonely, those one-man stations."

"They are. I hate it," answered Newman, bitterly.

And they were silent then, wrapped as one, while they moved together over the floor. Newman felt a curious strength springing into his arms and he held her more firmly round the waist, pressing her fingers very slightly and feeling his own pressed in response. He shut his eyes, and the champagne to which he was not accustomed mounted to his face, filling him with a pleasant sensation quite unknown to him. He wished the room to close in darkness, leaving him alone with the woman he had in his arms. He bent his head a little and some hairs of her head touched his cheek and the smell of her body rose up to him from the warmth of her breast. Some force was gripping him, rising in waves within him; the strength went out of his arms, surged back into the core of his being, and the spittle dried up in his mouth; it was not easy to dance any more.

"Shall we go and finish that bottle?" he said.

But Elsa did not answer. He looked down at her, and her eyes were shut and her face pale: he felt her a little limp against his arm.

"Shall we——"

"Oh, I'm sorry," she almost whispered, opening her eyes. "Had you been speaking? I think I must have been in a kind of dream! Silly of me. Yes, let's sit down."

Newman led her to their table and they seated themselves on neighbouring chairs.

"Sure you're all right?" he asked with concern.

"Yes, absolutely. You dance too well, that's all!" And she looked up at him and laughed.

They sat drinking champagne. Bright was still at a distant table. Newman lighted a cigarette with a hand that trembled. He felt as though he had been running in some exciting race and had not altogether recovered his breath. He was not sure what had happened in the race, but he knew that his heart was now beating with unusual vigour. There was a tight feeling in his chest, and his head thumped regularly to the beat of his heart. His thoughts were entirely submerged in his own body, then in that of the woman next to him. Tonight, in a moment, she would be gone: and tomorrow he—he would be gone. It was hard to believe he would be gone, away from here, away from her, for he felt he had known her a long time, all his life. There was no need to talk to her now: there was no uneasiness in her company, no nervous wondering as to what he would say next. She was there, for him,

with him, part of him, in the communion of their two selves. She
did not speak, but it was as though she were talking to him all the
time. And tomorrow. . . .

When the band struck up once more he got up and she rose
with him. There was no word spoken between them. And he led
her out and put his arm round her and clasped her hand in his.
And it was as if it had always been like that. Yet there was no
peace for him. The old force sprang up again, like a tidal wave,
possessing him with the strength of a vice, weakening him. He
gripped her tight and she melted into him: their legs were as two
legs, hers pressed firmly against his, advancing and retreating
with his own to the rhythm of the music. His mind became empty,
his vision a fantasy of indistinct figures, and the blood in his
head flowed down, drawn as though by a magnet, into the source
of his body. Dancing became impossible for him, and they went
back to the table.

Newman saw Bright standing there with his hat in his hand.
"Well," said Bright jovially, "all good things must come to an end.
I'm afraid we must be off now."

Newman stared at Bright without speaking. There seemed to
him nothing to be said, and yet the idea that this man should
walk away with the woman with whom he had just been dancing
sounded hardly credible. And yet—she was his wife; he meant
nothing to either of them.

Elsa fumbled for her coat on her chair, her head lowered, away
from the men. Newman bent down to assist her. Her coat was on.
She put out her hand. Half-consciously Newman took it and,
pressing it, was aware of the pressure of her thin fingers.

"Next time you are in town," she said in a weak, far-away voice,
"you must come and stay with us. We have a room."

"Yes, that's right," Bright added; "come along and spend a
week with us and we'll introduce you to some people. Love to
have you."

Newman managed to smile. He dropped Elsa's hand. "Thank
you," he said, "it's very kind of you. And, thank you, for this
evening."

He followed the husband and wife from the room. As they
reached the door Elsa Bright looked back over her shoulder.

"And thank you," she almost whispered, "for dancing so beautifully."

But Newman could find nothing to say. And waving, Mr and Mrs Bright passed through the swing doors and out into the night.

Newman sat down in the chair from which only two hours before he had risen to meet Elsa Bright. All that had happened since then raced through his head in a series of mind-pictures, over and over again. He was getting up and clasping her thin, lifeless fingers, looking at her red mouth set in the pale face. They were sitting at the table and suddenly he was happy, ordering champagne. "Oh, I'd love it," she had said, and beamed on him. Newman shifted in his chair. Then they were dancing. "Oh, dear, I didn't know you were as far away as that. They must be terribly lonely, those one-man stations." Terribly lonely! The one brick house, his bed, his table, his chair, the whisky bottle: the empty, friendless, silent days and nights of monotony! Lonely! "Yes, it is. I hate it!" And there had been silence then.

They were dancing: she was in his arms, pressed against him; he could feel her hair on his face; he shut his eyes; that unbearable force rose in him; she hung limp against his arm, and he could not dance any more. "You dance too well, that's all!" And they sat in silence, in a kind of mutual, silent communion. And they were dancing again, pressed together, melted into one another: but the force leapt up in him once more—as it was rising in him now—and Bright was standing at their table with his coat on. "Thank you for dancing so beautifully!" Thank you! *Thank you!*

With a groan Newman got up and went to his room. There was an acute ache in his loins. He sat on the bed and looked round the impersonal room. His pyjamas, his washing things, his riding clothes . . . nothing more. A detailed vision of the station appeared before his eyes: the little two-roomed, one-storey house, the table, the chair, the empty bed. . . . Tomorrow: in a few hours . . . ! He stretched out and rang the bell.

The same native girl who had answered his ring on the first night of his leave appeared in the doorway and smiled a recognition. Newman looked at her, smiling involuntarily at her friendliness, and ordered a whisky.

While he waited he began to walk about the room. The pain in his loins was increasing, and now and again he stopped and bent down for relief. But his body still trembled from the strange physical contact of the evening, and he could not be still. Raging within him, the force of his manhood allowed him no peace.

The door opened and the girl came in with his whisky on a tray. She passed near him to lay it on the table, and as she passed, Newman smelled the full hot smell of her body. But he was not repulsed. Desire overruled it. He closed his eyes, trembling violently. Then he took a step towards her, not knowing that he moved: he put a hand on her shoulder as she turned to leave, and he looked down into her dark, inscrutable face, and a wildness seized him with the suddenness of a thunderclap; a torrent whose power was irresistible surged up in him, possessed his stricken limbs as his arms went about her, and the rocks called colour were conquered as the man and the woman fell slowly together where they stood, on the floor.

Two Men

EIGHT MONTHS we had lived together in the only brick house at Fort Insezi, five days' ride from Bulawayo. Thirty-five years ago Lobengula, old, fat, obscene with disease and self-indulgence, no longer able to walk, had been carried through the village to his death, which will always remain a mystery. There had been bloodshed then: farther north Captain Wilson and thirty Englishmen were trapped and killed by natives on a vast ant-hill. A monument, overgrown with moss and fallen branches, more like a dead tree than a memorial, still stands on the hill to commemorate the occasion. Since then few white men had been seen in Fort Insezi; it was the headquarters of the Native Commissioner; nothing of any moment came our way. It was just a native village with one brick house outside it, where Maurice Macadam and I lived.

Behind our house stood two huts, where the two police boys slept. They wore uniform—khaki shorts, shirt and a wide-brimmed hat, like that of a Boy Scout. Beneath these their faces seemed even blacker than they were in reality. They were very proud, these two. The other natives saluted them as they saluted us: to an African Negro, as to millions of men, a uniform means much.

From the front stoep of the house we could see a great expanse of scrubby bush, flat to the horizon. Here and there a few mealie lands showed signs of native dwelling, but apart from this there was nothing on which the eye might linger, nothing but brown scrub.

The Fort lay in the centre of the district we had to survey. Our northern territory occupied a large part of it, between the Tcshangani and the Gwelo rivers, whither it was our duty to go during two months in the year.

Both of us lived for these months, although this fact, with so many others, we kept to ourselves, even in the evenings. For only at sundown did we dare reveal to each other the strain of monotony so evident in our faces and the manner in which we went about our work. We seldom smiled; we found nothing to smile at. I spent more time than I knew looking at Maurice and wondering what was going on behind those pained eyes. His yellow face was lined like that of an old man; two deep furrows started either side of his nose and ran down to the corners of his thin mouth, which drooped, saying more than he ever said. At the end of eight months, conversation between us had almost ceased. Unless something unexpected occurred (and my prayers were rarely answered), we spoke hardly at all. Yet, to escape from each other was impossible. Sometimes at sunset, with the aid of whisky and water, I found myself soaring a little above this quiet black village. Under its influence I became detached, two eyes in the clear sky, seeing two white men, one barely middle-aged, the other young, sitting together with a bottle between them, uttering a word, a sentence, then silence, then a string of words punctuated by strained silences as between men ill at ease, the lips not daring to utter the cry struggling so desperately within. Then, for a brief moment, something would melt in me—a mental hand stretching out to feel the fingers of another—when, before the mind could be reinforced with further stimulant, I would descend with a crash to earth and the bitter hatreds of the dying day. In all that time we learned nothing of each other. British, we lived our own lives, secretly harbouring every thought as though it were right for them to be so precious, allowing ourselves no relief in speech— the only outlet that was offered us. We did not actually fight; or we fought rather against fighting, each one knowing there was only the other. We lived on in a kind of desperate hope, waiting for the relief of walking away.

In silence the days grew nearer; the rains ceased; the sun began to burn the grasses; at nights I could hear the two police boys talking excitedly about the approaching departure. Hearing them, I myself experienced a curious elation. There would be freedom! There would be uncertainty in the days; in the mornings we would not know where we would sleep the night, nor how far

we should walk the next day, and every day something fresh to
see, no certainty ... the relief of not knowing. Something leapt
up at me at the thought. Maurice, in that listless voice I had
grown to hate, murmured: "Oh well, I suppose there'll be a little
shooting."

Ten days of walking through endless *vleis*, the grass in some
places reaching high above our heads, the two police boys carrying on their backs the little we needed, ourselves burdened only
to the extent of two shot guns, brought us to the banks of the
Tcshangani River.

In summer this river is deep and wide, filled with torrents
which sweep along with them anything, however huge, that dares
to approach beyond the brink of its shelving banks. But now, in
winter, during the long period of sunshine, we found it low and
docile in sleep. The dirty grey water lay sluggishly in the bed,
foul and stagnant. But water was an immediate necessity, and
Maurice decided to remain.

Slowly, during the days of walking and sleeping out, a curious
sensation of hopefulness, like the sudden appearance of sun
brightening the earth after days of rain, had begun to rise in me.
In the early mornings, when half-awakened by dawn to find the
white sky above growing gradually whiter, then a hue of pale
orange melt the white into a watery gold as though the heavens
were cast in snow, queer exciting thoughts, like those that enter
the head with opium, raced and re-raced through my brain. I
would fear to move under the blankets, lest full day should appear
with the swiftness of a light turned on in a dark warm room, and
a cold portrait of my real and sober self be thrown too clearly
before me against a background of the already rising sun. Yet the
quick-coming dawns were not easy to sleep through; now it was
night, now day. But one fought against waking fully in a moment,
if only for the subconscious thought that a day, like a life, is
so often more lovely in its beginning than in its fullness or its
end.

As for Maurice, I could not but notice a change of a similar
kind in him. Each day it seemed as if a little more weight were

being lifted mysteriously from his body. The afternoon before we
came to the river he shot two pheasants with a brilliant right and
left. His dog brought the birds and laid them at its master's feet.
Maurice smiled, patted the dog affectionately, and as we moved
on I could see that a new vigour had sprung up in him; he walked
fast and looked about him as though on the alert for fresh things
to see and enjoy. The same evening, while sitting over the fire
eating the birds and drinking from a bottle, he turned to me, and
his voice sounded as if it were coming from the lips of a man I
had never met. "I've wanted to say this for a long time," he began,
staring into the flames. "Till now I haven't been able, I really
don't know why... I ... I hate the Fort. I've been there five years
now, you know. There was Spencer, then Murphy, and now you
... it's always been the same. Often—oh, hundreds of times—I've
been on the point of quitting, but I know it's no good. I've seen
men go, fed-up, seen 'em return home, swearing all known curses
on this blight of a country, and ... what's happened? A year, two
years, back they are again, for no better reason than that they
couldn't stand the climate in the old country. It's no good." He
stopped, at a loss for words, took a long drink from the bottle,
wiped his face with the back of his hand, then went on. "Always
the same. The same with Murphy and Spencer as it is with you.
All right for a month, a few weeks, then ... oh, you know. I'm not
a man with a hell of a lot to say, but, good God, how can two men
go on talking night after night for months, years on end! I ... I
only wanted ... wanted to tell you I'm feeling a bit better now
that I've got away and ... and, well, I'm damned sorry if I've
made it none too good for you ... just ... just try not to forget I've
had five years of it at a stretch and ... well, sometimes ... sometimes .. I think I must be ... *mad*!"

For a moment I could not bring myself to look up from my
plate. While he had been speaking I had not moved, finding it
hard to believe this was the voice of the man I had known so
long; never had I heard him speak like this. As I heard the last
words I wanted to get up and run away, I was so filled with
embarrassment. But the hollow silence that followed was worse.
At last I looked up. Maurice was staring at me, his eyes bright
with tears, then the thin lips creased themselves up into a sudden

smile, and he stretched out his right hand towards me. Instinctively I leaned over and shook it—for the second time in my life. During the remainder of the evening neither of us spoke again, but the silence, so different from the dreaded, painful silences during the long days and evenings at the Fort, seemed heavy with the unspoken words that speech could not have made more eloquent.

And at last, when we came to the river on the following day, I felt as though an invisible enemy, so long endured and hated by us both, had been killed between us. Maurice began to talk and laugh and I to answer with a zest unknown to me, full of wonder at what a few words and the last days had accomplished. I found myself speaking without thinking, asking questions and advice as from a man I both respected and admired. Here, as though by magic, the brutal strife of living seemed curiously to fade away: it was like waking from a hideous nightmare to find the sun shining outside on a pleasant world: the desire to be part of all one saw, the mere quick awareness of once more being alive, seemed sufficient to give one a queer exultant happiness that was full. Of a sudden I found the breath of my tired body whispering one wish—to be left thus, in peace.

In the afternoon we began to cut down the bush to make space for our camp, while the two boys disappeared to collect dried logs for an all-night fire. From time to time I stopped in my work to glance at Maurice, and each time I became more aware of a softening in his face; I thought the hard look that had been always dormant in his pained eyes was beginning to pass away: there was a peaceful and easy tolerance in the way he bent over the small trees and cut them very carefully just above the ground. The vicious little twist to his mouth had gone, the gleam of cruelty which I was so accustomed to see in his face when he was working with his hands was supplanted now by one of strength applied by a man whose body and mind are evenly oiled with a sense of freedom and tranquillity. Just as I saw him he seemed to me to fit in so well with this world where there was no war: it was as though at last he had found some companionship, not in me, but in the very atmosphere of this place where the strange voices of alien men were as yet unheard. Such men were

we, but our lonely advent I could not help but consider rather as
our good sense and fortune than as a crime. Looking back on
that day, and almost unwillingly I do (for sometimes there is
pain even in thoughts of peace), I would return tomorrow and
have nothing altered, were it not for a superstitious nature warning me never to try to repeat a moment of happy time.

The camp we had made lay in the heart of some thick jungle,
on the edge of the southern bank of the river. A few natives,
having heard in their mysterious way of the arrival of white men,
hovered about in the background, peeping out from behind trees,
making signs to each other, the children gazing wide-eyed with
amazement at two beings so entirely different from anything
they had ever seen on legs, and the women, with naked babies at
their breasts, speechless with curiosity, watching our every movement as a dog watches a stranger in its home. Summoning one of
the men, Maurice asked him to show us the surrounding country.
It was late in the afternoon when we set out. The native, with a
spear which he carried over his shoulder as if it were an axe,
moved silently ahead of us, glancing about him all the time,
stopping to point out the spoor of an animal, then beckoning us
on with a finger over his lips. Almost unconsciously we followed
him in the very way he moved, treading lightly, expectantly, on
the look-out for we knew not what. We had not gone far before
the native suddenly stopped dead, and stood pointing in front of
him to a long, wide clearing in the bush. I could see that the trees
had been broken and trampled down, making a path that led to
the river. *"Ndhlovu!"* he whispered. "Elephant!" Blundering
across the parched land towards the sweet smell of water, we
could see where they had plunged down the slopes and immersed
themselves in the cool streams. With a look of fear on his face,
the native eyed their traces for a few moments, then all of a
sudden he jerked up his black head, sniffed the air, while his
eyeballs rolled round in their sockets with excitement and
pleasure. His lips parted, showing two rows of beautiful teeth.
"Lalela!" he murmured. "Listen!" Hearing nothing, I followed
the direction of his eyes, and then, amongst the trees some hundred yards ahead, I saw a long dark line of movement, like a
slow train seen through some thick bush, indistinct. A moment

later, as if from nowhere, the dark line appeared as a herd of eland. Behind me I heard Maurice draw in his breath. Incredible it seemed that so many and such heavy creatures, larger than horses, could travel with so little sound. Their feet, as they loped forward, moved with the precision and care of human thieves at night, creeping in and out among the shadows of the branches in the sun. A great bull, all alone in front, led the way, resting every now and then on three legs to listen, his pointed ears flung out sideways to catch the faintest note of a human voice, while his head was thrust forward, muzzle raised, to avoid the crash of his long horns in the trees above. Then, off again, stealing along slowly towards the river, each hoof placed on the earth with only a little less soft a sound than might be made by the naked foot of a child on mown grass. Trembling with a queer excitement, we watched them make their way to the water, in ones and twos, a seemingly endless line of eland. They reminded me of sullen cows walking down a straight road, aimlessly, one behind the other, yet the thrill of watching them was evident even in the native who had known and seen them all his life. Slowly they descended the bank to the river, and there, fetlock-deep, flank to flank on the water's edge, we saw them part their forelegs, lower their long necks, and drink.

I turned and looked at Maurice. He was leaning against a tree, his hands clenched, his eyes unusually bright, his lips twisted into a smile whose meaning I could not interpret. "God, makes you long for a rifle, doesn't it!" he said.

It was very warm and comfortable under the blankets; the heap of grass beneath them was as soft as a real bed; and the morning dew lay so thick on my hair that to move would mean allowing its cold dampness to trickle down into the warmth within. With only one eye open I could see the river below: beyond it rose an arch of gold, growing gradually larger, above the distant horizon. The stagnant water shone like a long sheet of brass, reflecting the black bushes on the farther bank where a duiker came walking slowly down the sand, its thin legs like sticks sinking deep as it moved towards the flaming river. I was acutely aware of an

unearthly stillness in the air, yet I knew that all about me a
million voiceless creatures were moving silently through the
undergrowth and trees.

A drop of dew fell from my hair, trickled down my forehead;
I was about to brush it away when I was startled by a cry from
Maurice. "Man! There're some duck! Quick, get your gun!"

Sitting up, I stared at the sky overhead. At first I could see no
sign of anything. Then in the far distance, following the course
of the river, a long line of specks coming towards us caught my
eye. I put my hand out for my gun, slung a bag of cartridges over
my shoulder, and got up.

"Get down, idiot!" whispered Maurice, excitedly, kneeling on
his blankets with his gun ready. "Don't move or they'll see you!"

We sat still in silence, waiting. The specks grew slowly into
living birds, flying very high, their necks thrust out, travelling
towards us at a great speed. They were almost over our heads
when Maurice, holding his gun, which was so dilapidated that its
broken triggers he pulled with the aid of string, whispered:
"Now! But yards in front!"

"Miles too high!" I answered, staring straight above me. At that
moment he fired. The line of birds, like sparrows in the sky,
parted in the middle, one half flying a little left-handed, the other
half continuing their previous line of flight, while from its centre
a single bird, doubled-up, leaving a few feathers hanging in the
air, came hurtling down. With a smothered plop it landed on the
sand between the camp and the river, and lay inert.

"Marvellous!" I cried impulsively.

For the first time in my life I saw Maurice look at me and really
laugh. He laughed outright, from sheer joy, as a child laughs,
inhibiting nothing.

Then a curious thing happened. No sooner had I seen the dead
bird crash on to the sand and heard Maurice laugh than a whirr
of wings made us instinctively grip the guns again. Looking up,
I saw that the same flight of duck, only a few yards over our
heads, had returned! Taking aim as they retreated in the direction
whence they had come, my eyes caught sight of another flight
advancing towards us, then another, and another—till the sky all
round was flecked with hundreds of birds, some coming, some

sheering off down the river, some swooping as if to land, then rising again only to return at a greater height, others flying in circles over our heads, but none going far before they whirled round and came back to the volley of shots we were firing into their midst. The more we fired the more birds appeared. Among them a flock of geese, large as swans, flew over us, round and round, croaking madly, never having known the sound of a gun. In the midst of this uproar an intense excitement seized hold of me. I was firing, taking hardly any aim; I let off shot after shot into the whirling maze of wings. Birds were dropping everywhere, some on the sand, some thudded into the bush close beside us, while others splashed into the river, where even a native refused to wade for fear of the crocodile that infested it. And all the time an increasing lust leapt up within me, depriving me of any thought but that I must kill, and kill quick, before it was too late. The fact that such a quantity of dead birds was useless, that we needed but a few to eat and that the others would not keep, never entered my head. I felt nothing save the overwhelming desire to continue shooting. And with the desire I could feel my whole body growing hot in affirmative answer; the gun shook in my hands. When I wished to reload my fingers trembled, so that the cartridges hovered round the opening to the smoking barrel, chattered on the edge before, by sheer luck, they fell into their appointed place, and I closed the breech and fired again. Each time I pulled the trigger a tight feeling in my chest surged up to my throat; I became breathless in a fever of orgiastic happiness; the barrel was growing so hot that I could barely grip it with my left hand; my head felt as if it were about to split as each report rent the air, which by now was filled with all manner of birds careering crazily above us in the sky . . . and yet some wild force over which I possessed not the slightest control drove me on, refusing to allow either thought or reason to intervene.

Not until the barrel had burned my hand was I at last compelled to desist; I dropped the gun at my feet and, trembling all over, turned to Maurice. He seemed possessed of the same frenzy as had overwhelmed myself. He was kneeling on the blankets, loading, firing blindly into the sky, unloading, loading again, his hands shaking, and on his face a look that struck me with horror as one of madness. His little eyes were screwed up till they were barely visible, the mouth twisted into a devilish, insane grin as though he were intent on repaying some unknown god for all the unhappiness he had known in his life. Had *I* looked like that just now? Or had these last five years . . . ?

"Just try not to forget I've had five years . . . sometimes I think I . . ." In horror I looked away from him.

By this time the birds, realizing the danger, had soared so high that they seemed no larger than hundreds of black stars in the sky. Yet even now they wheeled about in circles, their curiosity still unsatisfied.

Then what in the world was Maurice shooting at?

Following the direction of his gun, I saw, low over the river, a great cloud of pink birds, in thousands, with the golden flame of the rising sun full on their backs flying serenely, silently towards us. While they flew, the water beneath them turned slowly as if from pure cold brass into a cloth of the palest mauve. I caught my breath, never before having seen flamingoes. Two shots rang out in quick succession. Two long necks turned in and fell, followed by flying pink feathers, into the river. . . . A heavy lump rose in my throat, almost choking me, and all of a sudden great hot and blinding tears rolled out of my eyes so that I could not see.

Without thinking, before I was aware I had done it, I picked up my gun and hurled it down the slope. It landed on the last foot of the hill, bounced away, then dropped with a splash beside a dead bird into the water.

"What the hell d'you . . . you must be . . . *mad!*"

I turned to find Maurice staring down at me, shaking in every limb. His eyes were ablaze with anger; in them I could see the look of pain and hatred I had known so long. A wave of faintness swept over me; I felt very weak. The tears in my eyes rolled back, my throat relaxed, and, as I sat down, in a flash I saw Fort Insezi. All alone it loomed up before me, like a black spot on a brown table. It was just a native village, with one brick house outside it, where Maurice Macadam and I lived.

A Stranger Among Miners

THE WORKMEN'S BUS creeps through the endless Derbyshire villages, stopping every few minutes to pick up some men, drop some more. The villages are endless rows of houses, line upon line of small red-brick houses—with one outside lavatory-hut to every two—packed together as though seeking warmth from each other in the raw cold of early morning.

We creep into the town of Chesterfield just as full day dawns and a watery sun floods the mean, crowded streets. Over everything a curious, sinister silence reigns. Few men speak. In the market-square men and boys with white, pinched faces and red-rimmed eyes stand about, stooping slightly, hands in pockets. They lean against the walls of shops and public-houses, staring at their feet or out sightlessly into the square. Nothing is written all over their faces.

Through the square more men hurry to and fro: young men, old men, boys in their early 'teens—and perhaps one-quarter of that throng is maimed. Here is a man limping with a bent leg, there a man on crutches, here a man with his arm in a sling, here a boy with a bandaged head. . . .

A long crocodile of men fills one side of a narrow street. These stand, stamping their feet, one behind the other, swinging their arms, beating themselves in the raw cold. The head of the crocodile sinks into a doorway over which two words glare from a board: LABOUR EXCHANGE. . . .

The colliery bus is packed. The black-clothed, black-capped men and boys, with mufflers tied round their collarless necks, lurch in and fall into their seats. Others stand in the crowded gangway.

" 'Ow do, Dan!"

" 'Ow do, 'Arry!"

Then silence. No one speaks. The men sit, and stand, and smoke, and stare before them, while the bus roars out of the town, down a steep hill, towards the colliery.

I see it suddenly. Long lines of coal-filled trucks shine idle in the watery sunlight, huge lumps of coal sparkling above the brims. Beyond, jet-black smoke belches from two tall chimneys; and below, old, tall-funnelled engines snort backwards and forwards over the criss-cross maze of shining rails. And from the midst rises an immense black mound, a miniature mountain, from which the stock-heads, like twin cranes with two great wheels attached to their heads, rear themselves above the gleaming blackness, into the grey wintry sky.

The manager, in a brown suit with knife-like creases down his trousers, sits back in his arm-chair. "Well, I'll see that you're shown round . . . only too glad . . . we're not ashamed of conditions here. Of course, we're not exactly *proud*—the coal industry at the moment, you know, is not . . ."

His unnatural voice trails away and he picks up the telephone. "Er—is that Pit Five? Well, look here, I just want the deputy to take a visitor down the pit. . . . Yes, I'll give him overalls and cap —have a lantern and stick ready."

"We'll be goin' sixty miles an hour," says the deputy, as, holding lanterns in one hand and sticks in the other, we step into the iron-barred cage. A wild scream and my stomach seems to leap into my mouth and the world to slip from beneath me. Nose, eyes, and mouth are filled in a moment with flying black dust, as we plunge down through the pitch darkness into the earth. Water drips on us from somewhere unseen.

"Awl raht—'old on t'bar!"

The roaring noise and the wind is deafening. I shut my eyes, hold my breath, spit, then hold my breath again, clinging to a bar of the cage. . . . Suddenly my stomach seems to fall down into the pit of my belly. Are we rising, going back, instead of falling? No, still descending, but perhaps only at the rate of thirty miles an hour. *Crash!* A light!

"Duck yer 'ead! Now, keep it ducked, or ye'll smash yer skull!"

We step out into a low tunnel—a thousand feet from daylight. The air is hot and dry, puffs of hot wind blow into my face. We walk bent double, holding the lanterns, for a mile along a pitch-dark tunnel. Not a sound but the pad of our feet in the dust. That silence is like no other silence I ever heard. Above, the roof is supported by wooden beams: and more beams, every few feet—some cracked and splitting, where sinister boulders hang as though about to fall—support these on either side, like matches placed to hold up a house. We walk between two lines of rails, down the centre of which steam-driven "endless ropes" move silently over the ground like shining snakes. I step on one, and fall. My lantern drops and goes out. I stand up and bang my head on the roof.

"Keep down an' near me, so's you'll see."

We reach some wooden swing doors, beyond which comes a sound as of a rushing torrent of water. The deputy stands still in front of it, listening. Then he throws himself against it. The doors give way and—the noise ceases. It was compressed air whistling through the cracks in the door.

"Better take off yer vest 'ere—going ter be 'ot."

More doors. They give way to the deputy's weight, and we walk through into a hot wind that makes me catch my breath. I begin to sweat: little streams run down my chest and face. The roof is lower now; my back and neck ache as though a load were there; it is difficult to see without raising my head and banging it on a beam. There is a roar in the distance, like thunder, approaching.

"Hey, stand still! Keep on this side!"

There is no light but the dim glow of the deputy's lantern, and that roar is approaching fast.

"What's the noise?" I whisper, feeling constrained to whisper in the sinister darkness.

"Dunno. Here, get in this refuge—*quick!*"

Beside me is a hole hewn out of the rock. I crouch in it, in the dark. The deputy darts into another hole. The thundering roar increases.

"Awl raht. Only tubs. Come out, keep on this side, though."

A light flickering in the distance is coming nearer, accompanied by the muffled thumps of hoofs. A blinkered pony, straining forward, appears suddenly out of the gloom, harnessed to a load of coal-laden tubs. A teenage boy, black, naked to the waist, wet with sweat, stumbles along beside it, lantern in hand.

"Hillup, Nobby, hillup!" The tubs crash by.

We have been groping our way for close on an hour with the light of one lantern (once a lantern is out you cannot relight it in the pit) when we branch off down another tunnel where the rails and "endless ropes" cease. Here the roof is much lower and it is hard to crouch low enough and still manage to walk. I hate my six feet of body and long legs. Dirty sweat runs off my head into my eyes. A lantern hangs from the roof. Faintly in the distance I can hear a tap-tap, tap-tap—then a succession of many taps. A line of grimy shirts hangs from a wire on the side-wall, their tails on the ground. There is a strong smell of human sweat gone stale, horse-sweat and dung, in the dry, hot atmosphere.

Then suddenly several flickering lights in a line—it is the seam, the coal-face. . . .

I fall over a boulder of coal and rip open a leg of my overalls. Now we are forced to get down on our hands and knees and advance, like tired monkeys, over the debris of stone and shale and coal, into a tunnel a little less than four feet high—the coal-face.

The air is so thick with dust that only immediately round a lantern can anything be seen.

Crack, crack, crack! An oldish, half-naked man with no teeth and little hair, the whites of his eyes gleaming from his black and perspiring face, is kneeling before the four-foot wall of coal, crashing his pick against the surface. Crack! crack!

Next to him a boy kneels in black water and scoops out the muddy shale from between his knees, heaving it through the roof-props on to the "packs." Close to a splintered prop a sharp end of threatening boulder pierces the roof immediately above the boy's head. Every few minutes he stops and gives it a glance, the fear of a scared animal in his eyes. . . .

For more than half an hour we crawl past naked men and boys kneeling and sitting in water. No one speaks. Nothing but the crack of the pick and the noise of shovels scraping through the slime and shale. I keep spitting and wiping my face and body. I wonder how long I can go on without standing up.

I blink in the sudden sunlight which hurts the eyes and shines warm on our black and sweat-stained faces. I draw the cool fresh air into my lungs and think it's like drinking cold water on a hot day.

" 'Ullo!" cries the check-weighman, a large shock-headed man. "You t'lad bin down t'pit?"

I nod.

"Which one's tha' bin down?"

"Number Five."

"*Five!*" he shouts. "Why, tha's seen best conditions in t'colliery. Who sent thee down, lad?"

"The Manager."

"Ah!" and his eyes narrow and he clenches his fists. "Down 'ere, lad," he suddenly bursts out, "in Pit One—four hundred yards under where ah'm standin', is men an' boys workin' on theer stomachs, on theer backs, in two-an'-'alf-foot seams. They can't kneel, lad—t'ain't 'igh 'nough. Seven-an'-'alf-hour shifts—roof may fall in an' kill 'em tomorrow—fifty shillin's a wik w'en lucky ... wife, one kid, two kids, three kids ..."

He is shouting now and his eyes blaze. "Know wot ah think o' men as'll consent to work down there?" he yells, bending towards me. "Ah'd 'ave more respec' for 'im that took t'dole than 'im tha' crawls in theer on 'is stomach! ... Aaaach!"

And turning on his heel he spits in disgust and climbs up to the weigh-box.

There are not many like him.

II

His house is in a cobbled street of a village on a hill overlooking a mining town in South Wales, where the mines are not working and where in the distance rows of tall chimneys rising from steel factories are merely black question-marks crying: "How much longer must we wait, how much longer?"

The street is poor and the houses almost derelict. But the inhabitants do not think this, for they know into what state nowadays a house must fall before it is "condemned": and they also know that then they will suffer more than the house. . . .

In this street there is no pavement: the doors of the hovels open out on to the tiny cobbled lane down which drains gather in holes where stones once have been; and small children sit round the holes and play contentedly with garbage, the only toy they have ever known.

It is raining. There is no answer to my repeated knocks on the door, and I am about to leave when a pale woman in spectacles, carrying a baby, approaches me.

"I'm Mrs Davies," she says. "D'you want Bill?"

When I thank her she coughs, once, twice—deep coughs that bend her and shake her and stay her hand on the door-handle. The baby begins to cry. "Oh, dear," moans the mother. Then she straightens herself and we walk in.

"Bill's in bed," she says. "He's not usually up till midday, ye know—but there, ye can hardly blame him."

Then she coughs and begins calling Bill.

The house possesses two rooms, and there are four Davies children.

The dole provides them with twenty-seven shillings a week.

Bill Davies has nothing to do. He has had nothing to do for ten years—and his rent is ten shillings a week. They spend the day in one room and the night in the other, up a dark and tiny flight of stairs. The downstairs room is small; there is a fire and a little oven; there are three wooden chairs and two tables; on the walls hang old and odd pieces of clothing of no particular colour and two faded and framed advertisements taken from some weekly pictorial some years before the Great War. There is a leakage in the roof where rain drips through in a corner near an old pram, and there is a curious smell as of stale human sweat and of something else, I don't know what. Perhaps a small room of considerable age that has never been aired smells like this.

Mrs Davies receives no answers to her calls. "I'll wait," I say. She turns slowly, looks at me. She smiles. "Ah, but you ain't so good at that as we are," she says. She puts a comforter in the baby's mouth, and places it in the pram. Then she goes up the creaking stairs.

The rain floods the little window-panes. I look through the window, and through another on the other side of the street I can see the dim outline of a young man sitting with bowed head and a baby in his arms in front of the fire, just sitting. . . .

The baby in the pram behind me begins to cry: I go and rock the pram; it ceases to cry; there are voices upstairs. A female voice says: "Ah, Bill, it was one o'clock yesterday, an' it's nearly that now, an' a visitor downstairs. . . ."

Suddenly a child, dirty and wet, stands on the threshold of the open door, staring wide-eyed at me. I say, "Hullo," but the child just continues to stare. Then it goes out into the rain and returns with another. They both stand in the doorway and stare, and cough. Their noses are dribbling and their faces are covered with filth, their hair dank and wet with rain. Presently more children come and stand, some in the rain, oblivious, and some just inside. There is deep coughing upstairs. Then a boy of about sixteen with a large cap over one eye and half-naked chest walks in, push-ing the children aside. Suddenly he sees me and stops. He stands still with his mouth open; two of his front teeth are missing, the others are yellow. Then, without taking his eyes off me, he sits down near the door.

"They're all upstairs," I say, imagining he has come to see the Davies's. But there is silence; he just goes on staring.

"Have a cigarette," I say, and I offer him a packet. He takes one, with his eyes still on my face, and I light it for him, and he draws on it and sits back in his chair, but he says nothing, only stares. Two more youths have now joined the children on the threshold. Twelve eyes are gazing at me. There is not a sound but deep harsh coughing upstairs, the rain outside, and the monotonous drip-drip within.

Someone is coming heavily down the stairs. It is Mrs Davies with a child of two in her arms. She puts it under the table where it promptly begins to cry. Mrs Davies sighs. "Ah, shut up!" she moans.

Then, with a wooden spoon she starts mashing potatoes in a black bowl. She pays no attention to those in the doorway or to the boy on the chair, and they pay no attention to her, only stare at me.

There is more clumping on the stairway and Bill Davies enters. He is a big man, once a collier, with a white, but kind and open face. His hair is turning grey at the temples, but he cannot be more than thirty-five. He has nothing on but a pair of soiled trousers and boots. His ribs stick out of his white flesh.

" 'Fraid I kept you," he says, shaking my hand, his eyes cast down. He bends down over a bucket of water and begins to wash his body and face with a piece of soap. He dries himself on what was once a shirt and starts to lather his face with his hand. There is no mirror.

"Any tea, May?" he asks.

"Ah, w'en ye're ready." And Mrs Davies sighs and coughs and begins cutting bread. Bill Davies coughs every few minutes, body-stirring coughs that cause him to bend down.

The boy in the chair has smoked only half of his cigarette and puts the remainder behind an ear. He coughs three or four times, leaning over, as though in sympathy, then draws in his breath through his nose and wipes that part of his face with the back of his hand.

Both babies begin to cry. "Hell!" blurts out their father. His wife sighs and says, "Oh, dear." She picks up the baby from the floor and rocks the pram with her other hand. Two boys suddenly rush in and start fighting on the floor.

"Dan! Bert!" shouts their father with a razor held high over his head. "Stop that row!"

The two boys have just returned from school. They see me suddenly and promptly sit on the floor and stare. The room is now literally full. There is not space for another human being, however small. The two boys, hot and excited, start coughing. Their father dresses himself with old garments hanging from nails on the wall. He knots a scarf round his neck and brushes his hair to one side with a piece of comb.

"Cup o' tea?" he asks me. I thank him; he pours it out, and margarines four pieces of bread. For the first time the children turn their eyes from me to him, and watch his every movement as he bends over the bread. He pushes a cup towards me.

"Sorry about the condensed milk," he says, offering me a tin, "we 'aven't 'ad any fresh jist lately."

"How long have you been out of work, Mr Davies?"

He smiles. " 'Ow long! Ah, that's a conundrum, May—i'n't it?"

"Ah," says Mrs Davies, "our eldest, this 'ere kid, Dan, 'e's nine year old now, 'e's never seen 'is father go to work of a mornin', 'ave 'e, Dan?"

Dan sniffs, coughs, wipes his nose, and continues with the rest to stare at the bread as I put it in my mouth.

"But we mustn't grumble, we mustn't," his father goes on. "We ain't livin' in a slum like some o' these poor folk round 'ere, ye know—and that's somethin' to be thankful for. And thank Gawd we only got four kids, not eight or nine, eh, May?"

Mrs Davies coughs and smiles wanly, then goes on rocking the pram with her free hand.

Our tea finished, we go out into the rain and Bill Davies joins a group of men standing at the corner of the street.

"Well, s'long," he says, "an' if you come back this evenin' ye'll find me still 'ere." And he points to the kerb at his feet. Then he laughs good-naturedly and waves his hand.

Our Father

ALL WE KNEW OR CARED ABOUT was that she was grand. Nothing else mattered to us but that in our eyes she was perfect. I was seven: Hans little more than a year younger. Oh, we loved our mother, thought her so much grander than anyone else's mother. She was big-boned, with blue eyes and straight shining hair like smooth straw. We would sit on her knee and reach up to her head and stroke the softness of it and say: "Straw, Mum, straw!" And she would smile, a strange, sad smile, her lips would tremble a little, tears come to the brims of her eyes—and oh, I would wonder, why those tears, Mum, why? Why cry when we love you so?

So proud of her we were on the hot mornings when, Hans on the one side, I on the other, we would take a long finger of each of her hands and walk out of our gate, down the white street, to the swimming-pool. I can see her now in her plain white cotton dress with the scarlet scarf, her arms and legs bare and brown—and the men stopping to stare and mutter words of admiration at her beauty. We used to try and listen to what they said, and if I heard I would clench the long finger and look up at her and say: "Mum, that man said you were lovely; you are lovely, Mum, I say so!" But Hans would not be denied. Rushing forward he would plant himself before her to stop her and reaching up to her waist, cry: "No, Mum, I say so, I . . ." She would lower her brown face then, take Hans's cheeks between her large hands and look into his eyes, very close. And I watching would see her red lips quiver as she closed them down upon my brother's, see her pat his hair that was wavy and a shade darker than straw, and a dagger of jealousy would dart into my chest. We would move on then, our mother very quiet, I sulking a little and not holding her finger any more, but thinking of her lips trembling and hoping secretly for a moment that it was what Hans had said to her that made her look so sad.

But when we got to the swimming-pool and I saw the water and knew that Major Keller would be there joy leapt up in me, I would forget, and clutch our mother round the big part of her leg. I loved to clutch her leg, it was so firm and I could just get my arm round the part above her knee.

I never knew whether I loved our mother or Major more. Major was wounded: he lost an arm last year in the war, just six months after our father and he had gone to France with the Uhlans to fight the French and the English. We had seen them together in uniform, standing side by side, and our mother had taken a snap of them: they looked so grand, she said. Then they had got into the car and driven away, to the war.

The snap was a very good one: Hans and I agreed that our father and Major looked grand. We put it on our mantelpiece, next to a photograph of our mother. That seemed an awful long time ago now.

I don't know exactly when, nor precisely why—perhaps because we had seen that our mother had done it with her copy—we cut that photo in half, divided the two men, and placed one at each corner of the mantelpiece, with the smiling face of our mother between. And then one day the half whereon our father's figure stood disappeared—just vanished. That was soon after Major had returned with one arm, to live over the way in a little apartment, and to keep our mother company in our father's absence, for it was very lonely for her with us children and no man, and she never knowing. . . .

I asked Hans where was the photo and Hans asked me, but neither of us knew. We asked our mother, but she was only quiet and went to Katia about it—Katia cooked for us—but when Katia shook her head and said that the duplicate of the photo on our mother's table was also missing, we saw our mother go red and heard her say—"No, no, that's impossible!" And she rushed from the room upstairs, but the snap was not to be found anywhere, she said. We had never seen our mother go red like that before.

I asked Hans in bed that night why our mother went so red, but Hans said she didn't go red and I said she did, and we fought and didn't sleep for a long time. But soon the subject was dropped and forgotten.

A week later when we asked our mother why Katia had gone she bent down to pick some fluff off the floor and said Katia had gone to get married.

All that seemed a long time ago now, and since then we did not see our mother go red any more. All the summer days we spent with her and Major. We thought they looked grand together. He was tall and thin and had hair rather like our mother's, but curly. And whenever she was busy he used to come and take us out with him in his boat on the river. There we undressed and put on bathing-pants and we would watch him do everything with one arm, and marvel at his cleverness. The arm was cut off at the shoulder; there was just a lump of flesh hanging; we found it hard not to stare at it when he had nothing on but bathing-pants. His body was very sunburnt, for he spent all day without clothes, on the river and in the swimming-pool, and his curly straw hair shone like frail golden wires on his head.

In the stern of the boat he had a single rowlock, and with one oar he would steer and row as easily as we could have done with four arms and as many oars. We would sit fascinated while he rowed, and never tire of watching him doing with one arm all that other men did with two. When we were in mid-river, he would throw out the anchor, stand up in the stern of the boat, shout to us to hold on tight, raise his one arm above his head so that for a moment he looked like some huge bronze spear, then rise, his body curve in the air, and down he would come into the water with a little splash as porpoises make when they roll in and out of the surface of the sea.

Did we love our mother or Major more? I don't know. In our prayers at night we used to say "God bless Mum, Daddy, and Major" and my mind as I said it always saw a picture of our mother and Major sitting together in the swimming-pool, talking and laughing in low voices, or walking together down the street, her brown face and arms showing up against her white dress, his against his white shirt and flannels, both their heads gleaming like

gold in the sun, and people stopping as they passed, to look and
to wonder.

And when we had mumbled those words of blessing and passed
on to the Lord's Prayer, the first words of it showed me a man I
called Jesus, whose face was brown and beautiful and whose wiry
hair was a halo of gold such as I had seen in the Scripture books.

Often Major went into the town and brought us back little
presents. One unforgettable day he returned with a huge white
model of the liner *Stuttgart*. Hans and I gazed at it in wonder
while our mother looked at it, at us, at Major, and when he put
it down on the floor we ran at Major and hung ourselves round his
neck and hugged him. Our mother must have disappeared in the
midst of our embraces, for she was gone when we turned to ask
her to come with Major and us to sail the *Stuttgart* on the river.
So we set off without her, Major carrying the monster model
under his one arm and Hans, who was small and always had to
jog to keep up with him, holding on to his coat.

In the boat we undressed as usual, and launched the great
white toy on to the water. Then Major pressed a button and away
it sailed across the river, making a little thudding noise that came
from the clockwork engine within: a fan of tiny waves streamed
out behind it. Hans and I sat watching, thrilled. It was the most
marvellous thing we had ever seen, and it was ours, our very own.
Major had given it to us: no one else had anything like it.

The liner moved away from us, straight, across the current.
"Shall we go after it?" we asked Major, "or it will reach the bank
all alone, and then . . ."

Major was smiling, showing his white teeth. I think he had
been sitting watching us all the time we were admiring the lovely
toy. I believe he had forgotten about it for the time.

"Sure!" he said then, and looked quickly at the retreating
Stuttgart. "But, my Heaven, you two," he added, "we'll have to
hurry!"

I looked up. The boat was scudding away from us fast. Major
stood up and rowed with one arm, furiously. We gained upon the
liner, but it was still some distance off, heading straight for the
wall on the opposite bank. If it should hit that. . . .

"Oh, Lord, Major, we can't do it, can we?"

Fright took us. We clung to the Major, to his legs, clapped our hands, and I looked up at his face. It was very red and he was rowing with his one arm, furiously. His teeth were clenched. Hans and I were horribly excited. If that boat should crash, sink—the first day we had had it . . . ! Hans began to whimper.

"Oh, it couldn't—couldn't sink, Major—*could* it?" cried Hans.

But Major didn't answer. Instead, looking up suddenly, he stopped rowing. He was perspiring freely, the sweat running down his dark-tanned chest, glittering there on a few golden hairs. The *Stuttgart* was in front of us, still out of reach—and five yards ahead was—the solid wall, the river-bank. Then all at once we heard Major cry out: "Hold tight, you two!" And at the same moment we were thrown into the bottom of the boat. Major had dived. . . . Picking ourselves up we peered over the edge, and immediately Hans and I clasped each other. For the little thud of the liner's engine had ceased: it was heeling over to one side, the stern sinking quickly below water. Then one gurgle—and the *Stuttgart* was gone from sight. The water lay clear and motionless when Major's head shot up to the surface, a couple of yards from where our treasure had vanished.

Hans began to cry. I shouted, my lips dry and trembling. "It's gone, Major, it's gone—just beyond you! Oh, Major . . . *please!*" Then I, too, burst into tears. But the next instant through our tears we saw Major's head disappear, the seat of his scarlet pants rose for a second in its place, then the water grew calm and silent over it and there was nothing.

We sat motionless, holding our breath. The tears remained in us when—"Look—Hans!" I shouted, "look, there—by the bank!"

For just beyond us, close to the wall, we saw the white bows of the *Stuttgart* pierce the surface of the water, and then Major's head appeared close beside. We watched him give it one shake, as a dog does, his hand grip the wall, and he turned to us, smiling, his teeth shining, with the huge model, half beneath the river, under his arm.

"Come on, you two!" he laughed, "come and save your father!"

And we rowed, both of us, our four hands gripping and turning the single oar. Treading water, Major lifted the dripping *Stuttgart* up to us. We leaned over and stretched out our arms and hoisted it in. Then Major, like an acrobat, clambered up the side.

"We saved our father, didn't we?" we shouted when he was with us. And Major smiled. And we clapped our hands and laughed: all the way across the river we sat close to him, half-crying, half-laughing, clutching his wet legs, snuggling close to his thighs, thanking him.

"Oh, Major, you *are* grand," we said, "shall you always stay with us?"

And Major looked at us once and he put his hand on my head as the boat moved silently into the bank. He was about to say something, I think, when he looked up and suddenly gasped— "My God!"

"Well, you naughty boys, come and see who——" It was our mother standing there, our grand sunburnt mother dressed in white, her hair shining like soft straw. But her face! I shall never forget her face just as I saw it then. It drooped, sagged, her shoulders seemed to hang, like a dog when it knows it is about to be beaten. Then something seemed to happen to her, and she smiled—but that smile! We had never seen our lovely mother smile like that before. And as she smiled she turned, and it was then—only then—that I saw there was a man standing there, in the Uhlan uniform.

He looked very stern: his jaw was set, and he began to walk towards us, then stopped, looking down on us. He was looking at me. I glanced quickly at him and it was as though something suddenly melted inside him, for his jaw fell a little, his clenched hands unclenched themselves, his shoulders seemed to relax. But —I don't know why—fright took me in a flash and I glanced at our mother, and all I knew was that she was grand, and I ran to her and buried my head in her skirt and cried.

It seemed a long time that I cried there before I took one quick look at the boat and saw Hans sitting in it, closed between Major's knees, gripping his wet thighs, as though he were frightened. And Major—oh, Major, I thought, why do you look like that, stare like that, at the man in the Uhlan uniform?

It was terribly quiet. The whole world seemed to be standing still, waiting—for what? *I* did not know.

The Beginning and the End

When i was just short of ten years old I fell in love with a girl called Lena—Lena Morgan I think was her full name. When we grew up we were going to get married.

Her parents and mine were close friends, and we children saw much of each other, in the holidays.

Of Lena I remember first that she was two years older than myself, which set me worrying, for I knew my mother was three years younger than my father, and I was certain Uncle Patrick who lived near by at Donnybrook was at least ten years older than my Aunt Marjorie, because he not only had a beard but his hair was grey and hers was black. So towards Lena I could not help but feel a bit inferior. Again, if it were not actually a sin for a boy to marry a girl older than himself, I knew at all events it must be wrong; and very often between a Wrong and a Sin there seemed to be no difference. Also, God saw all things, punishing the sinful. He could see right inside your head, God could, so there wasn't much hope so far as He was concerned. But He couldn't prevent me loving Lena. And Lena said she loved me, in spite of God and her age. So we told each other we couldn't help ourselves, which was true.

Lena's hair was parted in the middle, brushed back from her forehead, and fell in two long plaits down to her waist. And I remember thinking that the skin on her face was like the pale pink china ornament on the mantel in the living-room at home. When I touched her face with my fingers it was cool, like the ornament, clean and without blemish from the top of her head to her pointed chin. I had never touched her face till a week before my second term at school. That was the day we fell in love, in the middle of a laurel bush behind my home, where our love was consummated in innumerable kisses. And all the time we lay there together in the discomfort of the laurels, Lena only spoke but once. "Lord!" she breathed, "what a lot of kisses, Sam!"

It was during this last week of the summer holidays, when every moment of each day I was living only in the ecstasy of loving and being loved, that my mother fell ill. The doctor came. He said he thought she had whooping cough. No, he said, not only children got whooping cough—anyone could catch it. The next day my father confirmed this, and forbade me to go and see her.

"You're going to school in a few days," he said. "They wouldn't welcome you back in Dublin with the whoop."

I supposed that was true enough, but I was thinking neither of my mother nor the whoop, but of Lena. So I said: "I suppose Lena can come over so long as we don't go into Mummy's room?"

Sticking his pipe into his mouth, my father said: "Lena? Yes, I don't see why she shouldn't—but oh, by the way, your mother doesn't want you to go into the cloakroom, the drains are out of order and the lavatory's going to be seen to. There's a bad smell in there. Understand—on no account go into the cloakroom!"

"All right," I said, and I was so relieved at Lena being allowed to come that I didn't think about the cloakroom, until she came. Then I remembered and told her. But she seemed more interested in my mother's whoop than in the smell of the lavatory.

"Does she whoop much?" asked Lena. "I've never heard a whoop."

I had to confess I didn't know, that I hadn't heard her whoop.

"What! You've not heard her!" Lena cried. "Oh, let's go up and hear a whoop!"

Her excitement was infectious, so when my father was safely out of the house we crept up the stairs and listened, at the top. My mother's door was facing us, and we stood together, bending over, our heads lowered, listening. But not a sound came from the room in front of us. We crept nearer. Silence. Finally we sat down, and waited. Once I very nearly got the giggles, but immediately I closed my eyes and thought of a funeral I'd seen a long time ago, the small troupe of solemn black men carrying the coffin in at the gate of the village cemetery, and a woman crying into her white handkerchief. I was all right then; at once the giggles subsided and there was silence again. Nothing stirred in the house. Only once, when a newspaper rustled, did my mother give any sign that she was there at all. She never so much as cleared her throat, and I felt that if she did whoop in that stillness we'd both jump or cry out from shock.

I looked at Lena and felt she was getting bored sitting there on the staircase waiting for a whoop that never came, so I whispered should we go, and she nodded. So we crept down the stairs again, into the hall. And it was then, as we were passing the cloakroom to go out, that I remembered what my father had told me. I stopped and looked at the door, and at the same time Lena remembered what I told her my father had said. An instant later she was walking up to the door and sniffing the air, like a dog scenting a rabbit. I burst out laughing, threw my arms round her from behind and kissed her neck between the plaits. I pressed her close to me and a wave of what I looked upon as Love flooded my body and my senses. But Lena seemed more interested in the cloakroom than in me. I stepped back, pouting, pretending to be more offended than I was. She turned round, flung one of her plaits over her shoulder, and smiled. "Here, Sam," she said, "I don't smell a thing. Is there a window on the other side?"

When I said there was, Lena ran out of the house, calling me to follow. I went out, but the window was shut and the glass was glazed, so we returned, frustrated again. But by now my own curiosity was roused; we had nothing of interest to do, and I fell to wondering just how bad was the smell of the drains.

"Listen, I know," I said, turning to Lena as we entered the house again, "the key isn't in the door, let's smell through the keyhole!"

When Lena agreed we both walked up to the door, and, heads together, bent down and began to sniff at the open keyhole. But we got the giggles, then laughed out loud, so that we couldn't smell. So I shut my eyes again and thought of the coffin on the shoulders of the solemn men, and the women weeping. My giggles ceased and I stooped, stuffed my nose half-inside the keyhole, and sniffed. But there was nothing more than the nasty smell of mackintosh. I told Lena this, looking through the hole with one eye, but I couldn't see anything but the door of the lavatory, which was open.

"Lena," I said, "the lavatory door's open. Surely if the smell's so bad they'd shut the door?"

She nodded and fell silent.

"It's a hoax," I said. "There isn't a smell at all!" Then I had an idea. "I know," I said, "I'll go and tell Maggie I've left my holiday task in there, can I have the key!"

Lena's eyes brightened. "Would she give it you?"

"She will if I tell her I must have the book to finish before I go back to school on Monday."

So we went into the pantry. Maggie was ironing. I told her my lie.

"Oh you and your books!" she grumbled.

"Sorry, Maggie," I said, "can't be helped. I have to read it before Monday, else I'll. . . ."

And Maggie reached up to a nail over the mantel and handed me the key. "There," she said, "but bring it back, mind!"

"Sure," I said.

We went back to the cloakroom, slid the key into the hole, and almost before the door opened we both had our heads up sniffing the air. But not only was there no peculiar smell, there weren't any mackintoshes or hats or sticks. In fact, the room was quite bare but for one thing—an empty cot!

II

Now it may seem strange, but it's a fact that although both of us knew my mother to be in bed with "whooping cough" and we both had seen the cot in the forbidden room, yet we did *not* think of the two facts as having any connection with each other. So far as I knew, up to the day I left for school, my mother still had "whooping cough" and the "drains" were still bad in the lavatory.

When I thought of the cot I did not think of my mother. I thought rather of my father, and his forbidding us to use the cloakroom, the coats and the hats being moved elsewhere, and there being no bad smells behind the locked door. Beyond this, thinking of the cot . . . my mind went blank. Of course it did suggest a baby, because babies slept in cots, but a baby suggested roof-tops and a stork. Yes, even at the age of ten. But vaguely; my mental picture was hopelessly dim. And in my heart I could not *quite* believe it, but no other picture or thought of any kind came as a substitute for the ridiculous and cruel fable, so I just went on half-believing, yet not with the power of fully believing what in my heart I told myself to be too tall a story to accept whole.

It was the same with Lena, in spite of her superior years. We talked of it, of the cot, the "whooping cough," and the "drains," very much in the same manner as I have said my thoughts ran, but not once did it cross our minds to connect the cot—even though it did suggest a baby—with my mother, and only with my father in so far as he apparently had not wished us to see it.

But so much does youth live in the present, with such unfailing and enviable optimism, and so quickly does it forget and forgive, that by the time Lena and I parted the subject was already a memory in our lives.

We parted on the doorstep, with not so much as a handshake, for my father was there to drive the trap to the station and put me in the Dublin train. But the vision I can still see of Lena standing there is the most vivid recollection of her that I possess. It was a warm sunny afternoon, and she stood alone, facing both my father and myself, dressed in a plain white frock. Her arms hung by her sides, but her hands were clenched so tight that her face looked cross with the effort. Her eyes stared out towards us, but unblinking, as though seeing nothing at all. Then, as my father got into the trap and beckoned me to follow, she reached out to me one of her hands, but I didn't take it, for I felt that if I did, not only would my father see but that I might not know how to leave it go. So I turned my head, seeing nothing, for my eyes were blurred, and made a rush for the trap.

And when I could bear to look back the pony had lurched forward, my father was waving his whip, and the last I saw of Lena was her small white figure sitting on the doorstep of my home, with her golden head bowed on her knees, her face in her hands, and her shoulders shaking with sobs.

My father told me since it was all he could do to bring himself to put me in the Dublin train that day—I looked such a miserable sight, he said. But I remember nothing whatever about myself, till I was settled again at school.

There, one of the first things I did was to write to Lena. It was a wild scrawl, written in pencil in the lavatory, the schoolboy's sole place of privacy. I don't know what I wrote, but I know I ended the letter by beseeching her to write to me every day, promising faithfully to do the same.

This promise I think I kept for two days. On the third day I know I wrote her a postcard, because later she rebuked me in a letter about my spelling. "Terribly bizzy. Love, Sam," was all I said.

On the fourth day I did not forget to write, but I did not write. As each hour at school went by I became more and more wrapped up in the business of the moment. I had my friends, I talked and laughed, played games, swam and worked, ate and slept. Lena's letters came, and were greedily read, but the moment one was back in its envelope I forgot it till another arrived. I thought of her when I was in the lavatory and I thought of her before I went to sleep at night, but when I was not alone her image faded further and further from my memory and I became engrossed only in the moment in which I was living. Geography, like Time—the two murderers of memory and love—played its inevitable part. In the totally different, exciting, and strange atmosphere of school even my home became a far-off place of weeks and months ago, though in reality it was but days since my father had put me unwillingly into the Dublin train.

I think it was at breakfast on the fifth day that a clear vision of that life I had just left was brought back to me, in an unexpected way. The school was a large one and at meals the boys sat at long tables running parallel with each other down a huge room. But the youngest boys in the school, of whom I was one, sat at a table placed across the room, beyond the others, with a master sitting at each end. I was the fourth boy on Mr Morris's right hand. He was a young clean-looking Englishman, who wore very smart suits. We admired and respected him for his looks, his age, and his clothes. He used to read at meals, and at breakfast he always looked through the morning paper. I remember it was after we had finished our lumpy porridge and were waiting to be served with bacon, while the hubbub of a hundred voices rose to its loudest, that Mr Morris looked up from his paper, said "Ha" in a loud voice, and shouted my name down the table so that everyone immediately stopped talking to hear what he had to say to me. In the sudden silence, with all eyes on me, I felt myself blushing scarlet and my hands going wet. Someone jeered "Beetroot!" and everyone laughed. Mr Morris said, "Shut up!" and as he looked at me I felt better, for his face seemed cheerful enough. Then he leaned over the table and said: "Did you know you had a brother?"

"No, sir!" I said, convinced. "I have not!" Everyone round me roared with laughter. Mr Morris smiled.

"Oh yes you have!" he said, and he gave me the newspaper, pointing at the top of the page to a column headed BIRTHS. There I read my name, my mother's and father's name, the address of my home, yesterday's date, and at the end the three words—*of a son.*

Still blushing, while the boys next to me were reading over my shoulder what I had read, I handed the paper back to Mr Morris, who laughed and said: "What d'you think o' that, eh!"

To which I felt too bewildered and self-conscious to answer. I looked down at my hands below the table, knowing that still all eyes were on me, while vaguely in the back of my mind a ridiculous stork, with a baby in its beak, hovered about over the roof of my home, fell in a miraculous fashion on to the lavatory window-sill, walked through the window, hopped on to the cot, and there deposited its burden that was my new brother!

The hush around me continued for several minutes. Everyone, I realized with a prayer of thanks to God, seemed as confused as I was myself. I was still the object of all stares, yet no one spoke to me; there seemed to be nothing to say; it was as though we'd all been told one of my parents had died. . . .

Then the boy next to me said: "What's your brother's name?" I looked at him blankly. "How the hell do I know?" I said. And someone laughed.

But the next moment the morning's mail was distributed and all but myself forgot about my new brother. There were two letters for me, one from my father, the other from Lena. Hers was long and full of a frantic desire to know why she hadn't heard from me for two whole days. At the bottom of the last page there was a P.S. "Mummy says your mother's whooping cough is much better."

Then I opened my father's envelope. As usual, his letter was short.

Dearest Sammie:

Wonderful news for you! You've got a brother, a grand little man, came this morning at six o'clock. What do you think of that, eh?

(Exactly what Mr Morris had just said, I thought!)

He's going to be called John Frederick Alexander. I hope we'll call him John, but Mummy likes Fred. Her whoop is much better, I'm glad to say. She says she will write to you in a day or two. We are going to try and arrange for the christening to take place during your half-term leave. Hope you're working hard. In haste,

Your loving Daddy.

I put the letters in my pocket and munched my bacon. Already the hubbub of voices had resumed as before. I looked up and down the table. Some boys were reading letters, others chattering with their mouths full. My new brother was forgotten: nor, during the ensuing day, did I think of him much. I had a vision of him in his cot, a tiny, ugly, uninteresting atom, rather repulsive because he was so small, and dribbled, and couldn't talk. It was impossible for me to think of such a thing as a "grand little man."

All day I was lost in the school again. Then in the evening I wrote to Lena. I apologized humbly for not having sent her a letter for two days; I was terribly sorry, but Sunday was the only day one was given proper time to write. Then I asked about my brother. Had she seen him? Funny not realizing a baby was coming when we saw the cot! And I asked her outright *how* it came, not mentioning the vision I'd had of the stork. I asked her to ask someone, because none of the boys I knew here could tell me more than: "Oh, you just get them when you're married!" It was important to both of us, I said, because if we were going to get married, what on earth would we do if we didn't know how to get a baby?

A letter from her, crossing mine, came the next morning.

> You've got a new brother. Mummy told me. He's going to be called Fred. Of course that was what the cot was for. Fancy us not guessing! I dreamt about a stork last night. Do ask someone at school about it. You know there's no one here who'd tell me.

So Lena was asking me to do what I'd asked her to do! I did think of asking the Senior who was Captain of my dormitory, but when I was in the dormitory that night I hadn't the courage. I felt, too, that even he might not know, and then I'd feel as much of a fool as if he'd told me and ridiculed me for asking him. So I said nothing and soon almost forgot about it.

When Lena answered my letter, she said she didn't know anyone to ask about the baby, but surely I could ask someone at school. She said it was no good asking her mother because when her mother had first told her about its arrival, she had added: "Now wasn't that a *nice* kind of stork to bring Sam a brother?"

And when, a few days later, my mother wrote to me, she said that Freddy was a wonderful boy, growing bigger every day, and looked "just like Daddy." She told me the christening was arranged for the last day of my half-term leave, and finished: "My rotten old whoop has gone at last, thank goodness, and I shall be out of infection in a week."

Slowly after this the subject of my brother slipped further and further from my mind. I had a brother, his name was Freddy, and that was that. As the weeks went by I became more than ever submerged in the curriculum of the school. Home, even Lena, faded gradually out of sight. Lena wrote regularly for a time; I answered spasmodically, full of apologies and excuses. But no longer was she uppermost in my thoughts during my daily visits to the lavatory, nor at nights did I see her image so often before I lost myself in sleep. My letters to her grew shorter, fewer, and ever more of a bore to write. So that when, quite suddenly, Lena's letters ceased altogether, I accepted the silence—although I was at first surprised and a bit piqued—without great regret, for it relieved me of what I felt was growing fast into an irritating obligation.

Then at last half-term came and I began to think of leaving school and going home. I thought of my mother and father, and, with curiosity mingled with resentment, of my new brother. And I thought of Lena—yet somehow I feared to meet her again; it would not be the same with us, I felt. For there was guilt in me for not having kept my promise. Was this why she had ceased altogether to write to me?

III

I had not been home more than five minutes before I felt I had never left it. Everything was just the same; even my mother's spectacle case was lying on the round table in the living-room, where I had seen it ever since I could remember seeing anything. There was no reason why it shouldn't still be lying there; there was no reason why anything should have changed, but whenever I returned from school I imagined things should be different; I imagined all the windows might be opened to welcome me, a hand waving from each, and my mother and father standing waiting on the doorstep. But instead there was always a great silence that never failed to depress me; the house seemed empty and dead; there were no voices; nothing stirred; everything was just as it always had been; Time had left no mark. Coming straight from the noise and bustle of school, the contrast of home always gave me a profound shock.

Yet, this time, after the first quarter of an hour, at the end of which I had exhausted all I had to say to my mother and father, and I'd taken in the sameness of everything so that I felt I had never been away—after this, I did begin to sense something different. There was an unfamiliar smell. And wasn't there someone walking about overhead in the spare room? Then, in a flash, it dawned on me.

"Lord!" I shouted, "my brother!"

And both my father and mother burst out laughing. "Why, I'd almost forgotten all about him!" cried my mother. "Come along and see Freddy."

"There!" said my father, "what about that for a compliment, eh?" He clapped me on the back and sat down again.

Not greatly impressed by what my father considered a compliment, I followed my mother upstairs.

There was a nurse in the spare room, and beyond her was the cot, the cot Lena and I had seen in the forbidden cloakroom. I smiled to myself, and longed to tell my mother I'd seen it there; but I couldn't, for I felt it would embarrass her—not wishing, I suppose, to accuse one I respected of deliberate deception.

And there, inside the cot, was the tiny, almost bald head of my brother. His eyes were closed, and I found it hard to believe he was alive. I thought of the stork and felt rather angry. Nor could I take any interest in the infant; he looked very much as I had thought he would look. That this thing could possibly grow up into a man the size of my father seemed to me quite incredible.

"Isn't he a sweet pet!" said my mother, making a baby noise over the cot. Then, suddenly turning to me, she said: "Sam, would you like to dine with us tonight, for a treat?"

Though delighted at this unexpected suggestion, I couldn't help feeling that my mother made it in a curious, unfamiliar, rather solemn tone of voice, as though she were half-afraid of something. Her eyes didn't look at me, but over my head, far away, at nothing in the room, I thought. Her face seemed very sad to me. It was pale, and I noticed for the first time lines down each side of her mouth, and when she smiled back at me there was no happiness in her face, only that far-away look in her eyes and a slight droop of her lips.

Then she suddenly frightened me. Swallowing, as though she were trying to choke back tears, she gripped my arm suddenly and said: "Come, Sam, into my room."

We went, my mother still holding my arm. She closed the door of the bedroom behind us. It was a large green room, and the windows were open, but there was a chestnut-tree immediately outside, shutting out the light.

"You sit on the sofa, Sam," my mother said. Her voice frightened me afresh. She almost whispered. I had never heard my mother talk like this. I sat on the sofa, my hands clasped together between my bare knees, my head down, wondering, frightened of what she was about to say. Sitting there, in the semi-darkness of the room, I thought of all my sins. God saw all things, punishing the sinful. My mother, standing there in front of me, had said that. He could see right inside my head, God could. So, anxiously, fervently, I sent up a silent prayer and thought of all my sins. But what could I have done that my mother knew?

But she didn't speak. She started walking up and down the room, slowly. Then she hesitated and stood still. Now she was standing in front of me. I glanced up as far as her waist and saw her hands clasped in front of her, her fingers nervously twining themselves in and out of each other. Then she moved and stopped in front of the mantelpiece, took a flower out of a vase and put it back again.

I sat on the sofa, scared, my hands hot, trying to think, but my head was empty. I dared not speak. My mouth was dry. The clock ticking in the corner seemed to boom out the seconds "—now— now—now, NOW!"

Then she spoke; almost in a whisper, standing in front of me, while I sat and stared at her ankles. "Sam," she said, "I've ... there's ... I thought I ought to tell you ... we've got ... some bad news. ..."

Her voice faltered, then stopped. There was a silence that I thought would never end. Perhaps I hadn't sinned at all? I watched my mother lift one foot over the other, then place it back again. Then she went on, still in a whisper. "It's about ... about ... *Lena, Sam!*"

My mother spoke our names so loud and suddenly that I jumped on the sofa, involuntarily. Then, walking away from me to the mantelpiece, she moved an ornament there, and when she spoke again her voice for the first time resumed its natural tone.

"Yes—Lena," she said, "she's gone away, she ... won't ever come back again, Sam!"

The clock went on ticking, but it did not seem so loud now. My mother began quickly to undress. For me, the strain of waiting had been such that when I knew she had said what she wanted to say and that it was nothing to do with my Sins—I felt nothing but a wonderful sense of relief. My limbs relaxed. My mother's words repeated themselves in my head. "Lena . . . she's gone away . . . she won't ever come back again."

I sat silent. For fully a minute only an image of Lena as I had last seen her passed through my mind. The clock ticked on; it was the tick I had always heard; my mother became real; she was undressing; her skirt was slipping down from her waist.

"Lena—she won't ever come back again." I knew. I knew what she meant. There seemed to be nothing for me to say. Lena had stopped writing to me. Lena had—died. . . .

I was lying kissing her in the laurels. Hundreds of kisses. I was at school. It was an awful bore writing. Lena had died; gone away; she wouldn't ever come back again. . . . There was a small troupe of solemn black men, with a coffin on their shoulders, filing in at the gate of the village cemetery. A woman in black was crying into her white handkerchief—Lena's mother. . . . Lena?

Hardly knowing that I spoke, in my ordinary tone of voice, I found myself asking: "Is she in the cemetery, Mum?"

I looked at my mother. She was smiling back at me. "Yes, dear," she said. "She's with God."

Lena was with God. God who saw all things. He was a big man, with a kind face, and a beard. Lena was with Him. . . .

Then my mother was sitting on the sofa beside me, in her dressing-gown. Her arm was round my shoulders. I didn't move.

"Now will you go and wash your hands for dinner, darling?" she asked.

"All right," I said, and I went out, thinking only of food, for I was suddenly violently hungry and I could smell eggs frying.

The next day but one, at the party after my brother's christening, I fell in love with a girl called Mary—Mary Jameson I think was her full name. . . .

Under the Beech Tree

THE LATTER HALF of our summer holidays my brother and I always spent with our Aunt Clara, at Sherndone Abbey. Our aunt was a curious woman. It was her boast that she had never been attended by doctor or dentist, never spent one day in her bed. She was one of those fortunate beings whom one cannot believe ever to have suffered; certain it was, in any case, that if she did suffer she never showed it. For us, for anyone who knew her to conceive of tears blinding those tiny stone-like eyes would have been as difficult as to imagine these same eyes aflame with anger—or, indeed, the unkissable mask in which they were set to demonstrate a semblance of any emotion or passion whatever.

Aunt Clara's face was pale brown, gaunt, with a weather-beaten look, and her nose was not straight. She possessed, so far as I ever knew, but two "suits"; garments of dull gaberdine, both identically the same, with the exception that the one was rather more worn than the other. In hot summer the iron-grey hair she covered with a stiff, sun-stained "boater"; in winter she went about in all weathers hatless. In this garb she lived her life, a life confined, as are the lives of a host of ladies and gentlemen in Britain, to what that country's natives have called "Sport"—sport of all kinds. Aunt Clara, indeed, lived—for sport.

I remember well having seen her play golf, lawn-tennis, croquet ("too slow for anyone under eighty," she would say), table-tennis, billiards, and hockey, which game was the cause of her crooked nose. Once I even saw her take part in a game of polo. But these —ball games all—were not what really filled Aunt Clara's thoughts from New Year's Day to Christmas of each twelve months. What did constantly occupy her mind and months were three pursuits,

dear to the hearts of many such as Aunt Clara—hunting, shooting, fishing. And of these three, hunting and shooting possessed
Aunt Clara's body and soul. Also, because of the hunting and
shooting, we boys were forbidden by her to do this, forced to
do that. In fact, what activity did not in some manner suggest
sport to our aunt, that activity she immediately detested as much
as she loved and admired those that did.

Pursuits, therefore, forced upon us were those, as may be
divined, appertaining to hunting and shooting. So on our very
first visit to Sherndone it was not altogether unnatural—and my
brother and I were somewhat impressed by the fact—that we
found two ponies at our disposal in Aunt Clara's well-filled stable-
yard. But we were more than impressed—expressions of astonishment and delight leapt to our lips—when that evening Aunt Clara
appeared at our tea table with a pair of brand-new rook-rifles (at
home we had been forbidden pop-guns, even water-pistols), one
under each arm; and presenting them to us, proclaimed in a loud
voice what at the time I was too overjoyed to realize was a sting-
ing insult to our intelligence: "Here, these!" she said in her gruff
manner, "to shoot with!"

In the midst of our stammered utterances of gratitude she cut
us short with the words: "Riding, nine to twelve—shooting, three
to six!"

Before we had time to take in the meaning of this, she added:
"I presume you know what to shoot!" Then, with greater emphasis,
"And what *not* to shoot!"

Wherewith, turning in the silence she had thus created, Aunt
Clara strode off.

And for the remaining weeks of those holidays at Sherndone
we rode and shot, shot and rode.

Of this constant riding, always up and down the same roads
and lanes, we soon began to tire; another week and we were quite
bored by it: and when we fully realized that riding was
compulsory we turned against it altogether, performing the
monotonous exercise almost with hatred in our hearts. But the
shooting—this for a long time was a different matter. It would be
no exaggeration to state that with the exception of human beings,
farm, domestic and semi-domestic animals, we shot, or certainly

shot at, everything alive in sight on the estate of Sherndone. It was not long before the cook objected to the influx of dead rabbits and duck piled high in her larder, and in even less a time that we chose a large beech-tree, not far from the Abbey, of whose branches we made a mortuary for the bodies of our (for the most part) harmless, useless victims. With curious avidity, almost with a collector's passion, we would stand under the tree and gaze up at our trophies. Arrayed there in deathly silence, row upon row, strung up by their skinny necks from every nether branch and twig, hung a specimen of every conceivable kind of animal and bird that the estate of Sherndone had to offer us. Our one ambition became not to leave alive a single species of anything that moved on legs over the property of our aunt. Thus, from noon to dusk, we continued our slaughter.

But the day came, during our second summer at Sherndone, when, so far as we could judge, our tree was "full," all manner of animals known to us there having fallen a victim to our fire; and with this knowledge we tired, and sought, as every being will, fulfilment of desire and appetite elsewhere.

My brother it was at this time who, as a means of diversion, was continually trying to make some kind of a garden. (In the eyes of our aunt, a garden was so far removed from the realms of sport that we were forbidden even to enter hers.) His enthusiasm I found infectious, and after much deliberation we decided the garden should take the form of a fernery. There was little convenient soil for such an enterprise outside of, and away from, our Aunt Clara's walled-in space full of vegetables and roses; and there, twice recently, my brother had been caught, with his gun beside him, in the very act of digging in the grassless turf with the gardener's spade. His punishment for this, on each occasion, had been two afternoons of disarmament, which penalty I remember he seemed to resent as though he been bidden to appear in public trouserless. However, to make a fernery became for both of us, from this time on, near to an obsession. We talked about it for days until, at last, we decided our only hope was to construct it in some remote place, to lessen the fear of detection. Our first thoughts coincided: we would make it in the wood near the river. The fact that such a spot, secluded, rarely approached by anyone, was also to us "out of bounds," made it all the more desirable in our eyes. We started in to work the next afternoon. To us, the spot we had chosen seemed at once filled with romantic possibilities. Close on the water's edge it was, and so surrounded by trees, overhanging branches, and huge wild rhubarb leaves, as to lie by day in a permanent state of semi-darkness; it was enclosed, indeed, by such thickness of brambles that at first it could be approached down the sloping bank of forest only with the greatest difficulty. Here, cut off, so it seemed to us, not only from civilization and all contact with the Abbey and Aunt Clara, but even from animal-life—so quiet, almost eerie it was—we started in to clear a space in the wild mass of undergrowth for our new enterprise. But for the fact that a few yards off, within sight of our chosen place a swan was nesting—had in fact already hatched two cygnets—we worked every day for a week, totally undisturbed. Even the huge white swan, sitting curled up on her young, seemed as little concerned by our efforts as were we by her peaceful presence. The space cleared, we began to dig; the earth was dark, almost black, smelling dank of the river water. And then, the ground sufficiently ploughed, we started off in search of all manner of fern.

It was late one evening, while my brother was absent on such a search, and I, having just planted my latest addition to this fresh collection, was sitting above our grotto, silently smoking a cigarette presented to me by one of Aunt Clara's gardeners, that I witnessed one of the strangest sights it has ever been my lot to see.

Beneath me now, in semi-darkness, lay our fernery, in its wild, unfinished state; immediately beyond, its head and neck hidden between its own wings, curled up in silent repose on a flat nest of rushes, slept the pure white ball of swan; and at my feet, as ever, my rifle. Finishing my cigarette I pressed out its smouldering end in the wet earth and sat there waiting for my brother's return. For a while not so much as a leaf fell to sever the hollow stillness that seemed always to possess the place, as though it were some vast cave; it was as if everything there were dead, decaying by interminable degrees, in utter silence: to move there, to break such noiseless solitude after a period of one's own stillness, would seem a sign almost of disrespect, as would games played over the grassy tombs of some human cemetery. Thus the sound of a twig snapping, elsewhere gone unheard by mortal ears, was here a shock, as is the sudden rising of a single fish in the spotless surface of a lake. The sound, as I say, was so slight that I would have taken little heed of it had it not been that in the same instant my eyes were attracted by something brown that moved, without further noise, among the brambles of the slope, on the far side of the sleeping swan from where I sat. Even at such short distance, so faded by now was the evening light, the object was at first indistinguishable. But whatever it might be I felt convinced it lived, and thus could only be an animal. Motionless, I sat waiting —my eyes staring at the spot—until soon there came once more a movement, noiseless, in the direction of the unconscious swan. By now I could see that the brown coat of that which moved was of a rich red colour. And then, poking out from under a mass of grass, light on its two eyes making it recognizable, I saw its head, the short sharp ears pricked for hearing. In a second the whole of the face was revealed to my sight, and I held my breath. (Would I have been my aunt's nephew had I at this moment breathed?) My first impulse (for was I not also a Briton born and bred; nourished in a land where vulpicide is murder most foul?)—my first impulse, then, was to spring to my feet, reach for my hat, and shout into the noiseless night one long and mighty Tally-ho-o-o!

But this impetus was followed immediately by another, stronger far than the first. (For was my aunt not a sportswoman with the proper thirst for blood; my father, her brother, a sporting soldier with many a Boer and Boche to his credit? Warriors all my ancestors on the Empire's far-flung lands and seas?)

And so, though still they did not stir, my two arms ached to add yet another specimen, the most revered beast in all Britain, to our collection under the tree.

And yet—I could not. Indeed, it was as much as I could do to breathe again, though breathe, at last, one must. (Had not my Aunt Clara once bidden me that whenever I saw such a sight as lay before me now—and no finer sight there be, she said—I must stand to attention, raise my hat, wish once, and offer up a prayer for the local M.F.H.?)

But here I have to admit I disobeyed my aunt's instructions in every respect but one. I neither stood to attention, nor

prayed, nor even raised hand to hatless head, but wish I did, my mind upon our tree—I wished the animal (God forgive me!)—*dead*.

Yet of more than this I was not capable. I sat numbed, in just reverence, watching the slow silent approach of this hungry-eyed, awe-inspiring vixen, intent on her sleeping victim. Her approach of the last few yards through the thick undergrowth, towards the nest, seemed to me, sitting there, hot with suppressed excitement, to take up an eternity of time. During it, my emotions, I remember, were somewhat mixed. Apart from the thrill of the spectacle, causing my whole body to tremble, my sympathies were at one moment so entirely with the unconscious mother-swan (is it not human instinct to back the weaker side?) that I felt, despite all possible consequences, I must shout aloud to warn her and her young of their impending fate. And then, an instant later, my inherited thirst for battle and blood (what else can it have been?) staunched any fear I had possessed for the bird's safety, and I remained sitting, breathless and trembling, terrified lest I should emit so much as an accidental sound of warning—warning such as only a moment before I had felt bound to utter, while the long red-brown animal only a few yards away crept stealthily nearer and nearer its dazzling prey. So close was it now I could smell its strong pungent animal odour, see the small dark fore-pads as they moved forward, inch by inch, bringing after them the body so low as to make it appear flat on the ground, and the head, with ears cocked stiff and brown eyes starting out of the fur with a look of frightening intensity, just clear of the earth.

Such was my excitement now that I myself felt deeply involved in the animal drama before me. All I need do, I knew, was to move and thereby save a life, possibly the lives of three; nor had I good excuse to act in any other manner, for never had we contemplated a semi-domesticated swan as a possible member of our tree. Moreover, as has been stated (would that print might whisper!), I wished the vixen dead. And yet, there I remained, dumb, transfixed, as though against a wall, faced with the terror of my own immediate assassination.

Not then, nor since (descendant of soldiers though I be), have I had the misfortune to find myself gazing down the barrels of a

line of loaded muskets, but even this sight as my last on earth—
if unnatural death must be my end—might be preferable to that
which the swan's eyes, had they not been closed between her
wings, would have looked upon at this instant. I have since, at
the finish of a sporting and murderous pursuit, beheld the awful
sight of a pair of haunted, hunted eyes gazing their last into the
slobbering mouths of hounds, but only this once—and I doubt it
has been the privilege of many another—have I witnessed those
brown eyes exulting in the prospect of dealing death unto others.
With my fists clenched, barely aware of a thumping pain in my
chest, I stared at the open pointed jaws, the sharp white teeth.
The tongue, like some limp wet dagger already stained with blood,
hung loose and dripping from the side of the mouth; the black
button of a nose inflated, deflated with the effort of suppressed
breathing and lust; the whiskered upper lip was curled, wrinkled,
so that both the needle-like teeth and crimson gums were bared
in an awful snarl. The eyes, glazed with greed, protruded from the
skull like lighted bulbs from an electric torch. The animal lay now
within a foot of the nest. With her fore-feet on the water's edge,
head down between them, ears flat, hackles up, the long red back
arched and trembling, the vixen sprang.

Much happened in the space of the ensuing second. Simul-
taneous with this last act, even while the vixen was in mid-air it
seemed, the ball of white opened like some gigantic flower: the
long pole of neck, as though it were the stamen, shot up perpen-
dicular from the centre; then, thrust out straight and hard, I saw
the arrow-shaped head jam itself into the very jaws of its assailant.
A frightful, choked groan accompanied the beating of wings, and
kicking wildly, the mass of brown fur dropped with a splash into
the water. And the water, a moment previously calm, was at once
churned from brown to a thick, black liquid.

Shaking, unconscious of my movements, I found myself on my
feet, rifle gripped in both hands. Below me, the nest bare, I saw
two dark grey cygnets, hardly bigger than blackbirds, thrusting
themselves away over the surface of the river. While beyond them,
in the black water already tinged with red, there raged a bloody
battle whose sounds made hideous mockery of the silence the
place must so long have known.

For a moment I could see little but two huge wings beating the water, two yellow webbed feet kicking out towards me with violent spasmodic jerks. Then, with what must have required untold energy on the part of the beast invisible beneath, I saw all that was white turn right over, fall suddenly back, in a manner I have seen happen only to men in the wrestling-ring. There was a splash, and with it a howl, as first the vixen's long thick brush appeared, black and dripping, and then the frantically struggling body broke loose. Leaping a foot from her adversary, mask a mass of blood, the vixen stayed crouched just long enough for me to see that from the streaming red jaws there hung now no tongue. And then, with a low strangled gurgle, once more she sprang. On this occasion the bird slightly altered her method of defence; although the great wings opened, and the long neck, now more scarlet than white, shot out straight, the proud curve of the head withdrew at the last second. Whereupon the vixen—whilst missing her mark—was struck a violent blow, with the full force of the swinging neck, and fell, stunned, across the empty nest of rushes. No sooner had she fallen than the whole of the body but the limp brush, the pale tag floating on the water, became once again invisible beneath white flapping wings. There, with harsh hissing sounds, such as are made by enraged geese, I watched the swan finish off her victim by a violent stabbing of her beak into the vixen's eyes. And then, as though taking stock of her battlefield, she sat back, panting, and gazed down at the corpse. Seeing no longer any resistance, she rose to her feet, slithered into the water, and made off in search of her young.

For fully five minutes I must have sat inert, exhausted, as though I myself had been a third combatant in the deathly struggle so recently ended. From the moment I had leapt to my feet I had stood as though in a trance, my body, all my muscles strained and taut. Now, suddenly, as I felt them slowly relax, a thought—forgotten since the beginning of the battle—returned to my mind. I smiled to myself, exultant with anticipation. Without further hesitation, rifle over one arm, I approached the vixen's body. At the sight of the mask I felt sick, and turned away. I hated blood; but reinforced with what was in my mind I bent down and lifted the body, gripping it by the brush. I remember, as I left our unfinished fernery, being astounded at the animal's weight. With sure, fast strides, rifle in one hand, vixen trailing from the other, I mounted the slope. Nor did I slacken my strides when from the top I caught sight in the distance of my brother, and another figure half-hidden by the trunk, standing under the beech-tree. I walked straight on over the lawn, waiting for the moment when he should look up and behold what I was bringing for the beech's branches. It was not, however, until I was within speaking-distance that he heard my approach, nor until that moment that the figure appeared from behind the tree trunk, and I found my-self walking straight towards Aunt Clara. . . .

But much nearer I did not proceed. For between the tree and my brother there stood staring at me an Aunt Clara I barely recognized. True, her clothes were the same as ever, the same old gaberdine, but what was strange—to me fantastic, frightening—was the attitude she struck. She stood, leaning slightly forward, one knee bent, as though about to spring, and on her face an expression I saw afterwards for many nights in my dreams. Gone was the expressionless, austere look; gone the rigid bearing of one who has led a passionless life—while, instead, the tiny stone-like eyes flashed and screwed themselves up with such venom as I watched them taking in first the body in my right hand, then the weapon, her gift, in my left, that, trembling, reminded of the last look I had seen on the face of the now lifeless vixen, my fingers unclenched themselves, and I let the body fall. Simultaneously, even as the weight sank to stillness at my feet, there came from the woman's throat a barely human, agonized moan. Terrified, I watched her head drop, her hands rise and cover her face, her whole body give one convulsive shudder as she burst into a paroxysm of uncontrollable weeping.

Something Wrong

STEPHEN, I've been thinking. Before you come here and stay till your job begins and I go back to school for one more year, I want to tell you something. It's something I've never told anyone, but now I know I must tell you. I've wanted to, ever since that evening at the end of last term when we went the walk along the river and you told me all about yourself. It was the day, you remember, when we came to the conclusion we liked being with each other so much more than with anyone else that we made our solemn pact: that whatever happens we'll keep together till, as you said, "death do us part."

But it's not only this that makes me want to tell you; it's also partly because I keep on thinking of another thing you told me the same evening: about how, one day when you were at a children's party, your father found you behind a curtain, kissing that girl-cousin of yours. And you said you'd never forget your father's face, nor the things he said to you afterwards.

If you hadn't told me that, Stephen, I couldn't write you this. But now I must, before you come. I'm afraid it'll be long, but if you are to know anything of it you must know all—all that I can remember, for it's ten years ago now. So try and be patient, Stephen, because I feel it's important to both of us that you should know.

Oh Lord, it's hard to begin; there's so much to say.

Well, the house we lived in at that time stood high up above Lake Corrib. It was an ugly house. I always hated the look of it. Last holidays I saw it again, for the first time in seven years, and it still scared me. But at the time I talk of it seemed terrifying. It had a face—no, two faces. It was grey, half-smothered in ivy, and when the blinds were up I used to think it looked like an old man dead with his mouth wide open (that was the hole of the open doorway) and when the sun shone the eyes of the man were red, like blood, from the drawn blinds. Then it looked awful. I imagined fire coming out of the holes in its head, and the door was another hole, a wide-open black one, where its teeth and its tongue should have been.

I tell you about the house, Stephen, only because whenever I think of it my thoughts turn on Bessie, and the other way about.

Bessie looked after me. And I remember one of the first things my mother told her I needed was "well looking after, mind, for he—sees things!"

My mother knew that I saw things because I told her so, over and over again.

At night it was I kept seeing things. Always at night. Way back —I suppose it must have been a year before, because Bessie wasn't with us then—I got so that I wouldn't stay in bed at night.

I walked in my sleep.

And each time, when I woke, I was crying. Life was miserable. I couldn't stand the darkness. When my mother put me back to bed again (my room was next my mother's and father's, with a door between), she kept telling me: "Boys don't behave like that, they go to bed," she said, "and sleep all night and in the morning wake up fresh." But I didn't sleep all night and I never woke up fresh, so I knew there must be something wrong with me.

Yes, I saw things—devils and horses and giants and wolves and snakes—and they were always chasing me in my sleep. I used to get out of bed, over the rail of the cot, and try to get into my mother's room. Sometimes I succeeded; but sometimes the door was locked; then I battered till they let me in. When it was open I'd walk to my mother's bed and try to get in with her. Then I'd wake up and begin to cry, but my mother always took me back to my bed, put me in it, covered me up, stroked my hair, asked me what was the matter. I'd try to tell her. I'd say: "I saw things, Mother—awful things!"

And she'd say: "Silly—where?"

So I'd wonder where I'd seen them, think back a bit, look round the room, but all I could say was: "In the dark, Mother."

And my mother—she had a brown face, blue eyes, with rings of black under them, and her hair was parted in the middle—my mother would crease her forehead and look worried, the long flat plaits of her black hair would fall down on me and I'd hold them and pull them so that she had to bend down and hug me. At night I always wanted her to hug me and kiss me; in the daytime I didn't seem to care about her much.

And then I'd remember where I'd seen the things. "Here," I'd say, "all round the room I saw giants and horses and devils. At the end of the bed there I saw snakes creeping towards me, and wolves barking and trying to clamber over the rail. And I was outside the house, and I saw huge men coming in through the red holes, climbing in——"

"Red holes?"

"Yes," I'd say, "the red windows, like blood——"

"Now then, child! You're silly, those are the blinds!"

Now of course I knew they were the blinds, but they were bloody and horrible when I saw them in the dark, and I told her so. But my mother would sigh then and tell me to go to sleep. "You'll never grow up if you don't," she said. And she knew I longed to grow up because then I wouldn't see things.

But I'd never let her go till I'd kissed her. And then I usually cried. Very often she cried too. I hated that. I was certain then she also saw things, only wouldn't let on to me she did.

Sometimes, in the middle of it, my father would come in, in his pyjamas—he was a fat man with a bristly moustache and he looked frightening in his pyjamas. He'd stand in the doorway and say: "Now, come on, what's all this about? Crying again? Watcher think's going t'happen when you go to school, eh?"

Now the moment my father said school, Stephen, my tears dried up and I felt scared. If I saw things at school they'd kid me and bully me and . . . it was then I'd see all over again those torture pictures in the history book I had.

My father knew how to stop me crying. But no one could make me sleep. Though I always did sleep, after a long time; I was so tired. And in the morning when I woke and saw the light and looked down across the field to the lake, I felt ashamed, but pleased—I was so mighty glad the night was over.

Yet I never woke up fresh, as my mother said other kids did.
So I knew there must be something wrong with me.

Well, after that, about six months passed by much the same;
and when at last my mother decided I must spend the nights in
her room and my father must sleep in mine—I did ask why my
father couldn't stay along with us two, but my mother didn't
answer—I thought I'd be better. But I wasn't.

Then they called in Doctor Finnigan to see me. He used to
come twice a week. He said I was run down; I must have a tonic.
A few days later he changed the tonic for another one; at least
the new one had a different colour. Then he changed it again.
I knew he was just guessing, and something told me he wasn't
trying, didn't really give a damn. Then he said I was too thin, so
they bathed me in cod-liver oil and gave me Virol and Kepler's
before meals and after meals half a tumbler of the blood of a
bull. I hated that; but I was good at taking things. And I was
given two pills which I swallowed with hot milk every night
before I went to bed; aspirins I think they were.

But still I was no better; still I kept seeing things at night, and
I began to walk again. Sometimes I woke up sitting in the fender
crying. Whenever I woke I got an awful shock; my heart thumped
in my chest, and my breath came short. Other times, more often, I
found myself trying to get into my mother's bed, but she never
let me in, always picked me up and carried me back to mine. And
I cried and tried to cling to her, pulled her down on me to hug
me—till my father came in and said something about school, and
then everything dried up in me and I lay still, and in a few
minutes heard my mother breathing in sleep and my father
snoring next door. Lord, how I envied them not seeing things and
being able to sleep like that, just turn over and sleep like that!

Then one night I walked farther than I had ever walked before.
I walked out of the room, down the stairs. Reaching the ground
floor I opened the door of the spare room. I didn't know the spare
room, had hardly ever been in it, which is maybe why I woke so
suddenly. Heavens, that was a shock! I woke, and didn't know
where I was. I couldn't smell where I was, because my mother's
smell wasn't there, nor the smell of the passage, nor the food-
smell from the kitchen. It was a queer, musty smell—and it was

pitch dark everywhere. I felt about with my hands, touched something, I didn't know what, certainly not what I thought I should touch, for in spite of everything I still thought I must be in my mother's room. I began to sweat and tremble. Then I started in to yell.

"Mother!" I screamed, "Mother!"

But there was silence.

I continued to raise hell, just shouting wildly. I turned round, felt the door, rushed through it—I thought from my mother's room into mine—then crashed my head against the passage wall. I collapsed on the floor shaken, holding my head. Somewhere a light was switched on. Pegeen, the kitchen-maid, appeared in her nightdress, her hair all over her face.

"Ah, Lord have mercy!" she cried. "Is it killed you are entirely?"

Then my mother appeared. Then my father. And there was a lot of talk; the doors must be locked in future, the doctor must come again.... And my mother put me back in bed, leaned over me, looked at me sadly, as though she were tired out and going to cry.

"Oh, Mother!" I remember saying, "I am sorry. I didn't mean to—honest I didn't!"

Then, suddenly, without warning, she fell on me, in a flood of tears....

So I leapt up, terrified. "Father!" I cried, "Father! Mother's ... quick, Father, there's something wrong ... Mother's—*seeing things*!"

So my father rushed in, grabbed hold of my mother, led her away into the other room, and locked the door. I kept the light on all night, out of fear.

The next day Doctor Finnigan came again. And that was the time, Stephen, when he said I must have a strong net over my bed, to stop me walking. (I've told you about this before.) They put it over the bed that night, fixed at all four corners, with me caged in under it. I fought and cried a good deal with my mother before my father had to come and lift me up and push me down in the bed so that they could fix the net over me, properly.

I had a dream that night I was in a hen-coop, and there was a fire, roaring, coming closer; I could see it coming, the flames creeping over the grass, towards me. And there were two bleeding holes in the middle of the fire and another hole, a wide-open black one, where teeth and a tongue should have been. Panic seized me. I battered at the coop; pulled at the wires in front; stretched up, and, lying on my back, tugged with all my might at the wires above me. Then something happened; the wires broke; and there I was—lying in the bed, wet with sweat, the string net gripped in my hands, and crying.

The light went on. "Mother!" I shouted, "it nearly got me, the fire. Oh, it was terrible in there——"

"In where, dear?"

"In the hen-coop. Mother! They won't—won't put me in there again, will they?"

I saw my mother trying to smile, but she couldn't. So I cried again and said I was sorry I'd broken the net, but I saw her lip tremble and I became frightened in case she should fall on me again and burst into tears. I couldn't stand that. So, with a great effort at courage, I said: "That's all right, Mother—never mind. I'm all right now—only, don't—cry!" I'm afraid I screamed the last two words, but I couldn't help it, I felt that way about her crying.

But all of a sudden my mother got up from the bed. I saw her shoulders give a heave as she put her hands to her face and sniffed. "I think I've caught a cold," she said, with her back to me. Then, staring into the mirror, she began wiping her face.

"Will you take the net off me, Mother?" I asked.

So she came and took it off the bed, and I pulled at one of her plaits so that I could hug her. While I was holding on to her, she said: "There now, silly!" and unclasped my hand from her plait and got into her bed and fell asleep with me looking at her with the light on.

I slept too, later on, when there was just a crack of day coming through between the blind and the curtains.

In the morning Doctor Finnigan came once more. But he didn't see me. I knew he had come because I heard my mother and father and him talking in the next room, while the door was shut and they thought I was downstairs. I didn't mean to listen, until I heard my father's voice.

"Well, so far as I can see," he was saying, "there's nothing for it but a wire net instead of a string one—the little devil couldn't break that!"

Going hot all over, I crept towards the door, reaching it in time to hear Doctor Finnigan say: "That's one way, of course."

But my mother said: "Oh no, we couldn't do that, he might hurt himself—anything might happen, you never can tell what——"

I found myself trembling. I didn't want to listen any more, but I couldn't help it, I had to.

"Well," my father said, "maybe if he did hurt himself it might turn out to be the one cure for the little blighter!"

"Richard—how *can* you!" my mother broke in.

"Well, my dear," said my father, "these nights aren't much fun for a man, you know!"

This seemed to anger my mother. "Ha!" she said, "you take pretty good care to get *your* sleep, don't you, though!"

They began to talk in low voices after that, and for the life of me I couldn't hear what they said. All I could catch was my father saying two or three times: "After all, my dear, we are married, you know—we are married!"

I thought about this remark for a long time afterwards. Why, of course they were married, whoever said they weren't! Often I'd think they didn't want to be married any more; that my father would go off and my mother and I would live alone together, perhaps go to a different house. And I wondered also did they, my mother and father, want to go away together, be rid of me, and leave me here alone. This I tried not to think about, but I did. And I went on thinking about that remark, but I couldn't make head or tail of it.

At last I heard Doctor Finnigan break in. "There's only one solution, I fear," he said, "and that's to get a nurse, a maid, someone to look after him. I know it's an expense, but—well, I'm thinking of your nerves and health as well as the child's. You mustn't go on having bad nights like this, you'll get run down and——"

Then I heard my father interrupt. "Right—done!" he said in a loud voice. "Right!" he shouted, "by gad, we will!"

I heard them all move then, so I darted from the room and down the stairs.

And that was how Bessie came. I liked Bessie from the very moment I saw her, loved her more than anything or anyone in the world, Stephen. I remember the day as though it were yesterday. All three of us were standing at the front door, waiting. I felt nervous, and stood by myself, behind my mother. The trap drew up. A girl with red hair jumped out. Without thinking, I came forward, walked out on to the gravel. And the girl with the red hair—she stopped and looked at me. Then she smiled. And when she smiled I smiled, because I loved the look of her. Then she said: "Hullo!"—just like that, nothing more, and took off the scarf that was round her neck. So I looked up and put out my hand and answered: "Hullo!" But she bent down and picked me up, looked at me close, and said: "My name's Bessie!"

Then she dropped me and put out her hand to my father. But he didn't take it. He just said: "The nursemaid, I presume?"

I glanced at Bessie, and her eyes were closed, her head tilted back a little, and for a second all the brightness went out of her face; then she smiled again and said: "Who the——!" But immediately she bit her lip and blushed. "I'm sorry," she said, "my name's Bessie Sheridan. Yes, the—er—nursemaid."

My father grunted and walked away.

Then my mother came forward and said she was glad to meet Bessie and Bessie said she was glad to meet my mother, and I could see by their faces that was all bunk—but it didn't matter. I was really rather pleased, for I knew I was the only one glad to meet Bessie and I felt she was more glad to meet me than my mother or father.

Well, Stephen, from this time on, life was different. That night my bed was moved down to the spare room, on the ground floor, and Bessie's bed was under the large window that opened right out on to the path leading down to the lake. It was a big bright room with white walls and a blue carpet, like velvet. Bessie, who had come all the way from Carriganass, said she had never been in a room like that, and before I went to bed that night she walked up and down the room and clapped her hands and laughed—I had never heard anyone laugh like that before—and picked me up, then dropped me, so that I too got the giggles and we both made such a row that my mother came in and said: "Well, what's up? You seem pretty happy, you two!"

And Bessie laughed out loud at my mother and said: "Why, yes, m'am, that's just what's up, we're getting on fine, aren't we, kid?" (Bessie called me that from the start.)

But I said nothing, for I was looking at my mother's face that was suddenly almost angry. It was then that she said to Bessie: "Now, Nurse, please don't get him excited. He needs well looking after, mind, for he—sees things."

But even at that Bessie laughed. "Sees things, does he!" she cried, "it's Bessie Sheridan'll teach him to see things, so it is!" And she grabbed me and flung me up on her shoulder. Then she pinched me in the ribs, making me laugh, though by now my mother's face looked angrier than ever. She made to leave then, saying over her shoulder: "I'll come and see you when you're ready for the night."

Stephen, there was nothing I hated more than to hear my mother say that. Ready for the night! If only she could have known what horror it meant to me! The night! Ready for it! The one thing on earth I had never been ready for was—the night, the awful silent empty darkness of the night.

Bessie looked up at me then—I was still on her shoulder—and I suppose I must have been looking pretty glum, for she said: "Now, kid, it's as though you'd gone and lost yourself, you look!"

So I gazed down at her and I forgot all about getting ready for the night. I said: "Bessie, why did you tell my mother you were pleased to see her when you came?"

"Why, because I was, of course!"

We looked at each other. She said: "Why d'you ask me that, kid? I like your mother. Don't *you*?"

I looked at Bessie again and I didn't know quite what to say. At last I said: "Yes, I like her, but——"

"But what?"

"But I like you better," I said quickly.

Bessie glanced up, surprised. "But you don't know me, kid," she said.

"Yes, Bessie," and I got down off her shoulder. "Yes, I feel I know you—at least I know you better than my mother."

"Silly!" said Bessie, "it's nonsense you're talking—why, your mother loves you!"

I stood away from her when she said that. "That's bunk, Bessie," I said; "my mother doesn't love me."

Bessie leaned back in her chair. "How d'you know?" she asked. "And who in the world learned you that word 'bunk'?"

"I know," I said, with my head down, "because my mother doesn't like hugging me, and she won't let me in her bed."

"But you've got a bed of your own, kid—and who learned——?"

"I don't like to sleep by myself," I said, "I see things. Last night——"

"Who learned you that word 'bunk'?" Bessie interrupted, and suddenly she burst out laughing, and when I saw her laughing I started to laugh and I ran at her and jumped into her lap and she clasped me round the waist and I put my arms around her head and my face in her hair, then on her face, and I kissed her, not like I kissed my mother, not on the cheek, but all over her face, her eyes and her lips, like I always wanted to but never could because there wasn't anyone but my mother, and somehow I couldn't with her because—well, she wasn't like Bessie.

When I'd got my breath again, I said: "Bessie, why did you laugh like that?"

And Bessie said because she thought "bunk" such an extraordinary word. "Where did you get it from?" she asked.

"Dan says it."

"Who's Dan?" asked Bessie.

"He's the man who works the pump down there by the lake," and I pointed out of the window, towards the engine-house.

"A young feller, is he?" she asked.

"Not he," said I; "as old as my father, probably."

"That isn't old," she said, laughing.

Then she was silent awhile, and in the middle of the silence the door opened and my mother came in. "Well," she said, "ready for the night?"

Oh Lord, I thought, why can't my mother be a bit happier? Why is life always so serious when she's about? And why—why must I always get ready for the night on the tick of six every evening?

Well, I started to undress slowly and when I got into bed my mother came and put a screen round it, and on the other side of the bed there was just a wall, so I could see nothing but the ceiling.

"Mother," I said, "I can't see anything!"

"What d'you mean, child—you can't see?"

"The screen, Mother——"

"But you're not supposed to see now, dear. It's night and you're going to sleep."

Then she bent down over the bed and kissed me on the forehead, but I didn't take any notice.

When she opened the door to go I heard her say to Bessie: "And, Nurse, if you have any trouble you know where I am, don't you?"

"Ah, that's all right, m'am," Bessie answered, "don't worry yourself!" And she said good night but I don't think my mother replied.

When she had gone Bessie came and folded up the screen. Then she brought up a chair and a book and began reading to me.

"I always read before I go to sleep," she said.

That had never happened to me before. While she read she held my hand and I looked at her but all I could see of her face was her nose, for her hair fell down over her cheeks and hid the rest. Lying there like that, listening to Bessie's quiet voice, holding her hand, I knew I had never been as happy before.

I don't know how long she read because after a while my eyes closed and I was in the garden hunting for something, I didn't know what, and I searched and searched, looked behind all the trees, in the flower beds, behind the green garden-doors, in the potting-shed and the greenhouse—when suddenly in the distance, walking down to the lake, I saw a girl with red hair, and it was Bessie. And then I knew I had been looking for her all the time, so I ran towards her, but when I got to the river-path she wasn't there, so I began to shout: "Bessie! Bessie!"

Then I woke; it was dark, and I forgot, and cried: "Mother! Mother!"

But the light went on and there was I in the spare room, and there—there was Bessie coming towards me in a green nightdress, with her hair flowing down her back to her waist.

"Oh, Bessie!" I cried, "I couldn't find you anywhere!"

"Couldn't you, kid?" she smiled, bending over me. "Well, you hadn't far to look, had you?"

I put my arms round her neck. "Oh, thank Heavens!" I said, "thank Heavens it was only a beastly dream."

"But, dear child," said Bessie, "there are good dreams as well as bad, you know."

"Oh no, there aren't!" I said. "I never had a good one in my life. But, Bessie, why do I dream like this? Please tell me. Is there —is there something—wrong with me?"

Bessie laughed. "Wrong," she said. "I can't find much the matter with you, silly. You just think too much, that's all."

"Think too much?"

"Yep, that's it."

"But how—how can I not think so much?"

She looked at me and smiled. Then she gripped me under the arms and said: "Shall I show you, kid?"

"Yes!" I said. "Yes!"

So at that she drew me up very quickly, out of my bed, and ran across the room with me in her arms, to her bed, threw me down in it, put out the light, and got in with me.

That had certainly never happened to me before!

She was warm and I clung to her, to her neck and her body, my arms round her neck and my legs either side of her body, and I kissed her face and told her I loved her, and she laughed and stroked my hair and crooned a song with words I didn't understand then because it was a Gaelic song. And I cried a bit, I suppose from happiness, and just before I went to sleep I whispered to her: "Bessie, I don't like to sleep in my bed, but my mother says all boys do. Tell me, Bessie, is there something wrong with me?"

As usual Bessie only laughed at this and said: "Hell, kid, let's go to sleep now, and don't you go on thinking a lot of—bunk!"

We both roared with laughter when she said that, and Bessie turned over and I clung to her back and fell into a deep dreamless sleep that way.

In the morning I woke up fresh. I felt so different I knew immediately that was what my mother meant by waking up fresh. I turned and looked at Bessie, who said: "Now go on, kid, get into your own bed—and you needn't let on to your mother you didn't sleep there all night."

"I won't let on," said I.

After this, Stephen, life was good. All the days I spent with Bessie. We did have meals with my mother and father, but somehow things were different now; my mother spoke to my father and he to her, and Bessie spoke to me, all through meals. And, for a time, I spent the nights with her, too; wonderful nights they were; until one day Bessie asked, rather seriously: "Kid, will you do something for me?"

"Sure," I said.

"Well," she said, "be real grown-up and try sleeping in your own bed all night—will you, kid—to please me?" And I did from then on, and I woke up fresh.

I took Bessie everywhere, showed her everything. We wandered all over the garden together and up the steep, rocky cliff where my mother always said I mustn't go, and into the haybarn where one day my father had caught me sliding down the hay and forbade me ever to go again. I showed her Joe Parsons, the gardener, Rory McBride, who milked the cows, and Phil O'Connor, the boy who brought the mail on a red bike. We went all over the place together and Bessie talked to everyone we met. At last I took her down to the lake, to show her Dan, who taught me that word "bunk" and who worked the engine that pumped the water up to the house. I never knew if I really liked Dan, because he always wanted me to come into the engine-house and I hated the engine-house. It was no bigger than a hut, it smelled, and there was such a noise inside you couldn't hear yourself speak unless you shouted aloud. The noise and the smell and the look of the engine with all those oily rods that popped up and down, slid in and out, while Dan just stood there and did nothing to make it work that I could see—it all frightened me, gave me a queer feeling in my stomach, made me feel slightly sick.

But Bessie—she didn't mind it; and she liked Dan the moment she saw him, and they got on fine. He was a tall man with a head of thick black curls. His hands were huge and always grimy with oil, the nails like lumps of ink. He wore filthy overalls and in one hand always carried some cottonwool stuff which he called waste. After a while we used to see him every day. Bessie would go into the engine-house, but I didn't; I just wandered about outside, stared at the minnows in the shallow part of the lake. Once I caught some in a net and put them in a jar and placed the jar on the window-sill in our room. I looked at them a long time and then thought they seemed to want to get out, so I poured them back again into the lake and caught some more. But Bessie said that was silly, to catch minnows, they were no good to anyone, why not catch eels? So I said yes, and next day we went down and asked Dan about catching eels, and he said sure thing, put out a line, he said, with a hooked worm on the end and you'll catch one sure as eggs is eggs, just here by the engine-house. So we did. (Bessie threaded the worm on the hook while I pretended to be watching, but I wasn't, because a worm gave me that queer feeling in my stomach and I couldn't bear to see a sharp hook being pierced into it.)

So next evening when we went down to the line we had laid in the lake, Bessie said: "Pull at the line, kid—and see!"

So I pulled and there was a kind of a tug at the other end, as though there was someone else pulling, so I dropped it, half-scared, and said: "Oh, Lord, there's something on it, Bessie!"

"Why, of course," laughed Bessie, "it's maybe an eel!"

Then Dan came out in his shirt-sleeves and Bessie smiled at him and he smiled at her and they stood there together, as though they'd known each other all their lives.

"Well," asked Dan, "catch anything?"

"I don't know," I said, stepping back from the water.

"Well, go on," said Dan, "have a see!"

"*You* see, Dan," I said.

"Why me?" asked Dan, and he laughed and glanced at Bessie and she looked at him, and for a moment I didn't like either of them, certainly not Dan.

"I don't like to," I said, though I didn't want to say it.

"Ach, man—that's all bunk!" he said.

Bessie laughed, and hearing her laugh I walked towards the line and gave it a quick tug and the line came right out of the water with a huge, glistening eel on the end and it fell on the grass beside me and wriggled and jumped and twisted itself in and out, trying with all its might to get free of the hook in its mouth.

Then Dan walked forward and picked up the wriggling, snaky, slimy thing by the middle, and I saw its glassy wide-open eyes. . . .

"He won't hurt," said Dan, as I turned away. "Come and feel what a nice hard body he has!"

"I will not!" I cried. And when I thought they would really make me touch it I began to walk away. Even when I heard Bessie say: "Ah, leave him be, if he doesn't want to, Dan," I didn't stop, but stalked back to the house, leaving Bessie down by the lake with Dan. She came up some time after, while I was having my supper, and, as usual, put me to bed and kissed me, and told me not to think about that old eel, for they were nasty fish, anyway, she said. So I hugged her, promised I wouldn't think any more about the eel, and fell asleep.

Now, Stephen, I know all these things sound very small and not worth talking about, but I feel I have to because whenever I think of that night my thoughts turn on that day; and all these things that happened during it stand out so very clear in my mind, and seem somehow to have something to do with what happened later.

I don't know what hour it was, but I think it must have been about dawn, because dimly I remember that when first I woke there was a grey hazy light that made the room seem cold.

At first I did not fully awake, so I shut my eyes and tried to get back to sleep again. Then I heard something, and held my breath, to listen. But there was only my heart thumping below me in the bed. So again I tried to sleep. But almost at once I was certain I heard a whisper, then something move, over by the window.

Then—Stephen, the memory!—there was a kind of sigh, then a groan, then breath coming and going very fast, hoarse breath. I sat bolt upright—but too terrified to yell: my mouth and throat were parched. I began to tremble. I looked towards the window, to Bessie's bed. And there—oh, God!—I could just see a man crouching over her on the bed, with his hands round her face and throat—strangling her!

And she—Bessie, my Bessie!—she was groaning, with her head thrown back and her eyes tight shut, her mouth wide-open, gasping!

Tears of fright suddenly shook me. I felt suffocated. I couldn't get any words out of my throat, and it was like my limbs were frozen stiff, for I couldn't move, only tremble like a terrified animal in every limb of my body ... and all the time I thought I was going to be sick.

Bessie was being murdered, murdered.

Then I saw the window was wide open! A man—in by the window—murdering Bessie, killing her! Oh, quick, quick, yell, scream ... anything ... but *save* her!

Then—just as I knew she was going to die, for she was breathing so fast and hoarse, and the man—the man was uttering some words as if he hated her—she cried out, my Bessie cried out: "*Dan, Dan—my Dan!*"

Now even today while I write this, Stephen, I don't know exactly what I did, I don't know what I screamed. But I did scream—at the top of my voice. This I know, because I remember just one thing, that is Bessie, with nothing on—so that in one flash at the age of six I knew women are not like men—with nothing on, I tell you, Stephen, and her hair flying out behind her, she rushed to me, knocked me down in the bed, stuffed my mouth with the sheet, and tied it round my head, tight.

And next I knew the light was on and I was lying under the bed-clothes. Dan was gone; the window was closed; Bessie was standing over me, calm, with her green nightdress on, and so was my mother.

And Bessie was saying to my mother: "Ah, that's all right, m'am, don't worry yourself, he's only been—seeing things!"

Well, that's all, Stephen. I'm afraid it's all very badly expressed, but I've got so worked up writing it that I found myself living it all over again, as though I were still that misery of a child. However, I'm glad I've told you at last—about *my*self. Perhaps it'll make things easier for us both in the future.

Come soon, and let's see each other as much as we can. I hate to think of school without you, but only a year, my Stephen, and we'll be together again.

Lord, I'm tired.

The Broken Leg

NEITHER DONALD NOR HILDA ARCHER had ever been aware that they spent rather more time and money on their animals than they did on their children. There exist a number of English homes where parental attention is divided, equally and unequally, between offspring and animals.

Not that Max and Elliot were neglected. On the contrary. Their parents' hunters had a devoted groom and stablemen, and were fed on the best oats and hay; while the father's shooting-dogs and the mother's poodles were nursed and trained by an experienced keeper. But the two boys possessed, and were incidentally possessed by, an expensive French governess. Each of them had a pony of his own to ride. They were dressed in fine clothes and fed on the best food England and the Archers could offer. Indeed, they were to grow up lacking nothing money could buy, and to realize above all that *horse-sense* means not only "plain rough sagacity," but a knowledge of horses, hounds and hunting—without which, the Archers considered, neither man nor woman is properly equipped for the business of living in this world.

It was said, it had even been written in the society journals of the time, that when Donald Archer married his wife she was "the loveliest girl north of the Tweed." Eight years later she was still very handsome in a big, masculine way; with strong brown hands and a mass of wiry black hair that seemed to make her eyes more blue than they were in reality. In that time she had grown into a woman of rigid principles, and of two outstanding passions, shared by her husband: she loathed physical cowardice and she adored fox-hunting.

That she who, until the day of her marriage, had never been

astride a horse, should take to riding to hounds in a manner that eclipsed even her husband's prowess in that art, no one in the county could have imagined. Even before Max, her elder son, was born, Hilda Archer was already known as the bravest and most intrepid woman rider throughout the shires.

"She puts all other women in the shade," her new friends and admirers had said. By the time Elliot was a year old, the sporting farmers insisted that if the scent were high and the going good "no man in England could catch sight of that Mrs Archer's face!"

Then, in the very same week as Max's eighth birthday, when much to his disgust he was presented with another pony, a terrible thing happened: Mrs Archer broke her leg out hunting. Her horse fell on her in such a way that her knee-bones came through the skin and breeches, smashed like broken sticks. She was not found until half an hour after the accident, by a local labourer, who said it was the most awful and the most wonderful sight he had ever seen. "While the poor creature was a'lyin' there as alive and conscious as me, there she was trying to straighten out the leg with 'er 'ands, so's she could put two feet to the groun'. An' when she sees me, all she says is: 'Did they catch my horse, man —did they catch my horse?' "

The labourer's words went the rounds, but the countryside was too shocked by the possible results of such an accident to pay proper heed to the story of the woman's amazing fortitude. For it was by now difficult for the hunting people to imagine a day's sport without the famous Mrs Archer leading them all in the field. For seasons now at covert-sides innumerable young men and women had sought her out in the crowd, furtively edged their horses nearer towards her, to see which way Mrs Archer would choose to go when the fox "broke"; and when it did, with tongues going dry in their mouths, to attempt to keep near her and so at the end of the day be able to boast they had seen as much of the hunt as anyone, since between them and the hounds there had only been one other—Mrs Archer.

At big Meets, to which many visitors and strangers came, she was the first after the Master to be pointed out in the crowd. "That's Mrs Archer," hosts would say to their guests, and seldom was any further explanation necessary. In the county itself, her looks, her modesty, her easy sociable manner, had endeared her to many people. Even her husband, always a silent unobtrusive man, had become more and more conscious of his increasing popularity. Secretly, though unresentingly, he knew this to be due to the people's admiration of his wife, for they were not a whit less proud of her than he was, nor could they reconcile themselves to the alarming possibility that this accident might deprive their sport of its idol and guide.

Their fears were by no means exaggerated. Within a week of Mrs Archer's leg being set, the bones of the knee had to be broken again. After much deliberation, during which the entire Archer household remained in a state of permanent anxiety—an anxiety communicating itself with extreme vividness to the impressionable Max, who was just old enough to be intensely aware of the grave faces about him and the curious "doctor" smells that issued from his mother's room and pervaded the house—the surgeon decided to insert a silver wire in the knee to keep the two parts of the shattered limb together.

A fortnight later the family doctor and the surgeon entered her room. The doctor, a friend since her marriage, and the man who had delivered her of both her children, walked towards her bed, sat down in the chair beside it, took his patient's outstretched hand. Mrs Archer looked at him, then turned her eyes on the surgeon. She saw him standing at the end of the bed, his body leaning slightly forward, his hands gripping the bed-rail, his eyes lowered. For a moment no one spoke. Then he looked at her. "Mrs Archer," he said slowly, "the operation has been successful."

She closed her eyes, laid back her head on the pillow and smiled, feeling on her hand the pressure of the doctor's fingers.

"In three months," the surgeon was saying, "you ought to be able to walk."

In a flash Mrs Archer saw herself walking out of the house, her dogs and children following her, walking down the drive, to the stables. . . . She was in the act of raising her leg to the mounting-block when her thoughts were interrupted by the surgeon's voice.

"But," she heard, and the word cut sharp, "but, Mrs Archer, I'm afraid you will never be able to ride again!"

A blinding light struck suddenly across her eyes, strength

sprang into her arms, and the next moment she was sitting bolt upright in bed, staring wildly before her. Her mouth opened to speak, but no words came. Her lower lip trembled for an instant while she fought against the hand of the doctor who was trying to make her lie down.

"No," the surgeon continued, coming towards her. "No, Mrs Archer, it would probably prove fatal. You've injured your pelvis."

It was then that Hilda Archer did what she had never done in her life before. She pulled up the bed-clothes over her head, and cried. She cried all night.

Although she recovered and could walk even before the surgeon's predicted time, Mrs Archer was left permanently lame. Her left leg was to remain misshapen for life, a deformity no dress but one of extreme eccentricity could hope to conceal.

The catastrophe affected her at first as many feared it might. During the whole of the following summer she seldom left her home. Her husband, in despair and on the advice of the doctor, tried to persuade her to go abroad. He talked to her of Switzerland and Italy, even of a trip to the West Indies. She refused to move. During the long midsummer days and weeks she rarely went out into the sun, never once approached the stables. Her own magnificent hunters she gave over to her husband, while hunting itself became a subject unmentionable in her presence.

Instead, she turned her listless thoughts more than ever towards her poodles, which she now groomed, fed, and kept upstairs in her room, cutting their coats into more and more fantastic patterns. But soon she tired even of them and bought a dog and bitch Sealyham, from which she bred a litter of four fine puppies. These she first kept in a kennel in the yard behind the house, visiting them at all hours of the day. When two of the puppies went down with distemper, she even made up a bed for herself in the loft above the kennel, where she tended the sick ones through the worst of their illness. For a long time she allowed no one, excepting neither her husband nor her children, to approach this kennel.

It was through and with these dogs, however, that she came finally to leave the immediate neighbourhood of the house and

start off for walks with only them as companions. After tea she
would escape by the back door, in a skirt covering as much of
her deformity as possible without attracting attention by its
length, and walk down through the avenue of yew-trees to the
rock-garden which, since the accident, her husband had made his
summer hobby. Here, when not riding or seeing to things on the
estate, Donald Archer worked and sat about, hoping thus to find,
if not a certain solace, at least an escape from the constant thought
of how his wife had altered, how she seemed to wish for nothing
more than to be alone all day with her dogs.

Some evenings she would join him there, and together they
would descend the last slope to the deep, sluggish river, where in
the silence of the golden summer light a single trout might startle
the world with an occasional leap through the surface and reeds,
or a cow on the far bank low mournfully for its calf, but where
otherwise no sound but the distant hum of bees in the limes ever
broke the wonder of the English stillness. It was on one of these
walks that Hilda Archer's thoughts were stirred into an un-
explored channel.

They were wandering together along the river-path, the four
white puppies running in and out of their legs. The last of the
sun's rays came slanting through the limes, dappling the dog-
wood's shining redness with glimpses of gold and the brown
water running over its roots with darting patches of pale yellow
light, when Donald Archer suddenly paused beside his wife.
"Oh," he exclaimed, striking his leg with his stick as though the
slight self-inflicted pain would help to remind him. "Tomorrow I
must remember to go and watch the boys ride the new ponies!"

To this statement, at the time, his wife did not reply. But in
that instant there crept into her mind a vision of herself and her
two children; and, with what came almost as a revelation, the fact
that she hardly knew her sons. A moment later she was able to
dispossess herself of this knowledge with that enviable facility
unimaginative people have for not thinking of what they do not
wish to think. But in this case she was incapable of ridding her
mind of it for long, for again that same night, when Max and
Elliot came to say their evening prayers and bid her good night
(lately she had been seeing them only in the mornings and even-

ings), she was conscious once more of the revelation that had
come to her by the river-bank.

As usual, the governess opened the door of Mrs Archer's room
as she lay on the sofa before taking her evening bath; she muttered something inaudible, and Max and Elliot came in. They
were dressed in grey flannel shorts and sweaters; their legs were
bare, showing fresh earth-stains on their knees; and they wore
open leather sandals. Between them there was that queer in-
definable family likeness shared by most brothers: their brown
curly hair was of a similar colour and texture, the eyes of the
same blue, and the tone of their voices, their little manners of
speech—always the most noticeable traits of similarity in a family
—were indistinguishable. But in no other way did these two
resemble each other. Max, the elder by more than twelve months
and a head taller than his brother, was lean, angular, pale, and
excessively shy. Elliot, though also shy in the sense that he felt
timid in the presence of strangers, was broad, strong, big-boned
and inclined to be fat.

Mrs Archer had one method, and one only, of greeting her sons.
When they came into the room, slowly, shyly, she would look at
them, turn away, then utter the word: "Well!"

This single word seemed always, especially to Max, a challenge.
And it was. Mrs Archer would have liked to see her sons burst
into the room, rush towards her and fling their arms joyfully
round her neck. But Max had only dreamed of boys so behaving,
while to Elliot's placid disposition such an abnormal demonstration of feelings had never occurred even in a nightmare—a noc-
turnal event as strange to him as it was well-known to his elder
brother.

For what, at first, seemed a long time to all save Elliot, who
stood staring, as he always did in his mother's room, at a photograph on the wall of Mrs Archer in the act of jumping a fence
in the middle of a hunt, there was, as answer to this monosyllabic
comment, complete silence. Max had walked to the window, and
now leaned there, staring out over the river, wondering what,
when he turned round, he could find to say to his mother. And
with this thought came another, ever present in her company, that
whatever he did when he turned, he must not gaze at his mother's

left leg. Ever since her accident—ever since, in fact, with a horror that all his efforts had failed to dispel, he had seen those grave faces, smelled those hideous "doctor" smells, and watched his mother's face of agony as she first began to walk on crutches—he had been totally unable to rid himself of the fascination that possessed him against the full power of his will, of wanting to gaze at the deformity of his mother's leg. He would see it in reality, and he saw it in his dreams that were nightmares; and every day that he rode his pony he was filled with fear, for then all the reasons of his dread rose in a vision before his eyes, clear and vivid as though the accident of his mother had been his own.

Of all this that went on inside Max, no one, least of all his mother, had the remotest idea.

While he was thus fighting with himself at the window, Mrs Archer's eyes remained on Elliot gazing at her image on the wall. For a time she had been hardly aware of him, piqued as she was at her sons' giving no answer to her own "greeting," but now she fell to studying his fat-cheeked little face turned up and away from her so that she saw it in profile. She noticed the intent and determined line of the lips, that were her lips half the size, at the one blue eye she could see opened wide, first with interest, then with genuine, unmistakable excitement. She watched the lips move into half a smile as the head remained motionless, so alive to what the eyes beheld in the photograph. Suddenly, with such overwhelming certainty that for an instant of time she forgot everything she had ever thought of, there came to her the knowledge that she must—that she longed to—devote her immediate future to her children.

Mrs Archer told not a soul, not even her husband, of her sudden resolution. It was an immense step for her to take; nor for many hours did she come to any decision as to how to set about it. You could buy a dog, and loving that dog, pat it, groom it, feed it, telling it of your love without any fear of embarrassment on either side; but to show a sudden, very definite interest in two boys whom you have known, and been known by, all their lives, and to whom demonstration of the extent of your love and interest has been but a peck twice a day on the cheek, was not so simple a proposition.

But Mrs Archer was determined to secure a mother's real affection from her sons, to win them over so completely that she would become indispensable to them, become the greater part of their lives, and they the whole of hers.

That night, for the first time in months, she limped up the stairs to bed with a light heart, the old expression of resolve and determination in her eyes. Once in her room she retraced her thoughts to the origin of her present state of mind, to what her husband had said on the river-bank, and instantly her face lit up. She called to him next door in a voice that had become almost strange to him. "Donald!"

He came quickly to the communicating door, and looked at her. He saw that her eyes were shining, and she saw that he saw, and smiled.

"What is it, dear?" he asked, puzzled, yet excited by the look on her face.

"Donald," Hilda Archer said, "did you say you were going down to see the boys ride their new ponies in the morning?"

Her husband nodded. "Why?" he asked.

She lowered her head, away from his gaze. "Because," she murmured, "I think I'll come, too."

II

It was one of those September mornings when even the beech branches overhanging the avenue seemed by their very lightness to be heralding a second spring. Where the sun had not penetrated the foliage the dark green of the wayside grass still shone with dew, and though the leaves of the chestnut trees had turned and nuts lay scattered brown and green over the drive, yet a biting vigour in the air came as a vehement denial of summer's dying days.

Even the dogs appeared aware of the keen morning air. With their noses to the ground they raced ahead of the family, tearing in and out of the laurels, rushing a few yards down the drive, each on its own, and then, before bounding off again, stopping to turn and wag their tails, as though to welcome the new advent of their mistress and the reunion of her family.

Mrs Archer herself, in spite of her limp, walked a little ahead of her sons, for flowing through her she felt a new life, a sensation now as uncommon to her body as all that she was seeing seemed strange to her eyes. In this new sense of well-being she had momentarily forgotten the prime cause of it, her sons. Close behind her on the one side Elliot half-walked, half-skipped along, his short legs unable to keep pace with those of the striding woman. His face was flushed with the eagerness of his one desire, to be on his new pony. From time to time he looked up at his mother, happy that she was to be present to see him ride. He loved riding, full of the knowledge that he could, and with the fearlessness of those in whom courage is misnamed. Lately, when they had returned to the stables after a ride, Sturgeon, the groom, had often whispered to him: "Fine, that bez, Mast' Elliot, fine— make two o' your big brother, you will!" And Elliot had glowed with pride.

On his mother's other side, even farther behind her than his brother, but not with his brother's excuse for that position, Max sloped almost wearily forward. Only in him was there no appearance of what the vigorous air and the prospect of the morning had given to the others. Only when, unconsciously (for the body is always slave to the mind), he lagged so far behind Mrs Archer that his lowered eyes became aware of her deformity, did he feel forced to increase his pace. Max loved horses, loved all animals, loved to look at them, watch them, play with them; but riding he hated with that deep hatred prompted by fear. And in England, as Max already knew so well, there are homes where to hate riding is to sin, to be oneself despised, even hated.

Donald Archer had already reached the stables when they arrived, having brought the news that at last his wife was to appear once more among them. The welcome she received there, though unostentatious and quiet, remained vivid in her memory long after the excitement of other happenings had faded from her mind into oblivion. At the entrance to the yard she saw Sturgeon, a broad grin splitting his jovial red face, coming forward with his dilapidated bowler in one hand, his other hand outstretched towards her.

"Oh, m'am," he breathed, staring into her face, "if you knew 'ow we've missed you!"

She looked at him, at this man who had taught her so much about the art of riding, who had helped her even more than her husband had, to experience the greatest enjoyment she'd ever known, and now would never know again; she looked at him, aware of the unveiled admiration and pride in his eyes, of the deep sincerity in his voice, and for a wild instant, sensing his knowledge of her grief, she almost gave way to her desire to sit down there and cry, as once, at the first realization of her tragedy, she had cried her heart out in the night.

But instead, taking in a swift breath, she bit her lower lip, gripped the man's hand. "Sturgeon," she said, looking away from him, "I've missed you, too." Then, glancing down at her children, she added: "But I'm all right now."

As the groom stepped away from her the other stablemen took his place, and one by one, touching their caps they shook Mrs Archer's hand, murmuring words of sympathy and welcome. In the distance, over their heads—for out of fear of revealing her emotion she would not look in the men's eyes—she saw the heads of her hunters staring out over their stable doors. Valiantly she fought with a strange feeling in her throat, and then, as one of the horses neighed, their heads grew blurred before her eyes, and she knew she must move on.

Alone she went off and fetched carrots, taking them to the horses that once had been hers. Each neighed delightedly at her approach, and she went in and spoke to them, laying her cheek against the downy softness of their muzzles, talking to them in whispers as though she were renewing an intimacy with human friends of long ago. As she closed the door of the last box she felt she had never been so supremely grateful for a few minutes alone.

"Two of the best ponies I've seen for a long time," Donald Archer was telling his sons when she caught them up at the end of the yard. The two ponies, one rather larger than the other and both of the same dark bay, were standing together, bridled and saddled.

"I like mine," Elliot said, turning to his mother, and smiling. "I'm going to call him Bay—isn't he a lovely colour?"

"Lovely," agreed Mrs Archer, patting the smaller pony's nose. "You *are* lucky, you two—I never had two ponies like these when I was a girl."

"You didn't ride, Mother—when you *was* a girl," Elliot said, arranging the reins on his pony's back.

Mrs Archer smiled. "When you *were* a girl," she corrected. Then she turned to Max who stood a little way off, shocked to find his new pony so much taller than the last he had ridden. Staring at it with a dry mouth, he wished his mother weren't there, that she wouldn't look so pleased. For a moment he envied her having a broken leg. "I could look pleased then," he said to himself.

"Well, Max," he suddenly heard her say, "what d'you think of *your* pony? I'm not sure he isn't the best-looking of the two."

"*Better*-looking," murmured her husband, but only Elliot heard and blushed for his parents.

Max watched his mother as she bent down and felt the pony's legs.

"Fine bone," she said. "Clean, too."

Max edged a little nearer, staring at the pony's head above him. He felt suddenly very small. His mother straightened herself and looked at him.

"Well!" she said, once more in that tone of challenge.

Max lowered his eyes in confusion. "Nice," he murmured.

"Nice! I should think he jolly well is. You'll be able to go cubbing on him next week. How'll you like that?"

Though Mrs Archer had no conscious desire to harass her son, Max felt certain that she, sensing his fear, was purposely baiting him. He blushed. Such a question as hers, which no adult asks of an adult nor should ask of a child, always made him blush. It was an insult. He hesitated, not knowing what to say, then lied, knowing it to be the easiest way out. "I will," he murmured.

"All right," said his mother irritably, staring down at his despondent appearance, "put your cap straight and don't look so glum about it."

She came a little nearer, bending down to him. "Is something wrong, Max?" she asked in a concerned tone, looking into his flushed face.

Max glanced up at her, trying to smile. But his mouth was dry, and the sudden strange tone of compassion that had crept into his mother's voice made him long to be able to clutch her and cry out to her all his fear. But fighting back the tears he clenched his hands. "No," he lied again, "no, 'course not."

"*That's* all right then," said his mother, relieved. "Now let's see you get on."

Surreptitiously wiping away one tear, Max walked towards his pony.

"By the way, Hilda," came Donald Archer's voice, "I forgot to tell you, I've put up one or two small fences in the Park field. The boys might as well try the jumping power of their new steeds."

Max heard the words from his pony's back, but now that he was high up there that queer bravado, a quality that has been the means of earning more than one Victoria Cross, possessed him suddenly, and for a moment he felt strong, almost happy in that sensation of being utterly without care.

"Good," said Mrs Archer, "let's go along."

Together the two boys rode out of the stables, the ponies' hoofs clattering on the cobbles, the three adults following on foot behind.

"Bez a fine pair o' ponies, sir!" said Sturgeon as they made their way through the yard.

"They are, Sturgeon," Donald Archer agreed. "Only hope the riders'll live up to them!"

"Ah," drawled Sturgeon, "that's what I'd like to see, sir. But that there Master Elliot—'e bez shapin' summat wonderful of late. Told 'im 'e'll beat 'is brother, I did."

"Hm," murmured the father. "I'm afraid Master Max doesn't look so strong on a horse as he might."

"Nah," breathed the groom, and he shook his head, peered sideways at Mrs Archer, as though wishing her elder son possessed more of that quality he so admired in her. He looked at her and thought of the past. "There now," he remembered saying to the other men as she rode out of the yard on hunting mornings. "There now, look at that for a bit o' courage! Taught 'er meself, too—ah, every bit, from 'ow to put 'er 'at on, to the way to shove 'er 'oss at a fi' bar gate! Ah, a beautiful bit o' courage, that—Gawd bless 'er!" Then he glanced away, saddened with memories of former days.

Since her accident Sturgeon had been more genuinely sorry for Mrs Archer than were even her closest friends. But she herself, far from thinking of her groom, now walked silently with the two men, heedless of what they said, for she was engrossed in a vision wherein she saw her husband fields away in front of the rest of the hunt, and her two sons galloping side by side, close behind. Vaguely she heard friends talking in the drawing-room afterwards, and out of the rabble of words she heard a loud voice exclaiming: "Oh, Hilda, you really should have seen your two boys today— they're marvels!"

Finding herself walking faster than the men she slackened her pace. Suddenly, out of her thoughts, an idea occurred to her. She touched her husband on the arm. "Donald," she said, "I think I'll get a pair of harness horses."

She noticed his face brighten. "What? And follow the hounds in the trap, Hilda?"

"Yes," she said. "It'd give me something to do."

"That's a great idea," he agreed. "You know the country so well you'd see everything."

"Why, m'am," said Sturgeon, "if I may make so bold, I think that's a very fine idea indeed—very fine. Why, fancy me not thinkin' of it before! Well, well." And he smiled to himself at the thought that he might be permitted to drive the trap for her.

When they had passed out of the stables they continued on down a lane flanked on both sides by huge barns of corrugated iron, where labourers were in the midst of stacking the new hay. At the end of the lane they turned a corner where there was a gate, and here they came upon the boys at the moment when Elliot, after many failures from Max, had at last managed to open it.

"Well done, Elliot!"

With a feeling of shame Max heard his mother's words in praise of his brother, and he blushed, envying Elliot his success and hoping it would not reflect too adversely upon himself. He was conscious, too, that his own efforts to open the gate might have been greater; for he had a very reasonable fear of gates, knowing well what the first feel of grass and the sight of a wide field mean to a fresh horse.

By the time the gate was open and the others had joined them the sensation of bravado Max had recently known in the stables had utterly forsaken him—a sharp, barely controllable fit of panic taking its place. Seeing the great expanse of field before them, with nothing between themselves and the grass, both ponies simultaneously pricked up their ears and began to paw the ground, suddenly impatient to be off. Max, sensing this in his pony even before he himself became aware that the animal's forelegs were prancing beneath him, quickly caught up the reins tight in his hands, thus immediately instilling into his pony the idea they were both out for a racing gallop. The feeling of fear is communicated from man to horse with a swiftness beside which silent interhuman contact is slow. Insidiously it descends with magic speed first from the hands, then the legs of the rider to the mouth and flanks of the horse; the instant the man is conscious of his own fear the animal is instantaneously and equally conscious of it.

The moment Max's breath came quick and he gathered his reins tight to his pony's neck and at the same time slackened the slight grip he had with his knees, that same instant his pony laid back its ears as though actually to hear the knowledge coming to him, cocked them again, then plunged forward through the gate.

"Don't hold him by his head, Max!"

His mother's shouted words were the last he heard before, panic striking dizziness into his head and a sickening sensation rising straight from his stomach to his throat, he felt himself thrown high into the air. He saw in a flash the pony's neck coming close to his eyes, and immediately the sharp contact sent a stunning pain into his forehead. A second later he was once more back in the saddle, tearing across the field at a pace that swept the very breath from his mouth.

A bolting horse gallops in an abnormal way, blindly, losing its head and all sense of direction. Max, whose arms felt so lifeless from fear that even to hold the reins required an effort, was horribly conscious of one thing only—that the pony, with its ears laid flat, its neck outstretched, its legs pounding away at the fast receding earth beneath him, had not the remotest notion where it was heading.

Only the most accomplished horsemen know how to deal with a runaway horse, and even they have experienced moments when their self-confidence has been rudely shocked by that fear which the very strength of an animal can infuse into the heart of man. Max's physical weakness, his ignorance, and his natural deep-rooted fear, all in one, combined to make him on the pony nothing but a terrified passenger, to whom even the idea of throwing himself off did not occur. Indeed, the human instinct for self-preservation bade him resolutely remain, somehow and at all costs, where he was. So there he stayed, little but a natural balance and a determination prompted by the power of fright keeping him in the saddle; for in its first plunge the pony had dislodged one of Max's feet from its stirrup, and that leg now hung as though partly severed from the body. With one hand he held desperately to the pommel of the saddle, while with the other he clung to the single rein of the snaffle bridle; but he no longer tugged at this, for with the effort it caused and the hopelessness of any result he felt his strength ebbing. In despair and with increasing terror he just held himself where he was, allowing the animal to speed madly on over the grass.

The Park field was large, used solely for grazing cattle. On all but one side it was bounded by a ditch and hedge; on the remaining side by a five-foot railing of plain wire. From end to end there was nothing in it but a circular wood, hedged in by a high bank on which brambles grew in crazy confusion. The field possessed but two gates, one at the end opposite the stables and the other one whose untimely opening had been the cause of Max's present predicament. Here Donald and Hilda Archer, with Sturgeon holding Elliot's pony by the bridle, were still silently standing when they saw Max and his pony making straight for the wood. The moment the pony had made that one plunge from the gate and got away, they knew there was nothing to be done. After Sturgeon had exclaimed "Little fool!" under his breath, a silence had fallen between them. To them a runaway pony was not a rare sight; it took much, where a horse was concerned, to scare them. The fact that Max was involved only made the spectacle a more personal one to his parents. Even Mrs Archer looked on with an air of one simply interested. For her there was no fear attached to a bolting horse in a field save in the possible event of the rider falling and being "dragged." That, she remembered, had once happened to her and she had suffered severe concussion. Landing on her head, a hoof had struck it as the horse galloped over her. She was now quite sincerely hoping this would not befall her son as she watched his pony making for the circular wood.

However, as the animal approached the enclosure they saw it momentarily slacken its pace and turn sharply away. For a second they all thought Max must fall at the pony's swerve, for it seemed that his body was actually hanging over the near side. The next instant, however, he appeared to be back in the saddle, clinging with both hands to the pony's mane.

Donald Archer uttered a short laugh; Mrs Archer smiled despairingly. "Crumbs!" murmured Sturgeon to Elliot, "'ow's that for a bad bit o' circus, eh!"

The words were barely out of his mouth when Sturgeon, tossing Elliot's reins to the boy's father, ran out into the field, waving his arms and exclaiming: "Lummy! 'e's 'eadin' for 'ome. Now we'll 'ave 'im!"

As the bolting pony approached, Mrs Archer caught a glimpse of Max's face, white from fright and weakness. "Silly old fool," she murmured to Sturgeon, "he could have thrown himself long ago!"

With surprising suddenness the pony was upon them, heading straight for the gate. Sturgeon started leaping about like a madman, waving his arms and shouting: "Hi, there! Hi!"

"That's no good," she cried, more aware than he that yells never stopped a bolting horse.

As the pony fled past them, it swerved sharply as though realizing that the gate was closed, and Max dropped from its back, with a thud, to the ground.

For an instant, while he lay there inert, nobody moved. Then Max, reacting to exhaustion and fright, burst into tears.

Mrs Archer strode towards him. As she came to him her face was set, almost fierce. Kneeling down over her son on the grass, she shook him.

"Max!" she cried angrily, "Max! What on earth are you crying for? You know you're not hurt!"

As he heard the tone of his mother's voice the flow of tears stopped: he swallowed once, then opened his crying eyes to her. Instead of her face, his gaze, against his will, sought out her leg, and there, with her skirt pulled up over her knee, he saw for the first time the whole of its terrible deformity, from the huge knee right down the curving bones to the swollen ankle. His body giving one convulsive shudder, he again burst into sobs.

"Stop it, d'you hear!" cried his mother, shaking him, "you're a man, aren't you? You don't have to cry like a—like a girl!"

On the last word she laid violent emphasis, as though she despised all it stood for.

"Can't help it!" gulped Max through his tears, "I—can't help it!"

By now Donald Archer had joined his wife. "Come on, Max!" he said, standing over him, "get up! We've all been run away with before now. But we didn't—*cry!*" he added in a tone of disgust.

Over the body of her son Mrs Archer looked up at her husband; and he gazed back at her, at first bewildered—for he saw her face flushed, her forehead creased, the lips drawn tight in one line, her eyes small with a gleam almost of hatred. Slowly she rose to her feet, stood over the whimpering Max, leaned towards her husband. He watched her expression in silence, never before having seen her look like this. Her face came close to his.

"Donald," she whispered, hesitating, "he's—he's a *coward!*"

The last word she growled out like a dog in anger; then, clenching her fists, looking away from him, strode over to where Elliot was walking his pony about near the gate. She smiled up at him.

"Come," she said, and she led the animal farther into the field, towards the fences her husband had made.

Though Max had not heard what his mother had said to his father he was conscious nonetheless, from the sudden silence above him and the fact that he had heard his mother go away, that there had been some communication concerning himself between them. That it was adverse criticism he had no doubt, but his ignorance of its exact nature plunged him in such fear of them that his tears dried up, and before his father spoke again he knew that he must move from where he so ignominiously lay.

"Come on!" he said, as Max felt himself grabbed roughly by the arm. "Come on—get up! Go straight home, and remember— you're in disgrace!"

Crawling to his feet, covering his face with his hands, Max moved off across the field. As he went he shivered with the cold of weakness, the horror of utter shame. He felt that nothing he did in the future could ever atone for the humiliating perform- ance his mother, father, and brother had just witnessed. He knew, moreover, that he had committed a great sin, two sins: he had shown fear while on a horse, and he had "cried before he was hurt." In the great hollow abyss of misery that only a child can know, he felt utterly, terribly alone; the whole of his tiny world was against him; there was none to whom he could turn; he was doomed. As he went up to his room the word rang out in his head as each foot mounted a stair—Doomed! Doomed! Doomed!

When he had flung himself on the bed, the phrase his father often used flashed across his mind: "Remember—the years of your youth are the best!" But he was too young to realize the falsity of the words; once more he gave way to his loneliness and misery in a fit of uncontrollable sobbing.

"He's really splendid!" exclaimed Mrs Archer, smiling at the memory of Elliot putting his pony over the fences. "I told him I'd give him a present of a new crop at the opening Meet. He's obviously a born rider."

Donald Archer came from his room in his pyjamas. "Obviously," he agreed. "Wonderful hands he seems to have for his age. You wouldn't think he'd have the strength——"

"It's not strength, Donald, that counts—as you know. It's— guts." As she almost hissed the last word the expression on Mrs Archer's face became suddenly cruel. Her husband looked at her, knowing she was thinking of Max. He came up to her, put an arm round her waist. "Never mind, dear," he said, "he's very young."

She lowered her face, her eyes still hard and relentless. "But he's ours," she muttered. "I'll not speak to him again till he proves he's a man."

"He will," said Max's father.

And they went to bed, both with a vision of Elliot jumping the fences on his new pony.

In the early hours Mrs Archer woke perspiring from a nightmare. Sitting up, she tried to retrieve in her conscious mind what had happened in her sleep; but all she could remember was being surrounded by hunting people in her drawing-room, and whilst she stood alone amongst them they raised their hands and pointed at her. "Max is a coward!" they murmured in chorus, "Max is a coward!"

Then, breathless and sweating, she had woken. She remained awake till after dawn.

III

When the first hound "opened" in the covert with a wild, haunting cry not unlike a human howl, something so sharp jumped in Mrs Archer's breast that her hands leapt on the driving reins.

"Steady, old man! Steady!" she said to the black horse which sprung swiftly forward in the shafts of the trap.

"Whoa, m'lad!" drawled Sturgeon, grinning with pride beside Mrs Archer. "Whoa, then—you bain't 'untin'!"

Dressed in black, a new bowler perched square on his head, Sturgeon was so pleased with himself and the world that a broad grin had not left his face since early that morning, the day of the opening Meet. Never in his life had he seen such a Meet. "Why," he had just exclaimed to a group of second-horsemen, "all those 'undreds, they didn't seem to've come to 'unt at all—more like the Missis 'oldin' a March Past, eh!"

When they laughed and agreed, Sturgeon spat. "Ah," he went on, "never seen the like. Blimey, must be awful 'ard on 'er, though! Seein' it all, like—and not bein' able . . . you know what I mean."

The men nodded, looking at Mrs Archer sitting in the trap, still surrounded by admiring friends welcoming her back among them.

"Just when 'er kids is beginnin' to 'unt, too," said one of the men.

"That's it!" Sturgeon exclaimed, his face lighting up with a thought. "Crumbs, though!" he continued excitedly, "you wait till you see that there Elliot—you know, the little 'un—on 'is new pony! Lummy—*ride*! The spit-image of 'is Ma. An' baint she proud! Like a struttin' peacock about 'im!"

"There's two of 'em, ain't there?" asked one of the men.

"Ah, there bez a couple," said Sturgeon, shaking his head till the new bowler toppled precariously. "There's that Max—but 'e ain't got an 'eart in 'im the size of a ruddy tanner!"

"Nah?"

"Narhh!" And Sturgeon spat.

It was then the first hound "opened" and Mrs Archer's groom, glancing up, put one finger to his ear, smiled broadly, and ran back to the trap.

"They found, then, m'am!" he said, excited.

But Mrs Archer didn't answer. Her eyes were busy searching among the crowd at the covert-side for her husband and sons.

"Oh, there's one of the boys," she exclaimed.

"Ah, I see 'un," said Sturgeon quickly, "at the back of 'is Dad."

Mrs Archer smiled. "But which of the boys is——?"

"Ah, that bain't so easy, m'am—like as a couple o' chestnuts in them brown coats o' theirs, bain't they?"

"Mr Archer really ought to have both boys near him, it's only fair——"

"Ah, that it be," agreed Sturgeon, "but there, 'untin's 'untin', bain't it, m'am? Sharp's the word and quick's the haction in 'untin', I always says."

As Hilda Archer bit her lip to repress a strong desire to laugh there came a wild, raucous yell from the far end of the covert, then another, and another—followed by a short silence, during which she had to hold her breath, a pain near her thumping heart was hurting her so. Then there rose on the air a deep, stirring, vocal sound that had in it something of both the sadness and madness there is in the hunting of all things, but which, to Mrs Archer's ears, was the most thrilling sound on earth. The huntsman was halloaing the "Gone away!"

Till the long drawn-out cry ended and rose again in an echo from yet another voice, Hilda Archer closed her eyes.

"There 'e goes, m'am!" Sturgeon suddenly cried, jumping to

his feet in excitement; and then, because the horse leapt forward in the shafts to the convulsive pull of its driver's hands, he collapsed on the seat again with a bump.

"Quiet, Sturgeon," Mrs Archer reproved him, "we'll 'head' him if you make such a noise."

"See 'im, m'am?" he whispered, too roused now to be silenced by a few words from his one-time riding pupil. "See 'im? There 'e goes! Gawd, bain't 'e coverin' the ground, eh!"

He was pointing to a large field beyond the far end of the covert. Mrs Archer followed the line of his arm and saw, against the dark green of the grass, an object like a brown bird travelling low in flight. She knew it, instantly, to be a fox.

"Heavens!" she murmured, "he'll be making straight for Ken Wood—a five-mile point."

Closing her eyes again, she saw the fields stretching away before her—every fence, every gap, every gate. Her thoughts followed the hounds and the fences immediately ahead. She knew the line the fox would take, the first flying-hedge away from the covert, the big "double" with the rail on top, the huge deep ditch just before the farm whose owner put barbed-wire round his land, the turn you must make to avoid that wire; and at last in the bottom of the field running into Ken Wood she could see the brook that either sent you home, or, as you sailed over it, gave you that feeling of ecstasy that only a horse and a fence can give. She was galloping hard in her vision when Sturgeon's voice broke the spell and she opened her eyes.

"Ah, there 'e is, there's Mr Archer," he exclaimed. "Nicely up at the gate as usual."

Following Sturgeon's gaze she scanned the dense throng at the covert-side. The dark mass of horses and men, flecked with scarlet coats, stood jammed together at one corner of the nearest field. In her blood she felt the thrill of the tensest moments of a hunt: those last seconds of waiting before, as the flag comes down at the start of a race, you not only know you can go but that you must. As though she herself were one of the crowd, her body trembled uncontrollably with excitement.

"Yes, I see him," she said, spotting her husband. "And there's one of the boys on his far side—I can see his hat."

No sooner had she spoken than there came the deep note of a single hound from out of the wood, and a moment later the whole pack broke into a screaming chorus of stirring sound that had in it shrill cries as of animals in pain and hollow inhuman roars, like echoes booming in a cave.

"Gawd!" breathed Sturgeon, "if them Sunday church bells'd chime like that, darned if I wouldn't go an' pray!"

"I've lost sight of Mr Archer," she said, ignoring the groom and scanning the crowd again.

Sturgeon looked up. "No, m'am," he said, "'e's still there, safe as a 'ouse, by the gate, see? An' there's the—young gen'lemen, m'am—there, see, close to their Dad? It's Master Elliot on the far side, and——"

"Yes," said Mrs Archer, "I see. And that's Max standing just behind his father. He seems all right, his pony quiet enough."

But she kept her eyes on Elliot, the thrill of maternal pride flowing through her. Oh, wait till this evening when the crowd comes in to tea and talks of him and his riding! On a wave of love she knew she adored her second son.

No one but Sturgeon himself had any idea that at six that morning he had galloped Max's pony ten times round the Park field. Yet even the calming effect this exercise had had on the pony did not dispossess its rider of the one realization that occupied the whole of Max's body and mind as he stood in the crowd by the covert-side—that, not even when his pony had plunged away with him in the Park field, had he ever felt so filled with fear. The combined forces of tension felt by all those surrounding him seemed in their intensity to have instilled themselves into him, to have crept in under his skin, causing the sweat to break out in the palms of his hands and his body to grow chilled with anxiety for the immediate future. Had there been fewer people present, had he known his mother was not watching his every move, were he behind or on the outskirts of the immense crowd instead of right up in front with his father—he knew he would try carefully, silently, unostentatiously, to lose himself, and so be at some safe distance from the hounds and horses when the former finally broke from the covert.

As it was, there appeared to be no escape. Not only were there hundreds of horses pressing in behind him, their riders trying to gain a better place for themselves in the crowd, but every few seconds his father looked round and increased his fear by saying: "Max, keep close to me—you'll only get knocked over and be a damned nuisance if you don't."

In his fear Max's eyes kept taking fleeting glances at the people about him; never in his life had he longed more to be anyone but himself. He gazed at a woman sitting calmly on a grey mare beside him, and he longed to be her, to be with her, inside her, to ask her—"Oh, why are you so calm—is there really *no* fear in you?" And with his torment of thinking there came back to him in a nauseous rush the sight of those grave faces, the "doctor" smells coming from his mother's room and pervading the house, the awful agony of her face as she first walked on crutches, and that one glimpse he had seen of the whole of her deformity as he lay on the ground in the field.

Suddenly out of the sweating stillness the first hound "opened" and he started, his tongue cleaving dry to the roof of his mouth. They'd "found": his last hope was gone. They'd go now, have to go, have to gallop at full speed across that field with the hedge at the end, have to race full-tilt over it, followed by hundreds of pounding hoofs; horses, bigger, faster than his pony, passing him, charging into him, their riders not caring, not knowing the horror it all meant to him, nor how, only lately, he'd been helpless and terrified on this same pony as it bolted with him till he fell from sheer exhaustion to the ground.

Of all this that went on in him not a soul among them knew. No one knew or cared; they were all out for themselves, selfishly; small, petty, uncivilized in their one desire to be there, to be there first, when at last one lonely exhausted fox was ripped to pieces by a pack of blood-lusting hounds. What was the good of it? Where was the joy of it, what the excuse for, hunting to a ghastly death one animal with thirty hounds each twice the size of that which they chased and killed and ate? He started again, and trembled, when with a roar in the covert they broke into their screaming chorus. What was music to his mother's ears was agony to his. People round him started whispering in excited tones:

"They're on 'im!" "Wonder which way they'll go!" "My God, it'll be heavy between here and Ken Wood!"

Not long now. Oh, Lord, this is enough of waiting, he said, and he went over his bedtime prayer to himself, adding a last fervent blessing on God if He would only steer him safely through the day. Anything in the world I'll do, Lord, if You get me through this day! But God? Who was *He*? What could He do? Why had He let him be run away with? Why? What had he done to be punished so? What had he done that his mother wouldn't speak to him any more? Why can't I be like Elliot, Lord? Be praised and admired and looked at the way Mother and Father look at Elliot? Why am I so different, Lord? Oh, make me a bit like him!

In his anxiety he glanced at his brother, and when he saw him calmly sitting there, alive, thrilled, on the alert at the sound of the hounds, actually smiling with anticipation, his former queer, placid acceptance of Elliot, his indifference to him, changed with the suddenness of sight, and for a second Max saw his brother through eyes turned suddenly cruel with dislike, envy, and a sharp, burning jealousy.

"He's gone!" someone shouted. Max's body twitched involuntarily in the saddle. Hounds screamed at the far end of the covert. The blast of a horn rang out in the sweating calm. Away! Away! Away-ee! A shrill whistle rent the air. Men cursed. Women said things they hated the country people for saying. Behind Max horses snorted and reared and stamped their forelegs. A man on a huge bay charged up beside him, past him, knocking his hat sideways with his elbows as he went. "God damn you, boy!" hissed the man.

"Max!" his father was yelling back. "Max! Come on! Keep close to me, for Christ's sake!"

A man laughed. "Amen!" he muttered.

The gate swung open. Max shut his eyes; set his teeth; leaned over; gripped tight with his knees; crammed down his hat with one hand; gripped the reins on his pony's neck.... (It didn't matter now; nothing mattered now. "God's on our side, to hell with the world!"—where'd he heard that?) With a roar of hoofs from behind him, the pony plunged forward.

"They're away!" cried Mrs Archer, and tapped the horse's quarters with her whip; the trap set off up the road.

"Gawd!" breathed Sturgeon, eyeing the hunt, "like a ruddy regiment at the charge!"

All his life Max would remember seeing his brother's coat out of the corner of one eye as their two ponies raced side by side across that field; all his life he would remember the moments, tense with excitement, his pony bounding along beneath him, of watching that coat gradually disappear behind him, of the withers of Elliot's pony taking its place, then the bridle, and at last the pony's nose receding from sight; of looking then to see nothing in front of him but the hindquarters of his father's horse and the line of flying-hedge immediately beyond.

And the moment his eyes caught sight of the hedge Max felt as though his heart were leaping high into his chest, into his throat, almost suffocating him. With the pace he had been going, the wind flat against him, the minutes of intense fear preceding the gallop across the field, his mouth was now parched, his breath came fast with apprehension at sight of the obstacle that loomed ever nearer and more huge before him. But slowly that old sensation he had known in the stables on the day of his fall rose in him again; the wild recklessness suddenly gripped his limbs, leapt to his head, and for a second it overwhelmed even his memory of fear. In this one high-pitched moment his reflexes worked with extraordinary speed and a clear sanity. The first thought that swept into his consciousness was that he must slacken his pace before setting the pony straight at the great bulk of hedge. With feverish haste, still at the gallop, he gathered up the reins and held his breath. Feeling the pony take the bit in its mouth, he tugged again. Changing its legs, the pony broke astoundingly from a gallop to a canter. In a flash, out of one eye, with the thunder of hoofs behind him, Max saw his father's horse on his left rise on a bound straight from the ground. A second later his pony cocked its ears, thrust out its head, and steadied itself beneath him. Max sat back; gripped with his knees . . . there was nothing but the great darkness of hedge between him and the roof of the world. As though by some rocket from behind he felt himself shot skywards, saw the top of the hedge falling towards him, caught sight of the next field from fifteen feet above the ground, then the black depths of a ditch as both it and the hedge fled from under him. An instant later, as with a jolt the pony landed, he heard his father's voice crying the most wonderful words he'd ever heard: "Bravo, Max! Bravo!"

The wild joy that beat in his heart as his pony galloped across that next field behind his father, Max never quite knew again. It was the first time in his life he had experienced the mad ecstasy of happiness, the soaring exultancy, that only hunting can give. He had but two thoughts—that he loved his pony more than any person or thing in the world, and that he intended to follow his father, no matter what he did nor where he went, till that hunt and day should end.

Vaguely, as he galloped over the following field, Max was aware of horses everywhere about him, some careering off to the left, some to the right, and others, a large majority it seemed, coming racing behind him. One or two men rode almost abreast of him, splashing the mud and water of the field out sideways, the flying drops hitting his coat and hat, raining on his pony's flanks. But Max kept his eyes only ahead of him, on the coat that covered his father's back. Somewhere in front he could hear the screaming cry of the hounds running to a breast-high scent, but he paid no heed, his thought and his eyes lost to all but the scarlet lead he was following.

"*Forrard—Forrard—Forrard! Awa-a-ee-ee!*"

The long, long cry of the huntsman ahead with his hounds rang in his ears, and with the thrill of its sound Max felt tempted himself exultantly to cry out the words in echo as he went.

At the end of a narrow lane his father turned his horse right-handed. Max reined in his pony to follow him, and together they trotted full-tilt through a gateway deep in mud. In the middle of it, with the mud spattering, hitting Max in the face, his pony pecked short in the deep slime. With the unexpected jolt one of his feet slipped from the stirrup and he almost dropped head-first into the bog. But with a supreme effort, for which the pony paid with a violent jag in the mouth, Max pulled himself back in the saddle again and spent the time crossing the next field in forcing his foot once more into the "iron."

"Well done, Max!" his father yelled back, "but don't come so close, boy!"

The hounds were near now. He heard them clamouring away immediately in front, while those followers who had not turned right-handed with the father and son were already fields behind on the left, having been held up by the wire Mrs Archer and her husband knew so well.

By the time Max and his father had floundered across a heavy ploughed field, through another gapway and into a wood, to get out of which they had to dismount and open a gate, hounds had overrun the line and were casting themselves less than a field away. Here Max, wet with sweat, found time to breathe normally for the first time since leaving the covert. And here, among half a dozen others, Elliot rode up, red in the face and covered with mud. Glancing at his brother, Max felt sorry and surprised he had ever thought ill of him. As though he were seeing him for the first time, he wanted to go and talk to him, as to a stranger whom he had known about, secretly admired, and now liked the look of.

"Good man, Elliot!" shouted his father, "thought we'd lost you!"

This brief check was nearly responsible for Max's undoing, for no sensation of recklessness such as he had just experienced can last long save under extreme stimulus, and he was just beginning to hope fervently this might be the end of his glory when suddenly the sun blazed out, one hound spoke, and immediately the whole pack raced away again at an even greater speed than before. Max jabbed in his heels and in a moment was once more behind his father. In a group they clattered down a narrow lane, the huntsman in front blowing his horn and crying, "*Get away on, then! Get away on! Yea—loo! Forrard—Forrard—Forr-ard! Aw-a-y!*"

The hounds fled along over the field before them, their necks strained forward, tongues drooping sideways from their jaws, sterns low, parallel with the ground, all screaming to the scent now made warm and strong by the sun. Almost invisible between two huge horses on either side of him, Max spurred his pony through a gap that gave from the lane on to a steep grass field running all the way up a hill to a long hedge at the top. Here, to his despair, he found other horses beginning to overtake him. The hill was steep and his pony blowing hard beneath him. As they mounted he could feel the flanks heaving between his legs. Near him he heard a man cursing his horse, and looking up, Max saw him bring out his whip and cut the horse twice across the quarters. Max flinched as though he himself had been hit, and a blazing anger came rising to his throat and eyes. Not for the world would he touch his pony to urge it faster up the hill.

He was half-way up the long, steep slope when he looked up to see his father nearly at the top, with several other horses between. In despair he almost burst into tears, but he would not touch his pony. He longed to cry out to his father to wait for him, to cry out to him his was only a pony, that he could go no faster. And just as he felt the tears of frustration and sorrow rising in him he saw his father slow down on the brow of the hill, turn round in his saddle, and beckoning to him, wave his arm in the direction of a gate in the far corner of the field.

Though Max knew at once what he meant, he clenched his teeth, and kept on, leaning over the withers and gripping with his knees to make the climb easier for his pony. As he approached the top he was aware that all those who had passed him were now standing either in front of the fence or galloping their horses along it, seeking a safer way over. Then Max looked at the fence and involuntarily he pulled at the reins; for there before him rose not only a high bank with a ditch in front, but on top of the bank a thick wooden rail.

"You can't get over here, Max!" his father was shouting, "go to the gate at the end and cross over the bridge—there's a brook this way! Hurry, old man!"

Then he saw his father turn, steady his horse, touch him with one spur, and make for the fence and rail.

Max watched him go, and seeing nothing but him, madness seized him: heedless of consequences, he jabbed in his heels. The next few seconds of time Max never forgot. As the father's horse rose from the ground Max's pony was in a straight line behind it, coming at a sharp canter with its ears cocked and the bit taken fast in the mouth. His father was in the air when there came a resounding crash—and, leaving behind them a large gap in the broken rail, both horse and rider disappeared from view on the far side of the fence. . . . The pony was half-way up the bank, atop the bank, through the gap and in the air again when Max, to his horror, saw his father and his horse both staggering to their feet immediately beneath him.

Whether his pony swerved in mid-air or simply cleared both man and horse, Max never knew. All he did know or care about was that his pony made a perfect landing.

"God damn you for a fool!" he heard, but in what seemed less than a few seconds his father was galloping beside him again.

"Max, Max!" he was crying close to his ear, "you're the grandest boy in the world."

As father and son raced on down the slope, with nothing alive before them but the screaming pack, and the covert of Ken Wood looming up on the opposite rise, Max grew suddenly aware of the pains of exhaustion and nervous strain. His arms ached, his legs ached, his seat smarted so that he could barely sit in the saddle, and there was a roaring noise in his head that made him want to cry out from both tiredness and joy. But his sense of weariness was even greater than his happiness, and, as they approached the bottom of the hill and Max saw the rushing water in the brook, he felt the tears well up into his face. He was on the point of shouting—"Oh, I can't, Father—I can't!" when Donald Archer turned quickly right-handed in front of him, crying, "Hurrah, we can ford it, Max! We can ford it!"

With a sinking heart Max watched his father's horse slip from the bank and plunge into the muddy torrent. Max shut his eyes, loosed the reins, and let his pony follow. He felt himself slipping, the pony under him slithering on the brink . . . there came a great splash, his face was streaming, his legs icy cold. Opening his eyes, he saw on both sides water flowing into the tops of his boots. Under him he felt the pony's legs floundering in a half-swim, half-walk. The water came soaking through his breeches, reaching his thighs. Then the pony was clambering up a steep cow-track onto the field.

"Well over!"

Max glanced up to find his father already on his feet by the covert-side. Near him stood his horse, its head hanging, flanks heaving fast, while clouds of steam rose on the air from its sweat-soaked body. And in front of his father the hounds were baying madly, furiously, as though in a bloody fight; all gathered together in a circle, heads to the centre, jaw to jaw, flank to flank, their sterns waving on the circumference like a mass of curved white sjamboks, they fought and growled over their dead, invisible prey.

As Max approached, he watched his father bend down and snatch something from out of the snarling pack. And now he was coming running towards him, crying, "Here, son! Here! And God bless you!"

As he came to him Max saw it was the fox's brush he had, and with one hand his father was wiping the stinking, bloody tag-end of it over his cheeks, while with the other he was hugging him, saying: "There now, go and show that face to your mother—you're the grandest son in the world—go and tell that to your mother!"

And he tied the furry, wet piece of the dead fox to the saddle.

As Max loosed his feet in the stirrups and was about to dismount his father stopped him. "No, no, Max," he said, "don't wait a second, you're too wet, old man. Take that road there and ride straight home, it's no distance. You know the way. And remember," he added, "jump straight into a hot bath, eh? I must go back now and look for Elliot."

Max turned his pony and rode off.

"And tell your mother I said you're the grandest lad in the world!" he heard his father shouting after him.

Now that all was over and he knew that throughout his life this day would never escape his memory, Max's exhausted spirits and body revived a little. Once on the road he spurred his pony into a trot, longing for the moment when he should greet his mother with the blood on his face and the brush in his hand.

He had gone no more than a mile when suddenly, to his surprise and joy, he saw at the end of the road in front of him the family trap. Reining his pony on to the grass-edge he stirred it into a canter. Soon he saw Sturgeon's figure sitting in the driver's seat.

"Where's mother?" he cried, approaching.

"Ah, she be gone through that there gate, Mast' Max—but I wouldn't—Hey!—?"

But Max didn't wait to hear any more. Steering the pony through the gate indicated by the groom, he cantered along the hedgerow of the next field. At the end of it he saw an open gateway, and in the next field another. Once through the second of these, a man came running in his direction, but since he made no sign for him to stop Max galloped on. The man shouted something as he passed but Max could make nothing of what he said. Then, at the bottom of the following slope, he caught sight of a group of people standing by a fence that Max recognized as one he had jumped in the hunt. Thinking of nothing but finding his mother, telling her, showing her, greeting her, Max galloped straight up to the crowd of men.

"Seen my mother?" he cried.

Though no one spoke and there followed a silence that, to anyone but the excited Max, must have seemed strange among so many men, yet those nearest the boy moved aside at his approach. And there, on the grass, through a gap they had made between them, Max caught sight of a piece of his mother's dress. Falling from his pony, his heart pounding inside him, disregarding several arms put out in nervous protest, he rushed through the group of speechless men.

"Mother!"

But as the word left his mouth and his hand was on his mother's shoulder as she sat on the grass, Max suddenly saw, beneath her bowed head, the brown coat of his brother. In terror he gripped her arm.

"Mother!"

But she did not stir, nor move her face from the palm of her hand. Max dropped to his knees beside her. And there beneath her, flat on the grass on his back, his eyes closed and his face yellow-white, Max saw Elliot.

Involuntarily his eyes followed the length of the prostrate body, then he uttered one piercing scream. . . . Between the knee and the foot, the boot on his brother's left leg was torn open, the lower half of the leg lying on the grass in the shape of a V.

For a few moments the world appeared to stand still in silent horror; there was a loud ringing sound in Max's ears, and his mother's eyes were looking into his; they seemed to be the largest eyes he had ever seen and they were enveloping his entire body; they passed slowly downwards from his face to his trembling fingers, thence to his knees. Max stood rigid, as though hypnotized; and then, as he grew aware of the eyes halting their gaze upon his own left leg, there came an ache at the back of his neck, his stomach rose, and, as the earth began to revolve slowly in total darkness, his whip dropped from his hand and he felt himself falling forwards into someone's suddenly outstretched arms.

On the Sabbath

THE THREE GURNEY SONS stood in the doorway of the little thatched cottage that was their home.

"Nay," growled Joe, the youngest, "I bain't a-goin' with 'ee over theyurr—t' see them gurrls!"

But his brothers mocked him: they stood either side of him, looked at him, half-smiling, taunting.

"Ah," said the eldest, "then bez 'ee afeard o' gurrls, Joe?"

Joe Gurney went hot; a flush sprang up his body, mounted into his face.

"Afeard!" he snapped. "I isn't, but I's got a bettur way of spendin' my day than suppin' cidurr with them blinkin' females—ach!"

And he spat. Then, blundering away from his brothers, he set off down the cobbled path, walking fast, swinging his arms, as though intent on reaching some particular place.

But when he came to the edge of the high cliff, out of sight of his home, he stopped suddenly and sat down on a patch of grass between two clumps of flowering heath. For he didn't know where to go.

It was Sunday afternoon, and Joe was sixteen. . . .

Drawing up his knees he clasped his hands round his legs and stared down between his thighs at the fork of his corduroy trousers, without seeing them. "Them gurrls," he muttered to himself, and it was at the daughters of the neighbouring farmer he was looking. He saw one in the act of crossing her legs as she sat on the sand with her back against a rock: as she parted her bare brown knees a gust of wind caught her white linen skirt, and lifted it. In the moment when her knees fell away from one another, Joe caught sight of a clean stretch of thigh, bare flesh, paler than the tan of the girl's knees and shins, and very clean.

His elder brother, drinking from the spout of a cider bottle, had looked at her and laughed; the girl had laughed, wickedly, Joe thought, and the two had risen together and walked off, his brother with his arm round the girl's narrow waist. That was last Sunday. "Them gurrls. . . !"

Below him, immediately below, over one hundred feet down, the sea gurgled in a deep pool, closeted between two huge rocks grey with barnacles. The languorous sea rolled in and rolled in on mounting, pregnant waves that never broke, for the water ran into the rock-trap on each wave's heaving rise, was caught there, gurgled deeply, ominously, then sank back with a low thunderous swirl, conquered—to gurgle once more before at last admitting its failure to overcome the solid fortress of rock.

Joe sat watching. Mute, with his lips drawn into a line that sagged a little at each end, he stared down at the ebbing tide. With one hand he pulled at the grass between his thighs, tugged a handful, threw it away, tugged again—with short, sudden, stabbing movements of his wrist and hand. He let his eyes wander out, beyond the rocks, to sea. The sun blazed down on the flat expanse, and the surface shimmered back at him, like a shining silver quilt of gigantic size, so that he had to screw up his eyes to see it. From afar it came surging in, in sinister silence; till at last it approached the rocks with a low growl, as a lion might before pouncing on its prey. He raised his head and looked up, but the sky was the same, colourless, filled with the sun's glare. It gave him a sharp pain behind his eyes so he closed them, opening them anew to find the horizon, but the sea and the sky were one, married at an invisible line. Only a stagnant blur of cloud, smoke from some ship beyond that line, marred the total absence of all things save the sea and the sky, and pointed to the neighbourhood of that line where the human eye says they meet.

Silence hung heavily on the air, still as the smoke-cloud over the sea: nothing but the swirl and the gurgle of the water below made sound. And Joe went on pulling at the grass, till within reach there remained no more to pull: while, from time to time, he kept muttering to himself: "Them gurrls . . . them bleedin' females . . .

starin', flirtin', 'ussies, I'd like to. . . ." But exactly what he'd like to do with them, or to them, he was not altogether sure.

Uppermost in his mind, and strong in his body, was the desire to handle them, handle them roughly. "Treat 'em rough!" he growled, and he wondered that the words sounded so huge in the silence; they seemed magnified, to echo and to mean even more than he meant them to mean, so that for an instant he himself grew larger and stronger, the girls smaller; he was attacking them, rolling them over in the heath, and they were laughing hysterically, half in admiration, half in fear, but making very little resistance to his flat-hand smacks on their bare thighs: "treatin' 'em rough, the kiss-an'-cuddle wantin' 'ussies. . . . I'd like to. . . !" There was a cruel look in Joe Gurney's eyes.

As he flung away the last few blades of grass, a shadow flashed in front of him across the brim of the cliff. He glanced up. A gull, gleaming white, swooped down as if from nowhere, wings motionless; then, seeing Joe move, it lifted the tip of one wing, rose like a silent rocket, and sped on. He reached out for something to throw; that was his immediate impulse; his eyes were hard and set. He looked quickly round him. A stone? But there wasn't a stone; there was nothing but grass and heath, and the gull was already almost out of sight. Balancing horizontally on the air he could just see it, a white fleck against the distant cliff-face, growing rapidly smaller, till at last it soared and was lost in the white distance of the sea and sky.

"Swine!" As before, Joe's voice sounded huge in his ears. He uttered the word viciously, feeling both the word and the tone of his voice were warranted. He told himself he was right to feel as he did towards the bird. It *was* maddening: the great evil beast, he said to himself, with its vicious food-seeking eyes and the carrion crook of its beak, flying off like that, sweeping effortlessly over the earth, untouchable . . . and he not able to raise himself more than a foot from the ground . . . mocking him, just as he felt the eyes of "them gurrls" mocking as they sat back with his brothers, eyeing him sideways, taking him in, sizing him up, aware of his years—on Sunday afternoons, when there was nothing to do. . . .

With a grunt Joe Gurney got to his feet. Raising his arms and clutching the back of his shirt between his shoulders, he pulled the garment over his head and stuffed it under a furze bush. He stood naked to the waist, his body tanned and hairless. Then shielding his mouth with one hand, he faced the sea and uttered a long, loud shriek. The cry, wild and haunting, not unlike the magnified scream of a gull, pierced the silence with such clear unexpected sharpness that Joe himself felt momentarily startled. It shocked him; it was a shock to realize he was capable of making such a noise, breaking thus so great a silence with the power of something so small as his own throat; but he was shocked even more when the one distant echo of his cry had died away, and looking round, found there was no living thing in sight that might have heard and taken notice of his haunting yell. The thought made him feel very much alone. He gazed down again at the gurgling water a hundred feet below him, then shrugged his shoulders and started off along the narrow sheep path that led eastwards for miles above the precipice of black cliffs. Below him was sheer cliff; but lower down sharp jagged rocks jutted out from the face of it, hung menacingly above the water or joined the smoother sea-worn and barnacled mass that was clear of the surface, even at full tide.

There were no houses, not even a sign of human life so far as the eye could see; yet sheep and the one-time wandering coast-guards had worn a thin pathway round the brink, frighteningly high above the sea. The path was so narrow that he had to walk by placing one foot immediately in front of the other, for only a few inches to his right was the precipice, while on his left the hill—covered with mossy down-grass, occasional dappled rocks thrusting through the green, clumps of sea-pinks, white convolvulus, fern, scabious and sweet-smelling crow's foot—this hill rose at a sharp angle from the very edge of the path, and towered above him, silhouetted dark against the colourless sky. In places the path ran so near to the edge that he would stop to unearth a large stone from the bank, drop it where he stood, and listen to it crashing as it ricocheted from one rock to another on its headlong flight down to the water. And when at last it plunged into the depths and the hollow resounding boom, echoed from the rocks below, rose up to him, he felt a wild thrill race through his body and head at the sound, making him feel somehow that digging up a stone and hurling it into the sea were admirable acts not easy to perform. That booming echo, like some prehistoric monster's roar...!

The sun shone hot on his back as he walked; he could feel the heat burning the rounds of his shoulders, smarting on his skin, tanning him a deeper brown. But soon the warmth and the heavy stillness of the afternoon began to fill him with a restless lassitude; his legs began to weary under him; the will to walk the five miles to the lighthouse was there, but his body lacked the effort to obey; his head was heavy, his eyes drowsy, and the interest to move any farther fell from him and left him lax. Yet he didn't want to sleep; he was restless. He sat down; stared out to sea; gave himself up. Why walk? What for? The lighthouse was not really an objective; he knew it well; he knew he did not really want to go there. Yet, what was there to *do*—on Sunday afternoon? His brothers—they were drinking cider now, sitting in the sandy cove near the village with "them gurrls." Let them; it didn't interest him. He never queried this; it never occurred to him this was the only thought that constantly did interest him. He assured himself that he was not and would not be "that kind of man," girls didn't interest him, he'd rather have the sea, watch the sea plunging against the rocks and the birds that his mother said he "doted on," he'd rather lay the pots, he said, for lobster and crab, even work on the land, be alone with himself—anything rather than be stared at by, and drink cider with, "them gurrls." Hadn't his mother always said, "Joe, 'ee bez a law unto 'izself, 'ee be!" And he told himself this so often that now he looked upon it as a recognized fact; he was *different*: he believed it, not thinking, yet never ceasing to think, in spite of himself, of his brothers in connection with "them gurrls."

Just then, with his feet dangling perilously over the edge of the cliff, he saw something move on a rock that was a little island over which the rising waves just failed to break. The object was small and black; it moved again, very suddenly, and he saw it was the small pointed head of a cormorant. He got up, the better to see it, and on tip-toe he could just make out its long thin neck. The bird stood alone on the far side of the rock, a foot above the rise and fall of the sea. Joe wondered if he could reach it with a stone again; it was his first impulse on seeing it, to heave a stone at it, to make it move: he wanted to see it fly, he told himself, but actually he could at that moment have experienced no greater joy than to have hit it clean and simply on the head so that it fell, with a plop, into the water, dead. Yet if someone had asked him: "Do you want to kill that bird?" he would have been greatly indignant. "Good God, no—" he'd have said, "—whatever for? I only want to see it move!" By climbing up the slope a little he could now see the whole of the cormorant. He decided it was watching for fish: swift as a dart it kept turning its head first this way, then that: standing up very straight, its long neck out-stretched, black, all alone, on the one little island rock, it was the only living thing in sight, this single lonely bird. Thinking of this, the bird became in Joe's eyes all the more desirable a target. He bent down and loosened a large stone half-buried in the grass by his feet. He pulled it out, a large grey stone that fitted perfectly into his fist. With this in his hand he felt immediately a strange power. It was a weapon, strengthening him; and he stood, exulting in the complete possession of the thing, as solid sporting English-men stand with their guns when waiting for the air to fill with the pheasants they themselves have reared.

Joe toyed with his stone for a moment, enjoying to the full the sensual pleasure of holding it tight in his fingers, drawing up his right arm so that the biceps bulged and the veins stood out big on the pale inside of his forearm. Then he leaned back with a smile, aimed, and flung it far out over the cliff, with the strength of his entire body. He watched the stone soar, curve, and come down with a sharp crack on a rock not so far out as that on which the cormorant was perched. As the stone landed Joe heard several cries come from under the cliff immediately beneath him, and a flock of gulls flew out, whirling wildly round in astonishment, but the cormorant merely spun its head, looked back once, then continued its lonely vigil unperturbed.

Joe stood watching, surprised by the sudden appearance of the gulls: then, concluding they must be nesting on the cliff-face, he returned his attention to the cormorant. It angered him that he had failed to "move" it; the cool defiance of so small, insignificant a creature riled him, deprived him in an instant of that strange power he was aware of when possessing the stone in his fist. He bent down again and looked about for another. Finding one, the strength in him returned and with it a cruel vengeful glare came into his eyes.

The gulls still swooped about wildly over the face of the cliff crying: Quark—quark—quark, cli, cli, cli, and rising suddenly and swiftly at each movement made by Joe, soaring high without effort, turning on the imperceptible drop or lift of a wing-tip, to glide away motionless and in silence, only to return again on a rise of the orange-hooked beak, dive like a falling star, then soar once more with one flap of the grey wings, and sail overhead, showing the snow-white of their bellies to the man at whom they mocked: Cli, cli, cli—quaark! knowing that standing there he was powerless to harm them.

Joe watched each one, admiring and hating, infuriated by the monotony of their cry, envious of their flying power, jealous of their life—he watched, with his fingers clenched tight round the stone. As each bird sailed over him, close, within reach, the muscles in his hand ran taut to clutch tighter the stone, and he was aware that even this movement was not concealed from the gulls, for at the very quickening of his sinews, the birds appeared to flash on speed and were away before he had time to raise his hand. He knew their little eyes saw everything and their cruel beaks missed nothing that was food.

Once more he leaned back, aimed, and flung his stone at the cormorant. This time it landed with a plop in the water, beyond the little island rock. The bird twitched its head, stared, and took no further notice. Gulls flew out again from the hidden cliff-face, raising a hundred wild cries, making out to sea, then turning, circling, swooping, some falling, and with a flutter of wings, landing gracefully on some rock far down at the sea's level, others coming back fearlessly to their nests beneath where Joe stood.

At his second failure to "move" the cormorant his anger and desire rose in him afresh. He came down again to the narrow path, sat on it, and worked his way by inches onto the brink, till his legs dangled over the edge. From here he leaned his head over till he could see a few gulls sitting flat on the jutting edges of rock.

Some rose and flew out at sight of him, screaming, leaving bare the brown speckled eggs on the roughly made nests. He remembered then his father forbidding him as a child ever to climb over the cliff-face, threatening him, warning him of its danger. And he remembered the day his brothers had defied this warning and succeeded in stealing two gull's eggs, "blowing" them afterwards in their bedroom at night. He had watched them fascinated, yet thinking with disgust, as his mother had taught him to think, how they had robbed the female gull of her children and two young gulls of life. Then he thought of the cormorant: his brothers had always lusted after an egg of this bird, but they had never found one. Long since they had passed on their egg collection to him, but Joe, while accepting it, did so with little grace, saying that robbing birds' nests didn't interest him, that it was a cruel, silly pastime; ask their mother. "I'se can betturr use my time," he had added.

But now, looking at the single defiant bird, sitting heedless of him on the rock, his desire grew. Had it laid there? The moment the thought entered his head he knew that he must know, that he would not rest till he knew.

He looked down between his legs, over the cliff. Height had never turned Joe Gurney's head; he had never experienced vertigo; and he was no physical coward when it came to rock-climbing. But he judged that to attempt to lower himself from where he sat was madness. Immediately under him the ground caved in, retreated several feet, then advanced again, in a series of ledges, like steps, and on almost every ledge a gull sat, or a nest was laid. No, from where he was it was impossible to reach the safety of these ledges. He looked eastward up the cliff and thought he saw a patch of sloping rock from which he might reach the ledges without too much risk of falling. Walking towards it he glanced at the island rock: the cormorant was still there, twitching its head backwards and forwards, intent on its own business. As Joe started to lower himself down the slope on his hands and back the gulls beneath him took flight again, screaming madly. He stopped to watch them, half-lying on the incline of rock; he made an effort at counting them but they flew and swooped and changed places with each other in the air with such speed that he soon gave up the attempt. It seemed that the nearer he came to their nests the more fearless they grew. Some rose over him and swooped horribly, frighteningly near; so close that he could hear the wind flashing through the small feathers in their wings and see the cruel little eyes warning him, defying him, and their curved beaks that sent a tremor of fear running through his body. He winced involuntarily when they swooped over him like that; they looked so huge and powerful, and so close; from wing-tip to wing-tip their shadow shut out the sun in passing, and for an instant he knew he was in the full shade of their flying bodies, lying on his back. He knew he was powerless should they attack. The thought angered him, forced a rabid hate into him. Yes, he must hate, he told himself, to convince himself he was on the side of the gods and that his actions were blameless. After all, he didn't want to hurt the gulls, he only wished to know had that cormorant laid over there on the island rock, and how else was he to find out? But should they attack, well. . . . Anyway, look at the advantage they had over him—they could *fly*!

Watching, his admiration of their effortless flight, the balanced and motionless wing-spread carrying them racing through the air, never wavered, but it increased his envy, his jealousy of them, and his hate.

He raised himself and descended the rock-face foot by foot on his back; then, turning over, he lowered himself over a steeper part of the rock on his front, grazing his chest at intervals, while he gripped with his fingers and groped for foothold with the toes of his rubber shoes, half-blindly, since the cliff-face fell too sheer for him to see anything below his knees.

As he approached the nesting ledges the cries of the gulls, now one incessant shriek, rang madly in his ears: their numbers had increased. Hearing the commotion others had joined them, flying from other breeding grounds along the coast, out of curiosity, full of their everlasting search for food. They circled round the boy in hundreds, screaming: Quark—quark—quark, cli, cli, cli, till he imagined the whole countryside must hear and come racing to know what it was that was causing the silence of Sunday afternoon to be shattered by such a noise.

By the time he reached the ledges the sun had fallen low in the

sky, coming golden in its setting over the sea that was magnifi-
cently calm, turning the water from silver to slate in the distance,
and beneath him from slate to a pale gold. The white of the flying
gulls' wings glowed in the light, and their beaks shone like little
daggers of fire as they opened them to scream, hurtling round
the boy who was now halfway down the cliff-face, in amongst
their nesting ground.

Strong as he was, the climb and his perilous position on the
precipice were beginning to tell on Joe's nerves and legs. All the
way down he had not found a single foothole large enough to
allow him to stand and rest awhile. The muscles in the calves of
his legs ached and there was a crick in the back of his neck from
constantly having to bend his head low to seek foot-room. It was
with infinite relief that he stepped on to the top ledge and was
able at last to stand still on both feet, keeping himself steady with
one hand on the cliff above his head. At his feet two nests were
laid, one with two brown speckled eggs, the other empty. Close
by he saw some grey fluffy thing move in a crevice of rock, and
he looked again. He shifted his position and saw the point of a
beak, dark grey, peeping out—a gull chick, hiding. He stared
down at it with mixed feelings; at first he wanted to pick it up
and fondle it, but a moment later the desire to grab it and fling
it from him possessed him strangely. In a curious way he feared
the little helpless thing, a kind of superstitious fear. He bent
down as far as he was able and peered into the dark crevice. The
chick sat hunched up in a corner, half-concealed, cowering, as far
into the rock as it could worm its little body. It sat there facing
him, frankly terrified, emitting a long sharp trilling noise of terror
from its open beak. Joe remained staring at it, hearing the wild
screaming behind and above him, and the whistle of the wind
racing through the wings of the gulls as they flew round within
a few feet of his head. He half-turned to see them, when at that
moment a gull swooped. He saw it coming, falling, as it sped
down straight towards him, its neck outstretched, beak wide open,
eyes wide with anger. He lifted his arm with a jerk to defend
himself: one of his feet slipped with the effort: his heart leapt
inside him: his throat went dry, and he could feel the blood
fading from his face. Clinging desperately with his fingers, he

shut his eyes and saved himself, hearing the tearing scream loud in his ear. He guessed how close the bird must have been, for he felt the wind from its rush fan his bare back as it skimmed over him in its furious flight.

He steadied himself and took a deep breath, and once the first fear subsided anger welled up in its place, his body revolting at the humiliation of having been afraid of a bird.

The chick still trilled in the crevice, infuriating him. He felt no pity for it now, only anger and a strong desire to destroy, a resentment of its weakness, and a resentment, too, of his own cowardice to destroy, the old superstition running deep in men, the fear of "I will repay." He wanted to frighten it out of its wits, to kill it with shock if he could, but lay his hands on it, his *bare* hands, kill its weakness with the power of his own superior physical strength, *murder* it thus, this he knew he could not do. And aware, acutely aware of this impotence, he was angered all the more. He bent down again to stare it full in the eyes, and as his face came nearer to the crevice the chick ceased its trilling, opened wide its beak and was promptly, disgustingly sick. The grey vomit sprang from its mouth and fell close to Joe's feet. Instinctively he recoiled, again losing one foothold. Shocked in his own stomach, his throat contracted and he came near to retching, but the perverted pleasure he received from having frightened the bird into sickness thrilled him, and he breathed freely again and steadied himself.

He turned and looked down; the sea gurgled in a deep pool still far below; long brown tongues of seaweed were flowing to and fro in the green transparent water; a fish darted and was gone. Beyond, a great black cloud loomed up from the horizon, darkening the sea, approaching, threatening. Behind him the sun had sunk over the hill and he could feel the evening chill on his naked back. He saw the cormorant still standing on the island rock, twitching its head. He must hurry; it would soon be dark; and how he should re-climb the cliff-face to return had not occurred to him in his desire to reach the island rock. But now, faced with the prospect, quite suddenly it did. He retraced in his mind the sheer precipice he had just descended and trembled at the thought of having to climb back again over the same glassy face. Then he looked below him at the ledges, and confidence returned at the thought of how easy they would be to descend. Once down, he thought, once I get there I'll get back somehow all right. But I must hurry.

It was simple work lowering himself over the ledges; grasping one with both hands he let himself down on his knees to the next, raised one leg to where the other knee was, stood there on one foot, then lowered the other leg. It was easy enough. The gulls still flew round him, crying, sometimes too near for his peace of mind. Once there was a crackling sound as he dropped his foot on to a ledge he could not see, and when he came in sight of it he saw that he had smashed an egg; the half-formed chick was a red and yellow mess in the nest; the oozing blood was trickling thick over the stone, down. . . . His stomach heaved for a moment as he was forced to pass his face over it on his descent. The gulls seemed to scream more wildly. . . .

The ledges ended more abruptly than he thought. No, there was still another, but it was far down, fully eight feet of flat vertical cliff, over which to lower himself. He stood, with one foot on the narrow ledge, and contemplated the difficulty. One thing was certain, he perceived; once down he could never return the same way; he could never hope to reach up the eight feet to the ledge on which he stood; that was certain. But the fact didn't greatly trouble him: he was far more intent on overcoming the difficulty of getting there, and from there farther, than he was thinking of his return journey. He stared down at the one remaining ledge. At last he made up his mind there was only one solution: he would have to drop the extra space separating it from his feet while hanging at full length. The possible consequence of this risk did not enter his head; he was a good climber and he was nerveless; he had never fallen, never so much as maimed himself on a rock: why should he now?

No sooner had he decided on this course than he began to lower himself, trusting his weight entirely to the strength of his arms and the grip his fingers had on the ledge. He let himself down by inches, till he hung in the air, from his hands. He gripped with his fingers till the veins stood out on his arms, and his finger-nails went white on the ledge from the strain put upon them: he drew himself up with the power of his biceps, to assure himself of his strength, his body flat against the rock-face, then lowered himself to full-length, stretched from fingers to feet.

Even in such a position, when he discovered he had not reckoned with the length of his arms—so that his toes now dangled within a foot of the last ledge—his self-confidence was such that he gave a laugh of glee, and dropped, throwing all the weight of his body against the cliff. He landed on both feet, his face and body flat with the rock-face, his arms at his side, and balanced there, still. Drawing in a long breath he let it out again in a sigh of satisfaction and relief, for he was tired and the strain had been more than he had expected to reckon with.

The ledge was just large enough and the cliff caved in sufficiently where he stood, to allow him to turn round. He did so, and stood facing the sea, his arms stretched out behind him, palms against the cliff. Then, lowering his eyes, he suddenly gasped and went white, in abject horror. All at once he felt his bowels turn loose inside him, his entrails writhe, and the water in his bladder flowed quick to the brim. For there, beyond him, was nothing but the open sea, the gulls crossing and re-crossing before him, while below—immediately under him—there was nothing but fifty feet of space, then a mass of sharp barnacled rock and the ominous gurgle of the sea. . . . He was cut off!

In one blind flash he knew that if he fell he would hurtle to certain death on the rocks, and he knew that even if he were able to spring from his position on the face he could not hope to fall in the sea.

Leaning over so far as he dared to see what there was immediately below the edge on which he was standing, he shrank back, for there was nothing. With a rush of terror he realized the dreadful fact: he was standing on the point of an overhanging crag from which it was impossible either to ascend or descend.

He was *trapped*!

Realizing to the full his position he began to tremble. His hand shook on the rock-face. His hand had never shaken before. It terrified him that he saw it shaking now, against his will. He looked at the fingers splayed against the stone; they were trembling violently. By clenching them with all his force he tried to stop them trembling. But he failed, for his fist trembled in their stead.

He looked at his other hand: it also trembled. Then he placed them side by side and they shook together. Staring wide-eyed at them he realized with the blood rushing from his face and the loose pain in his bowels growing every minute more acute, that for the first time in his life he was mortally afraid. Irrelevant thoughts raced through his mind, half-obeying his will, for he dared not allow himself to think. The gull-chick. He felt a wild pity for it now. It had vomited from fear—of him. The poor, miserable little thing, the cowardly beast he had been. Never again, never—if only he could see some chance of getting out of this . . . if only . . . his mother was sitting in the silent living-room, knitting, knitting . . . click, click, click, went her needles. She was knitting; it was dark evening; his brothers were out. Then the chair was empty; his mother was gone; the clock ticking on the mantel broke the silence. "Mother! Mother!" God in Heaven, would he never see his mother sit there again? But with a gigantic effort he pulled himself together. "Joe Gurney," he said aloud, "you're a man, stop trembling!"

Again he caught sight of his hands, but they unnerved him, and he looked away, down at his feet. Lifting one, he saw with renewed horror that it shook the same as his hands, violently. He let it fall back on the ledge and immediately his knees began to beat against the rock-face. The spittle dried up in his mouth, his tongue lay against his dry teeth like leather on stone. Aware that the horror of his plight was increasing with his thoughts and affecting him physically, he shut his eyes, but the moment they were closed he felt himself swaying, and, aghast, he opened them again and flung out one arm to hug the rock to him, as though the stone were the body of a woman. At the same time he uttered a despairing cry and burst into tears. But at once fear quelled them and he began to scream. "Help! Help!" His fear grew with his crying.

He leaned against the face of the cliff, with his head up, his eyes staring and watery, crying wildly, helplessly, in despair: "Help! Help!" But only the gulls answered his frantic calls: Quark, quark, cli, cli, cli, cli. They wheeled over and above him, closer now, screaming, as though fully aware of the man's impending doom. Joe, shivering, stared at them with a terrible envy, those *wings.* . . . Flat on the air they sailed, poised, motionless, heedless of the earth, held in mid-air, over the deathly rocks, on the power of a few feathers and thin bones, an expanse of grey and white wing, a little thing, more powerful than the human frame. His glassy, terror-stricken eyes stared at them hopelessly, watery with self-pity, silently crying out to them in his utter helplessness. But they only flew over his shivering body, raced close to his face so that he could feel the wind from their wings, crying their everlasting cry—Food—Food—Food! while he stood there, his limbs shaking, his teeth chattering, with horror.

It was dark now, and cold. A wind had sprung up and the huge dark cloud hung menacingly overhead, darker than night. Joe felt a heavy spot of rain fall on his chest, cold, sending an icy shiver through his body. Then another, and another. The cloud had broken. The wind fled through his hair. A flash of lightning ripped the sky, rushing fork-like into the sea. In the one brief white moment the rocks and the sea below were revealed to him in a light more clear than day, and he felt his strained nerves fail him suddenly; his muscles faltered in his legs; his bowels hurt him acutely and with a nauseating rush he lost control of his sphincter muscles; he held his breath, then let them free: simultaneously his water ran; he felt it down his shaking legs. The immediate weakness terrified him afresh; how much longer would he be able to stand? They must be hunting for him now; he was four miles from home: how long would they take, how long? *Were* they looking for him? Why should they? He had often gone out on Sunday afternoon and come home late. Had he? No, surely not! Yes, yes, he had. He could not get away from it, he knew he had. They were *not* looking for him. Oh God, oh God! Shivering, with rain running down his face and naked chest, he mumbled a prayer, with fearful fervour, praying to some God he had known at his mother's knee. At that moment a distant church bell came through to him on the wind. "God—God—God!" it tolled. Then he began to scream, "Mother! Mother!" But he could hear the increasing wind throw back the words at him. His strength was going; his arms against the cliff ached abominably and his legs felt numb, not part of himself any more. Another streak of lightning flashed out, wildly cutting the sky, then shot down into the sea. His empty stomach heaved, making him awfully aware of his complete emptiness. With effort he managed to turn his back on the rain and lean his head against the cliff-face, trying to summon his remaining strength. The rain beat against his back, ran down inside his trousers, down his legs, till he was drenched, and the cold water froze his limbs. Clenching his fists he began to scream again: he called into the wind the name of his mother, his brothers, one after the other, in terrible despair. At each cry he choked and retched, the grinding pain cutting through his body, from his chest into his empty stomach, forcing it to double up. But each time he recovered just enough to keep his balance, lean against the cliff, and cry again.

At last, in a hollow, failing voice he called the names of the girls he had refused to go and see with his brothers only that afternoon. He raised his head and called them into the night, his chin on the cliff, his arms stretched wide, fingers splayed. And his brothers' words came back to him mocking him. "Ah, then bez 'ee afeard o' gurrls, Joe? Bez 'ee afeard. . . ?"

And he screamed till the pain shook him. "I bain't afeard of 'ee—I love 'ee, I love 'ee . . . I love 'ee, Mother, I love 'ee. . . ." Then, as the last words rose into a mad shriek, his head went dizzy, his body wavered, faintness possessed him, his face blanched yellow-white, his back bent outwards, knees gave way, his arms dropped from the cliff-face, and, in a heap, he fell.

It was the gulls found him, his chest pierced by one rib and his skull smashed, one leg bent the wrong way; and the gulls told his brothers, soon after dawn; and by then the rain had washed the body clean of its blood and the gulls of its flesh. And the brothers returned to their home, one with a pair of trousers, the other with a pair of shoes.

Mister and Miss

"THERE NOW, KATHLEEN," said Mrs Bradley, "Mr Pringle's in for his tea—look sharp!"

"Oh, all right, Ma—I can't do everything at once!"

"Shish, child—Mr Pringle'll hear!"

Richard Pringle, standing in the middle of what was the Bradley's living-room when he was absent, did hear.

"*Mister* Hell!" he cursed, and flopped into the one easy chair. Staring down at his large farm boots, he picked off a lump of mud hanging from one of the heels, then started to undo the laces. He was tired; the process of "dipping" two hundred sheep, four by four, was an exhausting business; and even then each animal, separately, had to be held between his knees and thus escorted down the steps to the surface of the "dip"; and there, from the last step, each sheep was allowed to buck from the grip of his legs into the dark brown liquid, thence swimming down the narrow canal to join the grazing fold beyond. It was tiring work.

Dick lay back in his chair and began to reflect on what Ford, with one of his slobbery oaths, had said to him when first he had been put on the job, "Lord A'mighty, might think you weren't a man, the way you open them legs o' yours before you should, Mr Pringle!"

Mister Pringle! There it was again! Christ, he—Dick Pringle—he didn't say Mister Ford every time he addressed the farm-hand. Yet no one in the village, outside of the Norman family, addressed Dick Pringle in any other way than as Mr Pringle. And here he'd been living, in two rooms of the Bradley's cottage, for six months. All this time Mr Pringle: not even Mr Dick. No intimacy, no nearness, no friendship, other than that of the family Norman, who

owned and governed the entire village. A matter of wealth, of
birth, Dick reflected, pulling off his other boot and standing in his
stockinged feet. Here he was, a stranger, cut off, living in the home
of the Normans' groom. Colonel Pringle paying his son's rent and
keep. Dick Pringle apprenticed on the farm, learning to become a
farmer! Dick Pringle working all day with men whom in his heart
he feared, loved, then feared again. Did they—these men—did
they fear him? Did Ford, who cursed and blasphemed and told
him endless stories of fornication, did he fear him, Dick Pringle?
No, it was Dick's secret opinion that rather than fear him, Ford
probably despised him. Did Ford fear anyone? Yes, Ford feared
Ernest Norman, his employer. Everyone on the farm feared
Ernest Norman, who had made millions in Mexican oil, married a
wealthy wife, bought the Minster, the village, made the farm, the
model dairy, the bacon factory, rebuilt the school, founded the
Norman Hall where there was now a cinema twice a week and
once a month a dance. Everyone owed their manner of existence
to Ernest Norman, and everyone feared him; for he controlled
their very lives: on him, in these, the worst times of unemploy-
ment, they were dependent; and in the countryside it was an open
secret that Ernest Norman paid always slightly higher wages than
any other land-owner in the county. Feared, envied, admired by
a few, he was loved by none. Even Ford, bitter, blasphemous
English labourer, once a prize-fighter, caring for no man, feared
Ernest Norman.

Alone in the living-room, Dick was thinking of the day when
Ford had allowed the Normans' prize sow to be run over by a
passing motor, while he had stopped on the roadside for a drink
at The Crown. Tim Caley had handed him the glass through the
window, and Ford had thrown the liquid down his throat without pausing for a breath; nevertheless the damage, in that
moment, was done; and news of the reason why—as only gossips
in English villages know how—leaked out. The story flashed like
wireless from one mouth into two ears, from two mouths into ten
ears, and within one day it was being discussed, so Natalie
Norman told Dick, by her father in the dining-room at the
Minster.

Next morning Ernest Norman was in the styes leaning over

the rail where Ford and Dick were dunging out. Dick saw him first, but the man's silence, the expression on his face, the furrowed forehead, the tight invisible lips, the dark overhanging eyebrows, and the little eyes that stared as though they would pierce Ford's back, made Dick refrain from his customary polite greeting, and he continued to spade up the dung. Then suddenly the styes echoed one word, "Ford!"

Though aware of the man's presence, Dick jumped involuntarily. Ford dropped his spade, and gave vent to an oath. Dick watched him look up, then lower his eyes, in fear.

"Your wages are cut! I'll see you tonight at six-thirty!"

And immediately retreating footsteps echoed down the stone passage. Ford picked up his spade and, blaspheming, began belabouring a pig. He shook his fist in the direction his employer had taken, and growled:

"Wages cut, eh! And so'd your throat be, if only I wasn't a bleedin' coward!"

And the silence of the styes was rent with the howls of the unfortunate pig.

After his tea next morning, in the kennels, across the road from the Bradleys' cottage, Dick had told Natalie Norman of what had happened. He pressed her up against the wall of the retrievers' stall, as he always did every morning and evening when she came over the park to see the dogs and him. He pressed the length of his body along that of hers, pressed his lips against her lips, and told her: half in hate, half in frustrated desire—hate of what she was, daughter of her father, and desire of what he could not have, of what she would not give him.

Standing in front of the empty grate of the Bradleys' living-room, hands thrust deep in his trouser pockets so that the fingers met, Dick Pringle recalled what she'd said, and with the memory his hate and desire were rekindled. "Dick"—yes Dick from her, from Miss Natalie Norman—"Dick, I know—oh, you're hurting me, darling—I know, Dad was in a temper. And no wonder! Menelanda, our prize sow!"

Just as he had stepped away from her that evening in the kennels, Dick stepped back now, alone in the Bradleys' living-room—out of hate, and horror. It was on his lips now to utter

what he had uttered then, in his rage, "Ha! And no wonder!
Natalie! Our prize daughter!"

The vision of her leaning back against the wall sprang to his
eyes; she was staring at him, her small eyes full of fear, her rouged
lips, smeared from the strength of his kiss, quivering. Her eyes
dilated, then filled. "Oh, Dick, my Dick. . . !"

"*Your* Dick!" he had screamed. "I'd rather have—have my
Kathleen!"

With false triumph Dick remembered—false, for he was only
too well aware Kathleen Bradley had not been his any more than
Natalie had—how the girl had straightened herself, her eyes wet,
but shining now only with jealous rage, and attacked him with a
sweep of her arm at his face. Avoiding the blow with one hand,
and holding her wrist tight with the other, he saw himself flatten-
ing her against the wall once more, pressing his face on hers, till
he felt all her muscles relax and she hung limp in his arms, only
to quicken and resist as his hands moved from her waist to her
breasts. . . .

Dick Pringle took a step forward and laid his head on his hand
on the mantel.

"Your tea, Mr Pringle."

Far in thought, he started, and turning, saw Kathleen Bradley
coming through the doorway with his tea on a tray.

"Hullo, Kathleen," he said. "You gave me quite a shock." Strong
and healthy-looking, with dark brown eyes and straight black hair
cut short, Kathleen Bradley's figure attracted most of the male
attention whenever she emerged from her home into the village
streets. Having spent much of her childhood and youth with her
father in the Normans' stables, she was as capable as most men of
riding a young and spirited horse; she could groom and harness
them, and for a time she even helped in the forge where the farm-
horses were shod; she could drive the Ford van that was used for
bringing supplies from the station to the Minster; she could milk a
cow, make butter, play accompaniments on the piano, and turn the
undesirable attentions of men elsewhere without losing their
regard and admiration. Among other occupations that kept her
much at home Kathleen Bradley was now earning a small weekly
wage for attending to and feeding Ernest Norman's Labrador

retrievers; and when Natalie Norman was away or otherwise engaged, Kathleen would take these shooting dogs out for exercise, one couple on chains, the other two loose. Often Dick had watched her racing across the Park with the four great black dogs leaping ecstatically round her, and each time he had been forced to compare the energetic air of Kathleen Bradley with the appearance of Ernest Norman's daughter. Natalie Norman would always walk slowly behind the animals that raced away from her, or they pulled at the chains till Natalie, either from disinterest or laziness, would let them loose, while she herself followed at her slow, lackadaisical gait, her shoulders slightly drooping and her eyes all the time on the ground. Or sometimes, as Dick watched her come across the field, he would see Natalie savagely beating down nettles with her stick as she walked, giving him the impression something in her nature was for ever at war. It was in her face, he thought, this disgruntled bitter look, as it was in the face of her father, in the furrowed forehead and dark, humourless eyes.

In contrast, the clear brown skin of Kathleen's face was never ruffled by such signs of discontent, nor was this expression in the eyes of her father or mother; nor did Dick see in any of the labourers on the farm those traces of internal conflict suppressed behind thin closed lips and hesitant glances.

Kathleen herself would look at him straight, with her brown eyes wide, and there were times when their very open frankness intimidated him, so that he was aware of his own eyes hesitating to return her own candid gaze. It was then he found himself stung with a curious fear, as if sensing something mysterious and unknowable lying behind the girl's silent serenity. Yet he knew it was just this, the impression of health and strength she gave, that fascinated him. At nights, in his small bedroom, separated from hers by a single wall, he would lie thinking first of that day's meetings with Natalie in the kennels, but it was never long before that vision faded and gave way to another he had never seen, and which he knew to behold in reality he had but to open two doors. Yet every night he would lie on, thinking, thinking, till at last sleep came to succour his tired body, when he would dream of a fantastic world wherein he stood surrounded by women, he alone in the centre, tortured by that impotence to act, of which fear, ignorance, uncertainty, and long years of proximity with his own sex, were the cause.

And then, waking, he would dress and say to himself, "I'll see her at breakfast, and if I don't say anything to her today, I'll see Natalie after breakfast...." For he knew there was always Natalie; she was always there, to hold and to kiss and to love with frustrated, trembling words, but he was well aware that even while, with closed eyes, his tongue was uttering those words, that face whose lips his own were touching was not the face his eyes beheld. Instead, it was the face before him now.

He looked down at Kathleen as she stooped to lay the tray on the table, and thought for the hundredth time how much blacker her hair was than Natalie's. While she took the weight of the tray on to the points of her fingers he noticed the rising of her biceps under the short-sleeved jumper, and the pale skin on the inside of her hard brown forearm stretching taut over the blue veins. When she had settled the table the girl looked up, and for a moment he was caught staring straight into her eyes. Once more he was reminded of that something in her face which he found so hard to define. He could only think of it as her "cleanliness"; the skin was so clear, like the smooth, untouched surface of marble.

She smiled. "Would you like some of the toast Mother's made, Mr Pringle?" she asked.

Dick was about to refuse her offer when, hearing once again his name thus spoken, and on her lips, he stifled the reply in his mouth. He looked away from her, holding his breath, and with as much simplicity and as little self-consciousness as he could charge his voice, he said, "Kathleen, I—I've been here now nearly six months," he took a step back and looked at the ground, "I—I can't *bear* being called *Mister* Pringle any longer."

Feeling the anger of embarrassment within him, and with the knowledge that somehow he had managed to say so much, he was about to launch into a tirade of all his pent-up feelings, when in a flash he saw himself in his fury as the girl before him would see him, and he dug his nails into the palms of his hands and prevented the outburst. Instead, he said, "Can't you call me—" he hesitated "—oh, *anything* but that...?"

He raised his eyes to the girl's face and saw her looking at him.

He noticed her brown eyes were wide and serious, and that her lips drooped very slightly at the corners. Dick's heart seemed to fall within him; then it rose again, and he felt weak. He had never seen Kathleen look like that before. Was it really possible—that she had understood, from the few words he had spoken, what was going on in him? Again he looked at her; she was standing with her hands on her hips, and he saw that her expression had not changed. Their eyes met. She moved a foot as though preparing to leave. Then she smiled. "All right, Mr—Dick," she said. And before either had time to say any more she was close to him, and he found himself gripping her hand.

"It's all right," he heard the girl saying softly, close to him. "It's all right, only—try not to worry so. You do, don't you?"

"What?"

"Worry."

"Oh—not really, Kathleen."

Dick felt suddenly so happy he was ready to deny he had ever worried about anything. And in this state of happiness an idea sprang to his mind.

"Are you going to the dance in the Hall tonight?" he asked, looking down at the girl.

"Yes, I think we are all going," she said.

Dick smiled. Oblivious of all possible consequences, he said, "If I go for a short time, will you dance with me?"

Kathleen was smiling back at him, gripping his hand. "I'd love to," she said, and made for the door. With her hand on the knob she turned. "Oh," she said, smiling, "if you see Miss Natalie, I wonder would you ask her if she'd be so good as to feed the dogs tonight, as I have to go to the station to fetch a crate for the Minster?"

"All right, Kathleen," Dick said, "of course I will." When she'd closed the door he stood still, staring at the floor. "Miss Natalie," he repeated, "*Miss.* . . ."

II

Partly from force of habit, partly because he felt it was expected of him, but also for the reason that in spite of himself he wished it, his body urged it, Dick Pringle started off for the kennels as usual after he'd finished his tea.

Dusk was already falling as he left the cottage; yellow village lamps glittered here and there in the mauve, wintry evening; the cobbled pathway to the Bradleys' gate shone with dampness, reflecting the lamps. Dick noticed the oil-lamp was lighted on the Bradleys' kitchen table as he passed by their window; and he caught a glimpse of the family sitting round it, talking, drinking tea. There was Mrs Bradley's great shock of grey hair, her expansive bosom resting on the table in front of the huge tea-pot; Bradley himself opposite, his brown, good-tempered face smiling at Kathleen, who at that moment had raised her cup to her lips; and Tom Bradley, the Normans' second chauffeur, sitting facing his sister, his head concealed from view between the pages of the *Daily Herald*.

Dick was able to take in the entire contents of the room as he passed by the window, and a curious feeling of envy went through him. There seemed to be such peace in that one quiet room, no silent little wars waging, instead an understanding between the generations that in his own life he could not conceive of as possible. "What an odd world!" he said to himself. "To think that I can't go in there, say Hullo, and sit down with them. I like them; they like me. Yet I can't go in there. Why can't I? Why don't I? Because it would embarrass me. Why? Because I would embarrass them. Why...?" He ground his teeth in exasperation.

In his efforts to dismiss this seemingly insoluble problem from his thoughts, he merely found himself thinking of another not so very dissimilar, and nearer to himself. He remembered suddenly how, the last time he was at home, his father had passed by the kitchen door and seen him within, chatting amicably with the cook. Dick liked Mrs Preston, and had known her since he was a child. His father had stopped outside the door and silently beckoned to him. Dick had hesitated to answer, but thinking that he might, by ignoring his father, embarrass Mrs Preston, he had gone. He had followed his father silently down the passage. Then Colonel Pringle had stopped, confronted him, and on the Colonel's face Dick had seen that peculiar expression he had grown to know so well. He stared at his father's face, white and drawn, the pupils of his small eyes the size of pins. Here was a man who had helped to kill men, if he had not actually killed them himself, but whose face he had seen blanch at the sight of a frog being crushed beneath another's foot. Dick stared into his father's eyes, and saw the cruelty in them. He knew that the man's hands were clenched behind him, that he was not going to be able to say what he wanted to say, because when he was angry he became inarticulate, and that he was enraged more than ever because he knew Dick knew this.

"What d'you think you were doing in there?" he blurted out at last.

Dick pretended surprise. "Doing?" he muttered.

"Come on, out with it!"

"I've nothing to 'out with,'" Dick said, and he could feel the blood rising in his neck. His collar was too tight. "I was merely talking to Mrs Preston," he said.

"What about? When are you going to realize your place is not in the kitchen?"

Dick took a deep breath in order to control his voice. "I didn't know I had a *place*," he said.

"Well, you have," the man almost shouted, "and let me tell you once for all it's not in the kitchen." The Colonel was trembling. "Do *I* go in the kitchen?" he cried.

Dick felt certain his father had not meant to make this remark, but before he could answer the Colonel had made a curious guttural noise in his throat, and was marching away up the passage, swinging his arms.

At one time Dick would have brooded for the rest of the day upon this incident, but now, opening the gate on to the village street, he found himself muttering the same words as he had muttered at the time, "Poor Dad!"

Dick crossed the street and entered the wood that led to the kennels. He was no longer angry with his father, he was angry with something that made it possible for fathers such as his to think they were right to prevent their sons from standing in the kitchens of their homes and talking amicably with the women who cooked their meals. He supposed it was all part of this strange "social system," as Tom Bradley called it. And the fact that it had been thus in England in his father's and grandfather's time was not enough for him. It worried him. He seemed to meet it wherever he went. Suddenly he had a ridiculous vision of fathers, generations of them all over England, peering through kitchen keyholes at their sons talking to their cooks—and he laughed aloud to himself as he strode through the wood.

But immediately the smile passed and his face grew serious again as he remembered another father—the father of the girl he was about to see, Natalie Norman. Ernest Norman. And he thought of Ford, the farm-hand, and of Menelanda, the prize sow. . . . And with the memory of this before his eyes Dick felt his body grow hot with resentment. The Colonel, Mrs Preston, Ford, Ernest Norman, the Sow, the Bradleys, Natalie—he saw them all as though in the dark before him, and all seemed at war one with the other, and with him, when suddenly the sight of Kathleen laying his tea on the table rose before him, and the darkness vanished. He was saying, "If I go for a short time, will you dance with me?" and with a smile she was looking up at him, answering, "I'd love to."

As he smiled to himself he noticed the path at his feet grow more distinct, and he looked up to find the lights in the kennels burning yellow through the trees. He slackened his pace. Drawing near, he could see through a window the figure of Natalie Norman standing under the full glare of one of the lights, her head thrown back. He stopped. What on earth was she doing? He came nearer, peered at her through the window. Natalie Norman was in a curious position. Standing right under the light, she was holding something in front of her upturned face with her left hand, while the fingers of her right hand seemed to be applying some instrument to that part of her face between her eyes. This operation was apparently causing her some pain, for every few seconds her features became contorted in a grimace.

He turned the door-knob and walked into the kennel. He watched the girl jump back and stuff her powder-puff into her pocket as though ashamed of being caught with it in her hand.

"Heavens!" she exclaimed, her face flushed, "you did give me a jump, Dick! I never heard you coming!"

Closing the door behind him, Dick stood in front of her.

"Too engrossed in yourself," he muttered. She stared at him; then sneezed violently.

Suddenly he was angry.

When she had finished blowing her nose, he blurted out, "Why the hell can't you leave your face alone, like other people?"

The girl stepped back in astonishment.

"Like other people!" she exclaimed. "Why, Dick darling, everybody—er—plucks their eyebrows!"

"Everybody!"

"Poor Dick," she said, "you are naïve, darling. Didn't you know all girls pluck their eyebrows nowadays? Even Daddy says us girls should make the best of ourselves."

Dick clenched his hands, drew in a deep breath. Natalie watched his eyes grow smaller and she cowered away from him.

"Make the best of yourself, eh!" he cried, taking a step towards her. "Fatten yourself up, eh! Like your father's bullocks, getting fit for the market, eh! Like Menelanda!"

He was standing so close to her now she flinched, feeling his hot breath on her face. Suddenly, as she was reminded of the sow episode and what he had said to her then, she flared up and struck him full in the face with the palm of her hand.

"Take that!" she yelled, and retreated into the corner, her eyes wide with fear.

Dick, his cheek burning, made a rush towards her. The girl lowered her head and covered face and ears with her hands.

Catching sight of the cowering feminine form, the covered face, Dick felt his fury fall suddenly from him. With his body almost touching hers, his hands relaxed and his arms dropped to his sides.

"Oh, Dick darling—I didn't mean to, I didn't. . . ."

She put a hand out and touched his coat. He looked down at it, at the thin white fingers, the polished nails, then took her hand in his.

She looked up and smiled at him through her tears. Seeing the flushed mark her blow had made on his cheek, she closed her eyes and lowered her head onto his breast.

"Oh, forgive me, darling," she sobbed.

The scent of her body and perfume rose to Dick's nostrils, and, clasping her tightly, he buried his face in her hair. For a full minute they stood silently, holding each other. Then she raised her tear-stained face and looked at him. He wiped her eyes with the back of his hand.

"Dick?" she murmured.

He grunted his willingness to hear, for he didn't want to talk; he wanted to kiss her, but not in the way he guessed she wanted to be kissed.

"Dick, you do love me, don't you?"

Gently but firmly he drew her face back on to his breast.

"You do, don't you?" The voice reiterated from his chest. He forced a laugh.

"It looks like it, doesn't it?" he said.

She raised her face again. "Kiss me," she murmured.

He lowered his lips to hers, smelling the sickly-sweet rouge. Then he closed his eyes, and looked straight into the clear, smiling face of Kathleen Bradley. . . .

Immediately his body stiffened and he knew nothing but that he was holding another body and his lips were on lips. With his hands gripping her waist he pressed himself against the length of the girl, his face against her face, till he felt her fall limp between himself and the wall. Then with his left hand under her chin he brought her head down into the crook of his arm, and covered her face once more with his. With his right hand he slowly felt up her body for the shape of her breast. As his hand was upon her, suddenly she made a quick movement, ducked her head, and cried breathlessly, "Oh, Dick. . . !"

She stood away from him, back against the wall, a strand of dark hair falling over her flushed face. He stared at her, breathing fast, and he longed to strike her as she had struck him. Then he saw her face brighten.

"Oh, darling," she said, "I've something lovely to tell you."

Suddenly he didn't care; his body went limp and he felt tired. All he wanted was to get out. He turned without a word, about to leave. Then he remembered he also had something to tell her

—the message from Kathleen. He faced her again. "And I've something to tell you," he said.

She was smiling. "But I'm sure mine's nicer, let me tell you mine first, Dick."

"Well?" he muttered.

"We've got up a party for the dance in the Hall tonight, and Daddy expects you to dinner—and to come with us."

"What?" Dick was astonished. "You going to the dance?"

He began to think quickly. He would have to go to dinner: invitations of this kind were more like commands, and he would have to go to the dance—with the Norman party. And he was already going with the sole object of dancing with Kathleen; he wanted to talk to her in some environment other than those fleeting glimpses in her own home; he wanted to have the legitimate chance of putting his arm round her waist. . . . But now he would have to dance with her in front of the Normans—he had never known the Normans attend one of these village dances before— dance in front of Natalie, with Kathleen, and yet be with the Norman party! Be watched by Natalie as he danced with her father's groom's daughter! Natalie watching, all the Norman party watching! Already he could hear their questions, "Who on earth's that girl Dick's with?" He could see their eyes as they silently watched him—eyes, eyes all round him.

"Dick, you don't seem very pleased about it?"

He looked at her. She was smoothing out her hair, powdering her face.

"What time's dinner?" he asked, ignoring her remark.

"Eight, darling—black tie!"

Black hell! he thought to himself. He loathed putting on evening clothes. With his hand on the door-knob he watched her covering her face with powder. She produced a lip-stick, then looked up at him.

"Oh, Dick," she said a little nervously, "what was it you had to tell me?"

Dick tried to remember Kathleen's exact words. He said, "Kathleen wanted to know if Miss Natalie would be so good as to feed the dogs tonight as she—has to go to the station for Mr Norman."

Almost unconsciously he laid stress on the Mister and Miss. They looked at each other, saying nothing. Then Dick opened the door through which he had come.

"Well, see you later," he called back, and walked out into the darkness of the wood.

Inside the kennel the girl stood still, muttering to herself, " 'Kathleen wanted to know' . . . Did she indeed!" Stamping her foot with rage, she began preparing the dogs' food.

Dick walked fast up the High Street, turned to the right at the War Memorial, and entered the farm office, where after dark every evening he studied the science of Artificial Manure. A short young man named Slade, the bailiff's secretary, was sitting on the fender-seat, smoking a cigarette. Dick didn't like Slade's cockney facetiousness; he suspected, too, he was one of the worst of the village gossips; also, he knew he was an admirer of Kathleen; he had often heard his voice in the Bradleys' kitchen, seen him coming and going from the cottage.

" 'Ullo, Mr Pringle," he said as Dick came in, "your manure was nearly trottin' after you!"

Dick sat down at his desk. "Is it late then?" he asked.

"Gone six."

"Good Lord!" Dick felt himself flushing, wondering if Slade could possibly know where he had spent the last hour.

"Not for the 'op tonight, I s'pose, Mr Pringle?"

Dick could bear the "Mr" least of all from Slade. He always fancied the man slightly emphasized the prefix.

"Yes, I think I may go for a short time," he said. He knew this news would surprise Slade, since only once in his life, at Christmas, had Dick attended one of these monthly dances in the village Hall.

"Coo lumme!" was Slade's comment, "you becomin' a dancin' man, eh! Well, I never!"

Slade threw the stump of his cigarette in the fire and rubbed his hands together.

"Well, I'm off for a wet at Caley's," he said, taking his cap from a peg. "S'long, Mr Pringle, see you on the floor!"

"S'long," Dick murmured, and continued making notes about Artificial Manure.

III

Dick Pringle was slightly drunk. In spite of the tiresome dinner conversation, in which he had taken little part, he had eaten well of the rich food, drunk even better of the whisky. The Norman party was composed of six, three men and three girls. The two men, whom Dick had never seen, but who, judging from their conversation, had recently been gazetted to their respective regiments, wore small, rather inadequate moustaches, well-oiled hair, and talked in loud voices about their brother-officers, horses, Hunt Balls, and motor-cars. Instinctively Dick disliked them. He himself had been seated between Natalie Norman and a plump pink girl, called Primrose. As dessert arrived Mrs Norman had leaned forward from her end of the table and in a loud voice stated that the dance in the Hall was already about to begin. In spite of subsequent haste, however, the village band, composed of four men from the Norman estate, had already played through several dances by the time the party from the Minster arrived. As they trooped in, Dick sensed a hush go through the Hall, as though its occupants looked upon their entrance as an intrusion; simultaneously it occurred to him how conspicuous they must look, for no other man in the Hall was in evening clothes, nor had any of the women a backless dress such as that worn by this Primrose girl.

The room, decorated with paper lanterns, was crowded, and already a haze of smoke hung over the dancers' heads. When the new arrivals had left their coats with a man at the door, Dick watched Mrs Norman walk forward into the Hall on the arm of one of the young subalterns; he watched her smile greetings to those who passed, in a half-fearful, half-patronizing manner. Girls stopped laughing as they saw her coming, and young men postponed their mild flirtations as they bade her good evening. It seemed to Dick that everyone in the room was trying to avoid staring at their party and that not one among them was succeeding. "What business have we here?" he asked himself. He wondered what the Bradleys would think if he burst suddenly into their kitchen and insisted on sharing his meal with them. The thought filled him with embarrassment as he stood against the wall by the entrance, waiting for the girls of the party to finish powdering their faces in the cloakroom. Near him, the two subalterns were talking together. Dick nodded occasionally to men with whom from time to time he had worked on the farm, and to girls whom he had passed so often in the street and in shops that he had come to think he was actually acquainted with them. So far, he had not seen Kathleen nor any of the Bradley family; Kathleen he now longed to see; he longed to be dancing with her, and yet he weakened with fear at the ridiculous little scandal he was certain this action of his would cause. It would have been all right if he were alone, not in these absurdly conspicuous clothes; but with the Norman party, and with Natalie looking on, watching, with Mrs Norman eyeing him—and what would the odd girl of the party do if and when he danced with Kathleen? For they were a man short, Mr Norman having refused to come. With whom would she, the odd girl, dance? It was not as if people "sat out" at these monthly functions; left to themselves the people of the village recognized no such formalities in the dance hall, but now, tonight . . . what would happen to the odd girl if she were not introduced to someone? Could he, Dick asked himself, introduce the girl to one of the men of the village, one of the farmhands, one of the chauffeurs or a stableman? He'd like to do that; he'd like to introduce that Primrose girl to Slade, and hear what that little man would have to say to her, for Dick knew Slade considered himself not only a fine dancer, he also prided himself on his attractiveness to women. But what would Mrs Norman have to say if he did that? It was hardly his business, as a guest of the Normans, to introduce a fellow-guest to the secretary of their hostess's bailiff, who referred to a drink as a "wet" and a dance as an "op."

As though he had spoken his thoughts aloud, Dick heard a familiar voice beside him:

"Well, Mr Pringle, 'ere we are again! Enjoying yerself?"

Dick looked down at the little man whose breath smelled strongly of beer, and he wanted to slap his face. He grunted something, and Slade moved on. Then, realizing that he had been too long lost in thought, he looked round for one of the girls of the party. He caught sight of Primrose coming out of the cloakroom, and went over to her.

"Let's dance," he said. The girl placed a plump hand on his shoulder, and they waltzed in and out of the couples. With the constant turning necessary to the waltz, Dick realized once more that he was slightly intoxicated. He looked at the girl's waved hair before his eyes, at her plump white shoulder, at the serious, almost bored expression on her face, and he tried to think of something to say that would cheer her up. But before anything occurred to him the girl herself spoke.

"I suppose you know all these people?" she said.

Dick tried to catch the expression on her face, but he could only see it in profile. Was that contempt in her tone as she spoke the last three words? Immediately he slackened his pace. He began to dislike this girl. He thought of Natalie, and judged that they had much in common. He said, "Yes, I know a good many." Then he hesitated, wondering what he could say that would make it more clear whether that tone of hers had been contemptuous or not. Suddenly his eyes brightened.

"Would you like me to introduce you to one of them?" he asked.

The answer came quick. "Oh, no thank you," she said emphatically. There was no doubt about it now. Dick's right arm tightened with anger.

"Why on earth not?" he said. "There are some very nice men among them, and I'm certain all of them dance better than I do."

"Oh, I'm sure," she said.

Dick smiled to himself, aware that he had just stepped on her toes, not altogether accidentally.

"Well?" he said. He was now like a cat after a mouse.

"Oh," the girl muttered. She hesitated, confused.

"Don't you like being introduced to people?" he asked.

"Sometimes. It depends."

"On what?"

She looked up at him. "You're being rather rude, aren't you?" she said.

He smiled. "I'm sorry, I didn't mean to be. I was only interested."

"Well, if you want to know, I didn't realize it was going to be this sort of dance."

"This *sort* of dance!" he repeated.

At this moment, over the girl's shoulder, he caught sight of Kathleen. She was dancing with Slade, and it seemed to Dick he was holding her unnecessarily close, dancing with his left arm raised high, almost over her head. Anger stirred in Dick, and he steered his partner towards them. When they were close, he caught Kathleen's eye. She smiled, and a thrill of pleasure ran through him.

"See that girl there?" he said, nodding his head in the direction of Kathleen.

"Which?" asked Primrose, "the one with the black hair in the blue frock?"

When he said yes, Primrose said, "She looks nice," and for the first time he felt drawn towards his partner.

"She is," he said, "in fact, she's by far the nicest girl in the village."

"Who is she?"

"She's Kathleen Bradley, the groom's daughter," said Dick in a voice slightly louder than usual.

"Oh," muttered Primrose, and then, as though the words were meant as a challenge, "Why don't you dance with her?"

Dick's answer was prompt. "I shall," he said, and immediately, sensing that the dance was about to end, he steered Primrose towards Slade and his partner. When they were near, the music ceased, and as unostentatiously as possible Dick fell in close behind them in the queue that formed in the doorway leading to the refreshment room. He waited till Kathleen's partner was a little way in front of her, then reached out and touched her on the arm.

"Will you dance the next with me?" he said.

Kathleen turned, and smiled. "Thanks, Mr Dick," she said, "I'd love to."

While Dick stood drinking his lemonade, he tried to make himself as pleasant as possible to his partner, but try as he would he could not take any genuine interest in the conversation. Excited, not a little nervous, he stood waiting for the band to strike up. Mr and Mrs Bradley passed; they smiled, and Dick went over and shook hands with them. He watched Natalie talking with one of the young subalterns. The interval seemed interminable. At last strains of music came through from the other room, and couples began to move off. Dick thanked his partner and immediately went in search of Kathleen. Finding her by the door, waiting for him, he put a hand on her sleeveless arm and they went into the Hall. As his right arm went round her waist and they moved together across the floor, a curious feeling of peace seemed to pass through his body; it was as though the girl's own serenity were communicating itself to him, absorbing his anger and nervousness, injecting in their stead that tranquillity which marked Kathleen's looks and all her movements. He felt suddenly at peace, happy, even proud; and he found himself wishing with all his being that he were far away with her in a strange room where no one knew them, and that they could remain like this for an indefinite period of time. A sensation of infinite gratitude filled him, a gratefulness he had no idea how to express. At last, after a silence in which there had been no embarrassment, he pressed her fingers and said:

"Kathleen, I was so grateful for what you said to me today—I'm afraid I never thanked you properly."

He looked down at her looking up at him, and he saw she was smiling, her brown eyes wide and candid.

"Oh," she said softly, "I was ever so glad you said what you did, too." She paused, then went on, "I often think of it—how it must be for you, I mean. It doesn't seem right, somehow, does it?"

Not so much the words she used as the soft sympathetic tone of her voice thrilled him, and he longed to hug her with gratitude for her kindness and understanding. Nevertheless, he wasn't altogether sure what she meant.

"Doesn't seem right?" he repeated. "I don't think I know exactly what. . . ."

"Well," she said, coming to his rescue, "you living in our place like that, all alone, and . . . well, us all being together, next door, so to speak, and . . . oh, I don't know. Anyway, times Mum and I often think how lonely it must be for you, sitting there evenings . . . not that that's much consolation, I'm sure, but. . . ."

She broke off, and laughed, clearly a little embarrassed.

For some reason he didn't bother to fathom, Dick was suddenly aware that tears were frighteningly near the brims of his eyes. He raised his head and tried to think of something humorous to say, but he failed. Instead, he pressed Kathleen's fingers again, and murmured, "You are sweet, Kathleen. It's so rare to find someone who seems to understand things about other people, that when I do I. . . ."

Before he could finish the sentence Dick, over Kathleen's shoulder, found himself face to face with Natalie. For an instant he was forced to catch his breath. She was standing with her back to the wall—alone. And in her eyes—eyes that stared at Dick as though they would pierce his head, he saw such a look of venom, jealousy, even hatred, all combined, that for a moment he faltered and stopped in his dancing. As their eyes met there was barely a foot of space between their faces. Dick stared back, utterly at a loss to know what to say, or if he should say anything; and it wasn't until then, such had been his desire to dance with Kathleen and his readiness to accept Primrose's challenge, that it occurred to him he should, by right of courtesy, have asked Natalie to dance before asking Kathleen. The realization that certainly he was partly to blame for the look he saw on Natalie's face and the most humiliating position she now seemed to be in—Mrs Norman's daughter a "wallflower" in her own village—this realization at first shamed Dick, but soon the shame gave way to anger and resentment as he thought of the stupidity of allowing oneself to be thus humiliated. Why couldn't she go and talk to someone, the woman behind the bar in the refreshment room (who was actually her mother's maid) or the girl acting waitress there who incidentally was a housemaid, to whom Dick was sure Natalie had often chatted in the privacy of her own bedroom? Anything but stand up here like this and be stared at by the whole village! He could only suppose that here she considered none of "these people"— as Primrose had referred to them—to be good enough for her, or that she would have been too embarrassed to dance with anyone outside of her own party. Then it suddenly occurred to Dick she was standing there to watch *him*, watch him dance with Kathleen, to humiliate him, "show him up" in the eyes of the remainder of the Norman party. . . . So that was it!

He stared back at her over Kathleen's shoulder, wondering.

Then he remembered he was partly to blame for her position, and, coming still nearer to her, he forced a smile. "Dance the next?" he asked. But the girl only stared back at him, silent, her eyes still half-closed.

Kathleen turned as he spoke, and seeing Natalie, looked back at him. "Oh, Mr Dick," she said, frowning, "I expect you ought to be dancing with Miss Natalie."

Dick glanced away. "Maybe I ought," he murmured, "but I'm not."

"Oh dear," he heard her say. "I do hope she's not annoyed—did you think of telling her about the dogs' food?"

"Yes, I did," Dick said.

Here the music ceased and they went into the refreshment room. As he was offering Kathleen a glass of lemonade he caught sight of Natalie coming in through the door, alone. Handing the glass to his partner, Dick excused himself and went over to Natalie. He joined her and directed her into a corner of the room.

"Natalie, I'm sorry I didn't ask . . ." he began, but further speech was cut short by a violent outburst from the girl in front of him. She was facing him, her eyes like slits and her hands clenched into fists by her side. She leaned over towards him, her face within a few inches of his.

"Sorry!" she mocked him, "*you* sorry! You think you can lie, and insult, and hit, and be disgustingly rude—and get away with everything, don't you? You think I'm just a poor fool who will put up with anything from you just because I've once been idiot enough to fall in love with you. . . ." She paused, out of breath, her face flushed and her eyes blazing. "Well, this is enough for me," she went on, "and I'm through, see! You're a cad, that's all—a cad masquerading in gentleman's clothes! *You* a gentleman! Pah! What you've just done is proof you're nothing more than a village lout! I always knew it—you and your—your *servant-girl!*"

Expecting her actually to spit at him in her uncontrollable fury, Dick turned his face away, and when he looked back she was gone. For a few seconds he stood still. Only the last words she had uttered in her rage had had any effect on him, and the last of all kept ringing through his head, increasing his former dislike and anger to a pitch reached hitherto only on the occasion when he had told her of Ford and the accident fatal to Menelanda, the prize sow. ●

Realizing that he could not possibly stay any longer at the dance he went back to Kathleen. After one glance at his face, she said:

"Oh, dear, is something wrong?"

"Not much," he murmured, "but I've an awful headache; I think I'll be going home, Kathleen."

As he took her hand he noticed the worried expression on her face.

"I know it's not only a headache," she said, and he thrilled to the intimate, friendly tone of her voice.

"You're right; it isn't," he admitted, "but I must go all the same —really. I'll tell you about it—later, eh?"

He spoke the last words almost in a whisper. She nodded, significantly, he thought, and pressed his fingers. He smiled, pressing hers in return. Then, deciding that he would explain his absence by letter to Mrs Norman, he found his coat and left the Hall.

Once in the darkness he hurried home, anger forcing his legs to cover the ground at an unnatural speed. And as he went he came to a decision: never in his life would he set foot in those kennels again, never voluntarily speak to Natalie as long as he lived. He despised and hated her with all his being; never would he forgive her that insult to Kathleen. And as he was reminded of Kathleen, he spoke her name aloud. "Kathleen—thank Heaven for Kathleen," he muttered into the darkness, and he smiled to himself as a thought occurred to him. He would wait for her tonight, tell her everything—well, not everything, for he would never breathe a word of what Natalie had spat out at him at the end of her tirade of anger; but he would tell her what he thought of Natalie, and perhaps—perhaps he would be able to tell her what he thought of her, Kathleen. . . .

He reached the cottage, went into the sitting-room, and immediately poured himself out half a glass of whisky. Nearly all of this he drank at one gulp, and sat down. He shivered with cold. Should he wait here? It would be a long time before she came. Mr and Mrs Bradley would come home first and find him. No, he could not sit here. Finishing his whisky, he grabbed the bottle and went upstairs. He sat on the edge of the bed. Should he sit here, like this, dressed—for two, perhaps three hours? Thoughts that in turn he half-feared, refused to face for the reason that they dissolved in mystery, and to which the next instant the whole of his body thrilled—these thoughts flashed through his brain, causing him to perspire with impatient excitement. He got off the bed and, as though he were in a hurry to be asleep, he undressed very quickly, put on a clean pair of pyjamas, poured himself out another whisky and returned to the bed. But the cold soon forced him between the sheets. He sat up in the bed, leaning against the raised pillow, the glass on the table beside the candle, a vision of Kathleen as she had last gripped his fingers vivid before his eyes. Slowly his eyelids closed, his head sank sideways, and within a minute he was asleep.

In what seemed to him less than a few seconds, but in reality was more than two hours, he was woken by sounds from outside his room. Someone was coming up the stairs. Kathleen! Immediately he was fully awake. Holding his breath, he rose from the bed. He stood in front of the door, leaning over, listening. What was that? Someone's voice, half-whispering . . . it wasn't Kathleen's, nor one of the Bradleys'.

"Well, 'ere we are again, dear!"

How did he know that voice? He bit his lip to try and stop himself shivering; his hand trembled on the door-knob; his legs shook beneath him.

"Shish, be quiet! You'll wake Mr Pringle."

Dick held his breath again. That voice was Kathleen's.

"Oh, 'im!" came the other voice. Then Dick knew: it was Slade's.

Travellers' Tears

"MY LOVE, that certainly is bad. Your poor Ma." Mrs Awahnee's voice, like that of most Hawaiians, was low and very soft.

"I know," murmured John.

Two hours ago, John D. Crane had learned that his father had died suddenly in South Carolina. When the rotund, brown proprietress of their rooms in Honolulu had expressed sympathy with him, and John had answered that he "knew," he was wondering would there be any other guys of his age aboard the ship they were going home on.

"Fellows say you can have a wonderful time on that trip. . . ."

"How's your Ma taken it, John?"

"God darn that fly in my eyes—what's that you said, Mrs Awahnee?"

"Expect your Ma's feelin' pretty bad?"

"You bet, Mrs Awahnee. Say, what kinda tonnage is the craft we're makin' for home on, Mrs Awahnee?"

"Just how did your Ma get the news, John?"

"Cable, I guess. Say, you ever been in the States, Mrs Awahnee?"

"My love, that musta been a shock, poor woman!"

"I know."

Tired of standing, John sat down on the sandy porch, crossing his legs. His white pants were of the knickerbocker type, full and falling to within a few inches of his ankles. And his ankles were covered in grey socks, his feet in brown and white shoes. The sleeves of his white cotton polo shirt fell short of his elbows: the collar lay open at the neck.

In two years, when he would be thirteen, John D. Crane was

going to what he called "kahludge," in California, to get a degree, whatever that meant.

Like many young Americans, he possessed a magnificent skin: his face looked as though it had been chiselled out of fawn-coloured marble.

He crossed his arms and scowled—a habit he had acquired from not wearing a hat, and from living in the sun. Mrs Awahnee stood behind him, leaning against the portal, her folded arms resting on her massive breasts. She looked, as do most mature women of her race, full of a soft and melancholy contentment. Breathing peace and comfort, she gazed away into the sunny distance. Then she pulled a knitting needle out of her raven hair, and stuck it in her mouth.

"Will you be gone long?" she asked, after a pause.

"Search me, Mrs Awahnee," answered John.

"We'll sure miss you and your poor Ma, John."

"I know," murmured John, who wasn't listening. He was wondering if he could climb that coconut tree as fast as that coloured boy.

The brown boy, bent double like a monkey, was silently running up and down the tree, naked but for a gold-yellow bandana round his narrow hips. Beyond him the line of leaning palms ceased suddenly and gave way to some deep green grass; then that too ceased, and the white Atakuli beach glared fiercely back at the sun. Towards the sand the breakers came hissing siphon-like out of the blue, casting up white liquid diamonds that fell imperceptibly back into the blue again, where they were received without a sound. Closer, in the clear, more peaceful water, two Japanese women stood waist-deep, examining handfuls of olive seaweed. From round their bodies a warm breeze and the carry-ing tide ballooned their skirts into fantastic shapes. John could see the pale horizon line meet them at their elbows, and on that line a speck of a ship move like a fly on a thread of cotton up to the right-hand woman's arm. He shut one eye. "Guess I'll get my binoculars. . . ." He rose, glanced up at a window of the house.

"Say, Mother!"

"That you, John? Hey, we're sailin' in half an hour! Me all

alone packing! Ooh, if I'd your father...don't you *care*...at all?"

John listened to his mother's voice falter, rise, fall, then end on what sounded like a strangled scream.

"Your poor Ma!" groaned Mrs Awahnee.

"Ah, shucks!" muttered John, and he lurched away up the wooden stairs just as a Ford car drew up at the door.

"Baggage!" shouted Mrs Awahnee after John's retreating figure.

"Trunks!" said John, bursting into the room to find Mrs Crane sitting, red-eyed, on the bed.

People who looked at Mrs Crane thought of cooks, women who stand all their lives in front of fires, sweating, getting red, and fat. Even her women friends—and Mrs Crane had many women friends—thought that. Yet all recognized in her a charm that none could define. Her husband had had an haberdasher store in Dayton, Ohio. But the moment his business had shown signs of success, the Middle-West climate had suddenly failed to suit his wife. For the last three years she and John had lived on the Island of Oahu, first in Kailua Bay, then in the house of Mrs Awahnee in Honolulu. During that time Chandos Titus Crane had paid them three prolonged visits. But they had not been happy. Mrs Crane's women friends had not liked Chandos Titus; and he, unable to work or play Bridge, had pined for home.

This morning was proving the happiest Mrs Crane could remember for many years. She was filled with "emotion," with gratitude, with tears. Oh, if people only knew ... the sorrow, the relief, the heartache...the pity that, at last her due, she ought to receive, that she would welcome, with—oh, such seas of tears!

John stood in front of his mother, legs apart, hands on hips. "Want any help, Ma?"

"Help?" Mrs Crane sniffed, shouted, then sniffed again. Her face was purple, her eyes bloodshot.

"Oh, how I could *cry*...! she blubbered.

John gazed unseeing at her fat little feet.

"Trunks, Ma! The taxi's waiting."

Suddenly Mrs Crane rose, her neck the colour of blood. She planted herself in front of her son.

"Trunks!" she shouted, beside herself. "Trunks and taxis you say, when one half of my life—your own papa—is this moment lying dead! You heartless boy—that's what you are, and I don't mean maybe!"

"Well, for cryin' out loud!" murmured John, moving over to the window.

"Twenty minutes!" shouted the native driver from below.

"Baggage!" called Mrs Awahnee. "Shall I help your ma?" John turned into the room. He looked at his mother sitting on a suitcase, wiping her face.

"Trunks," he said, and staggered a yard with a huge portmanteau. "God!" he wheezed, dropped it and returned to the window.

"Hi, taxi, how about some help?"

The driver grunted and came up the stairs. When Mrs Crane heard his steps, she got up, seized the suitcase she had been sitting on, and heaved it out of the room into the corridor.

Dumbly, John gazed at his mother.

As the driver came into the room she sighed and leaned heavily against the door, a handkerchief to her eyes. While John and the driver carted the luggage down the stairs and out into the car, Mrs Awahnee stood weeping in the doorway. John looked at her and for the first time in his life felt sad. He liked Mrs Awahnee, though the fact had not occurred to him until this moment. His mother appeared in the porch, her face invisible behind a bandana. Her shoulders heaved. Suddenly Mrs Awahnee flung herself upon the other woman, burst out weeping on her breast. Together, clinging to one another, they tottered out into the everlasting sun. The white-ducked driver helped them into the back seat, then started the engine. John jumped in beside him.

"Only ten minutes," the driver said.

John looked up at him and noticed, unquestioning, that his eyes were filled with tears.

"I know," he murmured.

II

The customary crowd of tourists stood watching, waiting, listening, for the ship to sail. No one spoke. They had no friends on board.

> *Awa-hee-hoo!*
> *Ka-wah-na-lee, hehoo....*

It sounded like that, sung softly, sadly, slowly, under that sun. Though John had heard the melody a thousand times, he had never learned the Hawaiian words. Nor had his mother. Yet every time he heard them sung something happened to him. Something happened to everyone. He had often noticed a great deal happen to his mother. He felt thankful her friends were not present.

> *Awa-hee-hoo!*

Every morning, every evening, ships set out from the remote Pacific islands. And every morning, every evening, hearts of all ages and colours grew troubled. It immediately affected their eyes—eyes which, however small and hard, melted, suffused with a tearful longing to remain ... to remain within the hearing and sight of those dark girls on the pier, girls with flowers encircling their cool necks and scarlet hibiscus in their hair, girls whose fingers roved over strings of light ukuleles, fingers like long, pliant pencils, girls whose cool, soft voices kept murmuring, "I love you, I love you" ... languorous liquid balls of eyes whispering, "Stay, oh stay" ...

> *Ka-wah-na-lee, hehoo!*

"Say, Mother, you'll suffocate!"

"John, don't talk to me," murmured Mrs Crane. She was leaning against the ship's gunwale, Mrs Awahnee's arms about her, her head resting on the white woman's bosom of flowers. For Mrs Awahnee had just bought her six *leis* of fresh flowers. With tears rolling down her cheeks she had dropped them over Mrs Crane's neck—long, heavy, sweet-smelling chains of flower heads. A single *lei* held four hundred carnation-heads strung together. Flowers filled the woman's front: they mounted from the hollow between her breasts till they caressed her chin. They hung down like multi-coloured pythons below her waist.

Awa-hee-hoo!

"Oh, honey," moaned Mrs Crane in the other woman's ear, "wrung by death I am, wrung from you who've been everything to me, maddened by John, wrung from my kind friends in paradise, honey . . . poor Chandos, poor . . . poor Chandos . . . husband . . . gone. . . !"

Tears streamed down Mrs Awahnee's face as she clasped the white woman in her arms and breathed comfort in her ear. Then something seemed to happen to her. She allowed her arms to drop, stood up straight—big, and dark, in her full white cotton dress. A light flashed from her large brown eyes. Tilting her head slightly as though to listen, she gazed over the rail to where the string band of native girls was playing. Then she began to hum, her full red lips tightly closed. Her voice, deep in her throat, deep down in her body, rose soft and haunting, mingling, falling, following the ukuleles and guitars.

Ka-wah-na-lee, hehoo!

Slowly she raised her right arm before her, the fingers hanging limp. Her massive head fell back a little; the raven hair hung loose upon her shoulders; the long lashes closed over her eyes, touched her cheeks. She bent one knee, raised the lifted arm above her head, lowered her face to one side. . . .

John stood by the rail, transfixed, his eyes staring motionless from his marble face. "God, if she ain't going to *hula!*"

Mrs Crane, beflowered, bewildered, bereaved, leaned all her weight on the gunwale. Her eyes were dry again. She hardly breathed.

Dark men bustled past them up and down the rusty iron deck;

men laden with sacks, covered with grease, white with flour from the stores—shouting, blaspheming, laughing.... Somewhere on board chickens clucked. Querrrrrrk, kwuck kwuck kwuck kwuck querrrrrrrk! An imprisoned hog snorted from the stern. From below there rose the nauseatingly sweet stench of raw sugar cane: the hold was filled with it, and the hatch was still wide open. A mule, like a dead thing, sailed into the sky, hanging from the chain of the ship's crane whose summit towered immediately over Mrs Awahnee's head. The leaning standard whirled on its creaking swivel, hovered, stood still, while the mule hung helpless from the wide belly-band, its head and legs dangling, as though dead. Then, falling precipitously to within a few feet of the deck, it came slowly to rest, finding its legs at last on the boards behind Mrs Crane.

The coloured crew scurried hither and thither, half-naked, feet bare. The *Malukai* was a freighter carrying only emergency passengers in its specially converted officers' quarters.

But John saw no one but Mrs Awahnee. She was singing now, in her deep, full musical voice—the voice he had heard so often while she worked in the house, scrubbing, cleaning, cooking....

Awa-hee-hoo!

He watched her hips as they began slowly to move, her arms stretch above her head, the hands turn inward like the heads of cobras, while her shoulders, the entire upper half of her body, remained still as a rock. Slowly she cast her head from side to side, the face lowered, eyes closed. As the music on the pier grew louder, a little less slow, Mrs Awahnee's voice rose. Her hips moved faster, in and out, back and forth, in sensuous, tortuous movements; her feet, her shoulders motionless. Then she lowered her arms, thrust them straight out from her, the hands on a level with Mrs Crane's face, the fingers pointing at her. The Hawaiian woman ducked her head between her arms, the face invisible. John stared at her feet as they began to drum on the iron deck; he watched a young brown member of the crew suddenly stop behind her, smile a white flashing smile, then begin to hum. He stretched one arm out sideways, the other in the same direction across his body: his hips began to move, the arms stirred and rippled, writhed, like full supple snakes. . . .

Ka-wah-na-lee, hehoo!

John gazed at the boy in his white singlet and ducks, at the stomach muscles gathering and falling under the thin cotton. His own thoughts, curiously enough, affected him in much the same place.

Bor-baw-boooooooooor! The ship's siren, immediately overhead, shattered the world. Everyone jumped. Mrs Crane's jaw fell. John felt something give way inside him.

Bor-baw-boooooooooor! Four Filipinos with long shining black hair scampered down the gangway. The dancing boy had already begun to heave at a huge coil of rope, up in the bow. John clenched his right fist. God, *life. . . !*

"Any more for shore!"

He was suddenly aware of his mother being mauled by Mrs Awahnee. The two women were at grips. Large brown and white arms writhed together like loving pythons. Flower-petals rained to the deck from their embrace. Then, as though some referee had shouted "Break!" the two women fell apart. Staggering back with the words, "Everything to me!" Mrs Crane collapsed in a heap against the bulwark. Through a haze, John saw Mrs Awahnee's form spring upon the gangway. Then she turned and flung a handful of flowers in his face. He shouted apathetic last words at her, but she had already rolled down the bridge, between the ropes.

Ka-wah-na-lee, hehoo!

John blinked, clenched his hands, wiped a tear from one eye. As he approached his mother he saw the pier moving. Of a sudden words came into his mouth. He spoke, almost inaudibly, but in English.

"Our memory shall not fade with these flowers. . . ."

And slowly, deliberately, he began relieving Mrs Crane of her *leis*. Leaning over her on the deck, he picked the hibiscus and carnations, one by one, from her bosom.

"Say, Mother, Mrs Awahnee sure made a basket of you!"

"Don't talk to me, John."

As he pulled each flower John lifted his arm, squeezed the bloom in his hand, then threw it over the rail. He watched the petals spread fanwise in the air before they descended in a slow shower to the black and glittering water.

Ka-wah-na-lee, hehoo!

It was now like a woman crying far away, like standing outside a church, listening to an abiding hymn being sung by unapproachable voices within. There—between—stood the wall: here—between—lay the water, stronger, sadder, because of the sea's almighty strength.

"Our memory shall not fade with these flowers. . . ."

He flung out a handful of living confetti, wishing he knew the next line.

"Cast upon your laughing seas. . . !"

John turned as though struck, to look into the smiling eyes of the dancing boy. Something happened to him; he was acutely aware of his nipples; his chest felt tight. For the first time in his life he knew that he was blushing. . . .

He lowered his face and turned his eyes towards the land of idleness. Lush and luxurious, the huge green crater mounted out of the blue. And all alone, at the end of the pier, he saw a white figure standing, one arm raised over its head. John swallowed once, twice . . . then pulled two whole *leis* from his mother's neck, leaving but one remaining on the inanimate woman. Viciously he flung the coloured coils far from the throbbing ship. He watched them fall; then looked down on them as they lay—two bright circles—rising and falling, on the silent sea.

And when he turned to relieve the woman of her last rope of flowers he discovered her neck was bare. He looked about him, and half-way up the deck his eyes fell upon the disappearing figure of the dancing boy—round whose brown neck the last *lei* of white carnations hung.

III

"You just keep the indicator on that line, see, kid—and don't
go turning the wheel around, or we'll be landing up in Alaska!
Okay now? I'll go get me a rum!"

"Sure thing, Cap," said John, "you go ahead."

First Officer Poynton tilted back his cap and spattered down
the companionway. John, high up on the bridge, stood alone,
legs apart, steering the *Malukai* through deep waters in the direction of North America.

The ship throbbed its way almost silently through the night.
The sharp prow seared the sea like a great knife shooting through
black jelly, while on either side of it the white water kept swirling
up, making an eternal swish-swishing sound. John listened, feeling a world in the power of his two hands on the wheel.

Queer how they knew exactly where you were going; how
they could reckon your exact spot in the ocean right now, in the
darkness. Like a landscape, you might be going down a straight
road, but there ain't no road. Nothing but those twinklers up
above....

With his hands a little unsteady on the wheel he gazed out
through the thick plate glass in front of him, to right, to left; but
he could see nothing but ink-blue space relieved by a white half-
moon and a billion stars—a blue-black dome of a roof infinitely
remote and covered with countless silver specks that leaped about
each other, crazily. And beneath, all was black oil, immeasurable
miles of thick black oil. He reflected that if he were to draw his
finger across the surface of it the imprint of his finger would
remain there a moment before the oil oozed in again and it all
became once more a flawless jet mirror. Only when he leaned
over the side and saw the sprays of white and silvery phosphorus
flashing up from the cutting prow, was it all an immense Pacific
Ocean of water, as no other sea.

Wonderful, just standing up here by yourself, steering a ship ...
guess I'll chuck kahludge and snap in with this Navy business.
Wonder when Luani'll be coming up this evening.... One day
maybe I'll be able to play the uke like that ... it's queer about

him ... I never did feel that way before, kinda funny feeling all over.... Glad I don't have to share one of them bunks with Ma.... Golly, if she knew I was standing here driving her to California ... she's snoring down there right now....

John was interrupted in his reflections by a light step behind him. He started, looked round, and came face to face with the boy who had danced behind Mrs Awahnee and afterwards lifted from his mother's neck the *lei* of white carnations.

"Hi, Luani," said John, "I was just thinking of you."

Luani smiled down at him, his eyes half-closed. They always seemed to be like that, those eyes, veiled by long black lashes: even when wide open they gave the impression of being half-asleep. His skin was the colour of ivory stained with age—cool, without blemish; and the long black hair that he never brushed fell about his head and face in sweeping waves of beautiful disorder.

Approaching John, he laid a brown hand on the boy's shoulder. At the moment of contact, John felt again that sensation of tightness in his chest, as though something were moving swiftly under the skin, from one nipple to the other. It made him catch his breath.

They stood together, silent, gazing into the inky blueness.

"Shall I play?" asked Luani. Acutely aware of an intense intimacy in the Hawaiian's voice, John wished to return the compliment in a similar tone, but found himself incapable.

"Sure," he said, "play *Aloha lio*, Luani." But he felt ashamed of the coldness of his Western voice. Outside he heard the night-watch tramp up and down, up and down. Queer how he heard those steps so clearly just now. The air was like blue velvet out there, the world the moon shining silver on blue velvet, a silver sheen on dark blue velvet.

The Hawaiian brushed his fingers across the ukulele strings, once, twice: then he ceased, and glanced up. "Maybe I won't," he said.

"Don't, if you're tired," John said. He felt immediately delighted at his words; they came on impulse; and he considered the tone improved.

"Oh, I ain't tired, John. I was thinking." He spoke slowly, in a soft voice, as though men lived a thousand years and were happy every day of them. "I was just thinking—oh, crazy thoughts. Always at sea I think crazy thoughts. I was born at sea, John—in a sampan, off Papeete. My mother and father brought me up to Hawaii when I was a kid of two. So I'm Tahitian really, I suppose. I've been always on the sea. With sailing and fishing folk mostly. I love the sea, I could never leave it. I love the sun. I could never live where it's cold and rainy as they say it is other places. I loved to go swimming with the boys in the early morning on the island, before folks were out. When the sun was just up over the horizon we'd run out: we'd not dress ourselves more than put flowers in our hair and grease our heads a bit, then we'd swim out from under the palms of the Almoalini, with our boards, surfing—before folks were about, to watch us. All of us youngsters, oh, we had a fine life, John."

"I know," murmured John. He was surf-bathing with Luani.

The Hawaiian fell silent. Then, with his eyes on the boy, he began to play a few bars of an island song. Presently he ceased and went on in his low musical voice. "I was thinking. I was thinking maybe some day...oh, you can't tell...but...hey, John," he said quickly, "just what are you going to do, where are you going?"

"Me?" said John, startled. "Why, Mother and me, we're going to Carolina, bury Dad and all that. I told you last——"

"Ya, ya, I know that. I mean, what'll you be doing after that—what kind of a life——?"

"Dunno. Why, what d'you mean?"

"Oh, I was just thinking, see. Crazy thoughts. Always at sea I think crazy thoughts. I was wondering, really, will I ever be seeing...seeing you again after..." The voice faltered. John felt his chest tighten so that he had to catch his breath. He stared out in front of him, his hand unsteady on the wheel, feeling both infinitely sorrowful and incomprehensibly happy. He shivered in the warmth.

Suddenly Luani began to hum, then to sing, softly, slowly, his voice sounding both far away and very close.

> *"Let not our friendship fade with these flowers. . . .*
> *Cast upon these saddened seas. . . ."*

"Luani," John murmured, "you've changed the words."

Thoughts ran wild in his head, without form or sequence.

"I like mine better," he heard Luani say.

"How did you come to know those words, Luani?"

"Oh, I've known 'em a long time," the Hawaiian said. "I know the words of many island songs, in my language and yours. I change 'em sometimes, just as I'm feeling, see."

John wanted to add: "And as I'm feeling too." But he only murmured, "I know."

> "*I want you again to see our showers . . .*
> *Our sun, and the laughter we'd have—with these!*"

After a moment's silence John felt the hand on his shoulder again. In that instant he made, for his age, a very remarkable decision. And he knew that nothing short of death would prevent him from carrying it out.

The two boys looked at each other without speaking. Then Luani turned away and began to dance, accompanying himself by humming:

Ka-wah-na-lee, hehoo!

IV

In the intervals of his playing, voices rose up to them from Poynton's cabin. Poynton himself was sitting half-dressed, sweating, on the edge of the lower bunk. Behind him lay a young man, stretched, his face in his hands. And in the middle of the room, on fixed, revolving chairs, sat Mrs Crane and another woman. These three comprised the adult passenger list of the *Malukai*.

"You'd better get it out, lad—better get it off your chest. It'll make it easier for you. . . ."

Poynton hesitated and reached out for his glass of *okolihau*. He emptied it down his throat and licked his thick lips. The sound of his hand brushing across his unshaven chin reminded Mrs Crane of her dead husband. This thought caused her to shut her eyes, and when she opened them again she looked into the face of Emily de Ketteville. Mrs Crane had learned her name half an hour after the *Malukai* had set sail. She had just glanced at her, smiled, and five minutes later, sitting next to her in the ship's saloon, she had put her hand on the other woman's bare arm, stared solemnly into her brown eyes and said: "What *is* your name, honey?"

Emily de Ketteville was ten years younger than Mrs Crane, and in as many years—during which she had lived for the most part in Hollywood—she had made a small fortune, lost more than her first husband's large one, married another in Hilo, and was now hurrying away from him in search of she knew not what, but certainly not another man.

"*Men!*" she had just whispered to Mrs Crane. "My dear, don't ever mention that word to me!" And she had tapped her flat chest and rolled her eyes. She had magnificent brown eyes, a beautiful skin, and a deep, husky voice.

Inwardly purring, Mrs Crane wished officers' cabins had sofas, and demanded a drink.

"It must have been a ghastly business," Poynton was saying. "Poor kid, tell us though, it's better." He laid his hand on the head of the young man on the bunk.

"What's that, Mrs Crane? Why, sure. Say when."

"That's just dandy," breathed Mrs Crane, lifting her glass.

"What about you, Miss de Ketteville?"

"Emily to you, Officer," She flashed her bright teeth, shook her sleek blonde head. "I never was one to look a gift horse——" she said, and took a glass.

The two women looked at each other, smiled and, lifting their glasses, silently drank.

"Lord, but it's hot!"

"You said it," sighed Mrs Crane, and cast her eyes in the direction of the young man on the bunk. For the first time that evening he lowered his hand, revealed his face. Mrs Crane had not seen him before, and she received a shock. The face, though clearly young, was dead-white, cadaverous, with black hollows scooped out from under the grey eyes which peered up at Poynton in a frightened, hunted manner.

"Where is he now?" The voice sounded stricken with grief.

Mrs Crane, reminded once more of her dead husband, thanked her stars she hadn't been present at his death. All eyes turned on the young man.

"He's all right, kid," said Poynton soothingly, "don't worry about that. He's down in the——"

"*Down!*" The young man sat up, his eyes staring. Then he sank back against the pillow, put a hand to his face. Mrs Crane longed to leave the room but saw no easy way of doing so.

"Brave, kid—be brave," said Poynton, tenderly, laying his hand on the boy's knee. "Would you like to tell us now? Here, take this," and he handed the boy a drink. He took it, looked slowly round the room, gazed at a chart on the wall, then drank the spirit. His eyes brightened a little. "Damn it," he said, with an effort at a smile, "seems I'm nothing but a bore to you folks. I'd best clear——"

All three interrupted him with some form of protest. Poynton laid his hands on the boy's knee.

"You're all mighty kind," said the young man gratefully. He leaned forward on the bunk, drew up his knees, gripping them with his hands. As he began to speak a lock of hair fell over his forehead and he seemed to be seeing something infinitely sad and far away.

"As you probably know," his voice sounded dull and hopeless, "my name's Ernest Bate. My folks were from Colorado. Good, decent folks too, I guess. Though I never knew my dad. Just disappeared, they say, in Chicago; he never came back that I know of. Mother brought me up as best she could. . . ."

Bate hesitated and his lower lip quivered. He shut his eyes, to open them again as strains of an island song came filtering down from the bridge.

"Gimme another," he said, without moving his head.

Poynton reached out and half-filled four glasses from a bottle on the folding desk. He poured water from a jug and handed them round. Bate took his glass without moving his eyes, and drank. In the silent cabin smoke hung in blue static clouds above their heads; from outside came the faint faraway music of the ukulele, the deep throb of the engines, and the swish-swishing of the water as the ship purred its slow way east.

"Mother," Bate continued, "did her best. There wasn't much cash . . . no other kids, though—only me. The nearest town was Steamboat Springs, up above Denver, some two hundred miles up, not far from Rocky Mountain National Park. It's swell there. The tall firs and the mountains seemed like the walls of the world. But it was lonesome for mother. She had only me. No real friends. Wouldn't marry again, I guess, however long she'd . . . It got a bit lonesome for me, too. Mother worked in a store in Steamboat till I'd gone to day school, then she went down with pleurisy— and I had to quit. After that I was taken on at the store. I must have been around fourteen then. I wasn't even at that time—quite like other kids, not real natural. I'd get bouts of the blues, then it would be hell. I didn't get along any too well with the fellows at day school, kinda liked being on my own. Moochin' about. Though I was glad to have work in the store, I didn't take to the life indoors. But I stuck it, for mother's sake. She was never the same after that first sickness, took to . . . she drank a bit, stuff wasn't good either. She began staying in bed, getting up to sneak out for it, then going back again. Must have been just about that time I fell in with . . . with . . ."

Bate cleared his throat and passed a hand over his forehead. He thrust out his glass and sighed. Poynton filled it.

"You sure had it bad as a kid," he said encouragingly.

"*I'll* say he did," breathed Mrs Crane, her eyes full.

"Well," Bate went on with his eyes closed, "he was the finest-looking youngster I ever set eyes on, Al Jennings. My age about, with a head of long blond hair. We worked alongside each other for three years. Al never did get on with his folks; his mother was a wild hooligan of a woman, Irish; and his dad—they never could stand the sight of one another, he and Al. But if there was ever a kid with a heart and a dime to spare, Al'd be that one. When I was all in, he'd come along home with me and help look after mother. She was bad then, with the booze on her. Raving most days. After a while Al came to live with us. And I guess it was she who started him on the bottle. Anyway, he got fired from the store. I quit too. Then the trouble began. We didn't know what to do. No dough, no job—nothing, and mother raving. Well, one night, a night with no wind and a chunk of a moon, Al and me goes downtown swearing to God we'll not drink a drop, we'll just walk a bit we said, the night was so good. We sit outside a drugstore, on the sidewalk, when a tough-looking guy stops and says he's going down to Los Angeles to look for a job in the movies, so come along he says, jump a couple of trains and there we'll be inside of a week. He has a few dollars on him he says, and we're flat—maybe you know how it is to be that way, you do things then and don't think overmuch, you always think it can't be much worse than it is. It's better that way, maybe. It doesn't always do to think, I've found. Well, before we have time to say no we are in a bar, half lit with some bad stuff—but feeling pretty good. We'd not much in our stomachs, so it came quick. There's a coloured guy there playing an accordion, and though we weren't the dancing kind, I recall now feeling glad there weren't enough dames to go round . . . so Al and me ups and dances and the other fellows the same. And afterwards, sitting at a table, Al looks at me hard and says: 'Ern, we'll quit, eh?' And I feels—Jesus, don't know just how to say the way I felt—but I know I was mighty happy when I says straight out, 'Al, I'll go where you go, to hell with the world!' And Al puts his hand over the table, looks at me, and I take it. 'For keeps?' I says, and he grips my hand. 'Sure thing, kid,' he says, and I know he meant it."

Bate stopped and asked for another drink. Poynton passed the bottle round. No one spoke. The room was dense with smoke.

"Well," he went on, "we do quit, that morning, with the tough guy, but he's left us before we've gotten into L.A. We were there for two years, together, Al and me. Bad years they were, too. Work was hard to come by. Eight months we were in a lumber-yard. Slept out most of the summer. I sent what I could to mother. I went on sending months after she'd gone. I only heard of her going by chance, and I took to the booze again. Al did his best for me, then fell too. Things were mighty bad. We'd fight a lot when we were right out. But somehow—so long as we had each other—someways nothing seemed so bad it couldn't be worse. But we were in a mess. We'd no steady work, couldn't get it. At last we went on the road, headed for San Francisco, picking up odd jobs, lifting in stores when we were flat, but when we'd got up again we couldn't seem to lay off the darned booze. Then—in 'Frisco it happened. Al fell in with a dame.... Hell, pass the bottle. Thanks.... A fine-looking girl she was too, worked in the kitchen of the Mount Perkins Hotel. But it broke me up. I couldn't take that. He'd never done anything like that before, see. Kinda killed something in me. I never—never ... felt that way myself, and he ... why, he never let on to me he did, so ... I didn't know till then just how I felt about Al. Christ, if only he'd gone then ... But when you know he's likely to be hanging about on the other side of the world, round the corner or in the next room, and he's the guy you've spent your life with, known hunger and happiness and sickness with, been down and out with, the fellow that knows the number of hairs on your head—well, that's hard to grin at. Call me what you like —I was just about all in when one morning I knew he'd quit for ever. All he left was a note—I have it in my coat here——"

He hesitated, put his hand to his breast pocket, then drained his glass and lighted a cigarette without raising his eyes. The two women shifted in their chairs. Poynton refilled their glasses.

"It just says: 'Got to go. Can't face you, boy. God bless.' That was all. I really don't know what I did all the next year, all this last year that is, till—Jesus!—only a couple of weeks ago today! I hardly know myself. I do know I was in 'Frisco most of the time. I know I am in 'Frisco when the cops find me a couple of weeks ago tonight and give me the cable from Honolulu saying, 'All alone. Al.' "

"Two weeks tonight—in San Francisco!" All three listeners exclaimed at once. "Two weeks, kid!" repeated Poynton. "Why you can't have been on the island more than a few hours!"

"Just seventeen hours before I come aboard here," said Bate, with emphasis.

"My, my!" sighed Mrs Crane, perspiring.

"What do you know about that!" exclaimed Emily de Ketteville, which for her was not a flippant remark because she had seldom been so profoundly moved. "Me," she sighed to herself, "me with all those men behind me, but I never felt *that* way about anyone." ... She glanced at Mrs Crane, who smiled back at her, intimately, then dabbed her eyes.

"Go on, kid," urged Poynton. His feelings for Bate astounded him, and he wished he had shaved. He was aware, too, that he was not far from drunk and that he would soon have to go up to the bridge.

"Well, guess I'll cut how I got to the island, but I did, and I found Al." Bate suddenly started to speak louder, faster. "Yes, I found Al. I'd cabled; he was at the boat. But, Jesus, I hardly knew him for Al. He was—I guess you know the natives on the islands, brown as boards, wearing next to nothing. Well, that was my Al, with a scarlet sash round his waist and one of them big red flowers in his bleached hair. I wouldn't have known him only he smiled, but when he smiled I knew him all right and he leapt at me and I at him, and—God, I don't mind saying that was the happiest minute of my young life.

"He had a little car waiting—yeah, he had made some cash—and we raced over the crater, up over the green mountain that's covered with flowering trees, down to Kailua Bay and on to Tawanaloa, and there was his shack with fields of pineapples behind it and in front of it long palms leaning out over the shores of Kiawahnoo, close to the biggest breakers I ever set eyes on. Gee, I took one look at that water, Al caught me looking, and I had my clothes off and both of us in the ocean as quick as I'm trying to tell you what . . . what happened then.

"Though I guess there . . . there ain't a great deal more to tell. And if I skip some things I saw and felt in the next few minutes, maybe you'll forgive and understand. . . .

"Al was a wonderful swimmer: he was through the first breaker like a flying fish—with his head down and his long gold hair thrown back over his neck, in one leap he was through, near out of sight—and up, throwing himself into the next, like a porpoise, no effort, hardly seeming to move, yet gaining yards on me every time he leapt.

"I can swim—not too bad, either. I had a job once caddying on a golf course near Monterey and we'd swim there on the shore every morning—yea, I can swim, but I'd never seen breakers like them, and there was I trying to jump the crest of them, over the top and down as they came booming and rushing in on me from beyond there where Al was springing and leaping like a great shining salmon.

"Jesus . . . he'd gone out of my sight when the cry came. That cry—God, I never heard a cry like that, sent a shiver right through my body, down into my stomach. At first I couldn't find my voice, then I shouted back, and looked, ducking through the breakers and jumping high in the air between, to catch sight of him—but nothing, nothing more, not a sound, not a being in sight, nothing but those waves plunging at me and knocking me down.

"I went crazy, I tell you—and started in to holler. But not a sound above the crashing sea. Then—mad—I leapt head down into the shining breakers and struck out, demented with fear.

"I remember nothing now, till I was away beyond the last of the waves, and then I began to dive. . . . Folks, I'll never forget. Never again will I swim in the sea. The most terrible thing in the world the sea, never again will I go. . . .

"Did you ever see a drowned man? Did you ever see a body's lungs filled beyond a gasp with water, the face inflated, eyes staring ready to pop, mouth agape, hair flowing like seaweed—and all of it, the body I mean, upside down, the legs pointing up?

"That was the way Al was, the body I'd known as well as my own half my young life. . . ."

Tears of perspiration and tears from his eyes rolled down Bate's face; he had talked himself into a frenzy; his hands and voice shook as he resumed his story in the silent cabin.

"I dived again and caught him and clutched him to me, still warm in my arms, and up Al came with me to the surface, a dead weight. . . . I don't know how I got him back, I don't know. . . . Christ, why the hell did you?" Shouting, he raised his head, and those in the room started at sight of his face. For he was staring wild-eyed, at Poynton, with a look of hatred in his eyes, his body bent forward, taut, as though ready to attack the man. Poynton leaned back, scared.

"Why the hell did you bring it all back?" Bate hissed. "It's nothing to do with you; Al was *mine, mine*! Tell me, tell me now, where is he, *where is he*? He's *down*, you said, eh? Down, nailed into that darned box, eh—nailed *down*, eh?"

He was up on his knees, shaking, moving towards Poynton.

"Steady, lad, steady! I know it's bad, but he's all right now, lad."

Poynton sat still and put out his hand. The two women had risen, stood gaping, with linked arms, swaying slightly in the hot, smoke-filled cabin.

"He's nailed down, my Al—down under!" Bate's voice rose to a scream. Then he gave a wild despairing cry, and fell back, moaning. Poynton jumped to the boy's head, lifted it, put a cushion under it, stroked the long hair.

"Try not to take it too bad," he soothed. "Poor lad, there. . . . My, you been mighty brave, just try to keep it up lad—till we get ashore, then we'll see, eh—*you and me* . . . eh?" He lowered his face over that of the boy's. A hand, trembling, closed over his —and the two women, smiling sadly on the men, then benignly at each other, swayed slowly out of the room.

The cool velvet breath of the night caught them. They inhaled deeply, sighed, and walked up into the bows, leaning on one another. They stood silent, staring into the darkness. Then Mrs Crane cocked her head on one side, raised one fat finger. "Shish!" she whispered. And they stood, listening.

Ka-wah-na-le, hehoo!

The soft strains of the island song came floating down to them from the bridge, mingling with the throb of the engines and the everlasting swish-swishing sound of the water spewing up from the shearing prow.

Awa-he-hoo!

The benign smile crept over Mrs Crane's face. The presence of Mrs Awahnee was wonderfully, intimately close: she loomed up very big, and black, in her full white cotton dress. . . . Mrs Awahnee. . . . !

And slowly Mrs Crane withdrew her arm from round her companion, raised it before her, the fingers hanging limp. Her head fell back a little, her hair tumbled and hung on her shoulders; the lashes closed over her eyes, touched her cheeks. She bent one knee, raised the lifted arm above her head, lowered her face to one side.

Emily de Ketteville stood still, staring. "God, if she ain't going to *hula!*"

Through the thick plate-glass window John looked down on the jet form of his mother silhouetted against the inky blueness of the night. He watched her hips as they began to move, slowly. Her arms were over her head, the hands turned inwards like the heads of cobras. Slowly, face to face with the younger woman, she cast her head from side to side.

"Luani," murmured John, "play a bit faster." And the music behind him grew louder, a little less slow. Mrs Crane's voice rose up to them. Then John saw her lower her arms, thrust them straight from her, till the hands were on a level with the other's face, the fingers pointing at her.

Ka-wah-na-lee, hehoo!

Suddenly John was aware of his mother being mauled by Emily de Ketteville. The two women were at grips.

"My love," whispered Luani, close to John's ear, "they—must come with us, too."

John looked up at him and noticed, unquestioning, that his eyes were filled with tears.

"I know," he murmured.

At that moment Poynton appeared—arm-in-arm with Bate—and took the wheel.

Queeeeeeerrrrk—kwuck kwuck kwuck kwuck kwuck—queeeee-eeeeerrrr!

It was dawn.

The Woman Who Was Loved

THE DAY AFTER Miss Higgins had gone, nothing remained of her but her tennis racket. Ned and Miriam had found it in the attic— a soiled, slightly warped thing with a rubber grip, on which the now departed governess had inked her name in large square letters: ETHEL B. HIGGINS.

"It's a pity she got engaged to Dr Stimson," Mrs Turnbull said to her husband when the car had carried the woman away. "She was a good sort. It'll be hard to find a better."

"I don't like governesses who marry," grunted Mr Turnbull.

"She gave the children a wonderful time," his wife continued. "There's no doubt about that. I do hope they won't be too unhappy. Miriam's such—such a sensitive child. Under*neath*."

"Children," mocked the father. "They don't care."

"You never can tell," Mrs Turnbull said knowingly. "They were awfully fond of her. I wonder what the new one will be like. I wish I'd been able to see her. It's such a risk taking them on recommendation, and at such short notice. Women like Miss Higgins," she sighed, "don't grow on every tree."

Bored with the subject, Mr Turnbull relapsed into silence. The name of Miss Higgins, indeed, might never have been mentioned again had it not been for the tennis racket, which Ned and Miriam brought immediately to their parents. Mr and Mrs Turnbull were in the dining-room, sitting over their breakfast, when the children burst in.

"Higgy's left her racket behind!" they both shouted at once.

"Shish, children," admonished their mother, a finger to her lips. "Daddy's trying to read the paper."

Mr Turnbull peered over the top of the *Morning Post*. "Time the new governess came," he growled. "Never heard such an infernal din."

"Oh," asked Ned and Miriam simultaneously, "when's she coming?"

"Tomorrow evening," Mrs Turnbull said.

"What's her name?"

"Miss Whitmore."

"What's she like? How old is she?"

"I don't know, Miriam."

"On spec!" Ned said.

Mr Turnbull cleared his throat with irritation.

"Now leave the racket here," said his wife briskly, "and run up and clean your teeth. I can see you haven't touched them yet."

"And then what shall we do?" asked Ned for the fifth time since Miss Higgins' departure.

Mr Turnbull laid down the *Morning Post*. "God dammit," he shouted, with all the authority he could command, "did you hear what your mother said?"

The children looked away. Then, very slowly, shuffling their feet, they slunk from the room.

The periods between governesses—the family averaged two a year—were not easy days for Mrs Turnbull, for then she had to take charge of her children, a task for which she knew herself to be unfit and which embarrassed both her and them. It had been the mother's habit to see her children regularly three times a day: first at breakfast, when Ned and Miriam came to say good morning; then at eleven o'clock, during lessons, when she called on them in the schoolroom—a duty always the most painful for her to perform, for in the presence of the current governess she found herself invariably dumb. Each morning as she walked down the long corridor to the large bare schoolroom (which Mr Turnbull had had specially built "to keep out the din"), she would ask herself: "Now what shall I say today? I must think of something new." Yet, when the moment came, when, closing her eyes with embarrassment, she knocked, and shyly, carefully turned the handle of the schoolroom door, her imagination refused to function and for four long years the mornings of Ned, Miriam, and all their governesses had been interrupted with the same unanswerable greeting: "Well, how are we getting along today?"

The third visit, for which there were two alternatives, took place between the hours of six and eight. Should the parents themselves have visitors, then Ned was dressed in a tunic of white or blue, Miriam in muslin of the same colour, and the two "came down" to say How-d'you-do and eventually good night. But in the ordinary course of events, Mrs Turnbull would "come up" for this purpose, entering what was still known as the Day Nursery with that diffidence people reveal when in a strange house they open doors in search of a toilet. Once inside, she would bid good evening to the governess, and then, no matter what the hour, turn to her children and say: "Now hurry up, both of you, it's long past your bed-time!"

While they prepared themselves for sleep, she would gaze out of the window, stare at the view, move a stray toy from one place to another, remark upon Ned's untidiness, the prospects of the weather, the length of the children's hair, and occasionally whisper into their ears a question as to whether they had "gone somewhere properly this morning, dear." Finally, when Ned and Miriam were in their pyjamas and could think of no means of postponing any longer the last moments of their day, she would move into the Night Nursery where, with a peremptory "Now then," she would lower herself into the one armchair, lean forward, cross her hands in her lap, and close her eyes. From the habit of years the children recognized this performance as the signal for each in turn to kneel at their mother's feet, place their elbows on her knees, lock their fingers, and proceed to mumble two quite unintelligible prayers, followed by a smothered recitation of the hymn: *Gentle Jesus, meek and mild.* . . .

This always embarrassing duty accomplished, the mother would rise and follow them to the narrow twin beds, and there lean over and lay her face for a moment on their foreheads, pat their curls, bid good night to the governess in the Day Nursery, and leave the room as a burglar might escape from the scene of a carefully planned crime.

In one respect only was Mrs Turnbull's position less painful when a governess was not present: there was the absence of that ever-critical eye keeping watch in silence on her helplessness. It was never long, however, before realization of this fact served only as a reminder of her failings: her lack of contact with, and control over, the children infamous Nature had allowed her to bring into the world. Though unconscious of the fact that she behaved towards her own offspring as she would have towards another's, she did realize that they, aware of her helplessness, offered her no respect; and that she, in consequence, gained no authority. Harsh words had little effect, while her last resort, the threat of their father's name, produced only silence—a stubborn, unconquerable resentment, commonly known as "the sulks." When they disappeared between meals, she did not know where they were. She went out into the garden and in a high-pitched, bird-like voice, cried between her hands: "Cooo-eeee! Cooo-eeee!" During the ensuing silence she would stamp her foot, then call out their names: "Ned, where are you? Mirry—aaam!" As often as not they were within earshot, sitting in the branches of their favourite tree, the enormous lime behind the tennis court, giggling into fists stuffed between their jaws.

In the evenings, when she came to "see the children in their bath" (a duty she now performed only on Saturday nights), they would scream, at first with laughter and then with anger, crying out to her that no nurse or governess had ever washed them "that way." It was here in the bathroom, when alone with and close to her children in their nakedness, that the full realization of the gulf between herself and them made itself manifest as at no other place or time. She would stand over them and, to the accompaniment of the hissing sound made by grooms when curry-combing a horse, scrub their backs and legs and arms and necks in such a way that the soap splashed over their faces and seeped into their eyes. And when they howlingly protested, guarding themselves against her treatment by covering their smarting eyes with their hands, she would suddenly feel afraid, as though the two screaming children in the tub were not of her own flesh and blood, but some strange reptiles intent on doing her harm.

"Out you get!" she'd cry. "A little soap won't kill you! Get out and dry yourselves, before I go and fetch Daddy!" To which threat they reacted as they always did, by sulking silently. Beyond this, her behaviour had no consequences, bore no fruit; and the prospect of the next governess, of Miss Higgins' successor, of the return to normal—without which children, like adults, can rarely live content—was welcomed as much by Ned and Miriam as by the man and woman whose private incomes alone made the procession of governesses possible.

Yet not one of them was prepared for the shock created by Miss Whitmore. No one bearing the remotest resemblance to the new arrival had ever been seen inside the Turnbull home. At sight of the drawn yellow face, the veined and sickle-shaped cushions under the mournful eyes; the poor, lifeless, mouse-coloured hair raked up from the lean neck and rolled into a wad under the tiny hat of black straw—at sight of her the children, after a moment's incredulous stare, turned in their tracks and bolted. Not until they had reached the Nursery and slammed the door did they give vent to their astonishment and laughter. "The old hag!" choked Ned, throwing himself, convulsed, into the one armchair.

Although mirth was the last sensation Miss Whitmore's arrival created in the parents, it was nevertheless Mr Turnbull who, when the butler had left the room during dinner that night, uttered the remark which he continued to repeat long after the woman who caused it had turned her back for ever on its author. "I'm afraid, my dear," he half-whispered to his wife, "that Miss Whitmore is not a product of your agency's top drawer!"

But the outward appearance of the new governess, as the children were the first to discover, was far from the woman's only peculiarity. The second shock came when she spoke. From the lined and bony throat, encircled by a string of black beads, her voice came booming out, its tone as deep and powerful as that of a man. What Miss Whitmore said, however, punctually at ten o'clock on the first morning, proved no less unexpected.

"Put away all those books!" she thundered, and the command echoed round the schoolroom walls.

The children stared. They stood, opposite each other at the table, paralysed, dumb. Put away their books—those thumbed and tattered primers from which all their lessons had been learned! They glanced up at the woman, then furtively back at each other, with wide, bewildered eyes.

At the head of the table the thin frail figure in black, the worn yellow hands clasped over her meagre stomach, stood motionless. The children could not move.

"Dummies!" boomed Miss Whitmore. "Those books, I said! Away with them! Out with evil memories!"

Slowly, with the half-hearted motions of those faced with the incomprehensible, the children began stacking their worn volumes one on top of the other.

"Listen!" came the bark again. "I'll have you run up and down that terrace if you can't move quicker than that!"

But it was Miss Whitmore who moved first—moved so fast, in fact, so surprisingly, that the children stepped back bewildered, to watch, with consternation quickly giving way to awe, the long, bony hand shoot out and grab the books from the table. Fascinated, they stared at the woman as she then pitched each book with apparent recklessness but astonishing aim, into the empty fireplace.

"That," cried Miss Whitmore, when she had cleared the table, "is why you're dummies! You're bored, that's the trouble with you! No one should ever be bored!"

Still the children revealed no visible sign that they had heard or understood. Perplexed by what they had just been witness to, they stood gaping into the fireplace, at their thumbed and ink-stained books and papers—the living proof of all the facts and figures laboured over in that room—when suddenly Miss Whitmore's hand came down on the table with such violence that they were shaken, finally, to attention.

"Dummies!" she boomed again. "You're still asleep! Out you go onto the terrace! Out of this room! Out into God's air!" And turning from them, she steered herself stiffly, arms rigid, towards the french window. Gripping the brass handle, she opened the door.

"Now then!" she commanded, as though she were addressing a couple of puppies. "Out you go!"

The children followed her at a respectful distance. Then, drawing near, they sidled round her in the doorway, stepped out on to the stone porch. At the sound of their sandals on the stone, Miss Whitmore lowered her eyes.

"Shoes!" she cried, clutching Ned by the arm. "Shoes! Off with the beastly things! Away with one of man's silliest inventions!"

Still slow to comprehend the unexpected, Ned and Miriam stared first at their feet, then quickly at each other, finally up at her. At last, with the infinite precaution of those who fear to be made fools of, they began unclasping the straps of their sandals.

"Hurry, young man!" Miss Whitmore said, her hand still on his arm. "What's that they call you? Ned?" Suddenly she let out a chuckle of mirth. "Ridiculous!" she cried, her voice breaking, high. "That's what they call the donkey! Your name's Edward— perfectly good name. Now then, both of you, run!" and clapping her hands, she made a mock rush at them.

Stepping gingerly out on to the gravel, they took to their bare heels and, like bolting colts, tore along the terrace as though to prove to her that however inactive their brains might be, their limbs at least were in a very different condition.

Behind them, unseen, alone, the woman stood still, while there passed over her faded face an almost imperceptible transforma- tion: the pale lips slowly parted; the mournful eyes receded behind their surrounding web of lines, and a filmy substance rose and made them shine. Miss Whitmore was smiling.... But in- stantly the mask—the creases, the eyes, the lips—fell back into place, and she raised her hands to shield her mouth. "About— turn!" she thundered.

Halting near the end of the terrace, the children swung round, lifting their feet high at the sudden pain. As they drew up before her, flushed and panting, her eyes went over them, from head to toe. "Keep away from shoes," she said, "and you may grow up at least with decent feet. . . ! Now come in."

They followed her into the schoolroom. "Put those beastly things away!" she commanded.

Ned picked up the sandals and placed them on top of the piano.

"Now then," Miss Whitmore said, as she walked towards the table, "next thing you've got to do is to forget everything you ever learned!"

But before the children had had time to reach their seats, there came a faint knock upon the door and Mrs Turnbull stepped silently into the room.

"Well," her tongue said, "how are we getting along today?" But instead of advancing farther, as was her custom, she stood still on the threshold, staring mystified at her children as they prepared to take their chairs at the table.

"What on earth," she asked at last, "have you done with your sandals?"

They paused in the act of sitting down, then glanced, not for sympathy, but defensively, at their mother, at their feet, and finally—with the look of those who share a secret—at each other.

But Miss Whitmore had already risen from her chair. With one hand on its back, and the other fingering the black beads at her neck, she turned to Mrs Turnbull.

"Children," she said, as though quoting some well-worn maxim, "children should refrain from wearing shoes until bare feet cause them embarrassment."

Miss Whitmore sat down.

Ned and Miriam's eyes met, exchanging what no one but they knew were smiles. Mrs Turnbull, her face a study of astonishment, continued to stare. Then, as though someone had prodded her from behind, she turned and escaped rapidly from the silent room.

At lunch that day she said to her husband: "What do you think I found the children doing in the schoolroom this morning?"

Mr Turnbull hunched his shoulders, shook his head.

"Walking about the room in bare feet!" cried his wife. "Ned's sandals were on the piano—on the *piano!*"

"Peculiar," grunted Mr Turnbull.

Such was not the reaction his wife had desired. "If only that were all," she added quickly. "What d'you think that—that Whitmore woman said? Children, she said, without so much as giving me a name, oughtn't to wear shoes until they want to! Did you ever hear such cheek?"

"She sounds about as awful as she looks," observed her husband; and he added, "I never saw an Englishwoman look like that before!"

His wife breathed a sigh of satisfaction. She said, "I was thinking of the poor children." Then, pausing to let the subterfuge sink in, she murmured, "Poor darlings, they looked so unhappy. If only Miss Higgins hadn't—hadn't fallen in love!"

"Well, one thing's certain," said Mr Turnbull, with rare heartiness, "no one's going to fall in love with *her!*"

Because children are more adaptable than adults, because their memories are short and they are not burdened with responsibility or convention, Miss Whitmore at the end of a week was little more strange to Ned and Miriam than had been any of her predecessors at a similar period in their reigns. They accepted her violence, her code of values, as they would have a new home, or as, after a period of time short enough to shock the thoughtless, they would have accepted the death or disappearance of their father or their mother. The young are no less compassionate than their elders. Innocent, and therefore incapable of understanding the subtleties of hypocrisy, they live in the present, grieving only for the loss of those whom they sincerely love—a love, as often as not, bestowed upon a rabbit or a doll.

As the days passed it seemed quite natural, in fact, even perfectly sensible (as indeed it was) that this faded woman with the booming voice should fill their schoolroom hours with denunciations directed at everything that, by endless repetition and poring over primers, had previously been dinned into their heads. In language they could understand, she would inveigh not only against all accepted means of enlightenment, against textbooks, dictionaries, the practice of committing information to heart; but against false indulgence of the commoner human instincts: against the mania of acquisition, the hoarding of money, against the collecting of moths, butterflies and birds' eggs; against the hunting and shooting to death of wild animals; against the evil of ridicule ("Look into your own heart," she once boomed at them till they blushed, "before you laugh at another's face!")—and, above all, she would pound into them warnings against the danger of having being born an Englishman.

This last, they soon discovered, was Miss Whitmore's favourite subject. It was through it, in fact, that gradually her diatribes began to decrease and the mornings of invective to turn into monologues that led, at last, to horizons more familiar to the children, and thence to regions which, while geographically near, were in reality as remote from them as were the lives of those who spent their days there. The first sign that Miss Whitmore was about to alter the tenor of her verbal curriculum revealed itself one morning after she had been expounding her theories on what is known, among some adults, as the Myth of Racial Superiority, but which Miss Whitmore described as "all this nonsense about people in one country being better than those in another." She had just maintained, much to the children's surprise, that there was no such thing as an Englishman, when she suddenly broke off, rose from her chair, went upstairs, and returned with a book —an object so rarely used by her in the schoolroom that Ned could not conceal his desire to learn its title.

"Well, Edward," said Miss Whitmore, "I'm glad to see you don't believe curiosity is going to kill you any more than it did the proverbial puss! Curiosity is an excellent thing. So is this book. But that's not the reason I have it here. I brought it down because —just as I don't think you should go to church simply because others do—I don't want you to believe a word I say simply because I say it. I don't suppose I've uttered an original thought in my life. What's more, I doubt very much if you will, either. Well, anyway, the author of this book and I are great friends. We agree on most things. The fact that he died over two hundred years ago makes no difference. He was a man who said and believed what I've just told you: that there's no such thing as an Englishman—and don't you ever forget it. You happen to have been born of an old and wealthy family. Well, the sooner you forget that the better. This is what my friend had to say on that subject."

Raising her head and closing her eyes, Miss Whitmore was silent for a moment as though summoning her memory to obey her will. Then, in a low, steady voice, she solemnly recited:

> *Great families of yesterday we show,*
> *And lords whose parents were the Lord knows who.*

Miss Whitmore opened her eyes. "My Goodness!" she suddenly

cried, "write that down. . . ." While the children began hunting
for pencils and paper, she again closed her eyes.

Your Roman—Saxon—Danish—Norman English,

she quoted,

> *From this amphibious ill-born mob began*
> *That vain, ill-natured thing, an Englishman.*

"You can write that down too," Miss Whitmore said. And while
the children wrote, she slowly repeated the lines.

"Well now," she asked, as they finished, "shall I tell you who
my friend is? No, I won't. I'll tell you the title of one of his books."
And raising the volume in her hands, she stood it upright on the
table for them to see.

Both children exclaimed at once: "Robinson Crusoe!"

"So?" said Miss Whitmore, "then Mr Defoe is a friend of yours,
too?"

"Oh, yes!" cried Miriam.

"Oh, yes!" Ned repeated, "Hig—er—Miss Higgins gave us
Robinson Crusoe as a holiday task!"

"*Task!*" boomed Miss Whitmore, with a passionate energy that
still inspired them with awe. "What good a holiday if it has a
task in it? What good for that matter, to read about Man Friday
keeping himself alive on a desert island, if you can't boil an egg
to keep yourselves alive in a luxurious modern home?"

To which remark Ned, despite himself, let loose an irrepressible
snort of laughter. Whereupon Miss Whitmore, demanding to
know what was "funny about that," cuffed him over the head with
the palm of her hand, then dragged him off, convulsed between
laughter and astonishment, to the kitchen.

"All right, then," she said, planting him in front of the stove and
asking the flabbergasted cook for a saucepan and an egg, "all
right, Edward, boil this!"

"I—I can't, Miss Whitmore," stammered Ned, his face solemn
at last, his head lowered, and his feet scraping nervously at the
unfamiliar floor.

"Can't, eh!" snorted the woman; and while Ned watched, she proceeded to boil the water, then cook the eggs, which she and the children ate, later, for their lunch.

While Ned and Miriam were engrossed in a heated argument over Time and Consistency of Yolks (which Ned won because, as he said, "God dammit, I saw it happen, see!"), the elder Turnbulls were seated over another meal at the far end of the house. "What d'you think," asked Mrs Turnbull of her husband, "what d'you think Mrs West told me just now?"

Grunting, Mr Turnbull hunched his shoulders.

"That—that Whitmore burst into the kitchen, demanded a saucepan, and boiled some eggs!"

"Boiled some eggs!" repeated her husband, swallowing half a potato. "The woman's mad!"

"What's more, she said that poor little Ned had been dragged in there to watch. He was almost in tears, she said."

"Children," pronounced her husband pompously, "have no business in the kitchen."

"That's just what Mrs West said. In the middle of their lessons, too."

"I won't have a raving lunatic in the house," said Mr Turnbull with finality. "Not for another day. That woman should be certified."

"And do you know what she told Mrs West?" His wife lowered her voice as though she were about to confide to him a long-kept secret. "That one day the children will have to use their hands as well as their heads! She said that the days of governesses are numbered!"

"So far as she and we are concerned," cried Mr Turnbull, smacking his thigh with one hand and wiping his mouth with the other, "Miss Whitmore never spoke a truer word! It is for you, my dear, to see to that—at once!"

That evening, for the first time in several Saturdays, Mrs Turnbull mounted the stairs ostensibly to "see the children in their bath." She found them, to her surprise, alone—playing peacefully in the tub with a fleet of celluloid warships.

"Well," she said brightly, seating herself on a stool, "all alone?"

Her question was greeted with enquiring stares.

"Miss Whitmore!" said Mrs Turnbull in a tone of slight irritation. "Doesn't she come and see you in your bath?"

"Oh, no!" answered Ned and Miriam, as though the very suggestion were too novel to contemplate.

"But—well, hasn't she—ever?"

"Oh, no!" they repeated.

Mrs Turnbull rose to her feet. "Now, look here, children," she began in a tone that made Ned and Miriam exchange an apprehensive glance. "I want your—your honest opinion. You're"—she hesitated, out of her depth—"you're old enough now to tell me—what you think. Er—I'd like to know—do you—er—*like* Miss Whitmore?"

For several seconds the bath-tub water lay still; there was not an audible breath in the bathroom, not a sound throughout the house. Then Ned, with his head down and a splashing flourish of his arm, grabbed a warship and sent it spinning towards his sister. Miriam caught it and sent it spinning back.

"Ned! Miriam!" exclaimed their mother with an impatient stamp of her foot. "I'm asking you a question. Did you hear me? Stop playing with that—that toy!"

Miriam promptly held the warship under water, while Ned, covering a blind and wrinkled face with his hand, muttered: "She's all right."

Miriam slowly picked up a flannel and, without raising her head, started lathering it with soap. "Yes," she murmured, "she's all right."

"Well," said their mother, making small attempt to conceal her satisfaction, "it's pretty clear what *that* amount of enthusiasm means!" And with this, she pecked her children on the cheek and bid them good night.

The following morning, when Ned and Miriam came down to the schoolroom punctually at ten o'clock, Miss Whitmore was not at the table. "Beat the old girl this time," Ned said, and they settled down to wait. They pulled out some paper and started playing Noughts-and-Crosses. Then Miriam accused Ned of cheating and the game ended in a squabble.

Ned leaned back and yawned. "Perhaps she's ill," he said at last. "I'm going up to look."

"Me, too," Miriam said, and she followed her brother out of the room, up the stairs, past the Nursery, to the door of the Governess's Room. Outside, they stood still, their heads on one side, listening. They glanced at each other and stifled a desire to laugh. Then Ned raised a fist and knocked carefully on the door. When no answer came, he knocked again, louder. Then, quickly, as though half-expecting to be greeted by a corpse, he turned the handle and flung open the door. Before them, through closed windows, the sun blazed in on a spotless, uninhabited room.

They turned to each other on the threshold, their mouths open, their eyes wide. "Gone!" breathed Ned. Miriam said nothing.

Closing the door quietly behind them, they tip-toed away as though they had left someone sleeping there. Together, in silence, they passed along the corridor, down the stairs. They walked on silently through the schoolroom and out onto the terrace and from the terrace, never turning, they moved on soundlessly over the lawn of the tennis court, coming to a halt only when they had reached their favourite tree, the enormous lime. There, without a word, they climbed into its immense branches and sat down, hidden from one another by thick canopies of sweet-smelling leaves.

"Cooo-eeee!"

The high-pitched bird-like voice struck strangely across the country silence.

"Cooo-eeee!"

But still the children did not speak. Unknown to each other, tears were falling down their faces and their fists were stuffed between their jaws.

Next Door to Death

(To Kay Boyle)

THE FIRST I SAW of the hospital was the clean white ceiling of one of the rooms on the ground floor. That ceiling was without blemish but for a stain in one corner, and every detail of that stain I can still see better than I can see the features of my own face without a mirror. The Islanders called it the Chinese Hospital, for during the day the nurses were either Chinese, of Chinese extraction, or a blending of that great race with the Islanders. But the attending doctors were all from the States.

The man I had was yellow-faced with a long mauve scar down his left cheek, not at all my idea of a physician. He belonged, however, not to the hospital, but practised on his own; and among those who employed his services was the proprietor of the small hotel on the beach where I'd spent my first two nights before I fell ill and was forced to call him in. Vaguely I remember the sudden bright sunshine paining the sockets of my eyes, the heat of the sun after the room, the loud outside chatter of those mina birds in the palms, and then the shining blue-black head of a Filipino near to my face as his mighty little arms went about my waist and I was jerked up into the dark of a closed wagon.

I thought it must be evening, for a grey shadow seemed to be moving imperceptibly over the whiteness. I began to wonder where I was, thinking for a moment I was still on the ship that had brought me from San Francisco, when I remembered the scar-faced doctor had said something about a hospital. I was wondering would anyone come and take off these soaking pyjamas and dry the sweat from my body or would I make the seemingly great effort and do this alone, when near me I heard a low soft voice saying: "Well, how you feelin' now?" Then from where the voice had come a face appeared—one of the loveliest faces I'd ever seen, I said. I said that, and it was true, but I was soon to see so many similar faces that I find my memory holds but one or two differing sufficiently in that semi-Eastern beauty from any of the others that only these have remained, and will, singled out as sublime specimens of the human countenance.

All the face but the chin was shrouded in a cloud of hair so black that the creamy skin beneath and amidst it seemed in contrast as white and clear as the cap which appeared not so much like the concrete, tangible thing it was as some mirage-like halo of light finding its brightness, contrarily again, from those depths of darkness upon which it lay. When she came nearer she repeated her question and put the cold palm of her hand on the wet of my forehead.

"That's a bit of fever," she said softly, and I saw when she parted her lips, that were not Chinese lips but those of the Pacific Islanders, each full and red, that her rows of teeth were of the palest blue whiteness, without blemish from end to end, and straight, as though fashioned by a ruler in some steady, mortal hand. Yet, that they were not what nature gave her was as impossible to conceive as that her hair was not more to her head than is the canopy of the sky to a thunder-cloud.

I looked at the thin, jet-black wisps of eyebrows circling above the deep brown eyes, at the pallor of that skin between them and her cheeks, without discolour or a line of age, marvelling at the clear reality of her having been born that way.

"We'll change you first," she said, and she went out and came back with a basin of water and a long white sleeveless garment over her arm. She leaned over me till I smelled the scent whose origin I never discovered—a scent clean like lilies-of-the-valley— and with her small thin hands she laid back the sheets and peeled the soaking pyjamas from my body. When she had washed me with the warm water she tied the clean white garment around my neck. It was a long, blouse-like thing reaching to the knees, trouserless and sleeveless and made of cotton. I hated it, hated the look and the feel of it and not being able to get my arms out except through a slit that ran down the back.

"Horrid, isn't it?" she said, smiling. She spoke with that soft drawl of an American accent rarely heard in America. "But there —hospital rules. . . ."

I tried to smile, to show that I liked her, but no words would come into the fire of my mouth. Behind me I knew there was a window, and I wanted to see out, but I had neither the energy nor the courage to move.

"Now," she said, with the same smile, "you gimme your name an' address, eh?"

I gave her my name and that of the hotel on the beach.

"You live there?"

"Been there two days," I said.

"Hey, you kiddin' me," she said, and she smiled so beautifully I had to smile. "I mean where d'you live—your home—Antima, Paparato, eh?"

"No," I told her, "I don't live on the islands at all."

"Ah, you from the States then?"

"No," I said, "I'm from Europe."

"Europe! Eh, that's funny!" Her brown eyes opened wide.

"Why?"

"Why—I never met anyone from there. It's a long way, eh?"

"Hell of a long way," I said.

"Well, well," she sighed, "you mighty way from home!" And she eyed the chart as though she had no idea what to write on it. Slowly she shook her head, put the pencil between her teeth. Then quickly taking it out, she said: "Well, you better gimme address of friends here, eh?"

"I haven't any," I said. As I spoke the words I felt the first exquisite moment of self-pity, and my body went lax with wonderful hopelessness. "I haven't any," I repeated to myself, and for an instant the knowledge that I was the only person on the remote Pacific Islands without a friend or acquaintance seemed good in its utter truth.

"Haven't any!" I heard her exclaiming. "No friends! Hey, you kiddin' me?"

"No," I said abruptly, as though proud of the fact. "No, none."

I felt the heat come over me in great waves, the slow, unmistakable shivering fits, like rows of cold wet needles up and down my spine. I could feel the moisture rising in the palms of my hands, between my fingers, and my eyes coming aflame with fever. "No, sister," I said with a certain finality. "I'm travelling alone and I've no friends this side of New York City, and that's five thousand miles from here, as the crow flies."

"Well, just think o' that!" she said, and I did. "Five thousand mile! But you got father and mother, eh?"

"Oh, yes," I murmured with my eyes shut, "and brothers and sisters and aunts and cousins." I was tired, my body was burning and the light in the room seemed to be fading.

"Oh, that's all right then," I heard her say, "you gimme your father's address, then, eh?"

With a vision of my father sitting crouched over the desk in his London office, I told her his address, then had to spell it out to her, and when I told her it was the West Central section of London she began to giggle.

"My!" she laughed, "that is funny!"

But before she'd got it all I heard a male voice in the room. Opening one eye, I saw the scar-faced doctor standing at the end of the bed. The white garment was being untied at the back of my neck; the sweat was running cold on my scalp, a warm sponge going over me, the steely-pointed pain shooting down my back to my feet . . . my body was dry again, the skin burning only less hot than the heat in my eyes and mouth; there was a heavy ice-bag on my forehead, and now under my tongue I could feel the cold rod of a thermometer that seemed instantly to grow hot; the next moment I saw it was a poker aflame in a roaring fire.

I heard the doctor walk to the door. There he stopped and shouted back, "Can't stick you in a ward, young man—don't know what you've got—and you'll have to have a nurse tonight. Cost you six bucks!" Then he went.

"Just swallow this, then," a soft voice was saying. I swallowed, with two or three pills that were coals on the tongue, and very suddenly down I went, down—as though in a screaming mine-shaft—I and the bed and the room and the house and the island, into absolute blackness.

      ❈   ❈   ❈

That night was not dissimilar from those that followed: the effects of the daily drug would only deaden me and make my head feel as though some great weight were lying there, pinning it to the pillow; the permanent ice-bag became a mountainous rock. The nights were like silent ships moving in the darkness, tiny craft manned by none but the night-nurse and myself; and the great silences of the night became indescribably intimate, for both of us were on the same peaceful voyage, both intent on reaching the same place. It did not occur to me that each night might not be bringing me nearer to my destination; they were hours of a curious peace wherein, without thinking or asking, I imagined the ship to be travelling on through the darkness, always a little nearer a shore where the sun shone eternally and I should not have to lie on my back all day and night any more. The concrete fact of my remote loneliness seldom troubled my thoughts, for my mind was untormented by thought. By day the room became an island and I was a bit sick, and at night the little ship kept surging slowly through a calm sea towards a brighter, healthier existence.

The hospital, unluckily, had a tiresome rule prohibiting the night-girls from attending the same patient more than twice in a week, so that we never got to know each other there, and every third evening meant the effort of welcoming a new face and the trial of speech when even one word is hell to say. All these girls were white, from the States, a kind of wandering tribe, very young, who had done their training at home and then with a little money saved set out to whatever town under the American flag that most appealed to their imagination. There they would join that town's branch of their Nursing society and wait for the hospital telephones to summon them on night duty; I never came across any who worked by day. A great many found their way to the islands, where they lived cheap, mostly in huts on the beach, spending several hours of the day in the sea. Sometimes I found it hard to believe they were female; it was almost impossible to think of them bearing a child, or even conceiving. They seemed remarkably fond of each other.... Effortlessly, I would liken them to colts, with their immature boniness and their way of tossing back their hair from off their faces as though it were an unruly mane; very like colts they were, but with none of that animal's shyness or timidity. When I discovered that by forcing myself to keep awake at night I was more comfortable and sweated less, they encouraged this desire and I would find myself listening to a long half-whispered dissertation on racy American literature or a glorification of the plains of Arizona, the lately forsaken home of the bony, colt-like creature beside me. I would listen till my head began to reel, and just before I knew no more I'd hear a voice: "All right, honey—you go off then. Guess I'll get back to that story, else I'll go off, too! Happy dreams!"

But there were other, quieter hours in the darkness that were relieved only by the small night-light, when in a curious peace and feeling of security I would wake and resist the desire to disturb the girl for her towel and change, and instead lie watching her face under the dim yellow light of the lamp. In the darkness that seemed to me then so still I would follow the swift movements of the eyes as they raced backwards and forwards over the lines of the book: I'd gaze at the contour of her face—thin, pointed, with the clear smooth skin of the young American; at the curve of the forehead and back of the head where the hair descended close to the nape of the neck with the same fine precision as on that of a boy; I'd watch the lean fingers of her hand on the corner of the page as they waited impatiently to turn. I'd take a morbid interest that would, perversely, gladden my heart, in the cool clarity of her health, the sure rhythmical movement of the breathing in her straight chest, and the quiet easiness of her silent reading; and in some vague way I would admire, envy, and hate her all at once for being capable of doing without effort what I could hardly bear to contemplate. And all the time as I lay there staring, full of the knowledge of her thinking herself alone and unseen there reading, there would come, born out of the stillness and darkness, that intimacy of two souls, the woman strong in health and the man weak, inferior without it, confined together in a small space by visible walls—an intimacy so utterly private that for me a queer personal relationship would seem to form in the night, something as marvellous, as mysterious as the invisible formation of a child in the womb.

The early mornings—for at dawn the night-girls left me—were

easy enough after I'd managed to forgive Day for shattering the illusion of Night, for things happened then: the lovely pale presences came floating in, the air in the room became alive and scented, soft speech superseded the breezy American English, and silent slippers the high heels that clicked over the linoleum by night.... Slowly as the days passed, I grew more conscious of my condition by the different manner in which the bed was made. I was now incapable of raising my body without help; my arms lacked the strength; bed-sores had set in, and on being rolled over on my side by strong, frail-looking white fingers another pair of hands would rub alcohol into the back. Then over on to the other side—but now I knew no humiliation; rather I took pleasure in anything done for or near me, cherishing the company it meant. And the very knowledge that I desired company increased that desire a hundredfold, as a smoker's desire to smoke is increased when in the night he knows tobacco cannot be obtained.

Not every day at noon, but most days, the scar-faced doctor would come in at the doorway, stand there, then advance towards me in silence.

"You'll just have to take some grub soon, young man," he said one day. "You're slippin' down, you know."

But when I asked him what ailed me he looked away with a shrug.

"Search *me!*" he'd say, as though he were some casual acquaintance of whom I had asked an irrelevant and stupid question.

And then, as once more the room lay empty and white and I knew that for several hours I must lie alone sweating before a soul would come through the door, that for days and weeks, months even, I might lie there, not knowing what was going on in me, ignorant of that invisible something that was draining the body of its last resources—it was then, finally, that the mind could no longer slumber thoughtlessly, and on a gushing torrent of fear and self-pity panic would seize me in its grip.

The body is indeed a better pupil than the mind; nor was I ignorant of the fact that when the latter is also sick the former cannot heal. Now the tormented brain held sway; that I knew. For once the panic was in me, there it remained; I could not rid myself of it. On a flood of clear, sane thought the vision of myself slowly sinking towards the under-earth of this remote island flashed and reflashed across my brain. I would start suddenly out of this vivid revelation and dig my hands into the bed on either side of my body, to raise it, to insist that I was not so ill; then, overcome with the effort, sink back. I came with a shock to the state of knowing that my very life depended solely on myself, for I was now positive that nothing the doctor was doing had the slightest healing influence on the state of my body. And there was no one else; I knew no one; I could get no one; and soon I should run out of money. Everything, I knew, rested upon the strength of the will to conquer the disease undermining the body.

I now had the bed turned to face the window—in reality a door opening on to a veranda—and there, for as long as my eyes would stand the glare, I'd gaze out on to the dark green tropical growth covering the huge crater-hill that reared before me high into the dazzling blue of the cloudless sky. Here, on this hill, my eyes would seek some living thing, something moving, a man, an animal, a bird—with which to arrest the mind and so still the thoughts that raged there as rapids whirling in a pool before a fall. But I could see no sign of life, for though the darkness of the green seemed but a thick, short undergrowth no higher than tall bracken, it was, as my eyes learned through long hours of watching, nothing less than the lush verdant vegetation of innumerable great palms and plants like vast rhubarb, whose gigantic umbrella leaves served as waterproof roofs to the dense blackness beneath. Round and over these I could see the thick branches of the trees, brown and still as the sleeping pythons I imagined to be lurking there, circling and twining themselves in and out of the feathery green creepers that lay over it all, like the net of some monster spider spun on wild fields of grass.

Gradually, at first unconsciously, I began to strain my ears for the sound of a human voice, a movement, a footstep; and in this at least I was rewarded, for now, out of what in the past I had always thought so great a silence, vague noises reached my ears. In the middle of one lonely vacant afternoon when for the millionth time I was thinking of the street outside my home—of my mother as I had last seen her walking down that street, stooping under her umbrella with countless thousands of nails splashing round her on the pavement—I caught the faint sound of someone weeping near at hand. I held my breath to listen, but the sound did not come again. Instead, a few minutes later, I heard footsteps on the veranda, more footsteps of someone approaching, and then greetings as of two men well acquainted. The voices dropped a little, and, straining to listen, I heard one man saying: "Well, when can I have that bed?"

And the other voice answered: "Oh, that's all right—free tomorrow night."

"Tomorrow—sure!"

"Yes—he'll be gone by then."

"Really? Why, that's two this week in that ward!"

"Yes, he's goin' now . . . quite a death-trap, eh?" There was a short mirthless laugh; then a pause, during which I imagined the two doctors looking down reflectively at their shoes.

"Well," one voice broke out again, a little louder, brighter now, "well, that's fine. I'll be right here with another, tomorrow evening—may not be long either! Bye!"

"S'long."

I can recall that short conversation as though I'd heard it this very morning; every word of it, even the tone of the voices. Listening to the footsteps disappearing in the distance, I felt my face, hands and arms, the whole of my body, burning hot and wet. For in all the hours of tormented thinking I had not dared actually to look into the face of what is the final inevitability of all living things. Even during the last few days I had thought of it but dimly, of its grim yet still rather remote possibility in relation to myself, and that on one of these days in which I did little but stare at the ceiling my eyes should cease suddenly and for ever to look upon the everlasting shape of the stain there, I had not in its stark, and awful likelihood imagined. But now, with the words whose meaning I did not for a moment doubt, even that stain became wonderfully dear. I knew then, suddenly, fearfully, with what desperation, and to how little, men cling to life. And I now know, too, I said, what men think and say and do when their fellow mortals whom they have known can't open their eyes any more nor move their mauve lips to breathe a last supplicating word. . . .

"He's going now!" I heard again and again the casual voice, the short, mirthless laugh. "He's goin' now!"

Seized with panic, I started looking crazily about the room—at the ceiling, at the stain, at the white walls, the door, the screen, the window, the crater-hill outside, the end of the bed; and everywhere I looked I saw all the other hundreds of pairs of eyes that had gazed up at this same stain, seen this ceiling, this wall. . . . I saw all the bodies that had lain in this bed, stared out at that crater-hill, and now where were they all, those eyes, those bodies? I cried out loud in the silence; and the voice was like another's voice, alien, a voice I had never heard. It was the first symptom of delirium, and I knew it.

I knew it that night when such a storm raged round our ship that I woke and cried for help. Waves like small mountains rose with the shrieking wind into the black sky above us; the ship, one moment tipped up sideways on the surface of the heaving water, the next instant fell like a dead thing from the sky into the cavernous valley of the sea; the wood creaked everywhere in the howling storm, and water poured in on us in thick, dark sheets, like oil. "We're going!" the girl told me afterwards I cried. "We're going now!"

In a drenched state I woke suddenly to semi-consciousness, shaking, one hand gripping the side of the bed, the other above me waving frantically in a last vain effort to find something on which to clutch hold in the air. I was awake, yet the room was not the same; this was not a room; for a long time I lay out in the wet grass and the heat coming from somewhere unknown was intense; I was alone; there was no one else on earth. Then I felt an ice-bag on my forehead, a hand under my head: "Here, honey, you take this and go to sleep," and with a weight on my dry tongue I swallowed.

Now I knew where I was; I was ill. And, remembering how ill, I lay there, breathing fast. "D'you know, this is the eleventh change tonight?" What was that? Oh, the girl. She was talking again, and I lay still, listening, not to her, but to that sound once more, as of someone weeping. The sound came again, from just beyond the wall.

"What's that noise?" I said.

"What noise, kid?"

"There—that—hear it? Someone's crying."

"Oh, that!" the girl said. "That's nothin'."

I knew anger was senseless, but I had no control. "What is it?" I said aloud.

"Hey, now," said the girl, bending over me with a dry shirt. "Stop that yellin'—you'll wake the dead!"

"Wake the—wake the what?" I cried. As I turned I heard the weeping again. "What's the crying?" I demanded.

"There," said the girl, as though quieting a child. "There now, don't upset yourself, that's nothin' but the mother of the guy next door. She thinks he's bad."

At that moment I felt I'd been struck suddenly blind, for everything went black.

That dose must have been extra large, for when I regained consciousness the hill was dark, the light in the room already failing. The best part of a day and a night had passed. Maybe I wouldn't have woken then but for that noise coming from the same room where I had lately heard the weeping. I once travelled through the Gulf of Mexico in a storm in which every soul on board vomited continually for forty-eight hours, but the combined sounds of all those retching humans seemed now as nothing compared with what was going on in that room next door.

Every part of my body seemed forced to go with it there, as though I too must somehow share the pain of the sufferer; every thought and fear vanished in horror of what I was hearing; all my senses were concentrated there. Nothing like that can last, I said. Nothing like that can go on for long; no human being can stand that, I said. And as I said it the noise ceased, but the silence proved only a short-lived hollow moment, immediately followed by a long drawn-out moan, a groaning sigh as of someone's endurance of physical torture utterly spent. The moan ended on such a low, descending note of despair that I sighed with gratitude for the end of another's pain. And just as my muscles and nerves began to relax from the tension of listening, the low gurgling in the throat broke out again. I clenched my hands to prepare for, and withstand, the coming anguish; with my eyes tight closed and the bed-clothes drawn up over my head I imagined the sufferer's knees high and bent in resistance, the hands clutching the stomach, the face contorted. The throat sounds were replaced by such long heaving retches that my own entrails seemed to gather and twist in sympathy. After another agonized spasm of choking there came a tearing sound like the final heave of sickness, as though the stomach had risen to the chest, and then one long moan as the body was left lying in utter exhaustion. No more, I almost cried, no more!

Sweating, I pushed back the sheets from my head, and there by the bed stood a nurse, a young girl I had never seen. She stood there silently in front of me, her face turned sideways, while I lay saying nothing, and stared at her. I knew her at once for a pure-bred Islander: her body big and full, her eyes huge, round, and of that lustrous brown, sad like a spaniel's, but with none of that animal's look of submission. Nor was her complexion of that Eastern pallor shared by the other nurses, but brown, like deep sunburn. Her lips were the colour of the islands' common hibiscus flower, a natural blood-red, her hair a jet mass that fell thick to the collar and shoulders of the blue sleeveless overall she wore.

As I flinched at the sounds beginning again next door, she smiled and laid her hand on my wrist. With the touch of her flesh fish-cold on mine I looked at the long brown fingers, the white nails, and then the retching grew worse, and I shut my eyes.

"Does it trouble you much?" she asked, her voice a caress in its velvet softness.

"What is it?" I said. "Can it go on for long?"

As I spoke I thought I heard the sound of music in the distance. The light in the room had slowly faded: outside, the sky was hard blue, like bright ink. I looked up at the girl and her eyes shone like little pools in the darkness of her face, while over that face, against the grey evening light in the room, the cloud of her hair lay black as a halo of tar painted behind her on the wall.

"Not much longer," she said. "Poor woman—she's one of us. Quite young. Been ill a long time."

As she spoke I seemed to see the beautiful brown limbs of the native woman all caught up and contorted in agony. Again I remembered the conversation.

"What is it?" I said. "Can't they give her anything?"

"She won't take it," the girl said, then added: "We won't, you know." I sensed the pride in her voice. Then she smiled, with infinite sadness in her eyes. There was everything sweet and ineffably good in that face; a god-like, unearthly quality of peace —knowing, and accepting, all things. She was looking down at me. "You'd have something to worry over," she murmured, "if you had that!"

The retching began again, longer, worse than before. I closed my eyes, held my breath, lay waiting till it should cease. The girl's last words flowed through my head like a cool relieving stream, and for the first time in weeks I smiled, cherishing the truth of what she'd said. I thought of the weeping mother, her stricken son who had "left" the room next door while I had lain asleep; and now this young native woman in the agony for which she refused relief . . . and I despised myself. I am not ill, I said. I don't know, never have known, what it is to be ill. I lay there writhing, and yet glorying, in self-condemnation and shame.

"Listen!"

Again I felt my hand pressed, and I looked up to see the girl staring expectantly out of the window. I listened, and on the air came the strains of approaching music and the soft sound of Island voices singing.

"They're coming!"

"Who?"

"Her friends and relations," murmured the girl, moving over to the window.

But the music was drowned again by another long, heartrending spasm from the next room. When at last it ended the voices were close, immediately outside on the veranda; and there the soft low lilting notes floated on the air, sounding in my ears more like the music of flutes than words uttered by the human throat.

A moment later a procession of native girls, their hair streaming down their backs, passed my window, singing. They were dressed in straw skirts and scarlet scarfs; from their necks hung long *leis* of wild carnations; while in their hair, over their ears, huge single hibiscus gleamed dull-red in the gloom.

When they had passed I heard the slow tang-tang of ukuleles and guitars. I lay and gazed at the figure of the girl silhouetted there dark against the darker night in the open window. She too was singing, softly. From the room next door there came no noise but the sound of singing, and as I listened I thought that slow, clear-sung song the most beautiful and the saddest I had ever heard. In its very melancholy it seemed to soothe and still my nerves, and as I thought of the girl's words I laughed to myself in the presence of grief, marvelling how she in her wisdom and the woman in her last agony had lulled my mind to rest.

Presently I heard the procession of girls returning, still singing.

"What is that song?" I asked.

When the girl turned in the window, I could see the pools of her eyes were full. "That," she whispered, "that's the Island's Farewell."

She looked back just as the procession was passing. I saw the first girl stop, and, lifting her *lei* of carnations over her head, place it over that of the girl in the window. The two girls laid their cheeks for a moment one against the other. The singing ceased. The procession passed on in a new strange silence, and the girl in the window turned and came towards me.

"This is for you," she said, and bending down she took off the *lei*, lifted my head, and placed the long wreath of carnations round my neck.

"They're yours," I insisted, "not mine."

"No," she answered, smiling. "You give me a fresh *lei* when you're well again."

And I knew then that the body would swiftly join the mind and that soon, together, they would be sailing calmly out of the darkness into the sun.

Solitaire

I could call Dr Netzen about that neuroma case. Might have lunch with him. Or I could . . . Perhaps I'd better do that, get her over. She's been on my mind long enough. Stella Murphy. Odd little creature. Jesus, what a lifetime ago. Let's see, today's Sunday. She'd probably be home. And she'd like it—if she hasn't given me up since my promise to call her immediately after New Year's. What's today? February the fourth. My God, more than a month. In New York, days are like minutes.

"How about lunch, Patrick?"

"What's that, Betty?"

"About lunch. Ned and I are going to the Goodens. There's enough food in the icebox if you want to stay in."

"I was just thinking. I feel if I don't get that Murphy girl over soon, I never will."

"Murphy girl?"

"You remember. The girl I used to know here years ago, on my first trip. The one who wrote me in the summer, after seeing my article in the *Medical Journal.*"

"Oh, you must. After all, she sent you that Christmas card with the funny words. And didn't she call you on New Year's Day?"

"I know, I know."

Wish I weren't so damned tired.

"Well, I think it's only fair . . ."

"All right, dear. Hullo, Ned old boy? Dressed warm enough? Looks hellish cold out. Are you off immediately, Betty?"

"Yes, we're late already."

"All right, dear—*au revoir.* You can phone me at the Medical Centre after three-thirty."

"Try not to stay too long, Patrick. You look worn out."

I am. Well, suppose this must be done. Let's see, have I her number? Mavyrick, Merton, Murphy—Stella. Here she is. Scala 7—1834.

"Miss Stella Murphy, please."

"Pat?"

"Stella? How could you know it was me?"

"I'd know that voice anywhere, Pat."

"That's mighty clever of you. You've heard it only once in the last ten years."

"Eleven years on the thirtieth of next month, Pat."

"Lord, what a memory! Listen, Stell, forgive the short notice, but a doctor's life and all that, you know. Could you possibly make yourself free for lunch today?"

"I have no plans, Pat."

"Splendid. Let's see. It's twelve now. How about one o'clock? ... Where? Well, you're way over on the West side. Could we meet somewhere nearer, perhaps?"

"Sure, Pat. Where?"

Where? Somewhere neutral. American. Where you never go.

"How about Shore's—Madison and 89th?"

"I'll be there, Pat."

"A *bientôt*, then."

"What's that?"

Idiot, who d'you think you're talking to?

"In about an hour then?"

"Okay. Don't be late."

"I won't."

Hell, I don't feel up to having lunch with anyone—least of all with a virtual stranger. Really ought to sleep on Sunday afternoons. What could I find to say to Stella Murphy after all these years? How old was I then? Twenty-three. Jesus, wonder what I was like? Just bumming round the world. Remember now, there was that other woman, the married one—what *was* her name? —whom Stella never knew about. God, what a time that was! The intrigues, the subterfuges, the lying, disappearing, excuses. Will I recognize her? Tiny she was, and very young, and innocent. Worked in some fur store way up town. And no family; an orphan. That frightful rooming-house we lived in. Her room. Mine. Can't

have been much fun for her—for either of us. The stink of that
house. The crazy woman who ran it, always drunk. And the
Austrian who practised scales all morning. The oyster shop
round the corner; the snow piled high in the streets; the roar of the
EL overhead, and the Irish place which sold Guinness and "fresh
eggs straight from Dublin." Ireland? Didn't she come from there?
Some talk about Limerick. The people who remember you!
Americans. Several sent Christmas cards regularly for years.
Stella never missed a year. They reached me in the spring,
in France, Spain, Portugal, or Austria. And I looked at the gaudy
colours, read the name, never replied. This last one, which Betty
thought so odd. Believe she stuck it in my drawer. Here it is. On
the outside a basket of red tulips, tied with a piece of real red
ribbon. And inside:

> *I'd like so much*
> > *to see you*
> *I'd like to——*
> *But alas, I can't,*
> *And so this card must be*
> *A visitor, a greeting,*
> *And a loving wish*
> > *from me!*

Imagine! She must have searched for that. You'd seen them at it,
the Lonelyhearts. For someone she'd known for a week years ago
and was never likely to see again...! Must I put on that beastly
new suit? No, too thin; the trees are howling in the Park. Come on
then, Patrick Flannigan, raise yourself. One-fifteen.

God, it's cold. Got a nickel? The crowd in these Madison
Avenue buses. A poet should immortalize their drivers, the Devil
destroy the machines. 88th Street. Pull the cord. What am I going
to talk about? I'm an overworked physician, thirty-five years old
—not the bum with the wanderlust of eleven years ago.

Shore's. Curse the wind, the door—it won't swing. My God, that
must be her. Smile, man—she's smiling. She certainly is small.
Now I remember. Those magnificent teeth, wide blue eyes and
the ever-cheerful face.

"Why, Stell, you haven't changed one millimetre!"

"Pat! I don't know what a millimetre is, but—well, you don't look so old yourself!"

Now what? Odd, I'm suddenly nervous. What in hell am I doing here? I remember now—now that she's in front of me, walking away—that perky walk, like a bird, and the straight back, like a toy soldier. God, I feel old. She might be twenty-two, but must be—must be thirty. Are we going straight to eat? Shouldn't I suggest a drink? She has turned.

"Are you pleased to see me, Pat?"

"Stell, I hardly believe it's you yet!"

"Oh, Pat, and you just said I hadn't changed so much!"

"You haven't, Stell. Don't be silly. But when"—yes, that's a good one—"when you haven't seen someone all that time, you feel a bit tongue-tied. Listen, what about a little drink before lunch?"

"Ah, that sounds more like my old Pat talking. Let's get acquainted. Come, let's find a nice quiet corner."

A quiet corner in this array of aluminium, these shining rods, these reflecting mirrors, these dim lights that serve only to illuminate and exaggerate the gloom of fashionable hats all alike, the watch-chained waistcoats over the mass-produced paunches, the polished Sunday faces in the heart of the world's most capitalistic cavern of a city! Patrick Flannigan, M.D., moving through a human jungle, a forest of white tables, following a speck of his ridiculous past!

"There's no *real* corner, Pat."

"Never mind, Stell."

"This is very comfortable, miss."

"I think this will have to do, Stell."

"Okay. What's it matter where we are so long as we're together!"

Yes, I remember now, those teeth and eyes, shining, with never a hint of introspection.

"Stell, what'll you have—a Martini?"

"That would be lovely."

"Two Martinis, please."

"Oh, Pat, isn't it funny to be together again! Are you sure you're pleased to see me? Eleven years! To me it could have been eleven minutes. Tell me, Pat, tell me, what have you been doing all these last eleven minutes? Smile, Pat. I've not seen you smile for more than—more than a third of my lifetime. Think, Pat, I was only nineteen then. Imagine, nineteen—so young, so innocent, such a little fool! Oh, Pat, tell me I've changed! I was so frightened of you then. Pat the man, my man, my Irishman! But I *have* changed, Pat—I'm not frightened of you now!"

No, indeed! The tables have certainly turned. Pat Flannigan, European tramp, doctor, writer, lecturer, the specialist in nervous diseases—speak! Speak to the excited little girl at your side!

"Tell you what I've been doing, Stell? Lord"—don't sigh so wearily—"that would take a long, long time!"

"Pat?"

"Yes, Stell?"

"You don't look so—so terribly happy? Are you happy, Pat?"

"That's not an easy question to answer, Stell. Happy is not a word I use nowadays."

"Oh, Pat, what a thing to say! How come?"

Dear Lord, I cannot talk her language!

"Well, you see, Stell, in the first place there's a war on. To date I have had three friends killed. It's not a little war, nor even a big war in a remote place. There are no remote places any more. . . ."

"America's not fighting, Pat. Ireland, our country, is not fighting. . . ."

"Many Irishmen have died. Many Americans may."

"And is all this why you are unhappy, Pat?"

"Isn't it enough? But I didn't say I was unhappy, Stell. Can you read the headlines today and say: I am happy? The difference, you see, Stell, is probably that for years, ever since I last saw you, I've been forced to see things with my own eyes. Only a fool or a convict could have lived in Europe and not seen things, terrible things. What it amounts to, I suppose, is that I'm a European and you an American."

"We are Irish, Pat."

I have an idea the bum used to say that, eleven years ago.

"That, I think, is a dangerous thing to say, Stell. Nationalism is the disease of our time. I believe that if all of us could feel simply citizens of the world, this planet would be a healthy place to live on."

"You've changed, Pat."

"Isn't that inevitable, and even a good thing?"

"You're not so Irish as you used to be."

"Not so young, you mean, and not quite so foolish—and perhaps, just for these reasons, nowhere near so nice. . . !"

"I don't know—yet. You used to . . . Pat, d'you know what I'd like? You've guessed bang right. That's better. You smiled again! D'you remember, Pat——?"

"Waiter! Same again, please."

"D'you remember how you always used to say you must stop drinking?"

"A resolution that sounds horribly familiar, Stell! But did I, as long ago as that? Well, I confess I love it still, though not so much in the middle of the day. I'm a doctor now, alas!"

"Oh, but we'll have evenings together, won't we, Pat?"

What's this?

"Pat?"

"Yes?"

"Here's to the future—and you!"

"And you, Stell—and the United States of America!"

"The United States, Pat?"

"Why not? On them, Stell, rests the last hope of civilization!"

"Oh, Pat, must we talk like this—today?"

"No. But before we change the subject, Stell, let me say one thing. You Americans——"

"I am *not* an American, Pat!"

"But you've lived here for——"

"Twenty years. Yes. But I'm not a citizen."

"What?"

"No. No one knows—and don't tell anyone, Pat—but I'm not. I'm Irish. I was born there, in Limerick, and I want to die there, in Limerick. . . . Pat, don't look like that."

"I'm sorry, Stell. But I think that's naughty. Tell me, do you read the papers?"

"Why, sure. And books. I'm a member of the Book-of-the-Month Club. And I listen to the radio every evening. And every Tuesday go to lectures at Columbia. Oh, Pat, what do you think I am—an ignoramus?"

"No. Just a naughty girl!"

"Ah, Pat, smile—that's better. But your hand's quite clammy. Pat, you're not nervous at being with me, are you? Like I was, with you, eleven minutes ago? I have something more to say than I had then, haven't I? Pat, tell me more about yourself. Don't let's talk politics, not today. Is your wife nice, Pat, would I like her, is she tall, blonde, or dark and Irish and beautiful, how long have you been married, Pat?"

"Six years, Stell. We've a child of five. Ned. I was married before. Don't look so alarmed, Stell. I was."

"Oh, I didn't know that."

"Well, we've not been exactly corresponding, have we, Stell?"

"No. That's true. Your last letter was from Paris, in June, ten years ago."

"How d'you . . . You remember the date?"

"Of course. I have all your letters, Pat. Eight of them. I know them all by heart. They're lovely letters. I always thought you'd become a writer."

What's this! Knows my letters by heart!

"I believe even I thought that, once."

"Yes, you did—just about the time you last wrote."

"Did I? Well, I married a novelist. French. I suppose that was enough. What else did I say? I might as well get to know myself?"

"You said I shouldn't write to you any more, that you wouldn't, couldn't write to me, that you wouldn't forget me. And you didn't, did you, Pat?"

When she wrote me this summer it took me five minutes to remember who she was. How am I going to get out of this? What can a man do for her? She'd better not drink any more. Jesus, if I'd only known!

"Of course not. How could I?"

"Oh, Pat, it's so lovely to hear you say that! Pat, come closer."

"Stell, what damage you must do with those eyes!"

"Ha! That's just what you used to say. But Pat—Pat, dear?"

"Yes, Stell?"

"Spare me just one short kiss—just one. No, not there. Here's where you used to. . . ."

I remember everything now. Unfair? Still, wouldn't it be more unfair, more unkind, not to? God, I don't know. What's she saying?

"Oh, Pat, my lips were *so* dry!"

What? What bell is ringing now?

"Where did you get that—that gag from, Stell?"

"That? You're pretending!"

"I am not."

"From you, of course. You always said that."

"I really sound quite nice. . . !"

"You were the nicest person in the world. You always have been. You still would be if—if——"

"But you shouldn't, Stell. And I haven't finished mine yet."

"But *I* have. Pat, please light my cigarette."

"Well, you're not nineteen any longer. But I won't take any responsibilities, mind."

"You needn't, Pat. I guess I've looked after myself all my life. I can go on doing so. Waiter!"

"But you don't often drink all that, Stell. You couldn't look as you do, if you did."

"I don't *often* have lunch with Dr Patrick Flannigan. Pat, d'you remember the last time we had lunch together? Remember O'Reilly's round the corner, and the 'fresh eggs straight from Dublin' chalked on the window, which always made you laugh, and Tom and you singing:

> *You may ramble from Clare*
> *To the County Kildare!*"

"Stell, dear—not so *loud*! We'll be thrown out!"

Hell, there may well be patients of mine in this place!

> *From Drogheda down to Macroom*
> *And where would yer meet . . . ?*

"Pat, I *will* sing!

> *A fine widow like ME—E—E—E,*
> *Mrs Mull—i—gan, the Pride of the Coombe!*

"Oh, Pat, remember? You and Tom, with the line of empty Guinnesses on the bar? And the oysters we brought in because we were so poor, and you said oysters and Guinness were the 'th'only shtaple dyutt fer a poverty shthricken Irishman!' I went there for weeks after, Pat, and cried my eyes out on that darned bar— thinking, thinking of you—and old Tom, with the tears running down his moustache and his hand patting my back. 'There, there, Stell me gal, he'll be back, he'll be back. He'll be afther seeing what th'ould counthry is like, and 't is back he'll be, sure as me name's Tom O'Reilly!' And Tom's dead and gone now, Pat, God bless his soul—but he was right, he was right! You're here, Pat, sitting beside me again, after eleven long years, me holding your hand, after eleven years of waiting.... Dear Tom, drink to Tom, to Thomas O'Reilly's memory, Pat!"

This must stop. She must eat, or she'll soon be under the table.

"Stell, will you do something for me?"

"Anything, Pat."

"Just eat something. D'you realize it's two-thirty, and I have to be at the Medical Centre in an hour?"

"Oh, Pat, you're not going to leave me? Pat, it's Sunday, I've bought a bottle of Bourbon—planned we'd go home and talk quietly. And there's Mrs Dunn and all the others waiting to see you ... after all these years ... the whole house waiting to see you. Mrs Dunn, Pat, she has her camera out to take a picture of you for me...."

Holy God!

"Ah, she's so sweet, Mrs Dunn, like a mother to me. You'd love her. She keeps our house. I've been living there since a month after you left; I couldn't bear to stay in that place any longer after you'd gone. She knows all about you, they all know all about you, Pat. Oh, Pat, d'you know what Mrs Dunn and Daisy and Eileen had to do this morning? I shouldn't tell you, but I can't help it. They had to hold me up and almost carry me down the stairs and put me in a taxi to come here, I was so excited I couldn't walk, Pat."

Jesus, must quieten her somehow, or this will lead to hysteria.

"Stell, what about some *hors d'œuvres*, some fish, an omelette.

And then you must tell me what *you've* been doing all this time. How long were you in that fur store, Stell?"

"I'm still there, Pat."

Eleven years in the same fur store.

"Yes, I'm still there and making good money now, forty a week. Look, look what the girls gave me for Christmas, isn't that a nice compact?"

"That's beautiful, Stell. Listen, do look at the menu. There's not so much time, dear."

"How much money have you, Pat?"

"Oh, don't worry about that."

"Well, I'm going to have the most expensive thing on the card —a steak, a T-bone steak—to celebrate the greatest day of my life!"

"Two steaks, please, waiter—quick as you can."

Keep talking, Pat Flannigan.

"Tell me, Stell, what d'you do in the evenings?"

Fool, that's not so good.

"In the evenings, Pat? Well, I quit work at five-thirty, then I go and wash, gossip with the girls till six-fifteen, then I start walking home. On the way I stop in some place for supper, get home at eight, chat with Mrs Dunn and Eileen and Daisy and the others. Mr Dermot, too—he's a dear, asked me to marry him three times. Then usually I play Solitaire for an hour with the radio going. Oh, Pat, remember you teaching me to play Solitaire on the kitchen table? You with your Bourbon and me with my beer, and you saying I must learn Solitaire because sometimes I'd be lonely maybe and too much reading is tiring for the eyes, you said, and the black Mammy, remember, used to come in, and you said to her she'd nipped some of your Bourbon the day before, and she put her hands on her hips and said: 'Why, *Mis*ter Flannigan, a drop o' that stuff never went dahn this hole in all ma life.' And she opened her mouth so wide you had time to drop a bread crumb down, and then she began to laugh and choke till you banged her on the back so hard she collapsed on the floor! Oh dear, I often think of that night and laugh.... Well, after a couple of rounds of Solitaire I read the papers or a book, and then I turn in, and I lie there, thinking of you, Pat, thinking, till finally

I go to sleep, and dream of you, Pat. At seven in the morning I'm up again. . . ."

My God, how's she going to eat that great slab of meat?

"Seriously, Stell, why don't you marry? Not necessarily Mr Dermot——"

"Me *marry*!"

"Stella, dear, not so *loud*! I'm sorry if I——"

"I'll never marry, Pat. I've had nine proposals. Oh, don't you think I couldn't have married. I could have married nine times. Nine times, I tell you. Bill Rogers, he's a captain in th'army, he's been writing me a letter once a week for two years, and Sundays he sends me a telegram, he's the nicest man in the world—bar one. But I'd rather die than let him or any of 'em touch me. I know what I want, I've known for eleven years what I've wanted, so—so I'll not marry, Pat—*never*!"

"Ouch! That hurt, Stell!"

"Patrick Flannigan, I want to hurt you! For nearly eleven years I've wanted to hurt you. You've hurt me. And—now—here you are—*beside me*! Oh, I could——"

"Stella, *drop that knife*!"

Pat Flannigan, there are times when it's kind to be cruel. You've got to; there's nothing else to do.

"I'm sorry, Pat. Oh, Pat—Pat, my—my lips are so dry again!"

"Now, Stell, don't be a bad girl!"

"I've never been bad in my life, Pat. It doesn't cost you anything, Pat."

Doesn't cost anything? You don't need to be a doctor to know better than that.

"Stell, dear. Let me put my arm round you while I tell you something very hard to tell. See, Stell, I'm not only a married man, I not only have a child, but I've made a mess of my life more than once, or twice. I cannot—at my age, under the circumstances in which I live—I cannot risk, for anything or anyone, not even for you, making a mess of it all over again. See, Stell, if I hadn't got to work now, and I were to come home with you, it—it wouldn't be any good, dear. There's always tomorrow—and tomorrow. And both of us, alas, are human."

"I know. Even a week or a month wouldn't satisfy us."

Oh, God!

"Oh, Pat—Pat, my darling, I love you so!"

The doctor who cares for the sick has nothing to say.

"I have nothing more to live for now, Pat."

The doctor who can heal wounds, and relieve pain, and calm the dying, has nothing to say.

"We've-had-a-lovely-time-together-today, haven't-we, Pat?"

"I have, Stell. But I'm worried about you. And I'm worried about the time. Stell, dear, it's three-fifteen."

"Pat, do one more little thing for me? Drink a Bourbon with me before you go? Just one Bourbon—like we used to, in the old days. There were only seven of them. Seven days and seven nights, but they have been my life. And now they seem so very far away, so long ago ... I wonder——"

"Waiter, two Bourbons, please."

"I wonder how I shall be able to go on now. You see, I've had this to live for, to keep me going. I've worked so hard. Slaved and saved. I have two thousand dollars in the bank today. We could have done such a lot with that, I thought. And oh, I wanted, I always wanted three children—just three. I love children so; and I knew you did. 'The only decent people, children,' you used to say. I was selfish, of course. I didn't really think of you—though I thought about you every minute of my waking hours and I never had a dream without you in it. They say love is blind, I know that's true today. You see, I never doubted that I would get what I wanted, I had such faith. I compared everyone I met with you— and all of them seemed fools. That man in the Army I told you about—it's not true, I didn't give a damn for him. I knew when I saw your article at my doctor's—I've been subscribing to that journal ever since, Pat, but you've not been in it again—I knew the moment I saw that article that my dreams had come true, that you had come back, as Tom O'Reilly said you would. Even then I could not write you. I was afraid of what I might say, and I felt I would meet you in the street. Because you were a doctor I spent my Sundays walking the streets up-town where most of the good doctors live—I knew whatever you did you'd do well, Pat—and I walked round the Medical Centre, looking at every man going in and every man coming out. But I didn't have to look very close or carefully, for I'd have recognized your figure, your walk, a mile away. Then—every day knowing you were here, somewhere next door for all I knew, I couldn't stand it any longer, and I wrote you that note. It took me nearly a week to write. It wasn't a bad note, was it, Pat? It didn't annoy you, did it, Pat? You're not sorry you came today, are you, Pat? Oh, Pat, here's to our past, you won't forget it, will you, dear? And here's to your future, my—my lover!"

"Stell, I think you're the most courageous woman I know."

"Let me share that check, Pat. I ordered all those drinks."

"No, Stell, that you certainly will not do."

"Pat . . . ? Just one last one to keep me going, to think of and remember you by. . . . Farewell, my darling, and remember, if ever you are in trouble, if ever you want something, or just wish to talk, Stella Murphy will always love you and be there, for you, always."

"Oh, God, Stell, what someone is missing!"

"I'm the one who has done the missing. But I'm okay now. I can take it."

"Are you all right, dear? Here, hang on my arm. . . ."

"Indeed, no. An Irish gal has her pride."

"*Taxi!*"

"Get in, Stell. I'll drop you."

"No, Pat, I don't go your way. And I'm in no hurry—ever. But you are, Doctor Flannigan, you have the sick to tend."

"Good-bye, dear—and please take care of yourself."

" 'Bye, Pat."

The Face Behind the Bar

WE FIRST MET in the autumn of 1941. I had just rented a New York apartment in the East Fifties, off Third Avenue. He was a tall, thin man, with a high forehead and humorous watchful eyes behind thick spectacles—more like a schoolteacher, I thought, than the proprietor of a Third Avenue tavern reeking of stale beer.

"Lookat now," he was saying to a petulant customer as I entered, "why not take an honest man's word for ut?"

"I was only saying," argued the customer, finishing his drink, "that John Jameson has no business to be dearer than Johnnie Walker. It's no better and no older."

The man behind the bar leaned back against the shelves of bottles. "Only rarer," he said, and grinned.

What arrested my attention was not the senseless bar-room chatter, nor the man's appearance, but his accent, a brogue certainly neither Cork nor Galway, nor yet quite Dublin, nevertheless one so familiar—with its slight ironic inflection, the half-comic, half-serious tone uttered from the side of the mouth in an almost conspiratorial whisper—that it struck and bothered me all at once as does the face of a man known during childhood but never seen since, and to whom one cannot immediately put a name.

Only when I closed my eyes and listened, did what I heard create a vision of long ago. I was walking through my dirty native village on market day; the one wide street was packed with cattle, sheep and squealing pigs. Men in ragged clothes whacked at the backs of the animals with thin ash sticks, accompanying their assault with blasphemous oaths. Beyond them, women with their heads covered by shawls bargained over vegetables in a language that was the first I ever spoke. "Lookat now, why not take an honest woman's word for ut. . . . ?"

When I opened my eyes the customer had gone. By nature averse to asking direct questions, I ordered another beer and told the man behind the bar a story about how, when I first arrived in New York, a woman had burst into my hotel bedroom one morning to sweep out the room. "Be all that's holy!" she cried, "I thought it's out you were!" Bidding her to come on in, I asked her if she knew Dublin well. "Dublin!" she said, "sure I never set foot in Ireland in all me life!"

The man behind the bar grinned. "Well," he said, "I can't say the same meself, though it's a mighty long time since I was on the other side. Sixteen from forty-one—that's twenty-five years."

"That's a long time," I said. "But I wouldn't say you're a Dubliner."

"I am not," he replied, "but near enough. I'm from a wee bit of a place twenty-odd miles from the city. It's not likely you ever heard tell of it. Kilmessan's the name."

As he pronounced the word I felt as one does when suddenly remembering the name of a man known long ago in childhood. Kilmessan is two stations before my native village on the single line that runs from Dublin, through the green plains of Meath, to the ancient town of Kells.

"*Kilmessan*," I said, and I tried to imitate its one porter who used to scream: "*Change for Trim and Athboy!*" whenever the occasional train drew in at the station.

With pleasure I watched his eyes open wide, his hand go up to cover his mouth. Then he leaned slowly forward, laid his elbows on the bar so that his face was only a few inches from mine.

"Be all that's holy!" he muttered.

"I come from a couple of stations down the line," I explained.

"I'll drink to a man from Meath," he said, and he took down a bottle of Jameson, emptied my beer down the sink, and poured out a couple of drinks. "*Slainthe!*" he said. We raised our glasses and drank.

"And how is th' old place?" he asked, wiping his mouth on his hand. "When did yez see it last?"

"I left in 'twenty-two and was never back."

His eyebrows went up over the thick rims. "You were through the Throubles then?"

"I was and I wasn't—for part of the time I was at school in England. But I heard and saw enough."

"Me, too."

"You?" I said. "But didn't you leave in 'sixteen?"

"Oh, I did. But"—and he looked away as though the memory of those days embarrassed him—"well, a lot can happen even in a week."

"Sure," I said. "A lot happened in Easter Week."

"It certainly did."

"Even I have something to remember that day by," I told him, and I pulled up the sleeve on my left arm, revealing to him a scar running from the wrist half-way to the elbow.

"That looks more like a knife than a bullet," he said.

"It was neither. I was a kid of twelve at the time and all I saw of the fighting was a house going up in flames, and all I heard was the guns shelling Dublin and the talk of murder. It happened this way. Easter Monday there was a black frost, and I was trying out a new bicycle on one of the narrow garden paths at home. Round a sharp corner my rear wheel skidded, and I saw myself falling on to a cold frame which my mother used for growing violets. To save my head, I put out my arm and the glass ripped out a large piece of flesh."

"Musta been a nasty gash," he said.

"It looks bad because it was never stitched," I told him. "When my mother tried to phone for the doctor, she found the wires had been cut. At that moment we knew nothing about any Rebellion. So she put me in the trap, with my bandaged arm in a sling, and started to drive me to the nearest doctor, five miles away. Our place had an avenue and when we got to the lodge the gates were shut and there was a large wooden bar fixed across them on the other side. Behind the bar stood five strange men, one much taller and younger than the others, I remember, and they all carried rifles."

I stopped suddenly, for the man behind the bar had taken a step back. His hand was up to his mouth and he was gazing at me with wide-open, incredulous eyes.

"What's up?" I asked.

After a moment's hesitation, he said: "Oh, nothing—nothing at all. I was just thinking. Go on."

"Well," I said, "my mother knew none of the men and they wouldn't let us through. There was a war on, they said, and they were under orders to picket the place. When she got me out of the trap, showed them my bandaged arm and said that if I didn't see a doctor in a few hours maybe I'd bleed to death, one of the men put his face up to the gate and said: 'Lady, we have nothing against you personally, but we happen to know that your husband's a British officer in France. We also happen to know that your cowman's son, who lived in this lodge, was a member of the R.I.C. He tried to get away this morning, but we got him, lady—he's lying over there behind the house.'

"My mother gave a short cry and we got into the trap and drove home. There was a man in our stables who used to be a dog vet's assistant, and he bandaged up my arm with ordinary adhesive tape. At the end of the week, when the Rebellion was over, the arm was green and the wound was cauterized by a surgeon in Derry. Well," I concluded, "I guess that's all—but I'll always remember Easter Monday."

"I guess we all will," said the man behind the bar. I glanced up at him and he had his arms folded across his chest and a peculiar expression on his face. He stared at me hard for a moment; then he said: "I remember feeling mighty sorry for your mother that day. She was a nice-looking woman."

I stared at him in silence, blankly, for fully half a minute. Then he reached out for the bottle and filled the two glasses. He raised his drink, while his mouth slowly turned up in a grin. But I did not move. I was thinking: Just what kind of an Irishman is this? Then he said: "Lookat now, can yez tell me this? How in the name of all that's holy can we expect to smash the Nazis if those divils over there don't offer us the use of their harbours?"

"You know," I said at last, "you could easily be kidding me!"

"And why would I?" he asked. "I was afther thinking you had a good memory."

"You didn't wear glasses in 'sixteen," I said.

"You're right," he said, grinning. "And very likely your mother's hair is no longer red!"

"You're right," I said, and we shook hands and drank.

The next time I saw him was a couple of weeks after Pearl Harbor. Wandering down East Fifty-ninth Street one evening, I stopped outside a second-hand bookstore, where I noticed a large folio of old maps priced a dime apiece, three for a quarter. The maps were of European countries, many of parts of Germany, and almost all, I discovered, of German make. Among them, to my surprise, I found a coloured map of Ireland with detailed insets of *Dublin und Dublin Hafen* and *Die See'en von Killarney*, each drawn to a scale *zehn Mal grösser als die Karte*. With Christmas near I decided to buy the map as a present to myself or for a friend. With it rolled up in brown paper and tied with a string, I set off down Third Avenue.

On the way, I stopped in at the grocer's to buy some vegetables and before reaching home decided to visit my friend behind the bar, have a beer, and maybe show him the map of our native land. He, however, had taken a day off, so when I had finished my drink I went on home. I had not been there more than three minutes when I realized I had brought the vegetables, but left the map in the bar.

Returning immediately, I found the map had gone. I asked the barman. At first he said he had not noticed it, but when I described the appearance of the package, he recalled having seen, among the crowd at the bar, a man drawing a woman's attention to the fact that she was leaving behind her a brown paper parcel which answered to the description I had just given of mine. And the woman, whom the barman said he had never seen before, had departed with the package.

This is the kind of situation which makes me angry—not least because there was no one to blame but myself. Now what, I asked myself, does a woman do when she finds that her deliberate theft (and how else could I interpret her action?) turns out not something of value, but a useless old map of Ireland? More important, just when does she make this discovery? Does she open it right away, or does she wait until she gets home—a place 1 had already pictured as an evil hole littered with brown paper? If she takes the former course, I concluded that I must act quickly. With a vision of her grimace of disgust as she looked for some place to dispose of my map, I rushed from the bar and started scouring those tall wire baskets into which Third-Avenueites throw everything from old clothes and newspapers to empty liquor bottles and—I prayed—unwanted maps of my native land. After a vain quarter of an hour's search, I descended into the subway and poked about among the dark corners of those airless corridors. But all I found was a still-life of the inevitable, insensible bum and an empty pint that had slipped from his dead-looking hand. I thereupon abandoned the search and would probably never have given my map another thought had not the barman mentioned the loss of the parcel to his boss.

When I entered the tavern a couple of days later, the man behind the bar beckoned to me with his finger. I followed him into the back of the saloon. Near a juke-box there stood a single chair. "Take a seat," he said. I had never sat down in the bar before, and I wondered if he was going to offer me a shot of John Jameson "under the counter." But he stood over me with his hands on his hips and stared at me for so long in silence with such a serious expression on his face that I found myself asking if something were wrong.

"Maybe there is," he said, solemn.

"What's on your mind?"

"I've been wondering," he said, "just what kind of an Irishman you are."

I laughed. "I wondered that about you once," I said, and although my tone may have sounded jocular, I suddenly did not feel at all in a humorous mood. I did not like the look of his face.

"If you hadn't come in just now," he said, "I was coming round to your place."

"To my place! What the divil's up?"

"Lookat now," he said, "I'm always ready to try and get a friend out of a jam, but——"

"A jam!" I exclaimed, rising to my feet. "Who's in a jam?"

"Aizy now, aizy," he said, pushing me gently back on to the chair. "I just wanted to get a hold of you before the police——"

"The police!" I cried. "What the hell are you talking about?"

"Well, let me put it this way. D'ye think it's wise for a man in these days—to go around with a detailed German map of Ireland?"

I stared at him in silence, blankly, for fully half a minute. And he stared me back in hard, suspicious-looking seriousness.

This is the kind of situation that makes me sweat—not only because there was no one to blame but myself, but because it's just the kind of thing, I thought, that would and does happen to an innocent man in wartime. I saw the whole preposterous predicament in a flash: the row of cops, the plainclothes men, and over them all the huge invisible letters: F.B.I. Just why was I in possession of this particular map—a map of a neutral nation comprising a detailed inset of its capital and harbour; a map, moreover, printed in an enemy country whose leaders for years had been threatening to destroy the United States of America?

And I stood up and answered stupidly but truthfully that I had been in possession of the said map because I am a native of Ireland, and I like Ireland, and I like maps, and I found it in a second-hand bookstore, and I bought it for a dime for a Christmas present for a friend.

Oh yeah? snarled all the cops and plainclothes men together.

Suddenly my vision of the situation struck me as so utterly absurd that I burst out laughing.

"You know," I said, "you could easily be kidding me!"

"Why should I?" he asked in that almost conspiratorial whisper. "Why not take an honest man's word for ut?"

And then, before I had time to answer, I saw his expression change—his mouth go up in a grin for the first time, his eyes become slits behind the powerful glasses. He raised his hands to his hips, and throwing back his head, he too burst into peal upon peal of laughter.

"Thought you was had that time, eh!" he cried, leaning over and slapping me on the knee with an enormous hand. "The face of yez!" he roared. "Ye'd think they was about to put y'up agin the wall this very minnut!"

Though hardly in the mood to appreciate the joke, my relief was such that I could not help smiling.

"Listen," he said, his laughter spent, "d'ye know what? There's just two kinds o' Irishmen—them that take a wee drop, and them that don't. The dry ones are dangerous, t'others are dopes! Let's drink to the two of us!"

Then he turned, and with one hand reached for a bottle of Guinness, and with the other, from a shelf above it, for a brown paper parcel tied with string.

"I found it hanging on the door this morning," he said.

A Peaceful Place

AT EIGHT EVERY MORNING I used to set off in the jeep from what was once Nürnberg to what is still the University city of Erlangen, where I worked.

The distance is about seventeen miles, but my bump of locality is good, and I soon discovered a short cut. By ignoring the to me meaningless military roadsigns heaped one over the other on telegraph poles; by never asking the way of a German civilian and least of all of the sleepy Negro traffic-directors at the city's crossroads, I managed to find a crater-ridden lane which bumped me out of the ruins, through a pine forest, and on to one of those Hitler-made *Autobahnen* where you can sit back, step on the gas, and relax. Fifteen minutes later I was in Erlangen.

When the day's work was over, however, I seldom felt inclined to return too fast to the rubble of my temporary home. Instead, I used to wander about the rather dull, frantically overcrowded town. Since I had a pass allowing me to "fraternize," I used to stop and talk to Germans in the street. I would try and make myself behave as though I were a civilian, spending the day in a normal city in normal times, as though I were not a foreigner in uniform, an ex-enemy, gazing at a hungry, homeless, defeated people. But the effort was doomed to failure. They were still too stunned to enter into my innocent game of make-believe. They could not rub their eyes and wake from the nightmare of the past, because of the very real nightmare of the present, and the unpredictable, but no less certain nightmare of the future.

So, abandoning any form of escape into the world I once had known, I'd return to the jeep, purr slowly down the *Autobahn* and into the forest of pines. It was here in this silent forest, one sublime evening in June 1945, that I first saw a U.S. military sign that was not, to me, a meaningless letter or anagram, nor even a pseudonym such as "Garbage" or "Ashcan," denoting God knew what unit of American occupation. It was just a simple sign—large black letters on a white background, with an arrow pointing left—saying exactly what it meant: U.S. MILITARY CEMETERY.

I debated a moment, then turned the jeep left and scrunched down a cinder-covered lane. Suddenly the forest opened up to form a small circular space over which a floor of wooden planks had been laid. In the centre of this deserted place stood another sign: VISITORS' VEHICLES. Parking the jeep, I got out and walked towards an opening in the trees through which I could already see line upon line of neat white crosses. Reaching the fringe of the cemetery, I stood still and found myself admiring the good sense and taste of the man who had chosen such a spot to bury the dead. In a large, protected circle cut out of the pines, hundreds upon hundreds of crosses—all identical except for an occasional, surprising Star of David—gleamed white against a background of beautifully mown, very green grass. It was the first clean, orderly, peaceful place I had encountered in bomb-battered Bavaria. I stood for several minutes in the intense evening silence and thought: If I should die tomorrow, I suppose this is where my bones, if not my dog-tag, would lie for ever. . . .

The scene was so peaceful, so still, so lonely that I had begun to imagine it inhabited only by the dead, when suddenly, moving forward a few paces, I saw, just beyond the periphery of graves and set against the background of forest, a small house of stained wood. Approaching it, I noticed that its wall facing the cemetery had carved on it, criss-cross-wise, a series of sporting symbols—a tennis racquet, a club, what looked like a lacrosse net, and under these a ball, cut out of the wood.

While examining this example of "Aryan" art, from which I gathered, correctly, that what was now an American military cemetery had recently been a German *Sportsplatz*, I suddenly had the sensation that I was not alone. Looking up quickly, I saw above me a small window, from behind which there gazed down at me—sleepily, unenquiringly—a coffee-coloured face. I heard the sound of slow footsteps from within, and a moment later a door opened on my left and out came a lean, pleasant-looking Negro corporal.

"I was just having a look round," I said, by way of explaining my presence.

"That's okay," said the corporal. He then lit a cigarette, pulled up a stool, sat down and leaned back against the doorpost. Behind him I saw a pile of narrow wooden planks and a large can of paint.

"You lookin' for anyone special?" he asked, his glance turning on the sea of graves behind me.

"No," I said. "I was just passing by and saw the sign."

And then, more for the sake of conversation than from genuine interest, I asked him from what battle area these casualties had been taken.

"Battle?" he said, scowling. "Why the war's been over six weeks and more. . . ."

"But surely——" I began, but he cut me short.

"What with the dozen this morning, that couple at noon"— he put the cigarette in his mouth and began doing some mental calculation on his fingers—"that makes one thousand and twenty-six. Out o' that number, I guess there's no more'n a couple o' hundred battle casualties out there.'

"But what about the others?" I asked. "How come they——?"

"Oh, there's all kinds," he said, pulling on his cigarette. "Mostly on the road. We average about thirteen a day. Jeeps, trucks, weapon-carriers. Specially bad in wet weather. 'Careless drivin',' they call it. Guys get boozed up, you know. A long time and a long way from home, they do all kinds o' crazy things. There's what they call 'accidental deaths,' and others not so accidental. There's soocides—just had a couple this noon. . . ."

"A couple?"

"Well, that's the way I understand it," said the corporal. "These two were buddies, see. Ever since they left home, about three years back, they were always together. That's the way it gets some guys. . . . One of 'em was married and had just heard he'd got enough points to go home. He was all set to leave for one of them French ports end of this week—today it would have been. Then he gets a letter from his wife. A short letter. 'Just to congratulate you,' she says, 'on bein' the proud father of a beautiful baby boy....'"

The corporal hesitated, looked at me a moment, then continued in a toneless voice. "Well, this guy, after he reads the letter, he gets his gun and goes and looks for his buddy. I guess no one knows, never will know, just what was said, but anyway the bodies were found in a wood back of their billets, and the guy that wasn't married, he was holdin' the gun ..."

The silence that followed seemed endless. I gazed down at the grass between my feet, while my eyes watched a faceless girl writing a letter.... "A beautiful baby boy," I found myself muttering.

"Yep," I heard the corporal saying in his matter-of-fact way, "yep, that's the way it gets some women."

I turned and faced the graves. The sun, now sinking fast, came streaming through the forest onto the acres of crosses, painting their whiteness a delicate shade of pink. The trees, darkening in the evening light, seemed to be drawing closer, as though intent on forming a solid, intimate circle of protection against the oncoming night and all the nights to come.

"It's a peaceful place you've got here," I said, turning once more to the corporal.

His lips parted, and for the first time a smile spread slowly over his face. All of a sudden he beamed. "Glad you like it," he said. "Come again."

Then he rose from the stool, turned to go indoors. "Well, s'long," he said. "Guess I must be getting to work."

As I got into the jeep to drive to what once was Nürnberg, I looked back and caught sight of his dark figure coming out of the one-time *Sportsklub*. He was carrying a shovel over his shoulder with one hand, and pushing a lawn mower in front of him with the other. And he was singing.

Home

I FOUND KEMPTEN'S one remaining bridge, crossed it, passed the skeleton of what had once been a huge SS barracks (the only ruined building I saw that day) and relaxed only when I knew I was on the Memmingen road and that there were no more rivers to cross. Then I shifted in my seat, leaned back, and purred along at a civilized speed. The road was a driver's dream—a cement surface under a cool tunnel of sweet-smelling linden; it went into curves and see-sawed over low hills just often enough to prevent any possibility of boredom. At occasional cross-roads I would slow down and gaze at a wooden shrine of Christ on the Cross and wonder how long it had been there, who had erected it, then why it had not been desecrated. Once in a while, all by itself in the open valley, I saw the inevitable, motionless, already rusty train, abandoned in its tracks; and again I wondered on what day and for what reason it had come to rest just there. At sight of the *Gasthaus* in the village square I dreamed of cold beer and delivered a hearty curse at a vision of Hitler's face. This, and the lack of traffic, the loneliness of the road, were the only reminders of mankind's most frightful slaughter.

Even pedestrian traffic was sparse that morning. But for this fact, I probably never would have noticed that single girl. There was nothing remarkable about her, except that during that summer in Germany it was unusual to see a girl walking all alone, carrying nothing, on a deserted country road. I had a fleeting glimpse of her in a light green dress, striding along the edge of the grass, swinging her arms. I passed her and didn't look back. Half a mile farther on I came to a fork in the road and, not positive of my way, stopped the jeep. I got out, stretched my legs, and with a bottle of wine and a cigarette, settled down on the side of the road. The world of summer was utterly without sound. I sat smoking and drinking. I remember thinking of my apartment in New York, wondering if my wife were there and what she was doing at this moment in America, when I heard footsteps behind me. I looked up. Above me, one hand resting on the jeep, stood the girl in the green dress. Her legs were bare and she wore sandals. She was so heavy with child that several seconds passed before my eyes reached her face. It was a pallid, rather nondescript face, with sad grey eyes. Strands of longish blonde hair, pinned up in a loose bun, hung down her neck and over her forehead. She kept brushing back these wisps of hair with a hand that was hardened and coarse. The fingernails were black and broken.

"Excuse me," she was saying as I got to my feet, "but do you think you could possibly take me a few kilometres?"

Her voice was pleasant, perfectly calm.

"I'm sorry," I said. "It's *streng verboten*. You must know that."

She smiled—sensing, I thought, that she shouldn't.

"You speak German?" she asked, unable to suppress her surprise and delight.

"Yes," I said. "I used to live in Germany—years ago."

Her eyes opened wide. "Ach!" she exclaimed. Then her face fell. "It's hard," she said, "travelling in Germany now."

"It certainly is," I agreed. "Where have you come from?"

"Rome."

"What? Rome?"

"Yes," she said. "'I was getting on all right until a couple of days ago. In Italy things are different. . . . *Lieber Herr*, don't you think you could take me a little way, just a few kilometres?"

A hundred thoughts came rushing into my head at once.

"How long have you been in Italy?" I found myself asking without knowing why.

"Four years."

"Where are you heading for now?"

"Frankfurt."

"Frankfurt?" My eyes dropped from her face to her body. "Frankfurt's hundreds of kilometres from here," I said, "even as the crow flies."

"I know," she said. "But Frankfurt's my home."

"I used to look upon it as mine, once," I heard myself saying.

"*Was?*" she cried. "You know Frankfurt?"

In her excitement her hand went out to me. Then she quickly withdrew it. I found myself turning away. I leaned against the jeep and stared at my feet.

"Have you been in Frankfurt lately?" she was asking.

"No," I lied. "No, not for years."

"It's such a lovely city. . . . Do you know the Old Town, do you know the Kattgasse?"

"Yes," I said, "I knew the Old Town very well."

"And the Römer. . . ?"

"Yes, I used to drink *Apfelwein* at the *Schwarze Stern*. . . ."

"*Ach, der Schwarze Stern—so was!* How is it possible! We always stopped there when we came back from our climbs in the Taunus. Now I know you know Frankfurt. Ach, if only I were there again! *Lieber Herr*, could you really not take me just a little way?"

"What good would that do?" I asked her, looking her straight in the face.

"Just that much good," she said calmly. "Just that much nearer home."

"You realize that it's forbidden," I said. "No exceptions are made. If we are picked up, which sooner or later is certain, you or I or both of us may land in jail. All roads are patrolled. You understand?"

"I understand," she said.

"Get in," I said.

As we drove off, I noticed with annoyance that my hand was shaking on the wheel and that there was a faint smile on her pale lips. I drove slowly, feeling slightly sick, and prayed for an empty road.

"D'you mean you've been walking all the way from Rome?" I asked.

"Oh, no, I set off on a bicycle."

"When did you leave?"

"I . . . I don't know. I've forgotten. Perhaps three weeks, perhaps a month. It seems longer."

"Where's your husband?"

"He's dead," she said. "He was shot by the Fascisti. . . ."

I wanted to ask why, but it was hard to break that silence.

"He was Italian," she said at last. "He took me to Rome. I didn't like it. I was homesick all the time. I couldn't make friends. My husband spoke German. I could never learn Italian. I tried hard to stay on after he went. He would have wanted me to. But then the baby, it began to grow, and I thought and dreamed of home, and one day I thought it might be too late. . . . So I packed two little suitcases and my husband's rucksack and I rode away. . . . In Italy I got lifts. Things are different there."

"And where's your bicycle now, and all your luggage?"

"All stolen."

'Stolen? Who stole them?"

She hesitated, and during that short silence we turned a corner, and round the corner I saw a convoy—tractors, four-ton trucks, tanks, half-tracks, jeeps—coming rumbling in a thundering unending line towards us.

"See that!" I muttered, half to myself.

"Yes, I see," I heard her say.

Before the first truck was upon us I saw two officers leap to their feet in the front seat. As it thundered by, they shook their fists at me and yelled. The men behind, hearing the yells, yelled louder, howled together in a chorus that rose above the deafening roar of the engines. I wanted to step on the gas, but instead I changed into second, crept along at snail's pace, in an attempt to give the impression I had every right to do what I was doing and that I was not running the gauntlet I felt I was running. Like all convoys, it seemed to have no end. From behind every engine the screams and raucous cries of derision and shaking fists continued. Only one thought encouraged me: They can't stop!

When at last it was over, it was I who stopped. My mouth was parched. I uncorked the bottle and handed it to the girl. "*Prost!*" she said, glancing at me. "*Prost!*" I answered.

"This is the most comfortable ride I've had in a long time," she said.

I put the bottle away and drove on.

"You were telling me how all your belongings were stolen," I said. "Who stole them?"

"An American soldier," she said.

"An American? How d'you know? Where?"

"On the other side of Kempten. He wore the American uniform, like yours."

"What did he say? What language—?"

"He didn't say anything, only shouted. I was alone, and there was no one in sight. Suddenly he jumped from behind a tree, knocked me off the bicycle, pulled the rucksack off my shoulders, grabbed my handbag, and rode away on the bicycle. I screamed and hit him, but there was no one to hear and he was big. I've been walking ever since."

"It's very unlikely he was an American," I told her. "Americans don't need to steal bicycles. Most probably he had stolen an American uniform. Where have you been sleeping?"

"Anywhere. Sometimes people are kind. My condition helps, I think. Sometimes people prod me to make sure. When people aren't kind, or doors don't open, I sleep in barns. It's summer. That's a good thing. I was always a bit of a *Wandervogel*. And I'm pretty strong."

"What about food?"

"*Ja*, people on the whole are kind. Usually they spare me something. But it's different now. I have to beg. I have nothing to offer. I'm not used to that. Still, so long as I get home . . . My mother will look after me when my time comes. . . ."

"When's that?" I asked.

"Six more weeks. I'll make it, if I'm lucky. I've been pretty lucky so far. Except for my clothes. It's so hard to keep clean. And my bicycle. If only I had my bicycle. . . . I often rode seventy-five kilometres in a day. I could have been home in under a week. I know it's silly to be talking about home all the time, but I've been away so long. . . ."

"How long is it since you heard from your mother?"

"*Ja*, it must be more than a year now."

"Have you been reading the papers much?"

She laughed, almost gaily. "The papers! *Ach, nein*. They tell nothing but lies."

"I'll have to stop here," I said. Some way ahead I could see a stationary truck and a line of G.I.s sitting on the side of the road. "Don't you say anything," I said. "I'll do the talking."

As I came to a halt, all the G.I.s looked up and gasped: "Jeez!" I heard one of them mutter. A sergeant came up and I asked if there were an officer around. No, the captain had gone on ahead. I explained briefly why the girl was in the jeep, and he kept looking at the girl, then looking away. When I finished, he said: "Christ, that's certainly a tough one!" Then he informed me there was a garrisoned village not far along the road. "Try the C.O. there," he suggested. "Are you sure she's on the level?" he asked, smiling.

"Pretty sure," I said, thanked him and drove on.

In the village the jeep was immediately surrounded. A young, handsome captain broke through the staring crowd. I showed him my two impressive-looking passes, told him my story. He was extremely sympathetic, but apparently not sure what should be done. Finally he went off and conferred with another officer. In a couple of minutes he was back.

"You'd better take her into Memmingen," he said. "But be sure you turn her over to the AMG there. You say she has no pass?"

"No," I said. "She has nothing."

"How did she manage to get by the patrol posts?"

I repeated the question to the girl.

"Ach," she said, "they just looked at me. Most of them were very kind."

I translated for the captain. He smiled. "Guess it's hard not to be soft sometimes," he said. "You'll find the AMG in the middle of the square, can't miss it."

I thanked him, and as we moved on I remember hearing someone in the crowd shout out: "Why the hell did you pick on that one?"

I felt such relief at the humane manner in which we had been treated that I immediately passed on the news to the girl. Her reaction was more than surprising; it was positively frightening. She let out a gasp and grabbed my arm.

"Turn me over to the Military Government?" she cried. "But

lieber Herr, please—I know you'd never do that. You who've been so kind—!"

"But listen," I said. "The American Military Government is not the Gestapo. What d'you think's going to happen to you? You'll be properly looked after. You'll be taken to a maternity home. Memmingen, so far as I know, is not like Frankfurt, it's not been—"

"But *lieber Herr!*" she shouted. "Frankfurt's my home! You don't understand. Please stop. Please let me out. The Military Government would keep me. As you say, they would put me in a home. I would have to have my baby in Memmingen. In Frankfurt, at home, I ... *Ach, lieber Herr*, I implore you. ..."

Her cries had become hysterical. I stopped the jeep. Tears were flowing down her pale, unpowdered cheeks, and in her sad grey eyes there was a look of awful fear.

I took her trembling hand. "Listen," I said, "are you sure you're doing the right thing for yourself, for your baby? Supposing, in Frankfurt, you found ..."

"*Ach*, in Frankfurt," she murmured, closing her eyes. "In Frankfurt I know people. I have friends. I am home."

"Perhaps you are right," I said. "Perhaps you know best. Do you really want to get out here?"

"If I may."

She was out of the jeep and on her feet as though they had no extra burden to carry.

"Memmingen is an hour's walk," I said.

"*Ach*, that's fine," she said. She wiped her eyes with her wrist and smiled. The look of fear had gone.

I stretched out my hand. "Good luck," I said. "You deserve some."

"Thank you for your kindness," she said.

I didn't look back, but drove straight ahead, and probably very fast. I don't remember. I remember only seeing—as I passed under the arches in and out of Memmingen—what I had seen a month before: the battered remains of the few houses left standing in the Old Town of Frankfurt.